Chasing Fireflies

Chloe Fowler

Chasing Fireflies

To Jesse—my reason for everything.

1

RAINEY

EVERYTHING HAPPENS FOR A REASON. I can't count the number of times I've heard these words from the mouths of well-meaning strangers with pitying smiles. There are other phrases, too, of course. *Every cloud has a silver lining,* or my personal favorite, *It's all in God's plan.* The list of expressions people use to patch emotional discomfort like rags shoved into the hole of a sinking ship is a long and tedious one. And it's all bullshit. I mean, if everything happens for a reason, what is that reason supposed to be, and what kind of messed-up plan does God have, anyway? If you ask, I guarantee you won't get a satisfactory answer. A perfunctory cough, a muffled excuse to leave. Maybe if you're lucky, a pensive nod, as if your question was rhetorical (it wasn't).

"Rainey, wake up!"

A cold finger prodded my cheek. I cracked a reluctant eye to see the horrible clash of Maverick's flaming orange hair against her purple pajamas and rolled over, pulling my duvet over my head as I went. Undeterred, my sister jostled me as she crawled onto the bed, trouncing my efforts to sneak five more minutes of shut-eye. It was a good thing I loved her as much as I did, or I would have pummeled her with my pillow.

"Come on! I've been up for an hour, and I'm not even going to school. Aren't you excited?"

I made an indistinct sound that wouldn't have produced even the smallest blip on the Richter scale of enthusiasm. "Why can't we both be homeschooled?" I grumbled.

"Homeschooling is boring. There's no one to talk to."

"Exactly. It's perfect."

Maverick was our family's sinking ship. Of all the great and mysterious things I'd struggled to make sense of, she was the most unfathomable of them all.

I was five when Mom announced she was pregnant again. At first, everyone was thrilled. Especially me. I wanted a sister I could read stories to and play hide and seek with. But even before Maverick arrived, the doctors realized something was wrong. According to the ultrasound, the left side of her heart was too small to pump blood through her body. *Hypoplastic left heart syndrome,* they called it. I didn't know what that meant, but I knew it was bad because Dad stopped singing in the shower, and Mom smiled less. Our happy family dinners were replaced with hushed conversations and hastily wiped tears, and it seemed like everyone was holding their breath against some unspeakable, impending tragedy.

Maverick was born on a freezing cold night in February. My parents called her their little blue jellybean because her skin was the colour of a robin's egg.

"She's not getting enough oxygen," Dad explained. He held my hand as the two of us stood next to the incubator. Trapped amid all the tubes and wires, my sister was as tiny and delicate as a bee's wing. I stayed beside her while Dad talked with the doctors, my hand pressed against the glass, humming softly like Mom did whenever I was sad or upset. Dad was a doctor, too, but he worked with the brain, not the heart. Still, he seemed to know what was going on and asked a lot of questions.

Maverick had her first open-heart surgery before she was a week old. Her second surgery came six months later, followed by a third shortly after her second birthday. While the surgeries were successful, the doctors warned my parents there would be complications. For the next ten years, pediatric cardiologists closely monitored her heart, which meant Maverick spent most of her life in and out of hospitals. Not that she complained. Maverick never complained. She had more courage and grit in her pinky finger than I had in my entire body. Most days I wondered how we could be related.

Then again, only a little sister could drive me this crazy.

"You're wearing *that* for your first day of school?" she asked, eyeing the lumpy grey sweater I'd laid out the night before.

I crawled off the bed and snatched it from the chair. "It's comfortable."

"Nice clothes can be comfortable."

"Hey, this is nice."

"As a pillowcase, or a dishcloth, maybe."

"If I wanted your opinion, I'd ask."

Maverick wrinkled her nose at the shapeless bulge in my hands. "I'm calling an intervention. Jo will back me up."

Jo was my best friend and next-door neighbour. We'd been together since our sidewalk-chalk, sticker-trading days, and since her parents were bigwig lawyers who worked long hours, she came over a lot. My parents got so used to her being around, they eventually gave her a key.

She was sitting at our kitchen table when I came downstairs for breakfast, a bowl of Cheerios in her lap and our newspaper open to the crossword puzzle.

"What is a cotton-eating beetle?" she asked, spoon raised halfway to her mouth.

"Beats me." I grabbed the box of Cheerios and helped myself to a bowl. Jo was the kind of girl you couldn't help but love and hate at the same time—gorgeous, with thick waves of blond hair and the kind of figure you automatically compared yourself to, and inevitably came up short (quite literally in my case, being a humble five foot two, courtesy of my late grandfather). But it wasn't just her looks; Jo was a female Einstein, reigning captain of the volleyball team, and president of the student council. She was on the road to an Ivy League college and popular to boot.

I figured it was an only child thing. Both her parents were successful, career-driven types, and Jo had no siblings to help diffuse the pressure of measuring up. Thanks to Maverick, my parents were just happy I had functioning organs and didn't have a drug problem.

"Ten across: causation study. Eight letters."

"Etiology," Dad said, coming into the kitchen with his blue silk tie draped over his shoulder and a flake of toilet paper stuck to his chin, staunching a nick from a hasty shave.

"Perfect." Jo scribbled in the letters.

Dad bent down and planted a kiss on the top of my head. "Morning, sweetheart. Morning, Jo."

"You're wearing your lucky tie. Big day?" I asked.

"Operating on a glioblastoma. No harm in bringing along a little luck." He flicked the tie off his shoulder and filled the kettle with water. My dad was strictly a tea drinker; he left the strong stuff to Mom and me. "You girls excited for your first day of senior year?"

More like terrified, I thought.

"I want to go to school." Maverick propped her chin in her hands and gave a pout worthy of Scarlett O'Hara.

"You're not missing out on much," I told her. "Most of the time you're stuck at a desk listening to a teacher drone on about verb conjugation." I drank the last of the milk from my cereal bowl and put it in the dishwasher as I checked the time. "We'd better go or we'll miss the bus," I said to Jo. Slinging my backpack over my shoulder, I grabbed my lunch from the fridge and headed for the door.

"Good luck today, Dad. Catch you later, bean!"

"Remember you owe me a round of Snakes and Ladders!" Maverick shouted.

"Seven o'clock. Right after supper. I won't forget," I promised, crossing my heart with mock severity.

"Loser has to wash the dishes."

"Winner gets an extra helping of chocolate pudding." I shot

her a wink as Jo and I walked out to catch the bus at the end of my driveway. It was still warm enough that I didn't need a jacket. Jo was fearless in a pleated skirt and a delicate lace top. Her long legs were accentuated by a pair of purple pumps that I would have killed to wear had I not been so afraid of breaking an ankle.

"Do you really need all those books?" I asked, eyeing her backpack. The zipper looked ready to pop.

"I have AP calculus, AP English, history, physics, and economics this semester. All of them have textbooks that weigh a metric ton."

"Are you planning on having any fun this year?"

"I'm on the track team. Does that count?"

Last time Coach Gardiner had made us run hurdles, I'd smashed my shins so badly, they'd resembled bruised bananas by the end of class. "Nope. Not even a little bit."

"No pain, no gain." Jo grinned. "What about you?"

"I'm taking Mr. Greene's photography class." It was the one thing I was looking forward to this semester. Last year, I'd blown my allowance on a Leica M6. Mom and Dad had even given me permission to turn the basement storage room into a dark room. I knew they'd agreed because of Maverick. She took up most of their time and attention, and I suspect they felt bad for neglecting me, but I didn't mind. They were doing the best they could.

When we got on the bus, Jo and I headed towards the back row. Val, one of Jo's volleyball teammates, waved to her. "Looking good, Solano! God, I gained like five pounds over the summer. I'm so fat. I'm eating nothing but celery and cottage cheese for a week!"

"What are you talking about? You look amazing." Jo slid into the seat beside Val. "Rainey, come sit." She nodded to the vacant seat across the aisle. Val glanced at me but didn't say hello. I sat down while Jo and Val started chatting about their summer vacations. (Val had spent a month with her aunt in Auvergne. She was practically French now.) Holding back a major eye-roll at her terrible imitations of the French boy she was now dating, I pulled out a copy of my schedule from the front pocket of my bag. The nerves that had momentarily disappeared during breakfast returned in full force as my eyes zeroed in on my first class.

Math.

"God, kill me now."

LIAM

Mom banged on the door of my room.

"Get up. You're going to be late."

Fuck. It wasn't even eight, and already she sounded haggard and upset. I rubbed my face, the weight of my exhaustion anchoring me to the bed. For most people, the dawning of a new day carried the fresh scent of hope and possibility. As a Hayes, it carried the scent of stale beer and last week's garbage.

Heaving myself up off the bed, I grabbed my jeans. There was a hole forming over the left knee, but at least they were clean. Rooting around under the bed for a pair of socks, I hit my head against the wall and swore. To call the closet I lived in a bedroom was being Mother Theresa generous. If I stood in the middle of the room and stuck out my arms, my fingers could touch the peeling wallpaper on both sides. Not that I was complaining. Even though the mattress had a broken spring and the walls smelled like mold, it was mine, and last month, I'd fixed a deadbolt to the door, just in case.

Not that Ray tried to pull much shit these days. Thanks to a four-inch growth spurt and a summer of working construction, I'd gained enough weight to graduate from the scrawny ranks of easy targets and could now throw a right hook mean enough to make even Ray pause.

Mom stood over the kitchen sink, an unlit cigarette balanced between her fingers. She'd been trying to quit for years but could never hold out for more than a week, which was about the same record she held for avoiding a fight with Ray. If she was smoking, it meant Ray was in a bad mood.

Big surprise there.

"I made you some breakfast," she said, nodding to a plate on the counter. A fly buzzed over a mound of what might have been scrambled eggs next to a slice of burnt toast.

"Oh . . . thanks." I picked up a fork and extracted a cautious sample. The eggs were cold and overcooked. I braved another bite, then slipped the rest discreetly into the trash.

"Are you coming home right after school today?" Mom asked. Her attempt at indifference was undermined by the deep tension line etched between her brows. The cigarette in her hand twitched.

"Yeah, why?"

"Why don't you hang out with your friends after school? Maybe go to the arcade or something?"

I hadn't been to the arcade since I was ten. The building had shut down seven years ago. "Maybe."

"Or how about a movie? I think I have some money for a

ticket. Hold on." She reached for her purse.

"It's okay," I said quickly. "I don't think there are any good movies out anyway."

"Well, then do whatever. I don't care," she said sharply. "Just . . . just go have fun, okay?"

She could have just said she wanted me out of the house. It wasn't like it was a secret that Ray nursed his bad moods with alcohol, and when Ray was drunk, he was like a powder keg in a whiskey distillery. Unfortunately, I tended to be the match that set him off, but hanging out with friends after school required actual friends, and I didn't have many of those. There was always Mercy, but she didn't go to our school and was working a shift at the garage today.

"I'll see you later, then."

Distracted by her cigarette, Mom didn't reply.

Jumping over the broken front step of our trailer, I got into my truck, remembering that I had to make a quick pit stop on the way. Mercy had asked me yesterday if I'd give her brother a ride to school.

"And if you could, you know, keep an eye on him?" she'd added.

The Ramos family lived on the adjacent property, so it was a short drive to their house. Spotting Joshua on the front steps, hugging an old Spiderman backpack to his chest, I could see why Mercy was worried. The kid had yet to survive the shitstorm of puberty. Small, overweight, and wearing glasses that were too big for him, thanks to his parents shopping at the discount rack at the local drugstore, he couldn't be more of a target if he painted a bull's-eye across his back.

"Jesus Christ." I rolled down the window and called out, "Hey, Joshua!"

The boy climbed into the passenger seat without saying a word and turned to stare out the window.

"Morning to you too," I said, turning on the radio.

It was a quiet ride to school. When I pulled into the student parking lot, Joshua muttered a quick thanks and headed off in the direction of the school. "Good luck!" I shouted at his back. Fuck, he'd need it.

I waited in my truck, enjoying a moment of peace and quiet while watching the students disembark from the buses. They looked like puffed-up peacocks dressed in colourful designer clothes, some of which probably cost more than our trailer. Just another day in Springbank, I thought bitterly. The average family in this community had more money than Bruce Wayne. Most of it came from Alberta's oil-and-gas industry, but there were plenty of doctors, lawyers, and CEOs who had moved out to enjoy the mountain views on massive, multi-acre estates. Those who lived on the outskirts were the social outliers, myself and the Ramos family included. Joshua's father was the school's custodian, something I hoped these anachronistic classists never found out.

The bell blared, cutting off my thoughts. I got out of my truck and headed to my first class: math with Mr. MacAlastair. Great. Another shitty start to another shitty year.

2

RAINEY

AS I HEADED TO MY FIRST CLASS, my stomach started to knot. I wasn't terrible at math. I might have even enjoyed it under the tutelage of someone like Mr. Greene, who was so soft-spoken, you could barely hear him. But to my everlasting horror, I'd gotten Mr. MacAlastair, a six-foot-tall, white-haired Scot with an infamous temper and a scowl that could make the entire football team wet their pants. He sat behind his desk, watching the students enter his domain like a lion observing gazelles on the savannah.

Of all the teachers at Springbank High, I feared Mr. MacAlastair the most. Keeping my head down, I slipped into a seat near the back of the room, careful to avoid his gaze while I opened my notebook and scrawled the date with exaggerated precision on the top right corner of the first page.

"Is this seat taken?" a low voice asked.

I shook my head in response without looking up.

A boy sat down, pulling a pencil out of his back pocket. He twirled it absentmindedly between his fingers as students continued to file in. The motion distracted me and I looked over. It was Liam Hayes. I'd seen him in the hallways a few times, but never this close. My stomach did a strange sort of somersault, as if I'd missed a step going down the stairs.

He was kind of cute.

The thought took me by surprise. I had gone to school with Liam since fifth grade. Back then, he'd been a short, scrawny boy with dirt under his fingernails and grass stains on his knees. I remembered thinking he was probably wild and obnoxious, like all the other boys I knew. Not that I had any right to judge. In fifth grade, I was sporting chapped lips and a toothpaste stain down the front of my dress, a look immortalized in a photograph my parents insisted on displaying above the mantel in our family room.

A lot had changed since fifth grade, thanks to the miraculous phenomenon of puberty. Liam had grown at least a foot, lean muscle and high cheekbones replacing gangly arms and knobby knees. Unlike the rest of us who kept shooting Mr. MacAlastair nervous glances while fidgeting in our seats, he was leaning back in his chair, his gaze fixed on the patch of blue sky visible through the window, looking bored.

I wondered why he had decided to sit next to me. There were still plenty of empty seats available, including one next to Val and her D-sized cups. I looked back down at my notebook, swallowing a sudden impulse to say something. Having never spoken to Liam before, it would be weird to start now. What would I even say? *How was your summer?* It was a perfectly generic question, but maybe too trite, and I didn't want to sound trite. I wanted to sound interesting. Mysterious.

Maybe I could ask him if I could borrow a pencil? I considered breaking the one in my hand, just for the excuse, but that felt contrived. *Tell him you're writing a story for the school paper about hot guys and ask for an interview.* The suggestion came to me in Jo's voice, but I didn't have the finesse to pull that one off without sounding like a complete loser.

Quick, just say something!

"Did you know that hummingbirds are the only birds that can fly backwards?" The words left my mouth in a diarrheic torrent.

Liam turned to me, a bemused line appearing between his brows. He had the most vivid blue eyes. Like morpho butterflies. "I'm sorry?"

"Er . . . I was just—"

The bell rang, cutting me off, and before I could humiliate myself further, Mr. MacAlastair stood up from his desk. The room went so quiet, I could hear Coach Gardiner shouting drills at the football team outside. Wishing I could somehow erase the last minute from the collective memory of the universe, I watched Mr. MacAlastair scribble a quadratic equation on the board.

"Let's start with a quick review," he announced. "I want to see how much you remember from last semester. Who can tell me the first step to solving this equation? Rainey?"

I blinked. "Sorry?"

"This equation. How would you solve it?" He regarded me down the length of his nose, the marker poised beside the line of numbers on the board.

Oh God. My eyes scanned the configuration of symbols, but panic had snipped the wires between my eyes and my brain; I might as well have been staring at Egyptian hieroglyphs.

"Um . . . solve for *x*?"

Someone snorted.

Mr. MacAlastair frowned. "Yes. I'm asking *how*."

"Um . . ."

Given one failed attempt, any considerate teacher would have moved graciously on to the next student, but Mr. MacAlastair continued to dissect me with his glower while the rest of the class waited in awkward anticipation. My panic escalated. "I . . . I don't know."

The silence in the room rang in my ears, and a burning trail of heat scorched the back of my neck. Wonderful. Two minutes in and everyone thought Rainey Collins was a moron.

"Anyone?" Mr. MacAlastair asked tersely.

"Make the equation equal to zero, then factor," Liam said beside me.

Mr. MacAlastair did as directed, but not before shooting me a disapproving look. I released a long, slow breath, wiping my clammy palms on my jeans. Would anyone notice if I crawled under my desk, withered up, and died? Seriously, did the man have to call me out on the first day like that? In front of everyone?

I spent the rest of the class wallowing in the dregs of my shame, praying Mr. MacAlastair wouldn't call on me again, and when the bell rang, I heaved a sigh of relief, grabbed my things, and fled.

* * *

I barely spoke at dinner. Mom and Dad didn't seem to notice, but Maverick picked up on my mood and called me out during our game of Snakes and Ladders.

"What's with the perma-frown? You're going to get wrinkles," she said as I rolled the dice and slid down the longest snake on the board for the fifth time.

"I hate doing the dishes," I lied.

"Too bad. I'd break out the rubber gloves if I were you. There is no way you're going to win." Confident enough in her chances, she'd already eaten the leftover chocolate pudding. There was a ring of it circling her lips. "Was today that bad?" she asked.

I didn't want to make a big deal about it. I thought a guy was cute and had made a fool of myself in front of everyone. So what? I didn't care what people thought of me. I had repeated this to myself a million times since first period, but the scene of my epic embarrassment kept playing in my head like a record stuck on loop.

I groaned, hitting my head against the table. "There's this guy in my math class, and he's kind of cute—"

I wasn't even able to finish my sentence. Maverick let out a whooping screech that sent both my parents sprinting for the living room.

"What is it? What's wrong?" Mom's eyes flew to Maverick, sitting across the table from me, grinning ear to ear. The fear and anxiety drained out of her like air deflating from a balloon.

"It's all right, Cora. They're fine." Dad squeezed her shoulder. He shot me a chastising look before drawing her back into the kitchen.

I narrowed my eyes at Maverick. "Overreaction, much? I didn't even get a chance to finish my sentence."

Maverick was still grinning, oblivious to our parents' momentary panic, the chocolate pudding on her face lending a ghoulish edge to her excitement. "Oh come *on*. You can't say, 'There's this guy in my class and he's kind of cute,' and not finish with, 'and I want to marry him and have his babies'."

I rolled my eyes. I was now habanero levels of hot. "It's not like that. I just think he's . . . you know, mildly attractive."

"Are you going to ask him out?" Maverick asked as if this was no big deal. She rolled a seven and climbed another ladder.

"Are you kidding? He thinks I'm stupid."

"You are stupid." She ducked as I reached out to swat her.

"And even if I had the balls to ask him out," I continued, "it's a snowball's chance in hell that he'd say yes."

"Why should that stop you from asking him out? Just walk up to him and say, 'Hey, want to go out with me?' What's the worst that can happen? He says no?"

"Um, yeah. That sounds terrible."

"Compared to having a heart that might stop before the end of the year?"

The dice slipped through my fingers and rolled under the couch.

"Maverick." I stared at my little sister, at her narrow nose dusted in its coat of freckles, and her blue eyes fringed with pale lashes, and suddenly I couldn't swallow past the rock in my throat.

Maverick handed me a spare die from the box. "So . . . just how cute are we talking here?"

I snorted. Because snorting was better than crying. "Think Charlie Hunnam crossed with Ryan Gosling."

"Geezus, Rainey. You're screwed."

"I know."

LIAM

I would have gone straight to Mercy's, but I'd forgotten my student ID card in my room, and I needed it to take my textbooks out of the library. It wouldn't take long to get. Less than a minute. Ray might not even notice me if I was quick enough.

My hopes were dashed when I pulled up in front of the trailer next to a familiar '97 GMC.

Ray had company.

The only people worse than my stepdad were his friends. Wes, in particular, was a right ass. The man had the IQ of a dung beetle and a cruel streak that made him dangerous to any vulnerable creature in his line of sight. Paul was no saint either, and the three of them were usually soused by noon.

No wonder Mom had suggested I stay at a friend's.

I sat in my truck, debating whether or not it was worth getting my student card after all. If I left right now, I wouldn't be able to get my textbooks for another day, and I hated the idea of falling behind, but not as much as I hated sitting outside my own goddamn home, feeling like I couldn't go in because of some beer-chugging nobodies.

Gritting my teeth, I walked in, purposefully ignoring the three men slouched around the table littered with empty beer cans, a half-empty pack of Marlboros, and an ashtray overflowing with cigarette butts.

Ray had his flat cap jammed over his head, the rim dark with sweat. He leaned back in his chair, blocking the way to my room. "Where you goin', kid?" His eyes were already bloodshot, and it wasn't even four.

"Grabbing something."

"Oh? Grabbin' what?"

"Nothing."

"Nothin' eh?" he snorted. Wes chuckled as if this was some clever joke. "Why don't you grab us them beers in the fridge while you're busy grabbin' nothing?"

Fighting the urge to knock Ray off his chair, I edged my way around them. "Get them yourself."

"Ho now, that ain't no way to treat our guests!" Ray jeered.

Ignoring him, I went to my room. Reaching under my mattress, I pulled out the small tin pencil case where I stashed my valuables. There wasn't much inside: my ID card, an old picture of my dad, and about twenty dollars in cash. I used to keep my money in my wallet, but Ray had a nasty habit of rifling through it when I wasn't looking and taking whatever he could find. Tucking my ID card into my back pocket, I returned the case to its hiding place and went back to the kitchen.

Wes and Paul were laughing about something that had happened that morning with Mrs. Trenton's flowerbeds.

"Figured I'd water them for her, if you catch my drift," Wes said, crushing his beer can and tossing it towards the trash. It hit the lip and bounced to the floor.

Paul snorted. "That would have killed 'em. We all know there's more whiskey than water in your piss."

"Ain't that the truth!"

Keeping my face blank, I walked past them. I almost got to the door before Ray stopped me.

"Still waitin' on them beers, you know." A sharp edge had entered his voice, sending fingers of cold dread crawling down my spine. Wes and Paul went quiet.

"Get them yourself," I repeated, and before Ray could reply, I walked out, careful not to run or show any sign of how fast my heart was racing. I would probably catch hell for the lip later, but if I spent the night at Mercy's, there was a good chance Ray would get drunk enough to forget.

I kept my eyes on the trailer door in my rearview mirror as I drove away. I could almost hear Ray masking his anger with a hard laugh. "Fuckin' teenagers, eh?"

By the time I got to Mercy's, my heart rate had returned to normal. She was sitting on the fence next to the barn in a pair of cut-off overalls and a white tank top. Flea was rooting around in the dirt, one ear perked forward, the other flopping to the side. The moment the pit bull saw my truck, he gave a wild bark and pelted towards me, tail spinning like a helicopter blade.

"Easy there, boy," I said, getting out. I bent down to scratch him behind his ears and let him lick my fingers. I'd found Flea in a box on the side of the road last August. Some asshole had abandoned him, and judging from the scars on his hind legs and the ribs showing through his matted fur, the dog hadn't been cared for in a long time. I would have kept him myself, but there was no way I could keep a pet. Not with Ray around. I shuddered to think what that man would do if he found Flea while I was gone. Thankfully, Mercy had agreed to look after him.

"Hey." She walked up to me, her thumbs hooked into her pockets, her brown skin glowing in the evening sun. "How was day one of purgatory?"

I knew she meant school. "It was all right. Mind if I crash here tonight?" I asked. It wasn't the first time I'd sought refuge in the Ramoses' barn. While I was a welcome dinner guest, Mrs. Ramos didn't like me spending the night—not since Ray had shown up one day looking for me after I'd busted the side mirror of his motorcycle. He and Mom had gotten into a fight over a burnt supper. He'd broken her wrist, and at fourteen years old, I'd been too scared to do anything more than mess up his ride.

It was the angriest I'd ever seen him. It wasn't until Mr. Ramos threatened to call the cops that Ray had backed off. That night, I'd overheard Mrs. Ramos tell Mercy she wasn't allowed to see me again. She didn't want her children getting involved with 'rough people', but Mr. Ramos had told his wife that I was a good kid, and God demanded they give justice to the weak and the fatherless and deliver them from the hands of the wicked.

I hated that Mr. Ramos saw me as weak. I didn't want to be weak, and I didn't want the Ramoses' pity either. Mercy was different. She never looked at me like I was a charity case the way her father did, or like a potential felon, like her mother. It was her idea that I stay in the barn loft on nights when Ray was on the warpath.

"Avoiding the three stooges?" Mercy asked, sensing the tension behind my stoic expression.

"I figured I'd start the school year off without a black eye."

"Smart. You hungry? Mom made *mechado*."

"Yeah, sure."

We headed into the house. It was a nice place compared to what I was used to. Mrs. Ramos was an amazing cook who took immense pleasure in feeding people until their stomachs burst. Consequently, the house always smelled like garlic and roasted pork.

I wondered if Mercy knew what it felt like to walk into a house that smelled like a dive-bar dumpster, where the silence was so thick, you felt like you were suffocating. It was never quiet here. Mrs. Ramos puttered about with endless energy, listening to the Christian station on the radio, while Mr. Ramos watched the Golf Channel in the living room. I hated golf, but it was entertaining listening to him shout advice at the players, especially given he'd never held a golf club in his life, a fact Mercy reminded him of daily.

"Sorry about the mess," Mercy said, kicking aside the shoes that were blocking the front door. Mrs. Ramos was a seamstress, so there were always pin cushions, discarded patterns, and countless bolts of fabric piled up throughout the house. I didn't mind the clutter—the house was still *clean*. There were never day-old dishes piled up in the sink, or garbage littered across the floor. The ugly green carpet was always vacuumed, and the bathroom smelled like Clorox and bar soap, not a neglected outhouse.

"I wasn't expecting company this afternoon," Mrs. Ramos said, looking up from a swathe of blue floral fabric spread across the kitchen table. She regarded me with her usual air of disapproval, a pencil sticking out from the knot of her hair.

"Come on, Mom, Liam isn't company. Besides, you always make too much food." Mercy grabbed a chocolate-chunk cookie out of the jar on the counter and tossed it to me before taking one for herself.

"You'll ruin your supper!" Mrs. Ramos chided.

"I'm eighteen. One cookie isn't going to ruin anything."

Joshua was sitting on the brown wool couch, a pile of graphic novels stacked next to him on the coffee table.

I sat next to him. "What are you reading?"

"Sandman."

"Cool. Which one?"

"Volume one," he answered without looking up from the page.

"Is it any good?"

"I guess."

"He hasn't been able to put it down," Mercy teased. She turned on the TV, and we watched the last half hour of *Lake Placid* until Mr. Ramos came home.

"Awh, come on!" she groaned when he switched it to the Golf Channel.

"Sorry, dove, but Choi is playing the eighteenth hole at Whistling Straits. I can't miss it!"

Mercy rolled her eyes as her father turned up the volume. "In case we can't hear the crickets in the crowd," she said, shooting me a look. I grinned.

"I keep telling you, it's the great American pastime," Mr. Ramos said.

"Okay, first, that's baseball, and second, we're Canadian."

"Hush! Here he comes."

A man in a bright orange shirt and white shorts approached the tee and took his shot. I knew next to nothing about golf, but I thought his technique looked more than a little unconventional. The ball landed in a bunker. Mr. Ramos smacked his forehead and shouted something in Tagalog.

"Watch that language!" Mrs. Ramos barked. Getting up, she went to check the pot on the stove. I caught a whiff of something delicious as she lifted the lid, and my stomach growled.

"Dinner is ready!"

I followed Mercy to the kitchen, and we each grabbed a bowl of bubbling stew.

"How was work?" Mr. Ramos asked as we sat around the table, hastily cleared of Mrs. Ramos's sewing. He reminded me of a chinchilla: he had a round face that creased whenever he smiled and large ears that protruded beneath a mop of curly hair.

Mercy shrugged.

Mr. Ramos poured himself a glass of milk, not meeting her eye. "I thought you were going to sign up for some of those classes. Get your GED."

"I decided not to."

"Why not?"

"Because I'm busy working at the garage," she said, a thread of defiance lacing her voice. "It's good money, Dad."

"You could make more if you got a degree."

"Yeah, sure, and rack up a ton of debt while I'm at it. Look, can we not talk about this right now?"

Mr. Ramos frowned but let the subject drop. Mercy dug into her mechado, finishing her meal well before anyone else. I tried not to eat too quickly, but I hadn't had anything since the few bites of egg I'd eaten that morning, and the food was delicious. There were still leftovers in the pot after everyone finished, but I felt it would be presumptuous to ask for seconds.

After we cleaned up, Mercy grabbed a couple more cookies from the jar and jerked her head towards the door, motioning me to follow her.

"Thank you for the meal, Mrs. Ramos," I said before ducking outside. We headed towards the barn where the previous owners had hung a giant tire from the rafters. Mercy slipped her legs through the rubber ring and rocked back on her heels before passing me another cookie.

"What is it with parents thinking the only way to become successful is to get a good education?" she griped. "These days, all a university education gets you is a fancy piece of paper and a fifty-thousand dollar loan. Give me a paycheck instead. At the end of this year, I'll have enough money saved up to buy a one-way ticket to Europe."

"Europe?" My voice rose in surprise.

"Did you know you can take a ten-day hike from Mount Blanc to Matterhorn? I bet those views are some of the best in the world, and I'd rather see them in person than in the sticky pages of some waiting room magazine."

"That does sound amazing," I agreed.

"Right?" She sighed. "You should totally come with me. We can earn some money and get out of this shithole. I know you're just as eager to get away as I am. My uncle would hire you; we always need extra hands at the garage."

"Tempting, but I'm still in high school, remember?"

Mercy rolled her eyes. "You don't need school—you're already wicked smart. Besides, do you really want to stick around here for another year?"

I took a bite of the cookie so I wouldn't have to answer right away. Mercy was right: I'd dreamed of getting away from Ray ever since he'd moved in, but there was no way I was going to leave my mother behind, and unlike Mercy, I *wanted* to finish high school. I knew I could never afford university, but dropping out of high school felt a bit too much like giving up.

"I promised my mom I'd graduate," I lied.

"What, and she hasn't broken, like, a million promises she's made to you?"

True as that was, I didn't like Mercy pointing it out. "She does the best she can," I said.

"I guess." Mercy kicked at the ground, letting the tire swing her in a lazy circle. "I just know I don't miss high school. All that *drama*. Christ."

I couldn't argue that. I kept my head down at school and avoided people as much as possible. I had enough to deal with at home—the last thing I needed was people giving me trouble at school too.

3

RAINEY

FEARING THE INEVITABLE HUMILIATION of a repeat performance with Mr. MacAlastair, I went to math the next morning with all the enthusiasm of a condemned prisoner mounting the hanging block.

I wondered if Liam would sit beside me again, but I had my doubts. Afraid of being associated with the class moron, he'd probably cut his losses and move on to better prospects. I wasn't too bothered by this. Given my lack of experience with desire and all things related, I had convinced myself that the butterflies I'd experienced yesterday had just been a mild case of indigestion.

Then again, maybe not.

The moment Liam entered the classroom, my mind went fuzzy

and blank and my stomach hurtled towards the roof of my mouth. I could see why attraction and indigestion could get confused. I did feel slightly nauseous.

Keeping my face hidden behind the curtain of my hair, I stared at the doodles I'd drawn across the bottom of my page. I held my breath and counted to ten, then heard someone take the seat next to me. I didn't dare turn my head, but I tucked my hair behind my ear so I could see out of the corner of my eye. Sure enough, I spied a familiar khaki backpack with a broken zipper propped against the desk leg.

Trying not to groan out loud, I laid my head on my desk. Great. I was *that* girl now. The girl with a crush. And why did it have to be in math class, of all places—the scene of my daily humiliation?

"Absolute value and reciprocal functions," Mr. MacAlastair said once class started. "Who can tell me what an absolute value is?"

Liam's hand rose, along with a few others. I stared resolutely at my page.

"Ryan?"

"An absolute value is the magnitude of a numerical value, irrespective of its relation to other values," Ryan answered.

"Congratulations on having access to a dictionary on your phone. Yes, I can see it under your desk. Can you explain to me what that means in your own words?"

"Um . . ." Ryan floundered, and I felt a small swell of relief that I wasn't the only one who balked under the pressure of Mr. MacAlastair's interrogation. It wouldn't have surprised me if our math teacher had started his career in criminal justice or law enforcement before turning to education. A crisp black suit and a

Glock would have suited him.

"An absolute value is the distance from zero, regardless of if it is negative or positive," Liam said. I glanced over and noticed he had his textbook flipped open to the chapter ahead of us. He had written several questions out, his pencil flicking across the page.

He had nice hands. More specifically, he had interesting hands. They were slender and deft. Like an artist's hands, or maybe a musician's, only callused, with a few scars across his knuckles. He'd chewed his thumbnail down to the quick.

"Rainey?"

My head swiveled around, and I found myself once again under Mr. MacAlastair's penetrating stare.

Shit. Had he asked me a question? I scrambled to read what was now on the board, but Mr. MacAlastair didn't give me a chance.

"Less daydreaming, more focusing, or I will remove you from my class," he said grimly. I felt several pairs of eyes zero in on my burning face, including Liam's. I could have fried an egg on my forehead. I forced myself to look at the board and followed the lesson from there on in, my gaze never deviating from Mr. MacAlastair's marker.

* * *

When the weather was nice, Jo spent her lunch hour training for track. I sat on the bleachers, watching her jump hurdles, enjoying the early September sunshine while cheering her on. She had asked if I could take a few pictures of her mid-stride to help her analyze her technique, so I'd brought my camera out with me.

I snapped as many pictures as I could, hoping to get a few good shots while admiring her long legs and the exultant flush in her cheeks.

Why did some people get all the genetic luck?

I gave her a thumbs-up, and she waved back just as her teammates finished their heat and converged on her.

Peering through my lens, I turned and spotted a boy sitting further down the bleachers. He was alone, his ham sandwich lying forgotten on top of a brown paper bag, his eyes fixed and unblinking on the graphic novel in his hands. It felt a bit like I was spying, but there was something compelling about the intensity of his focus. I snapped a picture.

As I lowered my camera, Chase Buckner and his friend Carson Kozlowski appeared around the corner of the bleachers. Chase was the kind of person I tried my best to avoid. His grandfather was an oil tycoon, so his family had more money than God, and he made sure people knew it too. His parents had bought him a Porsche for his sixteenth birthday, an electric-yellow monstrosity that he drove to school with the stereo blaring at full volume. He had crashed it within a week, laughed it off, and become all the more popular for being crazy. Even the teachers disliked him; he always skipped class but never failed a grade even though his only strengths were football and making fun of the students on the bottom end of the social food chain. I suspect most of the teachers passed him just to get him out of their classroom as quickly as possible.

As he came around the bleachers, his eyes zeroed in on the boy reading his graphic novel.

Oh no. No, no, no.

"Look what we have here," he said. "A sweaty little laborer

thinking he deserves an education."

The boy's face flushed red behind his glasses. Carson snatched the graphic novel out of his hands and waved it over his head.

"A picture book? Does the idiot not know how to read?" The two of them laughed as the boy tried to take the book back, his glasses slipping down his nose.

Across the field, Coach Gardiner was watching Jo's heat with his back turned. I thought of getting his attention, but before I could move, someone strode past me.

"Back off, Buckner." Liam stepped in front of the boy with the glasses and grabbed the graphic novel out of Carson's hand with a deft swipe.

"Dude, get lost," Chase said, shoving Liam in the shoulder.

Liam didn't move. He didn't even flinch. "I said back off."

Had I been in Chase's shoes, I would have run for the hills, but Chase just snorted. "What are you, his boyfriend or something? Has the spic got himself a boyfriend now?"

Carson laughed.

"I won't say it again," Liam warned.

"Or what, you'll tell the principal? You know what, you do that, and I'll stay with your boyfriend here. We'll get better acquainted. What do you say, kid? You and me behind the school bleachers. Does the sound of that get you hot?"

Chase lunged to grab him, but Liam shoved him back. "You really are a knuckle-dragging Neanderthal, Buckner."

Chase's face twisted with rage. Without warning, he took a swing at Liam's head. It was like watching an orangutan go after a fox. Liam dodged Chase's fist and nailed him square across the nose. I heard the sickening crunch of breaking bone, then Chase let out a wild howl, blood splattering down the front of his shirt.

"Watch out!" The words left my mouth as Carson charged, but I was too late. He collided with Liam, tackling him to the ground. They grappled, arms and legs in a tangle, until Liam managed to swing his leg up and wrap it around Carson's neck. In seconds, Carson was on his back, trapped in an armbar, wailing in pain.

"What the hell is going on here? Break it up!" Coach Gardiner came running, his socks pulled up to his knees, sweat popping out on his beet-red forehead. "Hayes, get off him! I SAID BREAK IT UP!"

Liam rolled free of Carson and jumped to his feet, but Carson didn't move. He lay curled up on the grass, moaning and nursing his arm.

"You should be ashamed of yourselves!" Gardiner bleated, the vein in his throat pulsing. "All of you to the principal's office. You too!"

He was looking at me. Only then did I realize I was standing close enough to suggest involvement.

"I was just—"

"No arguing!"

I jumped like he'd stuck me with a cattle prod. Knees shaking, I turned and headed towards the school, trailing meekly behind the three boys.

"You are so dead, Hayes," Chase growled. The threat was muffled behind the hand clamped over his nose. Behind the spatter of blood, his face was the colour of curdled milk. Liam kept his distance from all of us, his hands shoved deep in his pockets. When we got to the principal's office, he took a seat as far from Chase as possible.

Given I had no desire to sit anywhere I might get Chase's blood on me, I took the chair next to Liam and stared decidedly at my shoes, my camera cradled in my hands.

Principal Jenner's secretary, Mrs. Tate, spotted us—or at least spotted Chase's bloody face—and sprang to get the school nurse. After a minute, Ms. Lynn came out and started to fuss over him and Carson. With a little cajoling, she herded them into a separate room to examine their injuries, leaving Liam and me alone.

My heart would not slow down. I felt like it would break through my chest at any moment. Pressing my hand against it, I closed my eyes and tried to focus on breathing while listening to the click of Mrs. Tate's nails against the keyboard. The office smelled like detention slips and stale coffee. Would I get detention?

"First time in the principal's office?"

My eyes snapped open. Liam's blue eyes were regarding me with a glimmer of humor.

Oh my God. He'd spoken to me. I swallowed the sudden ball in my throat, my fingers fretting with the dials on my camera. "Is it that obvious?"

The corner of his mouth twitched. "Don't worry. You didn't do anything wrong."

While this was true, it didn't make me feel any better. I frowned. "That's the problem. I didn't do *anything*. I should have done something."

"Against Chase?" Liam's eyes widened as if the idea alarmed him. "You were smart to stay out of it. You shouldn't get involved with people like that."

"You got involved."

"Yeah, well . . . Joshua is a good kid." Liam brushed his thumb over the barked skin of his knuckles. His brows, several shades darker than his hair, drew together. "And I know what it's like going to this school when you don't fit in."

I wanted to ask why he felt like he didn't fit in, but instead asked, "You two are friends?"

Liam's shoulder lifted in a slight shrug. "You could say that."

Before I could think of a way to keep the conversation going, Principal Jenner opened the door of his office, his grey, wiry hair set off against an inky-black face that was presently purple with fury. I instinctively sank back into my chair.

"I just got off the phone with Coach Gardiner," he said. "You two, in here, now."

LIAM

Jenner leaned over his desk, fingers laced and pressed to his lips. I imagined some augural music playing in the background, like in a scene from *The Godfather*, and fought back a smile.

"Would either of you care to explain why two of my students require medical attention this afternoon?"

The girl beside me looked unjustifiably cowed, staring down at her sneakers, her bottom lip caught between her teeth. I recognized her from math class, but I couldn't remember her name. I felt the urge to step in front of her, blocking her from Jenner's self-righteous anger.

"Well?" Jenner growled.

Her name popped into my head.

"Rainey doesn't have to be here, sir," I said. "She was just a bystander."

Jenner's nostrils flared. "I decide who should or should not be in my office, Hayes."

I managed not to roll my eyes, but only just. If Jenner wanted to assert his power, he'd have to do better than spew flimsy axioms. Still, I figured it was better not to provoke him.

"Ms. Collins, is that true?" Jenner asked, rounding on her.

"Yes." The word was barely audible.

"Good. Then you can give me an unbiased account of what happened."

Rainey blinked, her hands clutching a very expensive-looking camera. "I . . ." She glanced nervously at me, then back at Jenner. "I was taking pictures of the track practice when I saw Chase come up to a kid by the bleachers. Chase started bullying him. Liam stepped in and asked him to stop. It was Chase who threw the first punch, sir. Liam only acted in self-defence. Then Carson tried to knock him down, and that's . . . that's when Coach Gardiner came."

"You're sure that's what happened?" Jenner shot me a look of dark suspicion. He must have thought I'd pressured Rainey to lie for me while we were waiting outside.

"I-I'm sorry?"

"I'm giving you a chance to reconsider your story. As far as I can tell, there's a discrepancy in your account. You say Buckner threw the first punch, but Hayes here doesn't have a scratch on him."

If the man thought this girl was the colluding sort, he couldn't be a worse judge of character. I must have made an inadvertent sound of derision because he rounded on me with a silent glare.

The girl raised her chin and said more firmly, "No. Chase threw the first punch. He was just very bad at it . . . sir."

I bit my tongue hard to keep from laughing. Mr. Jenner's mouth thinned, and Rainey's face turned bright pink.

"Very well," Jenner said at length. "Collins, you can go. Just know that if I hear of you getting involved in anything like this again, I won't be so lenient."

Head down, she retreated from the room, shutting the door behind her. Once we were alone, Jenner pointed to the chair across from his desk. "Take a seat, Hayes."

I sighed and sat down.

"This is not a good start to the school year," he said. "I don't care what happened or who started it, violence is never the answer. Not in this school. Not on my watch."

"You're going to punish me for intervening when Chase Buckner was terrorizing an innocent kid? I didn't realize Springbank High endorsed such a hands-off approach to bullying. How very antithetical of you."

"Cut the attitude. I'm giving you a week's detention," Jenner said, circling his desk and taking a seat in his leather-backed chair. "And I'm calling your parents."

For the first time that day, I felt a small twinge of apprehension. "That won't be necessary, sir."

"Do you think this is a negotiation? Perhaps now you'll think twice before brawling on school property."

So much for social justice.

"What about Buckner?" I asked. "Does he get off, or does the Mustang's golden boy get a free pass?"

Jenner pulled a pen out of his desk and started writing a note.

"Of course not. I will be speaking to Chase after he's finished seeing Mrs. Lynn. Right now, we're discussing *your* actions, Mr. Hayes, and the importance of taking responsibility for them. One week's detention, and if I see you in here for assaulting one of my students again, you won't be scrubbing whiteboards. I will expel you, no questions asked."

Several arguments gathered in my throat, but I could see Jenner was past reasoning. Stubbornness and pride had their hooks in him, and if I pulled, they'd only dig deeper. "Understood," I said frostily.

"Good. You're dismissed."

I was hard-pressed not to kick the door open on my way out.

RAINEY

Jo was waiting for me on the bus after school. I sank into the seat beside her without saying anything, my palms sweating. I felt like I'd downed fifteen cups of coffee and was experiencing a heart-attack-level buzz. I wanted to find a place where no one could hear me, so I could scream as loudly as my lungs would allow.

Liam Hayes knew my name. He'd *talked* to me.

More than that, there had been a moment—okay, maybe only a brief one—during which we had fought for a mutual cause, the two of us standing up to injustice like Holmes and Watson, or Starsky and Hutch (though I was willing to admit my role had been somewhat less significant). In my mind, that moment had created a small, delicate bond between us. Like I could ask to borrow his pencil now and it wouldn't be weird.

"Hey, what happened to you at lunch?" Jo asked, derailing my train of thought. "I saw Coach Gardiner talking to you and some guys. He looked ready to rip out someone's teeth."

"It was crazy." I told her about what I had witnessed, keeping my voice low enough so no one could overhear. "I told Principal Jenner it wasn't Liam's fault. I hope he doesn't get into too much trouble. He was only trying to help."

I hadn't told Jo about my feelings for Liam. Jo had a poor opinion of boys in high school as a general rule. "They're immature and a waste of time. Better off waiting until college," she always said. I was afraid she would laugh at me if I told her I'd developed a childish crush.

Jo grimaced. "I don't know. Jenner's pretty tough on violence. Not that I'm condoning Chase for being a complete asshat," she said quickly, seeing my face. "I'm just saying, I doubt Liam will get a free pass. Did he really break Chase's nose?"

Remembering the sound of crunching bone, I shivered. "Yes, and I wouldn't be surprised if he loosened a few of his teeth too."

Jo grinned. "We should nominate him for a Springbank Humanitarian Award."

"Is that a thing?"

"No, but it should be."

I quickly erased my matching grin, afraid Jo would read too much into it, and switched topics. "Your birthday is coming up. Are we still on for our usual *Lois and Clark* binge night on Thursday? I'll order the pizza and buy enough candy to send us into diabetic shock. It'll be great."

Jo suddenly became very interested in the zipper on her backpack. "Oh . . . right."

"Where is the Josephine Solano enthusiasm I know and love? I thought you liked our *Lois and Clark* tradition."

"I do. It's just . . ." Jo shrugged. "Don't you think we're getting a bit old for that kind of thing?"

I dropped my gaze to my lap in an effort to hide my chagrin. What was so childish about hanging out and watching a classic? "Well, we don't have to watch *Lois and Clark*. We can watch something else. How about that new K-drama on Netflix?"

Jo bit her lip. "The thing is, my parents will be in Hong Kong on Thursday, so I've got the house to myself."

"They're travelling again? On your birthday?"

"It's no big deal." But I knew Jo well enough to know when she was putting on a brave face. Her parents had missed three of her birthdays in the past five years. "Anyway, I was thinking of having a party."

"A party? What kind of party?"

"The kind with people, dummy."

"Are we talking piñatas and pin the tail on the donkey, or Jell-O shots and beer pong?"

"Come on, Rainey."

I bit my lip. "I didn't think parties were your thing."

"They've never been *your* thing," she corrected. "Becca and Val think it'll be a blast, and it's my last birthday before university. I want it to be special."

"So this is Becca and Val's idea?"

"It doesn't matter whose idea it was. It'll be fun. Please come."

I groaned internally. I could never say no to Jo. "Okay. Fine."

"Yes!" Jo grinned.

When I got home, Mom and Maverick were in the kitchen,

singing loudly to *American Pie*, the aroma of basil, garlic, and tomato heralding pasta night.

"I'm home!" I called, dropping my bag and shucking off my shoes.

"We're in the kitchen!"

Mom was stirring a giant pot of pasta on the stove. She was smiling widely, the lines around her eyes soft and relaxed. My mother was a beautiful woman. Before meeting Dad and getting pregnant with me, she'd been on the path to becoming a world-class ballerina. She always said she'd never been good enough to make it into Julliard, but I liked to think she was just being modest. I loved watching her move. Even while performing mundane tasks like preparing supper, she moved like art. I could see why Dad had succumbed to her charm and married her after a month-long courtship.

"Rainey!" Maverick waved the wooden spoon in her hand, flicking pasta sauce across the counter. "You have to try this bolognese!"

"Careful!" Mom said, wiping up the mess.

I licked the spoon. "Oh my God, what's in this? It's delicious."

"The secret is in the pancetta," Maverick said, tapping the side of her nose.

Mom wrapped her arm around my shoulders, giving me a sideways hug. "We had our bi-annual appointment with Dr. Carter today," she said. "Maverick was a model patient, weren't you, sweetheart? She had an ultrasonograph of her liver and some blood work done. There were no signs of protein loss."

I had never been very good at understanding the medical complications of Maverick's condition. Mom and Dad had explained it to me several times, and from what I understood, the doctors had gone in like surgical traffic controllers, only instead of rerouting traffic around a nasty accident, they had rerouted the blood flowing from Maverick's lower body around her heart, sending it directly to her lungs for oxygen. Unfortunately, this placed a lot of strain on her circulatory system, which could lead to complications with her other organs.

"And after my appointment, Mom and I went and got matching pedicures." Maverick wiggled her toes, each nail a bright electric blue.

"Nice colour," I said. "You look like you've dipped your toes in Smurf juice."

"How was your day?" Mom asked.

"It was okay I guess."

She looked up from the pot of simmering bolognese, her eyes searching my face. "Maverick, sweetie, would you go set the table?"

"Sure." My sister hopped down, grabbed the cutlery off the counter, and disappeared into the dining room.

Turning the temperature down on the pot, Mom wiped her hands on the oven towel and reached for the glass of wine next to the stove. "Did something happen today?" she asked.

I plucked a piece of garlic toast off the pan and nibbled the buttery crust, not answering.

"Want to talk about it?"

Because my parents had enough to deal with, I didn't want to bother them with my comparably small problems. However, something was niggling at me, and I felt compelled to ask.

"Mom . . . if someone needed your help, but helping them

would get you in trouble, would you do it?"

She took a sip of her wine as she considered the question. "That's a difficult and complicated question, sweetheart. I'm not sure I can give you a straightforward answer. It depends on the situation and your own sense of morality, I suppose. Why? Is someone in trouble?"

"No, I'm just curious," I hedged.

Mom regarded me with a thoughtful tilt of her head. "If there ever comes a time when you have to make that kind of decision, you'll have to decide if helping the person outweighs the consequences. Sometimes you just have to trust your gut."

That's what I was afraid of. Most days I felt like my gut and I spoke different languages. The only thing we mutually understood was food. I could only hope that if a time came when I had to trust my gut, I had a translation guide at my disposal.

LIAM

Joshua was quiet on the ride home. I wasn't in any mood to talk either, but I figured I should say something. I considered teaching him how to throw a proper punch, but Mercy would rip me a new one if I even suggested the idea, and Joshua . . . well, Joshua was the kind of kid who carried spiders outside and saved his leftovers for Flea. He wouldn't hit someone if a gun was pointed at his head.

I looked at my hand on the steering wheel, my knuckles bruised and bleeding. Despite Jenner's irritating pietism, I didn't regret hitting Chase Buckner. In fact, the memory of his nose breaking under my fist was supremely satisfying. What worried me was waiting for me at home.

When I pulled up in front of the Ramos' house, Joshua made no move to get out of the truck.

"Something up?" I asked.

He shifted in his seat, eyes fixed ahead. "Can we not tell Mercy about today?"

"If you want."

He nodded, then said so quietly I barely heard him, "I hate that school."

"You and me both, kid." My opinion of Springbank was down there with Sunday church and telemarketers. "Which is why it's good to know I've got a friend who has my back."

Joshua looked at me, his eyes magnified by his glasses.

I nudged him. "You and I, we'll look out for each other. What do you say?"

Joshua's ears turned red. "Don't joke."

"I'm not joking. You're a smart guy, Joshua, and being smart is way better than being a loudmouth like Chase Buckner. Ten years from now, he'll be flipping burgers with a knee injury that messed up his plans to play college football, and you'll be a computer software designer earning a six-figure salary, and you won't even remember the name of the asshole who bothered you in high school."

"You can't know that," Joshua argued, but he looked a little less defensive.

"Sure I can. Chase is an idiot. He probably doesn't even know how to tie his own shoelaces."

"He called me a spic. I'm not even Hispanic. Mom and Dad

are from Mindoro."

"See? He can't even get his insults right."

Joshua smiled a little.

"Do you need a ride tomorrow?" I asked.

"No. Mercy has the day off. She'll drive me. Thanks though."

"No problem," I said as he climbed out.

Ray's truck wasn't in the driveway when I got home. Still, my feet dragged up the porch steps as if I were wading through wet concrete.

Mom was sitting in the living room, if that's what you could call the narrow space between the kitchen and the room she shared with Ray. The old upholstered armchair was the nicest piece of furniture we owned, and even that had scorched holes in the armrests where Ray had extinguished a cigarette during one of his drunken stupors.

The room was dim. We never turned on the lamp in the corner until after dark to save on the electric bill, and Mom had drawn the blinds. She was still wearing her work uniform—a blue polyester T-shirt with the logo for Mountain View Grocers on the right, her blond hair pulled up into a tangled knot. Her head turned as I approached as if I was a bad smell she wanted to avoid.

"Where's Ray?" I asked, dropping my bag by the door.

"Out."

I felt the muscles in my shoulders ease. "Look, Mom—"

"Your principal left a message on the answering machine," she said, her voice cracking. "He said you got into a fight. A fight? Really, Liam?"

"It's not like that. I—"

"I don't need this shit. Not from you! Can't you see I've got enough to deal with as it is? Damn it! I thought you were better than this!" Her voice dropped to a whisper. "You're going to end up just like him, aren't you? Like father, like son."

Her words felt like a rusty knife, carving out my insides. This was just so fucking typical. Whoever came up with the phrase *no good deed goes unpunished* must have been a Hayes. I wanted to punch something, to pick up the filthy ashtray on the table and hurl it through the window, to yell myself hoarse. But that would only prove her right, that I was like my father, or Ray, a man prone to violence, who would eventually lose control and end up in prison. I hadn't seen my father in years. He was serving time in Millhaven, a maximum-security prison in Ontario where he'd killed a man in a bar fight. The judge had issued a harsh penalty because the victim had been an investment banker and father of three, whose only fault had been getting a little too drunk after losing a major portfolio that day.

"I'm not Dad," I said emphatically. "I'm not going to end up in prison." I wasn't sure if I was saying this to her or myself.

My mother closed her eyes. Her hands were shaking, and I knew she desperately wanted a cigarette. "I'm trying my hardest to keep this family together. It's all we've got, Liam. We can't afford to mess it up!"

Looking down, I noticed several new bruises circling her wrist. A fresh wave of rage rose in the back of my throat, hot and bitter as bile. I looked back at the drawn blinds, blocking out the sun, and moved closer. Teeth clenched, I reached out and turned her head to face me. A livid bruise blossomed across her cheek, a day old, judging from the swelling.

"We're not the ones messing up, Mom," I said, my voice

shaking. "Ray is. And he is not family." He was a cockroach, a parasite I needed to exterminate.

But my words, like always, didn't seem to register. Removing my hand from her chin, she sighed as if she were hearing the petulant argument of an immature child.

"I know you two have your differences, but Ray isn't a bad guy. He looks after us."

"Looks after us? Mom, look at yourself!"

She flinched, but then her face went blank, her eyes glazing over. "It's fine, Liam."

"Fine? Are you serious?"

"Look, Ray said that if we can save up enough money, he'll take us on a holiday next summer. Somewhere hot, like Florida. Can you imagine?" She smiled, a sickening pantomime of happiness. I couldn't look at it anymore. I couldn't look at her.

"Ray says a lot of things."

"This time he meant it. He was really sincere. So please, *please* don't mess this up."

"Sure. Whatever."

She ignored the skepticism in my voice; she was good at that, at switching off. Like she was hearing but no longer listening. "Ray will be back soon. He went out with Wes and Paul, and tomorrow he's driving a load to Abbotsford, so he'll be gone for a few days. I have a meatloaf in the oven. I thought we could have a nice family meal before he leaves. I'll even make a cake. What do you think?"

She looked so happy at the idea of a family meal, as if the act of sitting around a table together eating a dry meatloaf would somehow make things perfect. "I'm not hungry," I said. Certainly not hungry enough to endure Ray.

But Mom had already taken a box of vanilla cake mix out of the pantry and was busy digging around in the cupboard for a bowl. "You don't have to eat much, and you can save the cake for later."

Arguing suddenly felt meaningless. I was too exhausted. "I'm going to my room." I retreated to my closet-sized bedroom and flopped down on my bed, relishing the darkness that embraced me behind my closed lids. Eventually, I heard Ray stomp up the front steps and kick off his boots.

"Oh, Ray! You didn't!" My mother's voice, muffled through the closed door, was bright with rare joy.

"Just a little something I picked up on the way home. Figured you deserved 'em for being so good to me. You like them?"

"They're beautiful. Here, let me put them in a vase."

I listened to her rummaging through the cupboards. She must have forgotten that Ray had smashed the one vase we owned last month when he'd come home to see flowers on the table from Susan, Mom's co-worker at the grocery store. He had assumed they were from an admirer.

"This will do. What perfect timing. Dinner is ready. Liam! Supper time!" she called.

I dragged myself upright. Just one dinner, I told myself. One dinner, and then three Ray-free days. It was enough of an enticement to get me out of my room. Ignoring Ray, I sat at the table and stared at the Radiance Bouquet from the local EasyMart propped up in an empty bean tin.

I heard Mercy's voice in my head, telling me to cut my losses and leave. Days like this made the prospect damn near irresistible, but then I looked over at my mother's bruised face and felt the weight of the chains around my feet, anchoring me to the floor.

4

RAINEY

I SPENT MOST OF THE NIGHT and the following morning hoping that Liam would talk to me in math class. Not that I had any grand expectations. I didn't expect him to spout poetic odes extolling my womanly virtues (though I might have caught myself fantasizing about various scenarios, one of which involved him announcing to the whole school how much he had loved me since fifth grade). I did, however, harbor a small hope that he would thank me for having his back the previous day.

It took all of ten minutes for me to realize I had read one too many Jane Austen novels. Liam did not talk to me during math class. He didn't even spare me a nod. I tried to catch his eye several times, nearly falling out of my chair in the process, but I might as well have been a ghost.

The stab of disappointment I felt was surprisingly painful, but rather than dwell on it, I decided to ignore him as well. I was *not* going to be pathetic. When the bell rang at the end of math, I scooped up my books and marched towards the door, until Val and Rashida converged in the middle of the aisle to discuss the hidden meaning behind an emoji text. ('Is that a horse? Is he saying I'm an adorable pony?')

Their momentary obstruction delayed my grand exit by ten seconds, which was the exact time it took for Liam to overpass me, and I ended up directly behind him as we left the classroom. No trouble, I thought. I would just ignore him . . .

We reached his locker before I realized I had followed him past the chemistry lab where I had my next class. Thinking it would be weird if I suddenly turned around in the middle of the hall, I kept walking and circled back, arriving at Ms. Bierman's lab just as the bell sounded.

As I was the last one to arrive, there was only one seat open. I cursed silently in my head and sat down next to Carson Kozlowski. Great. Our station was set up with five beakers, each one holding a different substance. Beside these were several apparatus, including a Bunsen burner, a conductivity meter, and various test tubes.

"In your seats, everyone," Ms. Bierman said, calling the class to order. She was the youngest of our teachers and wore brightly coloured skirts and the craziest earrings (today a pair of dangling peacock feathers). I would have figured, being a chemistry teacher, she would opt for less flammable attire, but I had to admire her commitment to fashion. Maverick would have adored her.

I chanced a peek at Carson. The guy was built like a two-ton gorilla; sitting next to him, I looked like a kitten waiting to be crushed by a single backhand. Even with his right arm contained in a sling and his left hand shoved in his pocket, I felt vulnerable. He kicked his chair leg idly with his heel, his eyes sliding over to me as I opened my lab book. Our gazes met for the briefest moment, and I saw a flash of recognition cross his face. His ears reddened.

I was terrified he would say something mean—he and Chase never missed an opportunity to degrade anyone in their vicinity—but instead, he turned his head to stare out the window.

"Covalent and ionic bonds," Ms. Bierman explained. "We discussed these last class. You and your partner will be tasked with identifying whether the substances in the test tubes are ionic or covalent by observing their solubility, conductivity, and melting point. Instructions are written out on the sheet in front of you. If you have any questions, I'll be circulating the class." She smiled widely as if she had just given us the most thrilling assignment.

Postponing the inevitability of speaking to Carson, I carefully read the instructions twice, and then a third time. Meanwhile, Carson switched on the Bunsen burner, cranking the dial until the flame became a roaring tower. I could feel the heat of it warming my cheek. I wondered if he would ignore me and let me do the lab solo; perhaps we wouldn't have to talk at all?

"Carson, Rainey, have you discussed the lab? This is supposed to be a joint effort," Ms. Bierman said, having noted the outward angle of our chairs. "Discoveries are made when minds come together!"

I tried to force a smile out of my grimace without much success. "Right . . ." I turned reluctantly towards Carson.

"Whatever." He raised his free hand. I could see he was about to whip it across the flame as if it were a tealight. I grabbed his wrist, my fingers barely making it halfway around its massive circumference.

"You really don't want to do that," I said, afraid he would burn himself.

He looked down at my restraining hand, and I saw a muscle jump in his jaw. I let go immediately, clearing my throat.

"Shall we get started then? The first step is to put a fingertip-sized amount of each substance into this spot plate and add water to see if they dissolve. Would you do the honors?" I held out the small silver scoop, then realized how difficult it would be for him with his right arm out of commission.

"On second thought, it'll be easier if I do it." I carefully doled out the substances, added the water, and recorded the results.

"Now we test for conductivity. Want to give it a try?" This required minimal dexterity, and having him do *something* was less awkward than having a silent audience observing my every move.

He stared at me, then at the meter. "What am I supposed to do with it?"

"You place the metal node in the solution, and if it's conductive, the display will read a number. Try it." Friendliness was my only defense, so I kept my voice light.

Holding the meter clumsily in his left hand, Carson dipped the needle into the first solution and watched a number appear on the display. "Okay. So?"

"So the sodium chloride dissolved in water, and it conducts electricity. These are both indicators of an ionic compound, which means the sodium chloride is ionic."

"I guess so."

"Let's try the next one."

Carson stuck the node in the next solution, but the display stayed at zero. "Why isn't it working?"

"It's just that this solution doesn't conduct electricity." I checked the label. "Glucose."

"So glucose is . . ." He thought for a moment. "Covalent?"

"You got it," I said with a smile.

The corner of Carson's mouth twitched. "Okay, cool." There was a faint note of genuine interest in his voice now. "I thought this was going to be tough, but this chemistry thing isn't that bad when your partner is a geek."

So much for the friendly defense. "Gee, thanks."

"What? No, that's not what I meant!" Carson's brows shot up in alarm, his ears turning pink again. "I was just trying to say you're, you know, smart."

I couldn't detect any derision in his voice and realized he was being sincere. "I'm not that smart," I said truthfully. I was a solid B student, though I got the occasional A in English, and I rocked photography, but that didn't count. Jo was the genius. I'd never seen her get anything less than an A on anything.

Carson snorted. "You're smarter than me." His ears were bright red now. "And I'd rather be partnered up with a geek than a complete loser like Trent," he said, jerking his head at the next table. Trent Ross was inspecting a test tube over the flame of his Bunsen burner, his mouth perched open. I could see why Carson had called him out: Trent was an overweight kid with an unfortunate case of acne. Easy pickings.

Usually, I was phobic to conflict and walked the path of least resistance by default. However, I couldn't get the image of Liam standing up to Chase out of my head.

I braced myself for impact. "Why do you do that?"

"Do what?"

"Belittle people. Tear them down."

Carson scoffed. "What, you think Trent over there isn't a loser? Figures."

"I'm just saying, I don't see what you get out of bullying others. Apart from a broken nose and a twisted arm," I added, eyeing his sling.

Carson stiffened at the mention of yesterday's fight. "Is that Liam kid telling people he messed us up? Because that is not how it went down. We were just hanging out and he went ballistic. The guy is a total freak."

"I was there. I saw what happened."

"He totally sucker-punched Chase and nearly broke my arm."

"He was defending a kid against two assholes who were being cruel."

"I'm not cr—" Carson stopped himself short, crossing his left arm over his right. "Whatever."

That was the end of our collaboration. Carson dragged his chair away from me, leaving me to complete the lab by myself. I barely finished in time. When the bell rang, I ventured a glance at his lab report. The only thing he'd written was his name at the top of the sheet.

Not my problem, I told myself as I packed up. Mom always said you reap what you sow. If he didn't want to work with me, that was his decision.

LIAM

Even though I had to endure Jenner's sanctimonious scowl during my lunch hour detention, my mood remained light. Ray had left for Abbotsford before I'd gotten up for school, which meant I wouldn't have to see his pockmarked, beady-eyed, greasy face for two whole days. Even Mrs. Burt's political lecture didn't totally suck.

It wasn't until PE that I felt my optimism flag. Undeterred by the grey clouds and damp drizzle, Coach Gardiner had us practicing discus in center field. I was waiting my turn behind the chalk line when my eye caught a figure moving past the benches by the parking lot. Chase had covered the bruises around his eyes with a pair of aviators, but there was no mistaking the taunting grin that spread across his face when he saw me. With a swagger, he turned around and headed towards the school doors.

A pang of unease ricocheted against my ribs. I did my best to ignore it and took my turn with the discus. Distracted as I was, it spun wide, nearly beheading Coach Gardiner.

"Watch it, Hayes!" he yelped.

"Sorry, Coach."

When the bell rang, we plodded inside to change out of our thoroughly soaked gym strips, and after stopping off at my locker to grab my books, I headed for the parking lot.

A large knot of students had gathered on the gravel. They were pointing at something beyond the press of bodies, talking in a swell of hushed whispers that stirred the unease I'd felt earlier. I pushed my way forward. Those who saw me moved quickly out of the way, eyes wide, their whispers growing. Finally, the crowd parted, giving me an unobstructed view of my Chevy.

Someone had smashed in the front windshield, and one of the wing mirrors was dangling precariously from the driver-side door, matched by a similarly lopsided bumper. But that wasn't what was drawing everyone's attention. They were pointing to the words carved into the side panel in crude capital letters.

MURDERER'S SPAWN!

My throat closed, and it felt like hot tar was spreading through my chest, making it difficult to breathe. Ignoring the stares and comments, I carefully opened the driver's door. The movement caused the wing mirror to disengage completely from the frame and fall with a crunch onto the gravel. This provoked a burst of laughter from a group of kids sitting on the cement barricade. I spied Chase among them, still wearing his aviators. If I'd had a discus in my hand, I would have thrown it in his face. You can't smile with a broken jaw, I thought savagely.

Refusing to meet his eye, I got into my truck, praying they hadn't messed with the engine. Luckily, it sputtered and roared the moment I turned the key, and I was able to back out of the parking space. It wasn't easy to see through the spiderweb of cracks across the windshield. I hollered at someone who walked in front of me and blared my horn. The culprit started like a spooked rabbit, and I realized it was the girl from math class. Rainey. She scampered back onto the sidewalk, cheeks flushing, and I felt an additional stab of remorse that only made the scalding rage in my chest flare hotter.

I managed to get to Mercy's by driving slowly with the side window rolled down. She must have heard the sound of the truck because she came out of the house as soon as I pulled up.

"Shit, did a herd of elephants escape the circus and trample you or something?" she asked, nudging the loose bumper with her toe.

Not in the mood for jokes, I didn't answer. I didn't need to yell at Mercy too. "Can I borrow a wrench?"

"Yeah, sure."

"Thanks." I walked past her and into the barn where she kept spare tools from the shop. Flea was rooting around in the tack shed, his grey fur covered in hay from rolling around in the loft. Mice ran rampant in the barn; they kept him busy, scampering along the walls and disappearing into crevasses too small for him to get at.

"Seriously, what happened?" Mercy followed me, all traces of humor gone from her voice.

"Just some assholes at school wanting to get back at me."

"Liam, that's serious property damage. You should report it. Get the police involved."

I scoffed. "Yeah, because that will make my life easier. Do you know how many times the police have knocked on my door? Do you think they'll want to help me out when Ray has an inch-thick file on their desk already?"

My ears rang as I rifled through the toolbox on the wooden workbench, searching for a deep socket wrench.

"Then bring it over to the shop. Ramil and I can fix her up, good as new."

"I can't afford that!"

"What about insurance? Don't you have—"

"Of course I have insurance, but if I make a claim, my premium will go up. I'm barely making the payments as it is!"

I'd picked up a weekend gig stocking shelves at the hardware store and tutored Casey Wilson from sixth grade on Wednesday nights, but the hardware store paid minimum wage, and Casey's mom was a single parent who ran a diner a few blocks from the school. She didn't have money to spare and paid me with free food.

I slammed the lid of the toolbox closed and kicked the workbench, rattling a box of nails. Flea whined.

"Easy, tiger." Mercy was used to my outbursts, this not being the first time I'd vented to her. "Look, I get it. We'll keep it off the books. I'll call Ramil and see if he can get us a deal on a new windshield. Your bumper is salvageable; we just need to reattach it, and I'm sure I can buff out the love note. Just don't expect me to get it all done in one night."

I sighed, pressing my palms into my eyes in an attempt to relieve the angry pressure in my head. "Thanks. I appreciate it."

"What are friends for, right?"

I nodded, managing a weak smile. A gentle hand touched my shoulder, and I looked up. Mercy had moved closer, her face inches away. I could see the flecks of amber in her brown eyes and smell her perfume—something sweet and slightly spicy that didn't quite mask the caustic whiff of the engine oil on her jeans.

I swallowed hard, caught in a dizzying panic, and took an instinctive step back.

Mercy's smile flickered, her hand dropping to her side. Not wanting to read her face too carefully, I kept my eyes trained on the workbench.

"Let's take a look at the damage, shall we?" she said, her voice bright. If it sounded forced, I chose to ignore it and followed her out of the barn. "The bumper should be easy enough." Not meeting my eye, she got down on the ground and shimmied under the truck to inspect the pinnings.

"Let me know if I can hand you anything," I said. Running my hands through my hair, I fought not to swear aloud. What the hell had that been? Why the sudden proximity, and why had it unsettled me? I'd been close to Mercy before. I tried to push the uncomfortable moment out of my head, but it continued to pop up like an overzealous jack-in-the-box.

After a few hours of working on my truck, filling the awkward space between us with the task at hand, the bizarre tension dissipated, and when Mercy wished me a good night with her usual perfunctory salute, I wondered if I'd imagined it all.

5

RAINEY

THINGS STARTED TO LOOK UP that morning. Liam sat next to me in math again, which made me hopeful it was going to be a permanent seating arrangement for the semester (one whole semester!). He also picked up the eraser I'd 'accidentally' dropped when it rolled under his chair, and handed it back to me without me having to ask. This exchange was enough to bolster my courage, and with a tremulous smile, I asked him about his truck.

"It looked pretty bad. I hope Chase pays for the damage." I didn't have to ask; of course it had been Chase.

Liam snuck a glance over his shoulder at Stacey, who was staring at him and whispering something to Rashida. In fact, several people were staring at him. Were they still talking about what

Chase had done to Liam's truck? Seriously, did these people have nothing better to do? I glared at Stacey until she looked away.

Liam's neck turned red. "I'm working on fixing it up," he said. "I owe you an apology, by the way."

"You do?"

"For what happened yesterday. I didn't mean to yell at you. I was angry at Chase, and I wasn't myself. I'm sorry."

I brushed it off. "It's okay. I have a little sister who can scream like a banshee when she's upset. I didn't take it personally, and it looked like you were having a seriously bad day."

I realized too late that I'd unintentionally compared Liam to a banshee. To my surprise, he laughed. I found myself transfixed by the way his eyes crinkled and his left incisor overlapped his front tooth.

"It was definitely that," he agreed. "But that's no excuse for bad behavior. Let me make it up to you."

"Huh?" The word came out somewhere between a squeak and a honk. What did that mean, exactly? My mind immediately conjured a scene from *The Depraved Duke*, my most recent late-night read, in which Horatio pressed Rosalind up against the wall and lavished her with kisses.

My cheeks burning, I tried to don a look of polite disinterest, but before Liam could elaborate, Mr. MacAlastair (the heartless blackguard!) doused my heated thoughts like a wet blanket by handing out a quiz, and at the end of class, Liam left before I could gather the nerve to revisit the subject.

Chemistry was stilted and awkward, as Ms. Bierman ordered us to sit with our partners from the previous class and work on a new assignment together. Carson shot me a look that read he would rather lick the underbelly of a toad, but it looked like we were stuck with each other.

"So . . . what do you think for question one?" I asked. I'd aimed to sound breezy and nonchalant, but unfortunately, my voice came out all squeaky.

Carson scowled. "What are you asking me for?"

I ignored the question and soldiered on. "The assignment is related to yesterday's lab. We have to determine whether the compounds are ionic or covalent, this time based on their chemical formulas."

Carson didn't look at me. He placed his pencil at the top of his desk and watched it roll down, catching it as it fell off the edge.

"Calcium chloride. What do you think? Ionic or covalent?"

He didn't answer, his pencil rattling as he continued to play with it. I eventually completed the entire assignment, talking as I went. When we handed it in at the end of class, Ms. Bierman stopped us at the door.

"It's not acceptable to let your partner do all the work, Carson," she said admonishingly. "And, Rainey, teamwork is important. You need to learn how to work together. I'm going to dock you both marks for that."

"But Ms. Bierman—"

"No excuses," she said, cutting me off. "It was supposed to be a collaborative assignment."

Shooting a dark look at Carson, I turned on my heel and marched out of the class, choking on the bitter dregs of injustice. Why on earth should I be docked marks for getting paired up with a crap partner? It wasn't my fault he was a pigheaded grump.

I marched off to my photography class and was just starting to feel somewhat optimistic again when Jo failed to show up at our usual bench for lunch. I'd brought her some of Maverick's white chocolate macadamia nut cookies for her birthday—her all-time favorite.

At first, I wondered if I'd mixed up her schedule and she was at a student council meeting, but there was no one in the library apart from Mrs. Spielman the librarian and a couple of students playing Candy Crush on the couch. I finally found her in the cafeteria sitting at one of the low tables with Val and Becca.

"Hey," I said. "I thought we were supposed to meet today."

Jo smacked her forehead. "Rainey! Damn it, I'm so sorry. I forgot!"

Not wanting to appear like the needy friend, while totally feeling like the needy friend, I shrugged. "It's okay. I was just worried."

Becca's and Val's eyes were boring holes into my head.

"Why don't you join us?" Jo shuffled over to make room for me. "We were just talking about who we're inviting to graduation."

Out of the corner of my eye, I caught Becca rolling her eyes. Small as the gesture was, it might as well have been a kick to the gut, awakening a sudden hornet's nest in my stomach. Clamping down on my nerves, I shook my head. "It's okay. I've got some pictures I need to take for a project," I lied. I couldn't remember the last time I'd lied to Jo.

"Rainey—"

"I'll see you later."

Eager to escape Becca's and Val's uncomfortable stares, I left.

* * *

On the bus home, Jo sat with me, leaving Val to sit next to Ryan. It was her way of making amends after standing me up, and I felt a little better for it.

"I'm so sorry, Rainey," she said, eyes round with contrition. "We were talking about our plans for tonight, and I got distracted. I'll make it up to you, I promise."

"It's fine. I get it," I said, but it wasn't, and I didn't. Not really. I just wasn't sure how I could explain how I was feeling and not come across as an insecure loser. "Here." I pulled the macadamia cookies out of my bag.

"My favorite! Thank you. You're coming tonight, right? Seven o'clock, at my place?"

"Who's going?"

"Lots of people. That's why they call it a party, dummy." Catching the look on my face, Jo sighed. "It'll be fun, I promise, and I can't have a party without my best friend there. That goes against the friend code."

She had me trapped. Trying and failing to summon an iota of excitement, I nodded. "Okay. Seven it is."

Jo grinned, her face glowing. "You won't regret it!"

Had I been the betting type, I would have placed a small fortune on the contrary.

When I got home, I went straight up to my room and lay down on my bed. It had been a weird day. The kind of day that started off well but somewhere along the way went a bit sideways. A *masquerade day*, Maverick called them. When everything is normal except for a subtle, unnerving sense that something is not quite right.

Six months ago, the doctors had told my parents that Maverick was experiencing arrhythmia. She was admitted into the hospital, and they inserted a PICC line, a catheter that ran from her arm to a large vein carrying blood to her heart so that she could receive injections daily with medicine that would help her heart rate normalize. When she asked how long she'd have to deal with a tube coming out of her arm, the doctor said, "A PICC can stay in for as long as twelve months. We'll monitor her progress closely and see if the medication helps."

So Maverick came home with a tube in her arm as if she'd escaped Frankenstein's lab. She insisted on wearing the brightest sleeve to cover it, with blue and green hummingbirds and bright purple flowers.

That first day home, my parents had wanted to make things as normal as possible so Maverick didn't feel bad about her permanent tube, only we'd tried a little too hard: Mom made her favorite dinner, we watched her favorite movie, and I was careful to laugh at all the funny parts even though we'd watched it a million times before and the humor had worn off. I was especially careful not to say anything about the conspicuous bandage around her arm. I couldn't even bring myself to look at it.

"Would you just stop!" Maverick screamed, hurtling one of the couch cushions across the room.

"Maverick, baby, what's wrong?" Mom asked.

"You're all being weird!" And with no more explanation than that, she shuffled off to her room. She would have stormed had she not been so exhausted.

"I'll go," I whispered, seeing Mom's dismayed expression. I

came up to find Maverick sitting on her bed, her shoulders hunched against the wall, and her stuffed rabbit, Carrots, cinched in a two-armed tourniquet.

"What's up, bean?" I asked, sitting on the edge of her bed.

"I hate it when you guys do this," she said, glaring at the top of Carrots's head.

"Do what?"

"Pretend like everything's okay."

"Everything *is* okay." But the words tripped and fell out of my mouth before I could wrap them in false optimism.

Maverick shot me a potent tween glare.

"Sorry." I sighed.

"I know what you're trying to do," she said, "but you're not helping. It's like everyone is wearing this mask and playing a part, and it's creepy! It reminds me of that circus we saw last year."

"The masquerade show?"

Maverick shivered visibly, and I didn't blame her. That had been a little ghoulish, even for me. All the dancers had worn leering masks with black holes for eyes.

"We're just trying to make you feel better."

"No, you're trying to make yourselves feel better, and it's freaking me out."

I bit my lip. She was right. Even though she was only twelve, Maverick had dealt with more than most people faced in their entire lives, yet here we were, treating her like she was still five years old.

"Fine. I don't like looking at that bandage on your arm. The fact that you have a tube sticking out of you makes me squeamish."

The corner of Maverick's mouth twitched. "Tell me about it."

"I also think it sucks that you have to take medicine every day, and we don't even know if it will help." Tears burned my eyes, but I wasn't going to cry in front of my sister. I couldn't. "We're just scared, bean. We don't want to lose you."

"I don't want to lose me either." She let go of Carrots and laid her head down on my lap, and after a few moments, I felt her fall asleep against me.

Since then, I'd tried to be as honest with Maverick as possible, even when it was hard. Especially when it was hard.

Listening to the comforting sound of Mom and Maverick debating the merits of pineapple on pizza (Maverick thought pineapple should be added to just about everything, including sandwiches and breakfast cereals), I peeled myself off my bed and changed for Jo's party. Given Becca's and Val's animosity at lunch, I seriously wanted to bail. Going seemed like the worst idea possible. How many times had I watched a horror film and yelled at the nerdy kid in the glasses not to go down the long dark hallway? This party was a hallway, and it was very long and very dark. And yet . . .

"It's Jo's birthday. It's Jo's birthday," I chanted. I headed down for supper.

"What time is Jo coming over?" Mom asked. "Shall I put the pizza in the oven?"

"Er . . . about that. Jo isn't coming over. She's having a party at her place."

"You're going to a party?" Maverick asked. I might as well have said I was joining a martial arts club and learning kung fu.

"If that's okay," I said, half hoping Mom would don the cap of parental authority and forbid me to go. At least then I'd have some excuse to stay home.

"Of course, sweetheart."

I'd forgotten how much my parents loved Jo—in their eyes, she was mature and responsible and destined to become the next governor general of Canada. Besides, Jo's place was literally next door. What trouble could I possibly get into a hundred yards from home?

"You look smokin'," Maverick said, giving my jeans and turtleneck sweater a once-over. I'd eaten peanut butter less thick than her sarcasm. "Please let me do your makeup."

"I wasn't going to wear any."

"Oh come on! You look like you're applying for a job as a librarian, not going to a party."

I stuck my tongue out at her.

"You and your sister look beautiful just the way you are," Mom interjected, tugging the end of my sister's braided pigtail admonishingly. "You don't need makeup."

Maverick pursed her lips in silent dispute. "Are boys going to be there?"

The question caught me off guard and sent my nerves on edge. "No. I don't think so," I added truthfully. "I don't think Jo's parents would agree to that."

Roused by Maverick's inquisition, Mom's parental instinct flared. "Make sure you're home by eleven and call if you need anything, okay? And absolutely no alcohol!"

"Ew, gross." Nan had encouraged me to try a glass of wine last Christmas, and I thought it tasted like poisonous vinegar. I wasn't interested in a repeat experience.

Satisfied, Mom put the pizza in for the three of us—Dad was

working a night shift at the hospital—and we watched an episode of *The Bachelor*. Come seven, I ran back upstairs and checked myself out in the floor-length mirror in the corner of my room. Maverick was right: I did look a bit plain, or as Nan would say, drab as a Highland October. Rummaging through my drawers, I found an old tube of mascara and applied a quick layer, then dabbed some gloss on my lips. It was no Hollywood makeover, but it would do.

Calling out a goodbye to Mom and Maverick, I slipped on my shoes and headed out the door. Crossing the lawn towards Jo's house, I could hear the beats of club music blasting through the Solanos' stereo system.

I was now walking down the long, dark hallway, but I couldn't stop. Was this how those poor suckers in horror movies felt? Compelled by forces beyond their control? I tried not to think about how much I wanted to be back home with Maverick, curled up under my plush blanket and eating my way through a package of Twizzlers.

It's Jo's birthday.

She's your best friend.

This is going to be fun.

I knocked on the door and waited for several minutes before realizing no one could hear me over the music, then let myself in. The noise was overwhelming. It pummeled my ears, shaking loose all sense of order and calm; I felt like a squirrel trapped in a taiko drum.

The press of bodies didn't help. Jo's house was packed with what looked to be everyone in our year. I even noticed a couple of juniors playing pool around the table next to the living room, the sporadic crack of the cue ball barely audible over the music.

The Solano residence always smelled like expensive leather upholstery and floor polish (their housekeeper came to clean every Friday), but tonight, it smelled like beer, nachos, and the unmistakable stink of marijuana.

I balked and almost turned tail, but Jo spotted me and came through the press of people, grinning from ear to ear.

"You came!" she yelled, throwing her arms around my neck.

"Of course I came," I yelled back. "This is quite the party!"

"I know, right?" she laughed, drinking something frothy from a red Solo cup. I caught a whiff of fermented wheat and wriggled my nose; I didn't know Jo drank beer.

"You look gorgeous, by the way," I said. She did, too, dolled up in a strapless pink dress and matching stilettos. I suddenly felt embarrassingly frumpy in my turtleneck and jeans.

Jo rolled her eyes. "My parents gave them to me for my birthday. I guess their solution to parental absenteeism is Jimmy Choo and Dior. Come on, let me get you a drink!"

"I'm good, thanks."

"What?" The music had changed to an ear-throbbing foreign club song I didn't recognize but probably should have if I was the least bit cool. Jo beckoned me further into the house, her voice lost to the pulsing beat. I squeezed past a group of people dancing, taking an elbow to the ribs as I maneuvered around a couple grinding in a way that made me blush. We finally made it to the kitchen, where even more people were crowded around the island eating a giant plate of nachos. Becca and Val were there, and Stacey from math class. To my surprise, Carson was there too, sling-free, his arm looped around Becca's shoulder. I couldn't fathom how her willowy, tall frame didn't crumble under his massive bulk.

Becca's and Val's smiles froze the moment they spotted me. Great. I wondered what I'd done to earn their hostility. It wasn't like I'd talked to either of them long enough to merit dislike. Was I breathing the wrong air or something? Did they have something against short people?

"As I was saying," Becca said, her ice-green eyes shifting back to Jo, "you have *got* to get the new Leiber. It is to *die* for. I asked my dad for one, but he said I already have too many. I mean, what would he know?" She rolled her eyes. "Oh well. I don't have a matching outfit for it anyway."

"What's a Leiber?" I asked.

"God, seriously? It's a purse." Becca looked outraged that I'd interrupted her, even though I hadn't really interrupted her.

"That Liam kid isn't here, is he?" Stacey asked Jo.

"God, I hope not." Val shuddered. "I do not like that guy. He gives me the creeps."

"Does he even have any friends? I've never seen him hanging out with anyone. He's always alone."

"With good reason. You saw what it said on his truck, didn't you?"

"Yeah, but that was just Chase having a laugh, wasn't it?" Stacey asked, eyes popping out of her skull.

"Who knows."

"Liam isn't that bad," I said before I could stop myself.

Five heads turned to stare at me, all of them wearing varying expressions of disbelief. Even Jo looked uncomfortable. I would have traded my camera for an invisibility cloak right then, but still. They were being unfair.

After a pregnant pause, Jo cleared her throat. "I could use a top-up. How about you guys?"

"Totally. This girl needs another drink. Carson, babe." Becca pushed her glass against his chest. He just barely caught it as she let it go. "Get us another tequila sunrise, would you. Hold the sunrise."

"Er . . . what is—"

"Jo, don't look, but Jake is totally checking you out right now!" Becca said, grinning mischievously.

Looking confused and more than a little irritated, Carson took the glass to the counter where Mr. Solano's alcohol store had been thoroughly pillaged.

"Jo . . . won't your dad get upset if you drink all his liquor?" I asked, glad the music was too loud for the others to hear.

Jo shrugged. "It's fine. He's always getting stuff from clients. He won't notice, and I doubt he'd even care."

"But—"

"It's a party, Rainey. It's supposed to be fun."

And *I* wasn't fun. She didn't say it, but the implication was there. I opened my mouth to speak, but I didn't know what to say. It was as if the threads that had bound us together for the past twelve years were snagging on invisible snares and starting to fray. Flashes of the Masquerade show played in my head, accompanied by an eerie lullaby.

Was this really happening? Was I losing Jo?

Another song came on, and Stacey screamed. "I love this one!" She grabbed Jo's hand and dragged her towards the hall where people were dancing. I tagged along reluctantly, standing with my hands pinned to my sides, bouncing my knees to the beat. I probably looked like a kid who had to pee. Meanwhile, Jo was singing along to the song, swaying her hips like a flamenco dancer, looking radiant and beautiful. I couldn't remember the last time I'd seen her so happy.

After one song, I felt hot and cramped and the opposite of happy. I spotted an open space on the couch next to the Solanos' massive limestone fireplace. A couple was taking up the majority of the sitting space, their arms entwined and their lips locked in a passionate exchange of saliva. Opting for the lesser hell, I extracted myself from the dance floor with a mumbled promise to return and shuffled over to the couch, sitting as far away from the engaged couple as the space allowed.

"Want a drink?"

I looked up to find Carson a few feet away, his brown hair brushed back in a cool wave. He really was a big guy. Not overweight, just big, and his brown eyes reminded me of a sad St. Bernard.

"No thanks." I looked down at my hands, hoping he would go away, but his sneakered feet inched a step closer to me.

"You sure? You look like you could use one."

He was probably right. "I'm okay. I don't really drink." With a rising sense of panic, I waited for him to get bored and move away, but he didn't.

"Why are you here then? You don't look like the party type."

I bristled. "What's that supposed to mean?"

"Whoa." He raised his hands in mock surrender. "I'm just saying. You don't look like you're enjoying yourself much."

Seeing Jo, who was like the old Jo I knew and loved, but not, and having to endure Becca's and Val's sidelong glances, along with the loud music, and the sour smell of beer and sweat—basically everything about this night—had put me on edge.

"Jo is my best friend," I said charily.

"Seriously?" Carson looked genuinely surprised. "I've never seen the two of you hanging out at school."

"She's busy." Why did I feel the need to justify myself? "We're neighbors. We've known each other since we were kids."

"Oh. Cool." He nodded. "Chase and I grew up together too. We're cousins, and his mom is a total whack job, so he—" Carson looked like he just bit his tongue. "Shit. Please don't tell anyone I said that about his mom." He raked his fingers through his hair, pulling it out of its relaxed wave into an anxious flop. "Shit. Chase will be pissed."

"It's okay," I said quickly. "My lips are sealed." I wasn't sure what Carson meant, calling Chase's mother a whack job, but I wasn't about to say anything that could land me in Chase's bad books.

Carson blew out a breath of air, his cheeks puffing out. "Anyway, I wanted to apologize for what happened earlier today. It wasn't fair that Ms. Bierman docked you points. I was the one being an ass. I'll talk to her tomorrow and try to get those marks back for you."

"Oh . . . er, thanks."

"The thing is," he continued before I could make an excuse to leave, "I could use some help in chemistry. I need to pass or I'll get kicked off the football team. I thought you could . . . you know . . ." He wasn't quite looking at me when he said this, his ears burning like embers; I half expected his hair to start smoking.

"You're asking me for help?" I asked, incredulous.

Carson shrugged, scratching the back of his head.

I hesitated. "I don't know. As I said, I'm not that smart. Why don't you ask someone like Jo? She's a genius. She'll be able to help you way better than I could."

"Yeah, well, I don't want to look stupid in front of people, you know? And I don't want Becca finding out."

I wasn't sure if I felt flattered by his confidence in me or insulted that he didn't consider me 'people', but I decided it was better to feel flattered.

Just then, I noticed Becca watching us from the dance floor, her face flushed in fury. Crap.

"Er . . . I think Becca wants to dance with you," I lied.

Carson glanced over his shoulder, his smile falling at the sight of his girlfriend's expression. It made me think of a documentary I'd watched with Maverick about hyenas.

The female hyena bares her teeth and snaps at the smaller male for getting too close to her kill.

I guess I was the kill in this scenario.

"Great." Carson chugged the rest of his beer and approached his girlfriend while I hunkered further down into the couch. Hot and Heavy were still at it and were becoming increasingly hard to ignore—was he trying to suffocate her with his mouth?—so I decided to relocate and headed for the kitchen. I was just thinking about getting myself some juice from the fridge when Becca walked by.

It happened so fast, I had no time to react. One moment she was holding a strawberry daiquiri, and the next it was splattered down the front of my sweater.

"Oh my God, Rainey, I am so sorry. How clumsy of me!

Here, let me get that." She reached out and smeared the sticky, ice-cold slush across my chest, smiling.

"Get off." I swatted her hand away.

"No need to be a bitch about it," Becca said, sticking out her bottom lip.

"That's the pot calling the kettle black." I pushed past her and ran upstairs to the bathroom, slush dripping from my chest. I tried my best to clean my sweater, soaking and dabbing it with a towel, but there was no way in hell I was going to get the stain out. It was my favorite sweater too.

I tried not to cry but did anyway.

Jo was still dancing in the living room when I came back downstairs, her stilettos discarded under the coffee table. Becca was with her, both of them waving drinks over their heads and laughing. I tried to get Jo's attention, but the music was too loud and there were too many people. I finally gave up and left.

Twenty minutes later, Maverick and I were curled up on the couch in our living room, eating cookie dough ice cream out of the carton and watching *Lois and Clark* in our pajamas.

"How was the party?" she asked.

"It was just a party," I said, shrugging. I didn't want to get into it. I'd managed to sneak upstairs and change the moment I got home so no one would see my ruined sweater. Even thinking about it now made my eyes burn with unshed tears. Every minute of the night was a splinter lodged between my ribs, making it hard to breathe.

It wasn't fair.

"Were there boys? Did you play spin the bottle and make out in a closet or something?"

I snorted. "Not even close." I pulled a Twizzler out of the package on the table and gnashed it between my teeth. If only I could be as badass as Lois Lane, intrepid reporter for the *Daily Planet*. She went toe to toe with scumbags like Lex Luthor without breaking a sweat. She would make mincemeat of girls like Becca. But I wasn't Lois. I was Rainey Collins, and I didn't know the first thing about making mincemeat.

"I wish I was like Lois."

Maverick snorted. "Lois is an idiot. Seriously, how can she not see that Clark Kent is Superman? It's so obvious."

"I guess so."

"Trust me," Maverick said, "you are way smarter than Lois."

I could always count on Maverick to make terrible situations bearable. "Thanks, bean," I whispered. But then I remembered that *always* is a very long time . . .

6

LIAM

"MERCY, YOU ARE A GENIUS!" I circled my truck, taking stock of the newly installed windshield and side mirror. She had even managed to buff out the words scratched into the side panel. "It looks brand new."

"That's a bit of an exaggeration," she said wryly. "It could still use a paint job, and your suspension is a little rough. You should think about replacing the ball joints."

Feeling light and almost giddy with relief, I waved off her concerns. "It'll be fine. How much do I owe you for this?"

Mercy shrugged, her hands tucked into the back pockets of her jeans. "Let's just say you owe me a favor."

I eyed her warily. "This was a lot of work, Mercy. I have to owe you something. At least let me pay for the windshield."

"It's okay. Really. I got a deal on the windshield, and the rest was just labor." She smiled, rocking back onto her heels.

"Are you sure?" Had it been anyone other than Mercy, I wouldn't have taken the handout, but I knew I could make good on the favor eventually, and in all honesty, I couldn't afford the alternative.

"I'm sure. I know where you live, remember?"

I smiled, but then I remembered the moment in the barn and felt a small tremor of misgiving. What if the favor Mercy called in was something I wasn't able to give? She was the only good thing in my life right now, and I didn't want to ruin it, but as cliché as it sounded, I just didn't feel that way towards her. What was I going to do if our friendship wasn't enough?

***

Rainey was already there when I got to math, doodling quietly in her notebook. She looked up as I entered the room, then quickly looked back at her doodle. I made her nervous, I realized. Given my behavior lately, she probably thought I was unhinged and dangerous. I couldn't get the image of her stricken face out of my head after I'd laid on the horn and barked at her to get out of the way. The quietest, most benign human I'd ever met, and I'd bitten her head off like a savage dog. The memory made me wince.

How could I make it up to her? When I needed to apologize to Mercy, I bought her a root beer soda and made sure I lost when we played at the pool hall, but that wasn't exactly a one-size-fits-all apology. Rainey could hate root beer. What did I know? The girl was a complete stranger.

I glanced over as I sat down. She had her chin propped in the cup of her hand, her bottom lip crushed beneath her teeth as she drew idly in her notebook.

"Hey," I said.

The greeting pulled her sharply out of her reverie, her lip popping out from between her teeth. "Hi."

Her eyes were a strange colour. Like pools of rainwater, wide and eerily serene.

"I don't know about you, but this first week back has been a disaster," I began, testing the conversational waters.

She gave a half-hearted smile. "You can say that again."

"At least it's the weekend, right?" I said this because it seemed the thing to say, but truthfully, I hated weekends. If I wasn't working at the hardware store, I was stuck at home with my mother and Ray. I much preferred being at school. "Do you have any plans?"

"Not exactly." She shot me a deliberative look—was I truly interested, or just being polite?—then added, "There's supposed to be a thunderstorm Sunday night, and I was hoping to take some pictures for my photography class. Mr. Greene gave us a project that focuses on light."

I recalled the camera she'd held in Jenner's office. "You like photography?"

She smiled again, but this time it reached her eyes, causing the light in those grey pools to shimmer. "I do. I'm not very good though."

"I doubt that."

The bell rang before she could respond, and MacAlastair stood up from his desk. "Everyone please pass in their homework from yesterday. We'll get started on today's lesson."

A small gasp erupted beside me. "Oh no!" Rainey started rifling frantically through her book, her face drained of colour.

"Everything okay?" I asked.

"I forgot about the homework! I was so distracted last night. Oh no, oh no, oh no. This can't be happening." She finally unearthed the worksheet from the mess in her binder with only the first few answers scribbled in and smacked her forehead.

"Here," I murmured. "You can copy mine." I pushed my worksheet to the far edge of my desk in plain view.

Rainey shook her head. "Thanks, but I can't."

"Why not?"

Everyone was passing forward their worksheets. Ryan turned around in his seat to take mine. "Dude, lay up."

"Hold on." I turned back to Rainey. "Just jot down the answers. Quickly."

"No. It would be wrong. I'll just have to finish it at lunch and hand it in by the end of the day."

"MacAlastair will dock you marks for that."

"I know, but I didn't finish it." Despite her words, Rainey's voice wobbled and broke. "And I should do the work, even if it is late."

I was surprised. It was obvious she was terrified of MacAlastair, but here she was, willing to take the hit of his disapproval on principle. After class, I watched her approach MacAlastair's desk, her incomplete worksheet clutched in her hand. The paper trembled like a reed in a hurricane. I felt bad for her. MacAlastair was a decent guy and probably one of the best teachers at Springbank High, but he could be a hard-ass when it came to deadlines.

Rainey looked one sneeze away from fainting when she returned to her desk.

"How'd it go?" I asked.

"He said I could hand it in at the end of the day, but he'd dock twenty percent."

The slight warble in her voice incited a pang of pity in me I wasn't expecting. I fought the urge to offer some kind of comfort, like a pat on the shoulder or a squeeze of her hand. I hated being on the receiving end of these gestures of sympathy, but maybe it would make her feel better?

"I've got to get to chemistry," she murmured. "I don't want to get in trouble for being late." She got up and left, leaving me with my hand half-raised, reaching for air.

RAINEY

Today was not going well. I couldn't believe I'd forgotten my math homework. Just thinking about Mr. MacAlastair's cold disapproval made me want to run for the hills, and that wasn't even the worst of it.

Jo wasn't at school.

The only time she'd missed school was in third grade after contracting chickenpox, and even then, she'd insisted on finishing her homework from bed. I sent her a text asking if she was okay as I sat down in chemistry.

"What's up?" Carson asked after catching me checking my phone for the fifth time. He sounded genuinely concerned, and I wondered if I had somehow, miraculously, made a friend out of Springbank's linebacker.

"I'm worried about Jo. She wasn't on the bus this morning, and I haven't seen her today."

Carson shrugged. "She's probably just hungover."

"Jo?" I shook my head. "You've got the wrong girl."

"I don't think so," he said, brows raised. "Becca, Val, and Jo got hammered last night. Becca called me and said she wasn't coming today, and I'm pretty sure she stayed with Jo last night."

It was impossible.

"You look like someone just stole your lunchbox. What's the big deal?"

The big deal was that Jo never missed school. At least not the Jo I knew. What the hell was going on? I sent her another text, the small bubble of anxiety in my stomach growing jaws that started to chew on me from the inside out.

Ms. Bierman gave a lesson on ionic formulas. I helped Carson as best I could but had trouble focusing. My mind kept returning to Jo, wondering if she was lying murdered in a gutter somewhere because that was the only thing that would stop her from coming to school. If she didn't text me back by the end of the day, I was going to call the cops.

My phone binged.

I'm fine. Just sick.

I blew out a sigh of relief. You should have told me. I was worried!

Sorry. See you after school? Rosie's?

Sure.

"She get back to you?" Carson asked.

I nodded. "Yes. She says she's sick."

"See, what did I tell you? That's what you get for partying it up on a weekday."

I couldn't bring myself to smile.

After class, Carson spoke to Ms. Bierman about our previous assignment and managed to convince her that I should be given full marks. Even though I was still hedgy about his taste in friends (the cousin he couldn't help), I was nevertheless grateful, and decided that the next time Maverick made her white chocolate macadamia cookies, I'd bring him one. He looked like he could devour a dozen without breaking a sweat.

* * *

After my last class, I delivered my homework to Mr. MacAlastair (I managed to thrust it into his hand without meeting his eye before scurrying away) then ran to meet Jo. She was waiting for me in her Mini Cooper in the student parking lot. I got in and scanned her face for signs of deadly illness: jaundice, gangrene, bursting pustules. But she looked completely normal, her face remarkably un-gangrenous and bright, her hair brushed into a high ponytail.

"What happened?" I asked, shoving my backpack into the well by my feet and holding my camera bag on my lap.

"What do you mean?"

"I mean, since when have you missed school like this?"

"I told you, I was sick."

"Yeah, but—"

"It's no big deal, Rainey. It's not like I can't make up the missed classes. Come on, I could really go for a chocolate milkshake right now." She drove us the few blocks to Rosie's Diner, and we grabbed a table near the windows. The diner was a popular hang for students, being close to the school and the purveyor of the best garlic fries in the province.

"You could have left your things in the car," Jo said as I struggled to fit my backpack and camera bag on the bench next to me.

"I can't leave my camera in your car. Someone might steal it. And besides, it would feel like I don't love it enough."

Rosie came over to take our order, her heels clicking across the black-and-white checkered linoleum floor. Rosie was the other reason the place was popular. She let us play whatever music we wanted on the player in the back corner, she stayed open late if we had a group study session, offering a special 'study' discount on the garlic fries, and she made a killer cup of coffee, an accolade which automatically put her in my good books.

"What can I get you hooligans?" she asked, flashing us her wide smile.

"I'll get a chocolate cherry shake, extra cherries," Jo said.

"And a vanilla shake with a side of garlic fries," I added.

"You got it."

When Rosie left, I turned back to Jo, noting the dark circles under her eyes, not quite concealed by a hasty application of makeup. "Jo . . . is everything okay?"

"What do you mean?"

"It's just . . . I don't know. Last night you were drinking, and today you missed school. It's not like you."

"Rainey, I'm fine," she said, rolling her eyes. "I just wanted to have a little fun. What is so terrible about that?"

"Nothing." I frowned, looking down at my hands.

"Look, Rainey, you need to learn to live a little. We've only got a year before we'll be in university. *University.*" She smiled, reaching over to squeeze my hand.

"I know," I said, pulling my hand back. "I get it."

"Do you?" Jo pressed. "Have you thought about what you're going to do after graduation?"

"Of course I have," I lied.

Jo narrowed her eyes disbelievingly. "And?"

"And I haven't decided yet," I hedged.

"Come on, Rainey. Don't you want to get away and explore the world? There's more to life than K-drama marathons and milkshakes at Rosie's. Think of everything you can do! You could learn how to make tea from a Buddhist monk or, I don't know, study stone carving from an Italian sculptor. Last semester, at the college fair, UVic boasted a pretty cool photography program. You skipped that, by the way."

I wrapped my arms around my chest. How had this suddenly become about me? "I don't want to leave. I like it here."

"So you'll, what? Graduate and ask Rosie for a job serving poutine?" Jo sighed, releasing her frustration in a giant puff. Then her voice went soft. "Is this about Maverick?"

I stared at the napkin dispenser, clamping my lips together so the bottom one wouldn't wobble. "Of course it's about Maverick," I whispered.

Jo was quiet for a moment; then she shook her head and smiled, her voice decidedly bright. "My point is, have you ever ordered anything other than a vanilla milkshake with a side of garlic fries off the menu here?"

"What's wrong with ordering a vanilla milkshake with a side of garlic fries? I like vanilla."

"But have you *tried* rocky road? Or cherry cheesecake?"

I shrugged. Jo already knew the answer. Just then, the bell over the door jingled, and I spied a now-familiar head of tousled blond hair over her shoulder. Noticing my captured attention, Jo turned, then swiveled back to me, her mouth hanging open.

"Oh my God. You *like* him! Rainey Collins, you have a crush!"

"Be quiet!" I hissed. "And I do not."

"Oh please. Look at your face! How did I not hear about this? Was this because of what happened with Chase?"

I shushed her with a spastic wave of my hand. Trying to be discreet, I watched Liam through the corner of my eye as he approached the counter and sat down on one of the stools.

Jo leaned conspiratorially across our table, grinning. "Seriously, why did you not tell me about this?"

"Because I know what you think about high school boys. I knew you'd make fun of me. Besides, it doesn't matter. I seriously doubt he's interested." God, I hoped the music coming from the stereo was obscuring our conversation.

Jo scoffed. "Oh please. One, I'm not interested in high school boys, but that doesn't mean I think they're all lost causes, and two, you don't know until you ask. Have you talked to him?"

"A little," I admitted. "We're in the same math class."

"Okay . . . well, that's a start I guess." For an inchworm. She glanced over her shoulder again with a look in her eye that made the bottom of my stomach drop to the soles of my feet. "Hey,

Liam!"

"Jo, don't!" I tried to kick her under the table but ended up stubbing my toe against the table leg.

When Liam looked over, I sank into the back of the booth, wishing I could disintegrate into a million pieces.

"Join us," Jo said, waving him over.

"Uh . . . sure."

My heart was pounding so loudly, I could have sworn he heard it as he sat down next to Jo.

"What's up?" He looked from me to Jo and back again with an expression of mild curiosity.

"Rainey and I were debating whether or not it's better to stick with a tried-and-true favorite or opt for the perilous unknown. What do you think?"

Liam looked at me, confused. My throat had gone very dry. I swallowed hard. "Jo thinks I'm missing out because I always order a vanilla milkshake."

Liam's expression relaxed into a half smile, and he raised his hands. "It's a classic for a reason."

"Ha!" I crowed, triumphant.

"But—" he continued, and my smile collapsed, "—I think trying something new once in a while is a good thing. Who knows? You might find something you like more than vanilla."

"I couldn't have said it better myself." Jo raised her eyebrows at me.

Rosie came by with our orders, and I accepted my milkshake, sending it silent reassurances that I would never betray our pact.

"Anything for you, honey?" Rosie asked Liam.

I blinked. I'd never heard Rosie refer to anyone as *honey*

before. She referred to all her customers as hooligans and ruffians.

"A steak sandwich, if that's okay."

"I'll have Hank hold the onions."

"Thanks."

Jo regarded Liam with a tilt of her head, her blond ponytail swinging to the side. "You must be a regular here if you've buttered Rosie up enough to tailor your order. She won't hold anything unless you have a doctor's note saying it'll kill you. What's your secret?"

"No secret. I just tutor her son."

"Tutoring youths, annihilating bullies," Jo said, ticking them off on her fingers. "And I *know* you're in the running to be this year's valedictorian because I asked Jenner who my competition was, and he might have slipped me your name. So tell me, Liam Hayes, is there anything you don't do?"

"Rotogravure?"

"Roto . . . sorry, you lost me."

"Sorry, bad joke. It's a technique in printing, but I'm guessing your question was rhetorical."

Jo snorted. "You're weird, but I like you."

I felt a nervous panic. I didn't want Jo liking Liam. That would spell disaster for me, the Velma to her Daphne. I wasn't even smart enough to be Velma. I was Scooby. I envisioned the two of them walking hand in hand, bantering wittily and smiling at each other like two beautiful people in a marketing campaign for toothpaste. I hated those commercials.

Jo suddenly reached into her pocket and pulled out her phone. "Hello? Oh, hey, Mom."

I narrowed my eyes at her. Jo had the kind of laser focus that made it impossible to get her attention when she was otherwise preoccupied, so she kept her phone on the loudest possible setting, and I hadn't heard it ring.

"Of course," Jo said into her phone. "No, I understand. I'll be there as soon as I can." She hung up. "Liam, I'm so sorry, but do you mind driving Rainey home? My parents caught an earlier flight, and I need to pick them up at the airport, pronto."

I would have applauded her for the lie's flawless execution, but I was too busy staring at her with my mouth hanging open.

"Of course." Liam glanced at me just as I snapped my mouth shut. "If it's okay with you?"

"Excellent," Jo interceded before I could summon a response. "See you guys tomorrow. Thanks, Liam, it's been a slice. Bye, Rainey!" She grabbed her purse, left a twenty to cover our bill beside her unfinished milkshake, and ran out the door.

Josephine Solano, I don't know if I want to kill you or kiss you right now, I thought fiercely.

"Do you need to get home right away?" Liam asked.

"Oh no, I'm in no rush," I said quickly. "You haven't even gotten your food yet." As if on cue, Rosie returned to the table with his steak sandwich, steaming hot and smelling like gravy and buttery garlic toast.

Okay, maybe I'd try the steak sandwich next time.

"Here you are, honey," Rosie said. "Say, how is your mom doing? I saw her at the grocery store the other day; she had a pretty bad shiner. Is she all right?"

Liam's head jerked up. "Oh . . . er, yeah. She slipped getting out of the shower."

Rosie winced sympathetically. "Wet porcelain is a death trap.

You should get one of those silicone mats. I have one, and it's saved me loads of times."

Liam gave her a perfunctory smile; I got the impression he wasn't thrilled about the topic of conversation. "I'll see if I can find one, thanks."

The bell over the door announced the arrival of new customers, and Rosie returned to the counter. Liam's shoulders relaxed as if he were relieved, but I only felt panic. I was sitting across from Liam Hayes with no idea what to say or do. I traced lines in the condensation forming on the table from my milkshake while chewing on the end of my straw, then remembered that Elizabeth Bennet never chewed on the end of a straw, and spat it out quickly.

"Thanks for taking me home," I said at last. Wait, had I said that already? I felt like I'd said that already. Maybe I'd just said it in my head? *Breathe, Rainey. You got this.* "I hope it's not too much trouble."

"It's no trouble at all. I owe you, remember?"

"You really don't." While I felt this was true, I was still disappointed that my one favor from Liam was being swapped out for a cab ride rather than a sordid encounter in a dark alley. This thought drew my attention to his lips. The bottom lip was full and pink, the top thinner and bowed. I wondered what his lips tasted like. Probably less like sunshine and ambrosia and more like a steak sandwich if I was being realistic.

"What?" Liam asked, looking up from his plate.

"Huh?"

"Do I have something on my face? You're looking at me funny."

I blushed. "No, I was just . . . I was just wondering if you were planning to go to the kickoff game at the end of the month."

God, was that the best I could come up with?

Liam gave a short, hard laugh. "I'm not sure if you've noticed, but I'm not exactly a fan of Springbank's football team. Why? Are you going?"

"Yes."

He looked surprised. "You like football?"

"Not even a little bit," I admitted sheepishly. I didn't even understand the rules. To me, football was just a bunch of guys in pads and helmets knocking into each other. Truth be told, I was dreading the event.

"Then why go?" Liam asked.

I shrugged. "Jo asked me to come with her. She needs me to take some pictures for the yearbook."

"So you're a masochist?" His eyes sparkled with humor.

I flushed. "No, it's called being altruistic."

He tilted his head as if considering something. "Huh."

Huh? What did *that* mean? I could have let it go. With anyone else, I would have, but Liam wasn't just anyone, and I cared what he thought, especially about me.

"What?" I pressed.

"Nothing." He took another bite of his sandwich.

"Liam—"

He gave an apologetic half smile. "I just think that altruism is a hedonistic desire for people to feel good about themselves. We do things for people not because we're selfless, but because we're seeking to gain something like friendship or self-worth. It makes me wonder if you have insecurities about your friendship with Jo."

His words struck me mute. I'd heard of snakes that could immobilize their prey with a single venomous bite; only instead of venom, I was struck with burning indignation. Indignation that Liam had just exposed one of my deepest vulnerabilities with such ease.

My feelings must have reflected in my face because Liam quickly backtracked. "I'm sorry. It's none of my business."

"You know, I think . . . I think I'll just walk home," I said, grabbing my bags.

"No, wait, Rainey—"

I walked out of the diner, my heart hammering against my chest. A hand grabbed my wrist, stopping me. "Please, Rainey. Let me drive you home."

"Why would you want to drive me home? You've known me for all of two minutes, and you think I'm . . . I'm hedonistic and insecure." I swatted his hand away, but he skidded around me, blocking my way. He looked genuinely distraught.

"Stop, please. That's not what I meant."

"I thought you were pretty clear." I tried to get around him, but he stepped with me, cutting me off.

"I didn't mean for you to take it personally. It was thoughtless pontificating, that's it. Seriously, you're one of the most decent people I've ever met. Can you just forget what I said?"

"No, and I don't even know what pontificating means," I huffed, feeling stupid.

"It means I was being an ass." He said this with a crooked, self-deprecating smile that prompted a swell of giddy emotion powerful enough to drown out some of my chagrin.

"Will you let me give you a ride home?" he asked. "Please?"

I bit my lip. It was a ten-minute drive home, which meant it would take me an hour, maybe two, on foot, and I wasn't wearing the best shoes. Being stubborn would seriously hurt. "Fine," I grumbled. "What about your food? Aren't you going to pay?"

"Rosie pays me to tutor her son with food," he explained. "She won't accept my money even if I offer."

His Chevy was parked on the side of the road, newly repaired if still a bit rusty. The door creaked as I pulled it open and got into the passenger side. The front seat was a single long bench in faded black upholstery, currently laden with a small mountain of tattered old books.

"Er . . . sorry about the mess," Liam said, moving them out of the way.

I glanced at the titles. Nicomachean Ethics. A Treatise of Human Nature. The Theory of Everything. Moby Dick. "Are these all yours?" I asked.

"Yes, well, sort of. I got them out of the library."

"Are you working on a paper or something?"

Liam shrugged. "No, I just like to read."

I liked to read, too, but you wouldn't find any of these titles on my summer-break reading list. I put my camera bag and backpack down by my feet, thinking of my bookshelf at home, filled with my tawdry romances, dog-eared manga, and a select few Jane Austen novels. "Which one are you reading right now?"

"Aristotle's Nicomachean Ethics."

"And does Aristotle think altruism is a hedonistic something-or-other?"

Liam smiled apologetically, hearing the sting in my voice. "Not exactly."

"What does he think?" I was curious. Not about Aristotle, but why Liam was so interested in a man who had been dead for a couple millennia.

"He thought morality was a practiced behavior. He believed that actions in themselves are neither good nor bad; it's whether the action is performed based on vice or virtue that determines its morality. But I'm not sure if he was right. He reduced human ethics to function, and I wonder if perhaps we shouldn't hold humanity to a higher standard."

"That sounds kind of heavy," I said honestly. And way over my head. I hoped he wouldn't ask me what I thought; I didn't even know what Nicomachean meant. "And you're reading it for fun?"

"More as an intellectual inquiry."

"An inquiry into what?"

"What it means to be good."

"It seems to me you've figured that one out already."

Liam grimaced. "Some days I'm not so sure. What about you? What are you reading right now?"

Thinking of the answer, I flushed. "You probably wouldn't know it."

"Try me. I read a lot."

I fiddled with my seatbelt, not looking Liam in the eye. I considered lying and saying something impressive like *War and Peace* (who had written that again?), but given my luck, Liam had probably read that, too, and I didn't want to risk getting caught in a lie.

"*The Depraved Duke* by Lisa Oswell," I blurted, then pinched my lips shut and waited for the chorus of laughter. But Liam didn't laugh. I glanced sideways, trying to read the sharp line of his profile. The ghost of a smile haunted the corner of his mouth.

"What, no pithy comment about low-brow trashy romance being a waste of time and intelligence?" I asked, echoing my father's much-repeated sentiments.

"Not at all. Though you're right, I haven't read it."

"Don't tell me you're not a fan of Lisa Oswell!" I said with mock horror.

Liam laughed again, but it wasn't mocking. "I'm not, but I also don't see why anyone should be criticized for their taste in books." He started the truck and backed smoothly out of the parking stall. "By the way, you're going to have to tell me where to go."

I was so busy trying to round up the butterflies flitting about my stomach, it took me a moment to answer. "Turn left at the lights, and then head straight for a few kilometers." I turned towards the window so he wouldn't see me grinning.

It felt strangely intimate getting a ride home with Liam. If Maverick were here, she'd be singing at the top of her voice, and Mom would be telling us to put on our seatbelts and asking if anyone needed to use the bathroom before we left. Even Dad couldn't drive without drumming his fingers against the steering wheel.

Liam was quiet. He drove with one hand on the wheel, his left elbow propped against the window, relaxed. There was a stillness to him that I found peaceful.

"You were right," I said after a while.

"About what?"

"Me and Jo. I mean, I am a little insecure about our friendship."

"Why?"

"I don't know. I guess because she's so accomplished and beautiful. It's intimidating. We're neighbors, and I wonder sometimes if that's the only reason we're friends." I'd never said any of this aloud, not even to Maverick, but I was still hurting from what had happened at Jo's party, and I couldn't shake the feeling that my friend was slipping away. It felt good to voice my fears.

Liam weighed my words in silence for a moment. "I don't think you're giving yourself enough credit, or Jo either. She doesn't come across as the kind of person who would pick her friends arbitrarily."

Maybe he was right. Maybe I was worrying for nothing. I just couldn't know for sure. I used to think Jo and I had a lot in common, but I was wrong about that, it seemed. Maybe I was wrong about our friendship too?

Seeking a distraction, my eyes roved around the cab of the truck. I noticed an old cassette case among the books and picked it up.

"What the . . . they still make these?"

"No. I found it at a garage sale. This old girl only plays tapes."

"You can get an after-market CD player installed, you know."

Liam scoffed. "And ruin the authentic experience?"

I looked at the cover and grinned. "Bob Seger?"

"You like him?"

"I love him. Maverick and I listened to his 'Greatest Hits' CD on repeat when my family drove to Kelowna to visit my grandmother last summer." Seven hours later, we knew every word to every song, singing with the windows of the Escalade rolled down, hands surfing over the wind.

"Maverick?"

"My sister."

"I didn't know you had a sister," he said, surprised. "Does she go to Springbank High?"

"No. She's only twelve." I wasn't sure if I was ready to tell Liam about Maverick. I'd be home in five minutes, and Maverick, small as she was, was far too important to summarize in so short a time. She was all the best chapters of my life, not a hasty footnote.

"Do you have any siblings?" I asked.

"No." He sounded almost relieved.

"You never wanted a brother or sister?"

A muscle in Liam's jaw twitched. "It's not that. It's just . . . complicated." It was all he was willing to say.

"That's too bad," I said. "I think you would make a great older brother."

He looked surprised, and maybe a bit touched. Or at least less grim. "Thanks."

We turned onto my street, and I pointed out my driveway. Liam pulled up and leaned forward in his seat, peering up at the white-framed windows. "Wow. Nice place."

"Is it?" I surveyed the familiar Edwardian red-brick facing, three-car garage, and large black door with its brass knocker. I guess it was nice. I just saw my home: the front lawn where I'd hosted childhood tea parties, the window Maverick had broken with her baseball, the driveway where I'd scraped my knees falling off my bike a million times. Next to Jo's house, which had an indoor pool and separate quarters for the housekeeper, I thought it was relatively modest.

"What do your parents do?"

"My dad is a neurosurgeon."

"Oh." Liam nodded, rubbing his hands over his jeans, his eyes fixed on the house.

"I'd better go inside," I said. I was stalling. I didn't want this short, stolen moment to end. What if he went back to ignoring me after this? "Thanks again for driving me home."

"Any time," he said with a smile that made my heart ricochet against my ribs. Terrified of what he might see in my face, I opened the door, leapt out, and raced up the front steps without saying goodbye.

I leaned my forehead against the front door as I closed it, letting out a long, calming breath of air. Now I knew why dogs wagged their tails when they were happy—I wiggled my bum, dancing from foot to foot as excitement shot from the crown of my head down my spine.

"Care to explain why you came home in some boy's pickup?" asked a mild voice.

I yelped and spun around to see Dad regarding me through the reflective glare of his reading glasses, a cup of tea in hand. My cheeks heated. "Um . . ."

"I thought you and Jo went to Rosie's." He didn't sound angry, exactly, but I was going to have to explain myself. The Collins family had a strict no-lying policy.

"We did, but she got a call from her parents and had to leave, so I got a ride home with Liam instead."

"Liam drove you home?" Maverick skidded around the corner wearing a green polka-dot dress and bright yellow stockings. "*The* Liam?" She ducked past me and pressed her nose against the window to peer out onto our driveway. "Awh. He's already gone.

I was hoping to get a good look at him."

"Liam, hey?" Dad's brows rose.

"It was just a ride home," I said hastily. "Is Mom still out?"

"Yeah, those Heart to Heart meetings can run long." The Heart to Heart meetings were for parents of children with congenital heart defects. At first, Mom had been hesitant to join the group. Now she saw them every week at the hospital as if her life depended on it. She loved those women like they were blood.

"You still have half an hour of music theory," Dad said to Maverick. "Go finish up."

Maverick sighed theatrically. "I'm trying *not* to die young. Another half hour of music theory will kill me for sure."

"Nice try." Dad was used to Maverick's hyperbolic jokes about death. She trudged dutifully back to her room, leaving the two of us alone. Placing his tea down on the side table, he removed his glasses and started to polish them with the end of his tie—a habitual action that betrayed a nervous agitation. I held my breath.

"So is Liam a friend?" he asked a little too casually.

Could I even claim that? It seemed a little presumptuous. "More like an acquaintance," I answered truthfully. "He's in my math class."

"Should your mother and I meet him?"

"I don't think that's necessary." God, I felt like I'd stepped into a time portal back to 1914.

"Fair enough. You know, though, that your mom and I are here if you ever want to talk about . . . you know . . . sex."

I now understood why some of the women in my books fainted from mortification. Staring at my shoes, I mumbled a quick, "I know."

"Okay then." Dad picked up his tea, then pretended he needed something from the kitchen and promptly fled the scene of 'most awkward conversation ever'.

Later that evening, when Maverick was brushing her teeth, I poked her under the ribs. "Would you mind not mentioning Liam to Mom and Dad again?"

"Why? I thought you liked him," she mumbled around her toothbrush, toothpaste dripping down her chin.

"I do. It's just . . ." A big dark ball of fear had subdued my elation and was now reigning supreme in the pit of my stomach. The rare, beautiful moments I'd shared with Liam were like delicate dandelion seed heads. I wanted to cup them in my hands and protect them, fearing the smallest puff of air would destroy them. "He's smart and good-looking, and I'm not exactly girlfriend material."

Maverick spat into the sink and wiped her mouth with the back of her hand. "I don't get it. You're a girl. Doesn't that make you girlfriend material?"

"Yes, but some girls are high-quality cashmere. Like Jo. She's smart, beautiful, adventurous. I'm . . . I'm corduroy."

Maverick wriggled her nose. "Corduroy?"

"Yeah."

"What's wrong with corduroy?"

"It makes you look like a sausage." I sat down on the edge of the bathtub.

"You do wear a lot of frumpy sweaters that make you look like a hotdog." When I didn't laugh, Maverick changed tracks. "He drove you home. Doesn't that mean he likes you?"

"He was just being chivalrous."

"Guys are only chivalrous to old ladies and girls they like."

I snorted. "Where did you read that?"

"In one of the magazines at the hospital. There was an article in *Sparkle* on how to read his signals. I was bored, and it was either that or a book about cranes."

As inclined as I was to dismiss the theory, a part of me wondered if Maverick could be right. Still, that didn't change the fact that I was . . . well, me . . . and I just wasn't brave enough to test the waters. I wasn't Maverick.

"Will you read to me tonight?" she asked.

"Of course." Maverick sometimes had trouble falling asleep. There had been several nights I'd woken up with a shriek to find that she'd crawled into my bed, her ice-block feet tucked against my legs. To remedy the problem, I'd started reading to her before bed. She said she liked the sound of my voice; she'd always struggled with reading, but she loved the stories—especially the adventure stories. We'd gone through *Gulliver's Travels*, *Robinson Crusoe*, *Treasure Island*, and *Huckleberry Finn*. We were currently reading *Peter Pan* for the third time. It was her favorite.

"Warm enough?" I asked as she crawled under the covers. Stuck to the wall beside her bed were several pictures I'd taken: Mom and Dad on the front steps of our home; Maverick sitting on Dad's shoulders, wearing a crown of daisies; Mom standing on the beach, watching the waves roll in as the sun went down. I snuggled in beside her, propping myself up with a pillow, and opened the book where we had left off.

"Overhead Tinker Bell shouted 'Silly ass!' and darted into hiding. The others did not hear her. They had crowded round Wendy, and as they looked, a terrible silence fell upon the wood. If

Wendy's heart had been beating, they would all have heard it."

I could hear Maverick's heart, but I could feel it beating doggedly, not yet ready to give up. I prayed it wouldn't. Not yet. It couldn't. Because a world without Maverick couldn't exist. It wouldn't make sense.

I continued to read until Maverick was fast asleep, weaving the words of J. M. Barrie around her in a cocoon of protection.

7

LIAM

AS I TURNED DOWN THE GRAVEL ROAD and crossed the cattle guard, I felt the dull pressure of a headache forming behind my eyes. It was like an anticipatory warning for the inevitable shitstorm waiting for me at home. I wondered at the sudden dip in my mood and realized that I had forgotten that Ray was back from Abbotsford, a fact that materialized when I saw his truck parked in front of the trailer.

I pulled up next to it, shut off my engine, and rested my head against the steering wheel. Mom was still working her shift at the grocery store, so Ray was probably inside, several beers in. Maybe I could stay here until she got home.

As I reached over to grab my biology textbook, I noticed the black bag in the passenger footwell. Rainey's camera bag. She must have forgotten it. I lifted it onto the seat beside me, surprised by the weight of its contents. There was a camera inside, a Leica M6, along with two lenses. I didn't dare contemplate how expensive it was. A small silver key chain hung from the zipper tab: a hummingbird decorated with green and blue jewels.

I could have called Rainey to let her know I had her camera, but I didn't have her number or a cellphone. Even if I found her number in the phone book, I'd have to use the landline, and I did not want Ray listening in while I talked to Rainey. It felt wrong. Like I'd be contaminating something pure and good with his vileness by even mentioning her name in his presence.

I could return the camera to her now, I thought. It was a perfect excuse to extend my time away from Ray. I grinned and started my truck again, but before I could pull away, Susan drove into the yard, dropping Mom off with a bag of groceries.

Susan was a well-intentioned woman with no husband, no children, and far too much time on her hands. I think she saw my mother as some kind of charity case she was compelled to tend as part of her Christian duty.

I hated Susan. She always sniffed her nose at me and made loud comments about never seeing me at church on Sundays, as if my absence were a crime against humanity itself. Mom went—usually after considerable browbeating on Susan's part—but I couldn't be bothered to join her. Sitting on stiff pews and listening to the reverend preach about piety for an hour every week did not a saint make. I knew some of the people in those pews: Paul, a man I'd seen climbing into his truck after drinking five beers with Ray and Wes and driving home. Mark Daniels, a police officer who I'd seen accepting a bribe from Wes after Wes beat a woman who had, according to him, stolen his wallet.

Did these people seriously think a sermon was going to absolve them?

"Liam, could you take this in for me?" my mother called, spotting me in my truck. I hesitated, noting Susan's pinched scowl and narrowed eyes peering at me through her window.

"Liam! Help, please."

I got out and took the bag from her arms. "Thank you, sweetheart. By the way, the oven doesn't seem to be working very well," she said with a laugh and a roll of her eyes, as if it was no big deal. "I was wondering if you'd be a dear and look at it for me."

I looked over her shoulder. Susan had her window rolled down and was listening to our exchange with ill-concealed fascination. No wonder Mom was putting on a Maria von Trapp act. Sweetheart? Really?

"Sure, no problem." I would return the camera first thing tomorrow, I thought.

* * *

I'd set my alarm for eight, but I woke up before seven. I had a shift at the hardware store and figured I could return Rainey's camera on my way there. Hopefully it wouldn't be too early to drop by. I rolled out of bed, grabbed my jeans and work shirt, and ducked into the bathroom for a quick shower. When I came out ten minutes later, Ray was sitting at the kitchen table with his back to me.

Gritting my teeth, I walked past him, deciding that I would skip breakfast and hope that someone brought muffins to work.

Sometimes my manager Sean stopped by Tim Hortons on his way in, if he was in a good mood.

"Morning."

Something in Ray's voice made me turn. On the table in front of him was Rainey's black camera bag, the zipper split open. It was like I'd suddenly swallowed an ice cube: cold tendrils radiated down my spine, prickling the hair on the nape of my neck.

"This is some nice piece of equipment," he said softly.

My hands curled into fists. "You went through my truck?"

"Where'd you get this, boy? It ain't yours." Ray's beady eyes narrowed, a leer peeling back the corners of his mouth. "You steal it?"

"It belongs to a friend."

He flicked the hummingbird keychain with his finger, making a soft tinkling sound, and the leer turned into a grin. "Pretty. A friend, you said? Or a girlfriend, maybe? Did she leave it behind after you fucked her in your truck?" His breath smelled like cigarettes and sour milk.

I was clenching my fists so tightly, my nails were digging into my palms.

"Girl should take better care of her things." He picked the camera up and turned it over. "This looks expensive."

"What do you know about cameras?" I asked, trying to keep my voice steady.

"Not much, but I know quality when I see it and this . . . this here could fetch a pretty penny, I guarantee it."

"Give it back."

Ray cocked his head to the side, placing the camera on the table. "Don't see why I should. In fact, I think I'll keep it. Teach ye to take better care of your things. Don't ever say I never taught you nothing."

"I said give it back."

"Or what? You gonna take it from me?" Ray's hand moved towards his hip, brushing the handle of the flick knife in his belt.

I tried not to look at the knife, keeping my eyes locked on his face, and made a lunge for the camera.

Ray caught my arm in a vice grip and slammed me against the counter. Gasping, I managed to twist myself free and drove an uppercut as hard as I could right under his ribs. He grunted, but it didn't slow him down, not even by a second. One hand grabbed me around the throat, and his other fist came flying. I jerked back but not quickly enough. The impact of his punch made my head rattle, and the iron tang of blood filled my mouth. By the time I regained my balance, Ray had me pinned, the edge of his knife pressed against my throat.

"Ray!" My mother appeared at the door to the bedroom in a pale yellow dressing gown. "Ray, stop!" She pulled at his arm. "Let him go!"

"Get your hands off me, bitch!" he growled.

"What are you doing?" she screamed.

Ray glared at me, and I could see he wanted to do it, wanted to carve my face with his knife, and through the rage, I felt a cold tremor of fear.

"Fucking pansy boy," he spat, releasing me. Shoving my mother out of the way, he stalked out of the trailer, leaving me standing against the counter, my throat tingling where the knife had been. I felt a drop of blood slip down my neck.

"What the hell was that? Huh? What did you do?" Mom said,

her voice shaking.

"What did *I* do? Jesus Christ, Mom!"

She started to cry, but I was beyond caring. I grabbed Rainey's camera, put it back in the case, and ran to my truck. I must not have locked the doors last night, I realized. Still, Ray wouldn't have seen the camera bag unless he'd been looking through the windows of my truck, which meant he'd been snooping around this morning, probably looking for spare cash.

Shaking with adrenaline, I drove to Rainey's. The cab of the truck was stiflingly hot. I rolled down the windows, letting the wind chill the sweat on my face. I could still feel the sharp edge of the knife against my throat, could feel the burn as it cut my skin and see Ray's face, inches from mine, filled with contempt; it was no match for the blind and wordless hatred that had me in its thrall now.

Fucking pansy boy.

I slammed my hand against the steering wheel.

To help settle my mind, I turned on the radio and tried to focus on the song that came on, 'Wayward Son' by Kansas. I blasted it as loud as it would go, feeling the beat pulse through me, but it didn't help.

I wondered if I needed to tell Rainey that he had gone through her bag. I decided—selfishly—that it wasn't necessary. The camera looked undamaged, and the thought of having to explain the disgusting disease that was Ray to someone like Rainey turned my stomach.

It was still only eight when I pulled into the Collinses' driveway. I cut the engine, the blaring radio leaving behind a quivering silence punctuated only by the distant honking of geese and the stutter of an impact sprinkler from the neighbour's yard.

I had no idea if the Collins family were early risers, but I couldn't just leave the bag on the front step—it would be too easy for someone to take it. Looking through the rearview mirror, I assessed the damage. The blood from the scratch on my neck had already dried. I pulled up the collar of my shirt to cover it, but there was no hiding the split, swollen lip, and my cheeks were flushed.

Closing my eyes, I took a few slow, deep breaths, counting up to ten and then back down to zero. It helped a little. I was still unaccountably nervous as I walked up to the front door and rang the bell. I heard it echo through the house while I rocked my weight from side to side, staring at the pristinely manicured lawn and neat flower beds, then down at my sneakers with their worn soles. I'd had to replace the laces with elastic bands after they'd broken.

I was about to leave, worried someone would mistake me for a thief, when I heard the pad of approaching feet.

A man—I assumed Rainey's father—answered the door. He wore a pair of chinos and a crisp, white collared shirt. Simply dressed, you wouldn't assume he was well-off at a glance, but I knew the signs, having been conscious of them most of my life: the cut of his clothes, the clean-shaven face, the whiff of expensive aftershave, the neatly barbered hair, the simple but expensive Blancpain watch.

Dr. Collins's eyes were a Xerox of Rainey's: a light, clear grey. Though where hers were guileless, his were keen and intelligent, framed by deep laugh lines and a pair of blue-rimmed glasses. He exuded a sense of competence and calm that at once put me at ease and made me even more nervous.

He smiled. "Can I help you?"

I cleared my throat. "Hi, I'm Liam Hayes," I said, acutely conscious of my two-sizes-too-large shirt and swollen lip. "Rainey left her camera in my truck yesterday. I just wanted to return it." I handed over the bag.

"That's kind of you. Thank you, Liam. Rainey is still asleep. I can get her if you don't mind waiting. Did you want to come inside?"

"Oh no, that's fine," I said quickly.

"You sure? You're welcome to stay for breakfast. I'm making my famous Nutella banana bread french toast."

My stomach growled. "I appreciate the offer, but I was just on my way to work."

Dr. Collins's gaze lingered for the briefest moment on my swollen lip. I saw a thought pass behind his eyes, but whatever it was, he masked it quickly with a polite smile. "Of course. Probably best to avoid the diabetic coma anyways," he said drolly. "I'll let Rainey know you dropped by."

"Thanks." I turned, hearing the door close behind me, and went back to my truck, eager to get away from the immaculate house before I polluted it with the dirt on my shoes.

When I got to work, I checked the break room. There were no muffins.

* * *

It was ten minutes to the end of my shift. I'd had worse days, all things considered. One customer insisted the box of hex bolt screws I was holding weren't actually hex bolt screws, and Evan, who helped me stock shelves, only dropped one bag of nails, which was a significant improvement from the previous week when he'd broken five dozen light bulbs.

I was sweeping up the nails when I heard a raised voice coming from the next aisle over. A loud crash and a curse followed.

Leaving the broom leaning against the shelf, I ran around the corner to see a woman standing in the middle of the aisle, blood dripping from her hand. The culprit—a small saw blade—lay on the ground at her feet.

"Ma'am, are you all right?" I asked, running forward. "We need to get you some medical attention. Let me take you to my manager's office. He has a first aid kit." The woman looked up at me, eyes wide with surprise before her face relaxed into an expression of recognition.

"I'm fine, Nathanial. Stop fussing. You always fuss."

"I'm sorry?"

"I was just coming to find you." She reached out, mindless of the cut on her hand, and patted my shoulder. "Your sister thinks I slept with Robert. Good God, I mean really. She has more imagination than is good for her. The idea is ludicrous."

The woman smiled at me, flashing a beautiful set of white teeth. I would have dismissed her for being drunk, but I couldn't smell any alcohol on her whatsoever. Her blond hair was done up in a bun, but much of it had fallen around her face in wispy flyaways, lending to the appearance that she was quite mad.

I looked up and down the aisle to see if anyone was with her. An older man with a balding head was inspecting the rotary blades further down the aisle.

"Sir? Sir, are you with this woman?" He looked at me and shook his head, clearly not eager to get involved.

"Ma'am, what's your name?"

"Oh please, Nathaniel, are you really going to play this game?"

"I'm not Nathaniel, ma'am. My name is Liam. Do you know where you are?"

"Of course! I was looking for Otis," she said matter-of-factly. "He ran away again. I'm not sure what I'm going to do with him."

"Otis? Is he your husband?"

"What? Heavens no, Otis is the dog, silly."

I spun around, wondering if we now had a dog loose in the store. But that wasn't the most pressing of my concerns. "Ma'am, you've hurt yourself. We need someone to take a look at it. Will you come with me?"

The woman sighed. "You don't have to make a fuss. I'm fine." But despite her protests, she followed me to the back of the store towards the manager's office. Sean was sitting at his desk when we came in, and I saw his face turn bleach white at the sight of the woman's bloody hand.

"What happened?"

"She cut herself on a saw blade. Can you get the first aid kit?"

Sean swore under his breath. These kinds of accidents always resulted in filed complaints and long-winded memos about safety protocols. He pulled the kit out from under his desk and opened it. "I'm very sorry about this, ma'am," he said. "Is there someone who can take you to the hospital? Do you want us to call someone for you? An ambulance?"

"Oh no, Nathaniel will take me home." The woman placed her head on my shoulder and looked at me with an unsettling degree of love and devotion while her fingers gently stroked my arm.

Sean stared at me, his mouth hanging open.

"I think she's a little confused," I explained in a quiet undertone. "Why don't you sit down," I said to the woman, smiling kindly. "Sean here will take a look at your hand."

She did as I asked, reaching her hand out while holding onto my arm with the other. At least she did not seem to be in considerable pain or distress. I searched for some clue that would lead me to her identity; she didn't have a bag and wore only a light jacket and plain slip-ons. The only jewelry she wore was a gold wedding band on her left hand and a silver bracelet on her right. I tried to get a closer look at the bracelet and spied the medical emblem on the narrow plate.

"Ma'am, may I see this?" I asked.

She blinked at me in surprise. "Certainly."

I turned the bracelet over and grabbed the phone.

"What?" Sean asked. "What is it?"

"She has dementia. There's a number to call." As I waited for the line to connect, I felt a mounting sense of unease press against my chest. Was it a coincidence? It was a common enough name. Besides, she'd called me Nathaniel, and while I couldn't remember exactly, I was pretty sure that wasn't his father's name.

Sean looked down at the bracelet after he finished wrapping her hand in gauze and tape. "Alice Buckner. Well, Alice, you might need a stitch or two, but I'm sure your family can look after that. Is that Buckner as in Hank Buckner, the oil guy?"

* * *

Fifteen minutes later, we heard the approach of several pairs of hurried footsteps. There was no polite knock; a large man with steel-grey hair and a hawkish nose flung the door open, causing it to hit the opposite wall, leaving a dent in the plaster. He took one look at the frail woman sitting at the desk and flushed scarlet.

"What the hell, Yates! You were supposed to keep an eye on her!"

"I'm sorry, sir," an older woman with mousy brown hair said to his right. "We were taking a walk and my shoelace came undone. I stopped to tie it, and when I looked up, she was gone."

The man scoffed. "How long does it take to tie a goddamn shoe?"

Alice was still holding my hand, and though she continued to stare with sedulous interest at the cracks on the floor, I felt her stiffen at the sound of the irate voice.

"Hank Buckner?" Sean rose from his chair, nearly knocking it over in his haste.

"Robert," the man said brusquely. "Hank was my father." He stood a foot above Sean, dressed in oiled brown leather shoes and a light wool three-piece grey suit. Cologne clung to him in a gag-inducing fog. "You said on the phone that she was hurt. What happened?" He barely glanced at Alice.

Sean hefted his pants up over the soft bulge of his stomach, sweat popping out on his brow. "Er . . . well, we didn't see what happened exactly, but we think she may have cut her hand on a saw." While Sean went on to explain how he had handled the situation with great competence, my gaze rose over Robert Buckner's shoulder to where his son stood just outside the office.

His face pale and drawn, hands shoved deep into the pockets of his faded jeans, Chase Buckner looked uncharacteristically meek in the shadow of his father. A flicker of recognition crossed his face, quickly swallowed up by a look of such savage rage I felt the heat of it burning holes in my chest. And at that moment, I knew—inculpable as I was—I was going to pay for what I had witnessed.

RAINEY

I poured myself a mammoth-sized coffee from the pot and added two tablespoons of sugar to curb the bitterness while slouched over the counter, propping my chin up in my hand.

"That's what you get for staying up all night taking pictures," Maverick said around a mouthful of toast.

"It was worth it." At least I hoped it would be. I would develop the pictures I'd taken of last night's thunderstorm after school today. The Leica was old-school. I had no way of previewing the pictures and had to wait for each frame to develop. Less convenient, maybe, but I liked the anticipation of watching the pictures appear like magic in the chemical bath. It made it all the more exciting when they turned out well.

"I'm just bummed Liam came by again and I still didn't get to meet him," Maverick said.

I was about to say *maybe next time*, but I wasn't sure there was going to be a next time.

"What's this about Liam?" Dad asked, coming into the kitchen.

"Nothing," I said hastily.

Maverick grinned. "I was just saying he should have stayed for breakfast. Are you sure you mentioned the Nutella banana bread french toast? No one can turn that down."

Dad wasn't usually one to dismiss a compliment, especially when it was related to his notoriously limited culinary skills, but he looked untowardly serious when he said, "He just came to drop off Rainey's camera on his way to work."

"Isn't he in Rainey's class? Why would he have a job?"

"A lot of kids his age have jobs, sweetheart."

Maverick looked at me. "Rainey doesn't."

"No, but your mother and I think it's important for you both to focus on your studies right now. You girls are lucky. You don't need to work while you're in school. Some families aren't so privileged."

I cringed at the idea of having to get a job. I wasn't qualified for any cool jobs, which meant if I had to work, I'd probably end up in the retail or service industry, and from what I could tell, those gigs looked like soul-sucking purgatories that required exchanging pleasantries with strangers on a daily basis.

No thank you.

Did that mean that Liam wasn't so lucky? I'd never given much thought to his family. Sure, his truck was probably older than my dad, but maybe he just liked vintage?

"What do you know of Liam's family?" Dad asked, echoing my thoughts.

"Nothing," I answered truthfully. "Just that he's an only child."

Dad pursed his lips as he put the kettle on for tea. Suddenly the conversation felt strained, and I wasn't sure why, but I felt the need to defend Liam, so I added, "He's really smart though. And kind." And kind of intense, I thought, but I kept this to myself.

Dad looked like he was going to say something, but then his eyes zeroed in on the giant mug in my hands. "That much caffeine will have you jumping off the walls by the time you get to school."

"Correction, I'll be able to function like a normal human by the time I get to school. At least, that's the goal."

Dad grunted. "You are your mother's daughter." Mom hated mornings. I was lucky if I saw her before the bus pulled up.

I checked the clock and realized I had to go. Grabbing my things, I nabbed one of the blueberry streusel muffins Maverick and I had baked the day before and tucked it in the front of my backpack for later, shouting my goodbyes to Dad and Maverick.

Jo was already at the bus stop when I came out in my red wool jacket—the temperature had dropped, and it looked like fall was finally here.

"Hey! So are you going to ask Liam out now?" she asked.

"Good morning to you too."

"That was implied. So?"

I'd received a barrage of texts from Jo Friday night asking how her genius setup had panned out. I'd stalled for hours trying to figure out what to tell her. *He said I was one of the most decent people he knew.* I mean, it was a compliment, and at the time I'd felt flattered, but I'd spent all weekend repeating the words in my head, and now I wasn't so sure. It felt a bit like how you'd describe your twice-removed spinster aunt with nine cats because you couldn't think of anything else nice to say. I'd also looked up the word *decent* in the dictionary, and it read: 'of an acceptable standard; satisfactory'.

Basically, the mashed potatoes of compliments.

"I thought that was the guy's job," I said evasively.

"Oh please. It's the twenty-first century. If you want something, woman up and take it."

"Yeah, I'm more of a camouflage hunter. I prefer to lie in wait."

"You know what Abraham Lincoln said. Great things may come to those who wait, but only those things left behind by those who hustle," Jo quoted as the bus pulled up.

While she had a point, the thought of asking Liam out felt a bit like jumping off a cliff without a rope, not knowing if there was a soft cushion below to break the fall.

* * *

I smiled when Liam sat down next to me in math class. It was an involuntary response now. I just hoped he didn't find it creepy, like Jack Nicholson in *The Shining*, or any child in any horror film ever made.

"Thanks for bringing back my camera on Saturday," I said. "Here." I thrust the paper bag with the blueberry streusel muffin at him. "Maverick and I made them."

While it had seemed like a good idea at the time, it felt a little stupid giving a seventeen-year-old boy a muffin. (Exactly what your twice-removed spinster aunt would do, I thought). As Liam opened up the bag and looked inside, I caught a whiff of vanilla and cinnamon and reminded myself that they were really delicious muffins, and maybe it wasn't such a dumb idea after all.

Some emotion flickered across his face, too fleeting to read. He didn't say anything.

"You don't have to eat it if you don't want it," I said quickly.

"No, I do. It looks delicious. Thank you." He scrunched the paper bag closed and put it in his backpack.

I grinned. "You're welcome."

I think the lesson was on linear equations, but my mind kept wandering, and I found myself looking over at Liam more than my math grade could probably afford. Near the collar of his shirt, I noticed a faint scratch several inches long. Had he walked past a low-hanging tree branch? Or maybe he had a cat that had clawed him?

"How did your project go last night?" he asked after the class finished.

I was surprised he remembered; I'd mentioned my project only in passing. "Well, I think, but if I don't get more coffee in me, I'm going to sleep through my English lit class this afternoon." We walked together to my chemistry lab. I wasn't sure where Liam was headed, but he seemed content to accompany me. This ignited a small ball of warmth in the pit of my stomach, and I instinctively walked more slowly.

"I'd love to see them sometime," he said.

"See what?"

"Your pictures."

"Oh . . ." Outside Maverick and my parents, and my photography teacher Mr. Greene, I didn't show my pictures to anyone. Not even Jo. Sharing them was like exposing my innermost soul to the world, and I wasn't sure I was ready for that. "Why?" We stopped in front of the chemistry lab.

"Because," Liam said with a tilt of his head, "I'm curious how Rainey Collins sees the world. But I get it if you don't want to, if it's too personal."

I hugged my books closer to my chest. *Personal.* The word sounded at once deliciously enticing and terrifying. I liked the idea of things between Liam and me getting personal. "Maybe."

"Is that a yes maybe, or an over-my-dead-body maybe?"

I laughed. "It's a maybe maybe."

Carson appeared then, and the look on his face when he saw Liam turned stony. I saw the muscles in Liam's jaw clench, and suddenly the air felt alive with a pulsing tension. One tiny spark, and flames would engulf the entire hallway.

"I should get going," I said with sudden cheerfulness. "I'll see you later?"

"Sure." Liam's icy gaze flickered to me before returning to Carson.

After a moment's hesitation, Carson followed me into class. I could feel him watching me as I set my books down and opened my pencil case. After a while, I couldn't take heat vision any longer and looked over. "What?" I asked a little rudely.

"Are you and that Liam kid a thing?" he asked bluntly.

"A thing?"

"Are you, like, dating?" He didn't look particularly happy as he said this.

"No, not exactly."

"Good," he said, his scowl softening.

"What's that supposed to mean?" I asked, stung.

Carson shrugged. "It's just . . . look, he's bad news, okay? I wouldn't trust him."

"That's rich coming from you, don't you think? You and Chase were the ones who attacked him."

Carson flushed. "That's not the point. His family is messed up.

Did you know his dad's in prison for murder?"

I did my best impression of our disapproving librarian, Mrs. Spielman, and tsked loudly. "Chase just scratched that into Liam's truck because he's a jerk."

"It's true! I heard someone mention it."

"I once told my sister that movies used to be in black and white because the world was actually black and white. She was only five, and even she wasn't dumb enough to believe everything I said."

Carson held fast. "Ask him yourself if you don't believe me. Look, I've done some stuff I'm not proud of, but murder? That's messed up, and apples flock together."

"Don't you mean apples don't fall far from the tree?"

"Whatever, you get the point."

I didn't believe it. Rumors were more contagious than the flu in high school, and most of them were half-imagined fictions plucked off graffiti in the boy's bathroom. I was pissed at Carson for propagating it. He must have seen as much on my face because his expression turned sulky.

"I just figured you should know."

"Because your intentions were totally pure," I huffed.

"Don't be mad." He smiled, his cheeks creasing into deep dimples. "Please?"

I pursed my lips.

"You'll still help me with chemistry, right? You promised."

"I didn't promise anything," I said, but I felt a smile creep onto my face and knew I'd lost my battle trying to stay mad. I was terrible at keeping angry, especially when the person my anger was directed at insisted on looking at me like a puppy with his tail tucked between his legs. A massive, two hundred-pound puppy.

"There's a test on Friday," I said. "Did you want to meet at lunch in the cafeteria to go over some practice questions?"

Carson bit his lip. "Do you mind if we meet somewhere with fewer people around? I don't want Becca getting the wrong idea."

"You don't want her to know you're getting help in chem?" I asked, confused.

"No. I don't want her to get the wrong idea if she sees us hanging out together. She can get kinda jealous."

"Why on earth would Becca be jealous of me?"

Carson shrugged, not meeting my eye.

"If you're embarrassed to be seen with me, just say so."

Carson looked at me in surprise. "That's not it. Really."

"Okay, fine. How about we meet in the library? It's quiet there." Becca already hated me. I didn't want to add any more fuel to that fire, so we'd play it MI6-style if that's what Carson wanted.

After class, Carson headed for the water fountain for a drink. Parched, I followed suit. I was waiting my turn when Chase came over and threw his arm around his cousin's shoulders. "Yo, get the team together," he said.

Carson wiped water from his mouth. "For practice? I thought the field was booked for javelin today."

Chase pulled Carson close and whispered something in his ear, a smile lurking in the corner of his mouth.

I couldn't hear what he said over the babble of student voices, but Carson suddenly looked like he'd licked vinegar.

"So? Are you in or out?" Chase asked.

"I don't know, man."

"Come on, Kozlowski." Chase's hand dug into Carson's

shoulder. "You don't want to get kicked off the team now, do you?"

Carson looked down at the floor, then glanced over his shoulder. Seeing me, his mouth pressed into a grimace. "Fine."

"Good man." Chase grinned, and they headed off towards locker rooms. I watched them until they disappeared around the corner, feeling inexplicably anxious. Anything devised from the dark hell of Chase Buckner's mind could not be good.

LIAM

The muffin was delicious. I managed to scarf it down between second and third period, my stomach cramping at the sudden intake of food. I'd stayed at Mercy's on Saturday, but had come home Sunday night for a change of clothes, and to wait out the storm. The barn served well enough as a shelter from the wind, but the roof was a lattice of split-timber planks and rotting beams haphazardly overlaid with well-aged shingles. Staying would have meant spending a miserable night subjected to the bone-chilling damp.

Ray had ignored me when I'd come in, polishing his Marlin rifle, a wad of chew shoved in his lip, while Mom fussed and asked if I wanted any leftovers. There was a pot of beans on the stove with some cut-up hot dogs.

It was like nothing had happened. Like he'd never hit me. Like he'd never held a knife to my throat. I might have hated her for willfully forgetting, for masking the tracks of her tears that were visible down the hollows of her cheeks with tremulous smiles. For flinching every time he spoke. But I was too tired and too hungry, and there wasn't much left in the pot, just a few mouthfuls.

When I'd opened the bag Rainey had given me and smelled the muffin, I'd been hard-pressed not to ravage it like a starved animal. At lunch I bought myself chocolate milk and a turkey sandwich from the cafeteria—I figured I had about ten dollars in my bank account after I'd fueled up that morning, which just barely covered the cost—and headed out to my truck where I wouldn't be bothered.

I'd spent most of Sunday trying to wrap my head around the acutely uncomfortable information I now had at my disposal. I didn't think it was public knowledge that Chase's mother was a long-term patient at Cedarpointe Psychiatric Treatment Facility, and I was the last person on earth Chase would have chosen to confide this to. Of course, I hadn't meant to find out, but I doubted Chase cared about intentions or happenstance. He would make sure I kept quiet, one way or another. Until I knew what he was planning, I intended to keep as low a profile as possible.

Sitting in the warm cab of my truck, I ate my sandwich and read *Moby Dick*. I found myself relaxing, wishing I could somehow extend this peaceful feeling beyond this miraculous wrinkle in time, when a flash of colour caught my eye. Looking up, I saw Rainey in a bright red wool jacket standing under an elm tree next to the parking lot. She had her camera out and was peering up into the branches through her lens with a look of fixed concentration.

I watched her, wondering what she found so mesmerizing. There was something captivating about the intensity of her gaze. It was a chilly day; her cheeks were flushed from the cold, and a leaf had fallen into her hair, caught in the loose braid she'd tied with a blue ribbon.

The words of Blake rose from the recesses of my memory: *Did he who make the lamb make thee?* I laughed abruptly at the grim validity of the poem. Laughed while bracing against the sharp sting of some painful emotion. Was it envy? I couldn't deny there was a lot I envied about Rainey: her family and station in life, her goodness. I doubted she went to sleep at night haunted by the anger and violence that hounded me, unrouteable and intrinsic.

She was like a firefly. A delicate glowing light that transfixed me.

Without thinking about what I was doing, I put my book down and got out of my truck. She didn't notice me, absorbed as she was.

"What are you looking at?" I asked.

She let out a sound of surprise and stumbled over a tree root. I caught her arm as she fell against me and tried to steady her. She was small, but surprisingly sturdy, her head knocking against my chest. "Sorry," I said, trying not to smile.

"It's okay. You startled me is all," she said, eyes wide. She pulled away from me hastily and checked her camera, her cheeks flushing. "I was looking at the nest."

"Nest?"

She pointed up into the branches overhead. Following the line of her finger, I spotted the matted mesh of twigs balanced in a small cleft in the trunk. "There are hatchlings inside. You can hear them. I think I might have gotten a picture, but the angle is all wrong. I'm too short." She said this last statement with frustrated vehemence.

"Shall I?"

She spun round, eyes lighting up.

Fireflies.

"Would you?" She handed her camera over and stepped aside.

"Do I need to adjust the dial at all?" I asked, holding the camera gingerly, afraid I would do something wrong and break it.

"No, just click the shutter button and then pull the film lever."

I raised the camera, the zoom lens bringing the nest into focused detail. I could see the tiny beaks reaching up, helpless and hungry. After I took the picture and handed the camera back over, Rainey wrapped the strap securely around her neck. "Thank you. It really sucks being short."

"Don't they say the best things come in the smallest packages?"

Rainey wriggled her nose. "Arguable. Wasps are small, and they are the evil peons of Satan."

I laughed. "Fair point. More legroom?"

"I never thought of that." We smiled at each other, and once again, I found myself struck by the luminous quality of her eyes. The bright orbs of her irises were trapped in a dark rim, darker even than her lashes. I realized I was staring.

"Thank you again for the muffin, by the way," I said suddenly. "I devoured it. You like to bake?"

"I do. Well, Maverick does. I think I appreciate the end results more than the process itself."

I'd noticed the few times Rainey mentioned her sister, her voice softened unconsciously. "You two sound close."

"We are." I got the sense she was wrestling with some indecision when she finally added, "Maverick is . . . special."

"Special?"

"She has a congenital heart defect. Hypoplastic left heart syndrome. That's why she doesn't go to school. I mean, she's not an invalid. She's not bedridden or anything, but she can't overexert herself, and there's the constant threat of complications and heart failure."

I tried and failed to control the look of surprise on my face. "That sounds terrifying."

Rainey nodded. "It is, but she's Maverick, so she doesn't really give it a second thought most days. Me, on the other hand . . ." Rainey's smile faded, and a delicate line appeared between her brows.

I wanted to say something comforting, but I couldn't think of anything to say. I'd had no idea. I suddenly felt a little stupid for assuming she was some miraculous creature untouched by suffering.

"I'm sorry."

"Me too." She looked down at her shoes, but when she looked back at me, her face was clear. "What about you? Are you close with your family?"

The question caught me off guard, and my mind immediately went to the message Chase had carved into the side of my truck. "Why do you ask?" Without intending it to, my voice carried a sharp edge.

Rainey blinked; I could see my tone register with her and watched her shoulders hunch slightly. "I was just curious. I thought . . . never mind."

Feeling like a jerk, I forced a smile to my face. "There's not much worth knowing about my family." This was true, in a sense. The whole Hayes line wasn't worth much of anything.

"I think you're worth knowing," Rainey said, looking down at her camera.

The words did something funny to my stomach, but just then, the bell rang, saving me from answering. I let out a measured breath of relief. "We should go. I have biology, and Mr. Yu kicks you out of class if you're late."

We walked back inside in a stilted silence.

I didn't have many friends, and for good reason; I knew they wouldn't like what they saw once they got close enough to see it. Rainey would be no different. It would be better for her if I kept my distance. It wouldn't be hard. I'd just ignore her in math class and avoid her in the halls until she got the message.

I spent the rest of the day more irritable than usual, and I had a short fuse on the best of days. After PE, I headed back to my truck, thinking I would go to Mercy's. I didn't want to risk a run-in with Ray when I felt this on edge.

The potholes in the parking lot were still full of water from the previous night's storm, the oppressive clouds overhead a reflection of my piss-ass mood. I was driving down the back road towards Mercy's when I noticed a black Silverado in my rearview mirror. As I watched, the driver accelerated until they were trailing inches from my bumper.

"What the hell?" I slowed down and moved to the right. The truck swerved around me and roared past, black exhaust billowing up behind it. The windows were tinted, so I couldn't get a good look at the driver, but judging from the silhouettes against the rear window, there were several people in the back seat.

I waited for the truck to speed off, but the moment it pulled in front of me, it jerked to a stop. I barely had time to slam on my breaks. I swerved, hitting the ditch and burying the tires in a mire of mud as I lurched hard against the locked seat belt.

"Shit!" I checked my rearview mirror, worried I would be rear-ended. Distracted by the truck, I hadn't noticed the bright yellow Porsche behind me. The driver opened the door and got out. At the same time, all four doors of the Silverado opened, and five guys climbed out, all wearing hoods. I noticed the rear window of the truck had a Springbank Mustang sticker, and recognized one of the boys from Chase's gang, Carson.

My heart racing, I popped my truck into reverse and hit the gas. Shouting, the guys ducked as my tires spun, kicking up a shower of mud and rocks. The Chevy didn't budge. I swore. I looked around for some kind of weapon, but the only thing in my truck were books. Why hadn't I seen this coming?

Chase came up to my door and pounded on the window. "Get out!"

I hesitated, wondering if anyone would drive by and notice a kid being harassed by a gang. With a twist in my gut, I realized what it would actually look like: a truck stuck in the ditch and a group of guys trying to help him out, and there weren't any passing cars, only a field of cows who couldn't give a shit. My hands clenched around the steering wheel. Had there been two, I could have fought my way out. Maybe even three. But there was no way I was getting out of this unscathed. Not one against six.

A panicked laugh ripped out of my chest. I closed my eyes. Were they going to kill me? Was this the last, pitiful chapter of my life? Fucking hell, if there was a God, he seriously had it out for me. There was no other explanation for the shitshow that was my life.

"Get out of the truck, Hayes!" Chase shouted, pounding on

the door. The others jumped onto the rear bumper and started rocking the truck.

Adrenaline pounding through my body, I unbuckled my seatbelt. Trapped and cornered, I felt the anger in my chest rear its head, and this time, I didn't try to subdue it. I let it loose until I shook with it. Shoving the door open, I knocked Chase backwards. I managed to land a kick and punched someone in the mouth before hands grabbed hold of me from behind, reefing my arms back.

A fist sank into my stomach, knocking the air out of my lungs, followed by another to my face. Stars exploded across my vision. I lashed back, kicking out at anything I could reach.

"Fuck him up!" Chase jeered.

My foot connected with someone's groin just as another fist landed on my side. This time I felt my ribs crack. Pain shot across my body, and I sagged. I couldn't remember much after that, awash in a haze of pain as they continued to hit me. I covered my head and took each fist, each kick.

"Stop. That's enough," someone finally said.

"What are you talking about? I want to teach this piece of shit a lesson."

"Are you serious? Do you want to kill him?"

Heavy breathing.

"This is fucked up, man."

"Shut it, Carson! Just shut the fuck up!"

"What happens when he goes to the police?"

"That won't happen, will it, Hayes?" a snide voice whispered close to my ear. "One word about this or what you saw the other day, and I'll kill you. One. Word." A wad of spit hit my eye, but I couldn't move to wipe it away. Each breath I took shot a streak of agony through every inch of my body. All I could do was lie there, my mouth full of blood, my cheek resting on the asphalt, the gravel digging into my skin.

"The same goes for you," Chase said, standing and facing the others. "If you say anything, you can kiss a football scholarship goodbye. Jenner will kick us all off the team."

"Chase—"

"I'm serious!"

"Let's get out of here before someone comes," another voice said. "Come on."

They finally drove off, the Porsche ripping away with a violent screeching of tires. I guess I should have been glad they didn't drive over me and finish the job. I lay there for a long while, too sore to move. No one drove by, and I lost track of time. The wind picked up, and I started to shiver, which only made the pain worse. Finally, I managed to haul myself up to my knees, and then to my feet, holding onto the door of my truck to steady me.

I could feel the swelling in my face and didn't dare look at my reflection in the window. Luckily, my legs were functioning— nothing broken there. I couldn't say the same for my ribs. Several of them had to be cracked.

I couldn't get the truck out of the ditch on my own. I'd have to get help. I was only a few miles from Mercy's. Pressing my hand to my side, I turned down the road and started walking, each fumbling step fueled by a deep and blinding rage.

8

RAINEY

I CAME TO MATH CLASS WITH a spare print of the baby bird picture. After fussing to get the correct concentration and time in the developer, I'd managed to get the result I was hoping for. I wanted to give Liam a copy as a memento for his help, but he never showed up.

I kept stealing glances at his empty desk through class, wondering where he was or if he was sick. The hour crawled by, the only perk to his absence being that he wasn't there to witness my humiliation when I got Mr. MacAlastair's question wrong, again.

Chemistry was even worse. I wasn't sure why, but Carson was in a lousy mood. He barely spoke to me, and when I asked to borrow his eraser, he said, "Get your own damn eraser," before jerking his chair around and facing away from me.

"What's eating you?" I grumbled.

"Nothing, I'm just trying to focus, and you keep interrupting my thoughts."

"Sorry. Geez."

We didn't speak for the remainder of the class, but when the bell rang, I had to ask, "Are we still meeting today at lunch to study?" Given his bad temper, I half hoped he'd back out. Locking myself in a small room with an irritated gorilla seemed like a very bad idea.

"Why, do you have something better to do?" he asked, scowling.

I was starting to tire from the grouch act, and my own mood sparked. "I do, actually, but I said I would help you. I'll be in the library. Show up if you want."

I was more than a little surprised when he did. I was waiting in one of the study rooms for less than five minutes before he arrived. He had his chemistry textbook under one arm and a box of Smarties in the other.

"We're not allowed to eat in here," I said reflexively.

"Relax. It's not like I'm eating spaghetti and meatballs." He sat opposite me, slouching against the back of his chair. "So . . . what first?"

I suggested we review the periodic table.

Carson rolled his eyes. "What's there to know? It just lists all the elements."

"Okay then, can you give me an example of a multivalent element?"

He stared down at the table, expression shuttered.

"Carson?"

He shoved his book away. "I don't know, okay? That's why I asked for your help. You're supposed to be teaching me, not asking me questions! Forget it. This was such a dumbass idea."

"No it wasn't, and I'm asking questions so I can figure out what you know and what you don't."

He went back to staring at the table in seething silence.

I slammed my book shut. "All right, what is it?" I asked. "Something is bothering you. Do you want to talk about it?"

"Nothing is bothering me. And even if it was, why would I talk to you?" he snapped.

"I don't know," I snapped back. "Because I'm the only one stupid enough to care, even when you're being a dick about it?"

He glared at me, but I heard a breath catch in his throat, and when he looked away, I caught a flash of desperation in his face.

"Carson—"

"Just drop it, okay?" Without further explanation, he grabbed his book and stormed out of the study room, leaving the box of Smarties next to my notebook.

I sighed. "Okay."

* * *

Liam didn't show up to school the next day either. Or the day after that. Or the day after that. I started to worry that something had happened to him. Was he in the hospital, dying from a rare tropical disease? Was he a secret agent who had left the country on a highly dangerous, top-secret mission and was stuck fighting drug lords in Russia? I pictured Liam as an undercover spy, extracting secrets from his informant in fluent Russian. (This seemed more than possible given his intellect and fighting acumen.)

It wasn't like I could tame the creativity of these ever-escalating scenarios with a quick text or phone call. I didn't have his phone number or email, and despite hours of searching, I'd had zero luck finding him on social media.

I considered going to the principal's office and asking the secretary if Liam's family had informed the school of his absence, but I doubted Ms. Tate, with her permanently pinched mouth, would disclose personal information to the FBI, never mind a student.

Math once again became my most dreaded class, followed closely by chemistry, which was unexpected given how much I used to enjoy it. I wasn't sure if I could blame it on my own deteriorating mood, but Carson's grumpiness seemed to be getting worse. On Tuesday, he didn't even acknowledge my greeting at the beginning of class, and on Wednesday, when we had to partner up for another lab, his hand slipped, and he dropped our test tube on the floor. It smashed across the tile, spattering hydrochloric acid everywhere. We had to jump out of the way to avoid getting burned. Swearing explosively, he stormed out of class, leaving Ms. Bierman and me to clean up the mess.

Despite his obvious distraction, he continued to show up for our lunch hour study sessions, each day bringing a snack—a Snickers bar, a bag of chips, gummy worms—and leaving it like some kind of ritual offering on the table between us. I figured it was his way of thanking me, though I was making little progress as a tutor, as far as I could tell.

"So how many moles would we need? Carson?"

He didn't answer.

"Carson?" I tapped the back of his hand with my pencil. "Hey. Anyone home?"

He blinked and rubbed his eyes with the palms of his hands. "Sorry."

I sighed and closed the textbook. "Look, I know it's none of my business, but if something is bothering you, you should talk to someone."

"I told you, nothing is bothering me."

"Right."

Carson opened his mouth as if about to say something, then snapped it shut again.

I waited, bracing for the snarky retort. Had he looked any less tortured, I would have left well enough alone, but I couldn't.

"I can't talk about it," he said finally, the words barely audible. "If I do . . ." He left the sentence hanging.

I felt a deep pang of unease. "Did someone hurt you?" I asked. It seemed unlikely. Carson was as close to the top of the social food chain in Springbank High as you could get, but that didn't mean there wasn't something going on outside of school.

Carson buried his head in his hands. "No."

"Is someone else being hurt?"

Nothing.

"Carson—"

"I did something bad, and I'm regretting it, okay?" His hands muffled his voice.

"Oh." I bit my lip, thinking. "Well, owning up to a mistake sucks. I remember when I was eight, I stole my mom's favorite butterfly brooch and lost it after she told me expressly that I wasn't allowed to play with it. At first, I lied about taking it, but lying felt worse. I felt *so* much better after telling her the truth. I mean, sure, I was grounded for two weeks, but after that, I was able to apologize, and it felt amazing."

I looked over at Carson, wondering what he thought of my little tale of woe, but his face was still buried.

"I can't," he said at last.

"Suit yourself."

* * *

On Friday, we had our test in chemistry. I wished Carson luck as Ms. Bierman handed out the papers. He responded with a short grunt. I managed to do quite well, even though I was now seriously concerned about Liam's continued absence, and my mind kept wandering to the horrific scenarios I'd envisioned earlier.

Come the end of class, I decided to take action. Liam had mentioned that he and Joshua were friends, sort of. Maybe he knew where Liam was. I spotted him between third and fourth period taking books out of his locker and made a beeline in his direction.

"Hi, Joshua?"

He looked at me the way someone would look at a talking bear in a hat, then slowly returned to rifling through his locker. I took this as a tacit invitation to continue.

"My name is Rainey. I have math class with Liam. I was wondering if you know where he is. He hasn't been to class in a while and . . . er, I have homework for him." This last bit was true, in a sense. I'd kept a list of all the pages we'd covered in math with all the relevant questions.

Joshua shrugged.

"Is Liam out of town?" I pressed, hoping for a more direct response. This only prompted another shrug, and I started to wonder if the boy was mute. "I'm just worried about him. Have you spoken to him at all this past week? Do you have his phone number?"

Joshua shook his head, pushing his glasses up his nose.

I was about to label my endeavor a failure when he said, "I know where he lives. He's down the road from my house."

"Really?" My heart sprang into overdrive. Would it be completely crazy if I orchestrated a casual drop by? What would Liam think if I suddenly showed up at his place unannounced? Innocent as my intentions were, there was a significant chance he'd see me as some deranged stalker.

"Do you think I could come home with you after school?" I asked Joshua. "I'd like to give him the homework he's missed." I smiled, trying to look harmless and totally un-stalker-like.

Joshua closed his locker, his eyes hooded beneath the fringe of his hair. "Sure," he said at last.

"Great! Awesome. I'll meet you here after school?"

"But—"

"Excellent, see you then!" Before Joshua could voice his concern, I scooted off to my next class.

* * *

I didn't realize Liam and Joshua lived so far away. In fact, there were a lot of things I hadn't really thought through. I'd sent Mom a text to let her know I was going to be studying at a friend's house after school and that I would get a ride home and not to worry. However, after Joshua's bus dropped us off on the highway heading out of town, and I was left staring down a seemingly endless gravel road framed by deep ditches, barbed wire fences, and a few docile cows, I realized I hadn't foreseen the possible complexities of my plan.

Like getting home.

Did taxis come this far out? Where exactly was I? How would I know to tell the driver where to pick me up?

One thing at a time, I said to reassure myself. Blowing out a sigh, I looked at Joshua. "Lead the way."

Hiking up his Spiderman backpack, he proceeded to guide me at a sedate pace down the road. I'd always considered myself a shy person, but having met Joshua, I realized I had to reassess my definition of social timidity.

"How long does it take you to get home?" I asked.

His narrow shoulder bobbed. "A while."

"That must suck in the winter."

Joshua pushed his glasses further up his nose. "My sister drives me most days, or Liam." We walked for fifteen minutes, covering what I estimated to be less than a mile, but given I was used to being dropped off twenty yards from my front door, it felt infinitely longer.

Finally, I spotted a driveway, marked by a red, lopsided mailbox and a planter filled with the long-dead remnants of what might have once been a profusion of flowers.

"Is this where Liam lives?"

Joshua shook his head and pointed towards a hill off to the left, beyond which sprawled thick woods. "Liam's place is that way."

"Oh." This was starting to feel like a terrible idea. What the hell had I been thinking? The answer to that was obvious. I'd been thinking about a pair of piercing blue eyes and broad shoulders.

You've come this far, I thought, you can't very well turn back now. "Is it much farther?"

"I'll show you." Joshua headed up his driveway, but after passing the fence, he veered left through the grass. I hesitated for a second, then followed.

It was a narrow deer path, worn through the grass and underbrush. I had to watch every step, minding rocks and the odd gopher hole. By the time we reached the trees, I was sweating, my feet were sore, and even though I didn't have access to a mirror, I knew my hair was a complete nest.

"What's that?" I asked, noticing something up ahead. It was a wooden structure, similar to a treehouse.

"A box stand."

"What's that?"

"It's for hunting."

"You hunt?" The incredulity in my voice was palpable.

Joshua shook his head. "Liam's stepdad does."

I didn't know Liam had a stepdad. Were his parents divorced? *Murderer's spawn.* The words popped abruptly into my head, and despite my previous conviction, a niggling doubt started to weasel its way into my thoughts.

The wind picked up, knocking a tree branch against the hollow edifice of weathered wood. The sound was eerie, like a gnarled finger tapping against the lid of a coffin. The hair on the nape of my neck rose, and I shivered.

"How much farther?" I asked, hoping to keep the fear out of my voice. The sun had gone behind a cloud, and despite the long walk, I felt cold again.

"Not long."

To my relief, it wasn't. The trees started to thin, and we came out into another field, in the corner of which sat a trailer. I figured Liam's house had to be close. I looked around, waiting for Joshua to carry on, but he stopped.

"There."

"What, *there*?" I pointed at the trailer. "You mean Liam lives—" I stopped mid-sentence, swallowing my disbelief. "Did you want to come with me?"

Joshua shook his head. "I'm not allowed. Mom doesn't like it."

I wasn't sure what to make of this, but nodded as if it made perfect sense. "Okay then. Well, thank you for bringing me here. I appreciate it."

Joshua made a small sound of acknowledgment and turned back the way we'd come. I hoped I'd be able to find my way back to the highway alone. I only just stopped myself from asking him to stay. "See you around," I said instead as he turned to head back. I couldn't tell if he heard me or not.

Gripping the straps of my backpack a little more tightly, I struck out across the field. The trailer wasn't quite as small as I'd first thought. From a distance, it looked like an abandoned shed with broken steps mounting a narrow porch which slanted at a suspicious angle. However, when I got closer, I noticed small signs of occupancy. Dull yellow curtains hung in the window, and Liam's truck was parked out front. I could hear voices inside and suddenly felt terribly nervous.

As I climbed the steps, my foot knocked over an empty bottle, and the voices inside fell quiet. I licked my lips and knocked on the door.

LIAM

"Well look here, boys. We've got company," I heard Wes say, his voice muffled through my bedroom door. I stopped reading and listened. No one ever came here. Not anyone who knocked, anyway. Wes and Paul always walked in like they owned the place.

I heard one of them open the door, the screen screaming on its hinges. "Hello there, darlin'. What can I do you for?" Ray's voice was as greasy as an oil slick.

"Hi . . . I-I'm Rainey Collins. I'm looking for Liam. Is he here?"

The voice pierced my stomach like a hot iron, sending a shudder of horror through to my core. I was hearing things, or maybe I was dreaming, because it wasn't possible. She couldn't be here. *Here.* The place I could pretend didn't exist because no one else ever came, proving its ugly, horrid existence. Not now, not with them here.

"Is he home?" The soft voice shook a little.

"I don't know, darlin'. How about you come in and sit for a bit. I'll see if I can find him for you."

I nearly ripped the door to my room clean off its hinges. Ray was standing in front of the entrance, blocking my view of her, but I could hear the leer in his voice and could only imagine the way he was looking at her. Wes and Paul were sitting at the table, peering out the window to see who it was.

I shoved past Ray, grabbed Rainey's hand, and dragged her down the porch steps and around the side of the trailer where there were no windows, so Ray and the others couldn't see us. I was shaking so hard, I was sure every bone in my body was going to come loose.

"Liam, I—"

"What the fuck are you doing here?" I snarled.

Even though I couldn't bear to look at her, I felt her flinch.

"I-I came to bring you your math homework," she stammered.

"I didn't ask you to. And how the hell did you know where to find me?"

"I asked Joshua. He brought me." Her voice was barely a whisper.

Damn it, Joshua!

"Please don't be angry with him," she pleaded, reading my expression. "He was just trying to help me."

I closed my eyes. The pressure in my head was excruciating. "You had no right to come here."

"I know. I just thought—"

"Go! Just go, okay? I don't ever want to see you again."

"But—"

"Did you not hear me?" I yelled. "I said get the fuck away from here!" I finally looked at her. She was staring at my face—the bruises and cuts—and to my horror, tears were coursing down her face, dripping from her chin. The guilt was nearly as bad as the initial shock of seeing her on my front doorstep.

"Y-you're holding me," she whispered.

I looked down. Sure enough, my fingers were still wrapped in a vice-like grip around her wrist. I was holding on so tightly, it must have hurt. I let go, and like a startled rabbit, Rainey backed away from me, then turned and sprinted away across the field, her red coat a bright flame of colour against the dry grass.

"Pretty little thing, that," a voice said to my left.

I looked over to see Ray leaning against the corner of the trailer, beer in hand, his gaze locked on Rainey's diminishing figure. I wanted to gouge his eyes out so he could never look at her that way again.

"She your girlfriend?"

"No. She's no one."

"Well she ain't that. Else you wouldn't have your dander up now, would you?" He pressed the bottle to his lips and tipped his head back, downing the last of his drink. "Doubt she'll be interested in you now." He snorted, regarding me with bloodshot eyes, the corner of his wide mouth curling up in a sardonic smile. "And you call *me* an asshole."

Chuckling quietly, he disappeared around the side of the trailer, the screen door slamming shut behind him. I heard them laughing from inside.

I crouched down on the ground, covering my face with my hands. The world around me was spinning, filling my ears with a chaotic howl that churned my stomach. God, what had I done?

You showed her the real you, a cruel voice answered. And now she was gone, and I doubted that she would ever speak to me again.

Standing, I looked out across the field. Rainey had disappeared into the trees, her bright coat long gone. She'd come with Joshua, probably on the bus, and then by foot, which meant she had no way of getting home. I cursed, kicking the ground hard enough to leave a divot in the dirt.

Just let her go. She'll be fine.

Would she though?

The thought of letting her walk all the way home after how I'd treated her chewed up my insides worse than my shame and embarrassment. Did I dare go and find her? After a moment's indecision, I ran to my truck and took off towards the highway. I reached the head of Mercy's driveway and slowed down. Had she come this far already? I didn't think it was likely, but I couldn't be sure. I crept along, keeping my eyes on the side of the road for a flash of red. I didn't have to go far. She was walking along the side of the road, arms curled around her body. I passed her, pulled up to the shoulder, and got out of my truck, leaving the engine running.

She froze at the sight of me, lambent eyes filled with tears. Words crowded my mouth, choking me. What could I possibly say?

"Get in. I'll drive you home," I said at last.

Something flashed across her face, fierce and hostile. "No."

"Rainey, please."

She walked past me, shoulders hunched against the wind. I could hardly blame her for wanting nothing to do with me. If I were her, I'd hate me too. I hated myself. And here I was, saying nothing, asking her to come with me.

"Rainey, I'm sorry. I know you probably don't ever want to see or talk to me again. That's fair. I deserve that. But let me drive you home. It's going to take you all night at this rate."

"I called my dad. He's coming to get me," she said without turning.

Of course. I hadn't thought of that. "Well, then, I can stay with you until he gets here."

Without warning, she spun around to face me, that fierce hostility burning her cheeks. "Why? Geezus, Liam, you told me to get away from you! I'm trying! What the hell do you want?"

"I don't know!" I shouted back. But I did know, and it burst out of me in a rush of anguished frustration. "I want you to forget what just happened. I want you to forget what you saw, so that I can keep pretending like life isn't as shitty as it really is. I wish I didn't constantly wonder what it would be like if things were different, if I was the kind of person who could be with you and not feel like the lowest kind of scum!"

Her brows snapped together in a devastated crease. "I make you feel like scum?"

"Yes! I mean, no. Sort of. It's complicated!" I was breathing hard. My ribs, still not fully healed, were starting to complain with sharp spasms of pain.

"That's totally unfair!" Rainey shouted, flushing even further. "I don't think you're scum! Can't you see . . . isn't it obvious how much I like you? God, I'm such an idiot." She covered her eyes with her hands, her lips trembling.

As her words pierced through the fog of my anger and confusion, I felt the ground disappear under my feet, leaving me precariously suspended. Any moment, I was going to come crashing down. "What?"

"I said I'm an idiot."

"Rainey . . ."

Her hand dropped, and her beautiful eyes snapped open. "I like you, damn it! Why else would I have come? I was worried about you! And what the hell happened to your face? You look terrible!"

I barely registered her question, focused entirely on the first half of this furious speech. It didn't make sense. What could she possibly see in me that would make her feel that way?

I must have fooled her into believing I was a good person more thoroughly than I'd intended. At least now she knew the truth. Realizing this, I felt a fresh stab of pain, a new kind of pain. The loss of something inestimable I hadn't even known I'd had.

Suddenly all my anger was gone.

She waved her hand in an *it-doesn't-matter* kind of way. "Look, it's clear you don't . . . can we just forget I said anything? We can pretend this never happened, and I won't bother you ever again."

It was exactly what I had wanted, only a moment before. Yet now, the thought of never speaking to her again made my chest tighten. "Rainey—"

A black sedan drove over the hill and honked its horn. Rainey turned. "It's my dad." She took a step back.

"Wait. I just . . ." The words faltered. I'd never felt at such a loss before.

"Just what?" she asked.

Don't leave. But I couldn't bring myself to say the words.

Rainey shook her head. "Goodbye, Liam." And without looking back, she walked over to the sedan, got in, and drove off.

RAINEY

"Do you want to explain to me why I'm picking you up on

the side of a highway, ten miles away from your school?" Dad asked.

"I was giving someone homework that they'd missed," I said quietly. I explained how I'd taken another bus here but hadn't really thought about how to get home.

"I see," Dad said in his stern-father voice. "This student wouldn't happen to be a dead ringer of that actor from *The Notebook*, would he?"

"You've seen *The Notebook*?"

"Your mother made me watch it with her three times," he said with an air of pained martyrdom. "But let's not get off topic with my marital sacrifices. That was Liam's truck on the side of the road. Why didn't he give you a ride home?"

"It's complicated." Geezus, why was everything so complicated? "I don't really want to talk about it right now." Tears started to dribble down my cheeks again. I wiped them away, sniffing.

Dad was quiet for a moment as he weighed my words. To my relief, he didn't argue. "I'm just glad you called me. I hope you know you can. Any time, under any circumstances."

That was why I'd called him; he was the first person I thought of in a crisis. Always calm, always comforting.

"I didn't interrupt you in the middle of a surgery or anything, did I?" I hadn't really thought about whether or not I had caught him at a good time.

"I was just heading home," he said, smiling.

We shared a moment of silence, punctuated by the drumming of Dad's fingers against the steering wheel and my occasional sniffs. I hoped the silence would last so that I could bury myself beneath it and hide away from what had just happened, but it didn't.

"You don't have to tell me what happened between the two of you, but I will say one thing. I like to think I give everyone a fair chance, but when it comes to my daughters, I have a right to be protective—"

"Dad—"

"And I'm not sure if I like Liam for you, sweetheart."

"Dad, you don't—"

"No, hear me out. I think he's a hard-working, well-meaning kid, and those are great things, but I think he might also be dealing with quite a lot right now, and it might be best if you give him some space to sort that out without getting involved."

Dad's words propelled everything I'd seen into the forefront of my mind, things I'd not yet had time to process. Tears pooled in my eyes as if my body were trying to relieve the pressure of my emotions in any way possible.

"You don't have to worry, Dad. Liam doesn't want me around either." My voice shook at the end, and the tears came in earnest. God, why couldn't I stop crying? It wasn't like I'd expected Liam to be overjoyed at my unexpected arrival.

But then I realized that's exactly what I'd expected. Or at least hoped for. And it had all gone so horribly, horribly wrong.

Dad looked over and, seeing my face, said a word I never thought I'd ever hear him say—at least not in my presence. "It's his loss, sweetheart. Clearly the boy isn't as smart as you think he is."

I laughed, wiping my eyes. "You said I should stay away from him. Now you're saying he's an idiot?"

Dad shrugged and smiled at me with sympathy. "I'm your father. It's my prerogative to have two dissonant thoughts when it comes to the men in your life."

"That makes no sense."

"It makes perfect sense." He reached over and squeezed my shoulder. "Hey, want to stop off for ice cream on the way home?"

"We'll ruin our supper."

He nudged me. "Spoilsport."

* * *

When we got home, I escaped to the backyard. We had a porch swing tucked next to the lilac bush in the corner of our yard, under the giant poplar tree. It was the perfect place to sit and daydream, especially in the summer when the scent of lilacs hung heavy and warm in the sun. Today, I just wanted some peace and quiet so I could settle the tangle of thoughts that were twisting me up in knots, and maybe cry without anyone watching. I sat down on the bench, rocking it slowly forward and back with my toes.

"You're home," a phantom voice chirped. I looked around, then tilted my head up and spotted Maverick's bright orange hair and blue coveralls high up in the branches directly above me.

So much for peace and quiet.

"Maverick, get down from there!" I hollered. "You're going to break your neck!"

"No I won't. See? No hands." Legs wrapped around her perch, she waved both hands at me.

"You know Mom and Dad hate you climbing up there."

"But it's my hideout."

"I'm serious, Maverick. Get down."

She huffed a giant sigh and started to climb down. I watched

150

with amazement as she moved with perfect surety, and upon reaching the bottom, jumped the last few feet, landing lightly on the balls of her feet.

"I swear you're half monkey."

Maverick straightened and brushed bits of bark off her knees. Despite her confidence, she looked frighteningly pale.

"Why didn't you come home on the bus today?" she asked, sitting down on the grass; I could tell that climbing the tree had tired her out more than she wanted to show.

"It's a long story," I said.

"I like stories."

I hesitated, but figured that talking to Maverick might actually help. She was a good listener, and I knew she'd tell it to me straight, whatever she thought. So I told her what had happened, or at least an abbreviated version. "Then Dad picked me up and drove me home," I finished.

Maverick wriggled her nose. "Why was he so upset?"

I'd been wondering the same thing. "I don't know, bean. I think maybe he was embarrassed because he lives in a trailer and not a nice house like this one."

"That's silly."

"It is," I agreed. I really didn't care that Liam was poor. Money didn't mean anything; Chase's family was loaded, and he was a total jerk. But then I remembered the man at the door, reeking of alcohol. I didn't think I would ever forget the way his beady eyes had crawled across my body, or that slow smile, exposing small, stained teeth.

I hadn't told Maverick about him because I was afraid it would frighten her. It frightened me. Had that been Liam's stepdad? And then there were the bruises on Liam's face. I hadn't told Maverick about them either. They'd looked several days old, and they weren't the kind of bruises you get from a fall—I'd fallen plenty in my life to know. When you fell, you bruised your hands and knees because you instinctively did everything you could to protect your head. Liam's face had looked like he'd gone ten rounds in the ring with a rhinoceros. Was that why he'd missed school? Would he be back Monday? Would he ever come back? What would I do if I saw him again?

I had so many questions, and no answers, and not even the dappled light coming through the leaves or the gentle rocking of the swing could settle the sick feeling in my stomach.

"Dinner is ready, girls!" Mom called through the window. Even though I had no appetite, I followed Maverick inside just as the sun disappeared behind a cloud, its comforting warmth vanishing.

9

RAINEY

"YOU WERE RIGHT," I SAID to Jo as we rode the bus to school on Monday.

"I usually am. What about, exactly?"

"Boys are headaches best put off until college. Or better yet, middle age." I'd had a couple of days to recover from Friday's disaster and my mortifying confession thereafter, but despite wishing on every star in the sky, and scrounging around the bottom of the washing machine for a lucky penny, a magical time machine had yet to materialize in my bedroom to take me back so I could undo everything that had happened.

"Things didn't go well with Liam?" Jo asked.

"Not exactly."

Jo draped a consolatory arm over my shoulder. "Well if you want, we can hit up Rosie's after school and drown our sorrows in vanilla milkshakes and double-whammy garlic fries."

"Don't you have student council meetings on Mondays?" I asked.

"Pfft. I can skip out."

"I thought you were the president."

"Countries run better without a president," she said blithely.

I smiled. "Thanks, Jo, but I'll be fine."

I wasn't though.

In math, I settled down in my seat while trying not to look at Liam's empty chair. Maybe he wouldn't come today either. The emotion that accompanied this thought was either profound relief, staggering disappointment, or a conflicted mess of both—I couldn't tell which.

Relief won out; when the bell rang, I blew out a sigh, not realizing I'd been holding my breath. It was, however, pre-emptive. Just as Mr. MacAlastair rose from his desk and approached the whiteboard, I caught a flash of movement in the corner of my eye, a familiar glimpse of blue jeans and sneakers. I shifted in my chair, turning as far away from him as possible. Would it be too obvious if I balanced my textbook on its edge and hid behind the wall of paper?

The following hour passed slower than a herd of turtles. I managed to keep focused on Mr. MacAlastair, and even though I felt Liam look at me several times, I refused to return the favor. I was afraid looking at him would prompt a painful reliving of all the scathing rejection and hurt I'd endured on Friday.

Why oh why did we have to be in the same class? Why

couldn't I just sink into the floor and disappear? Maybe I could drop math? So what if I needed it to graduate? In the long run, did graduating really matter?

I could picture Jo's answer to this; the eye roll would have bowled me over with the force of its derision.

When the bell rang, I leapt out of my seat and hurried off to chemistry, bumping into several people on my way out the door. Not that I was looking forward to chemistry either. However, to my relief, Carson was marginally less surly than he had been last week, and even acknowledged my existence with a nod.

"Hey."

"Hey?" My response was almost a question. Clearly, whatever had been bothering him last week was no longer weighing as heavily on him now.

At the beginning of class, Ms. Bierman handed back our tests. I got an eighty-seven. Trying to be inconspicuous, I glanced over at Carson's paper and saw he'd gotten a sixty-nine. I was about to apologize for my appalling tutoring skills when he raised his hand.

"Give it up, Collins! You rock!" He high-fived me so hard, my hand flew back and hit my face.

"I do?" I gaped, rubbing my stinging palm.

"Totally! I passed."

I guess it was true what they say: the key to happiness is low expectations. "That's great," I said, feigning enthusiasm.

He scratched the back of his neck and shot me a sidelong look. "I know you only agreed to help me get through this test, but maybe we could keep it up? Meeting in the library and stuff?"

"Won't that interfere with your football practice?" I asked.

"Yeah. I mean, I guess. It's just . . . to be honest, I'm not sure

I'm going to keep playing football."

"Why not?" Hadn't the whole reason for passing chemistry been so that he could stay on the football team?

Carson didn't answer right away, struggling to formulate his thoughts. "Ah, forget it," he said at last, giving up.

"We can keep studying together if you want. I'm just surprised. That's all."

Carson's face crinkled as he smiled. "Awesome. What would you like today? You've got your pick of anything from the vending machine that doesn't cost more than . . ." He dug his hand into his pocket and pulled out a fistful of spare change. "Three dollars and fifty-five cents."

I laughed. "You really don't have to keep bringing me things."

"I want to. So what'll it be? Gummy worms or Fuzzy Peaches?"

I capitulated. "Fuzzy Peaches." Maverick loved Fuzzy Peaches.

LIAM

I never thought I would hate someone as much as I hated Ray, but I was starting to think Chase Buckner was shaping up to be a fair contender. I'd expected some sort of retribution after our encounter at the hardware store. Some secrets are just too momentous to bear their exposure, and I'd stumbled—albeit inadvertently—upon the motherload. I also knew that Chase, who had all the discretion of a howler monkey and measured everyone by that standard, would never trust a stranger to keep their mouth shut.

Ironically, I was probably the one person who could rightfully understand Chase's fear. Being ashamed and embarrassed about one's parents was a specialty of mine.

What I couldn't let stand was the fact that Chase and his cronies had attacked me, six against one, leaving me on the side of the road like a broken hubcap kicked off the back of a truck. I'd spent the past week waiting for the bruises to heal, envisioning with sickening pleasure the moment of my revenge, of wrapping my hands around Buckner's neck and squeezing the life out of him.

It frightened me how naturally the promise of violence took root, as if it found my mind an ideal environment in which to flourish, like an organism that finds a habitat free of predators. I was a Hayes, after all. How many times had my mother warned me that I would take after my father, no matter how hard I fought against it?

But now . . .

Lying on the cot in the loft, I stared up at the beams of the barn roof, one hand tucked behind my head, the other stretching Flea's ears, and I wasn't thinking about Ray, Chase, or his mother. I was thinking of a girl in a red jacket who had shown up on my doorstep out of nowhere and had knocked my head into a cosmic tailspin with a universe-altering confession.

I kept hearing her say it over and over in my head: *Isn't it obvious how much I like you?*

No, I felt like shouting. No, it hadn't been obvious! I wished it had. Then maybe things would have turned out differently. Or maybe I was kidding myself. Even if I had known Rainey liked me, it would have only been a matter of time before she saw the ugly, angry, bitter person I knew myself to be. I'd just sped up the process and skipped to the end.

"Anyone home?" a voice called from down below.

I considered staying quiet but eventually called out. "Up here."

Mercy's head appeared over the edge of the loft as she came up the stairs, her hair wet from a recent shower. "Still brooding?" she asked. She came over and sat down on the edge of the cot, displacing Flea. The pit bull eyed her reproachfully as he resettled on the floorboards.

"You look like you could use a distraction," she said. "Why don't you come down to the house? Dad has relinquished control of the remote, and *Die Hard* is on."

"I'm good, thanks."

"Or we could head over to Watervalley and play a game of pool? I need to reclaim my title as reigning champ."

When I shook my head, Mercy grimaced. "When was the last time you left this bell tower, Quasimodo?"

"It's for the greater good."

"Oh please. Since when have you cared about the greater good?" she said, poking my side. I winced.

"Oops, sorry. How are you feeling?"

"A little less like a sack of mulch."

"The bruises are fading." She brushed my jaw with her finger but withdrew before I could move away.

Wanting to divert her attention away from me, I sat up. "I heard yelling coming from the house a while ago. Is everything okay?"

"Oh, that." Mercy rolled her eyes. "Dad was at me again about the college thing. I wish he'd drop it. I'm happy where I am. Just because he's unhappy with his life doesn't mean he gets to interfere in mine. God, just a few more months and I can get out of here."

I didn't say anything. In many ways Mercy and I were similar. We were independent, stubborn, and resistant to authority, especially when that authority proved incompetent. I knew that was part of the reason why Mercy fought with her parents. At the same time, it galled me how ungrateful she could be, having two parents who cared about her, who actually gave a damn about her future, and wishing them away.

Mercy waited for a response. When one wasn't forthcoming, she punched my leg. "Seriously, what's bothering you? Is it just that dickwad who painted your face? Because I'm all for busting his ass if you need backup."

Mercy wasn't being glib. When I'd first shown up at her place after the football team had jumped me, she'd been ready to go after them with a socket wrench.

"It's a tempting offer, but I can't risk getting expelled. And it's not just Chase."

"Is it Ray? Has he done something stupid again?"

"No." I was reluctant to tell Mercy about Rainey. For one, I hadn't had time to figure out what my feelings were, or what I was willing to admit—I only knew that Rainey's current frigidness towards me was unexpectedly excruciating, and I would rather get beaten up by Chase's band of merry delinquents than endure more of her apathy.

For another, I wasn't sure how Mercy would take my interest in someone else. While I'd been blind to Rainey's feelings, I wasn't blind to Mercy's, and I didn't want to make things awkward.

"Let me guess," Mercy said, eyes narrowing. "Girl trouble?"

I looked at her sharply. My expression must have been guarded because she waved her hand flippantly.

"It's okay. I'm not mortally wounded that you like someone else. It's a good thing. Pent-up sexual frustration makes men irritable anyway."

"I'm not . . . that's not—"

"Calm down, Charlie Brown. What's her name?" Her tone was mild, but I couldn't discern if it was an act or not.

I got up off the cot, swatting a spider off my shirt sleeve. "Rainey."

"I take it she goes to your school?" At my nod, Mercy groaned. "Please don't tell me she's one of those rich preppy types."

I snorted. "Rich, yes. Preppy, no. Not that it matters. I messed things up before anything even started."

Mercy laughed, but not unsympathetically. "I'm not surprised. You're bright, but when it comes to romance, you're not exactly a Casanova. Less a surgeon with a scalpel and more a drunkard with a scythe."

"Harsh."

Mercy shrugged. "It's a part of your charm, and to be fair, it isn't like you've had the best role models when it comes to healthy relationships."

I hadn't had the best role models period. "I'm not sure if I should be reassured or insulted."

"Take your pick."

"Like I said, it doesn't matter. Even if I could fix things, it would never work. We're too different."

"So you're giving up without even trying? That's weak."

"Do you have anything useful to say, or did you just come up here to insult me?"

Mercy affected a look of exaggerated patience, which I tried not to let irk me. "You like her, right? Enough to take a chance?"

I bit my lip. More than anything, I didn't want to hurt Rainey more than I already had, and I was afraid I would do just that if I did anything other than walk away. And yet . . .

"Look," Mercy said impatiently, "give her some space, and then apologize, but don't just say you're sorry and expect her to roll over. You have to show her."

"And how exactly do I do that?"

"I don't know," Mercy said, waving her hand. "What do rich girls like? Buy her two dozen roses and a pony. Feed her chilled grapes while reciting some sappy poetry."

I couldn't picture Rainey appreciating any of that, but what did I know? She'd admitted to reading romance novels. Weren't all the men in those books tall, handsome, and completely loaded? "I can't afford any of that."

"You'll think of something." Mercy stood and headed towards the stairs.

"Thanks," I said.

"What are friends for, right?" She smiled, but it didn't quite reach her eyes. I opened my mouth to ask her to stay, but she turned quickly and left, Flea following her down the stairs.

* * *

The following day was no better than the one before. Rainey ignored me in math class, keeping her gaze trained on the whiteboard during the entire lesson, and turned her shoulders away from me while we worked on the assignment. I watched her out of the corner of my eye. She'd tied her hair back with the same blue ribbon she'd worn Friday, the silk double-knotted and lopsided as if it had been done hastily or with frustration.

A ruler tapped the corner of my desk. "Having trouble with the assignment?" MacAlastair stood over me, brows raised in a sarcastic arch. We both knew I could do the assignment in my sleep, but I got the point and tried to focus on my work.

During our first break, I bumped into Rainey coming out of the girls' bathroom. Her books spilled out of her hands and across the floor. "Sorry, I didn't see you." I bent to help her pick them up, but she snatched them off the floor and ducked out of my way without responding, her cheeks flushing red. I passed her again in the hallway on the way to economics and noticed her shoelace was untied. The compulsion to stop and let her know was overwhelming. What if she tripped?

It was odd. I'd noticed Rainey before in a detached sort of way, as one observes a part of a familiar landscape, but now I felt like she was everywhere I turned. Was she doing it on purpose?

Come lunch, I decided to bite the bullet and confront her. Having finished the reading on scarcity and its impact on free markets in Mrs. Burt's class, I ducked out early and waited for her by her locker. I spotted her walking down the hall, talking to Carson Kozlowski. Maybe it was because of how I felt now when I saw her, but I recognized the look on his face. He was laughing at something she said, his hand grazing hers, his fingers curling as if he wanted to hold it.

The memory of his fist hitting my face came back with sudden sickening clarity, and my mouth filled with the copper tang of blood. I realized I'd bitten my tongue and tried to relax my jaw, but I couldn't control the anger in my expression before she looked up and saw me.

Her reaction was immediate. She stopped dead, made a 180-degree turn, and ran in the opposite direction. Stranded and confused, Carson scanned the hallway, looking for the cause of her sudden departure. Seeing me, he quickly averted his eyes and followed after her.

* * *

I had a shift at the hardware store after school. Work was usually tedious, but it was better than being at home, and today I was glad for the distraction. Someone had even brought a platter of cookies in during the lunch break. There were two large oatmeal raisins left out on the table. I grabbed them, eating one and shoving the other into my apron pocket for later.

Sean asked me to check the inventory in the lighting department, so I grabbed a clipboard and headed over. I was counting boxes of bulged reflector bulbs for the third time when I heard a familiar voice to my left.

"Maverick, get down."

"But I'm pretending to be Helen of Troy riding her chariot into the city."

"How about you pretend to be Sisyphus rolling a rock up a hill instead?"

"That sounds boring."

Glancing over my shoulder, I spied a young girl with bright orange pigtails climbing off a cart. Her father was inspecting our

163

selection of incandescent bulbs; I recognized the neat profile, currently obscured by the glasses balanced on the end of his nose.

I instinctively turned away so he wouldn't see my face.

"Helen of Troy ran off with the first pretty boy who caught her fancy and started a war that killed thousands of men. I would be more selective of your idols, my girl," Dr. Collins advised.

I chanced a second look over my shoulder and saw his daughter considering this thoughtfully. "Then I'll be Joan of Arc riding her trusted steed into battle."

"Joan of Arc was burned at the stake for heresy."

"Brilliant! I want to have an epic death too. I want poets to write stories about me so that I'll be remembered after I'm gone. Say, if I'm going to be Joan of Arc, I'll need a castle to defend against the hordes of my enemies."

"Sorry to disappoint, but there aren't any real estate listings in the area featuring moats."

"I was thinking more like a sanctum above the ground. Someplace high where I would be protected against swords and spears and have an excellent vantage point."

Dr. Collins returned the box to the shelf and tweaked his daughter's nose. "Nice try, but the answer is still no. We already discussed this."

"Aww, come on, Dad! A treehouse isn't dangerous. It's safer than climbing the tree."

"You shouldn't be doing that either unless you want to give your mother a heart attack."

"I wouldn't if I had a treehouse. Please?"

"Sweetheart, I don't have time. Maybe next year." There was a brief pause, then, "Liam?"

I turned to find Dr. Collins regarding me with a faint smile.

"I thought that was you," he said. "It's nice to see you again."

"Dr. Collins."

He held up his hand. "Matthew, please. Only my patients call me Dr. Collins."

I nodded stupidly, wishing my curiosity hadn't delayed my escape. The last time our paths had crossed, Rainey and I had been arguing on the shoulder of the highway. I doubted his opinion of me was high enough to crawl under. At least the bruises on my face had healed.

"Liam?" Maverick scooted around her father and proceeded to stare at me with unabashed fascination. I suddenly understood how the gorillas at the zoo felt. Then her face split into a wide gap-toothed grin. "You're Liam? Rainey's Liam?"

Hearing this made my throat close up.

Before I could respond, she stuck out her hand. "I'm Maverick, Rainey's sister."

I smiled—it was impossible not to when confronted by such uninhibited affability—and shook the proffered hand. It felt small and cold as a bird, and I was mindful that she was extremely sick, despite the defiant radiance of her grin. "Hi."

"You work here, at this hardware store?" she asked.

"Yes."

"Brilliant!" I might as well have said I was a lion tamer.

"Are there any perks?"

"Not really," I answered honestly. Sean was far too cheap to offer anything more than a ten percent discount off tools and hardware. He'd given us coupons for free pizza once. They had expired the previous month.

"If you work here, you must know your way around a hammer," Maverick said nonchalantly. Matthew regarded his daughter with indulgent amusement.

"Don't even think about it, bean."

"What? You said you were too busy. Maybe Liam can help me?"

"I'm sure Liam has better things to do than cater to your whims."

"I'd be happy to help," I said, almost involuntarily. I could have said Maverick's artless enthusiasm was impossible to say no to, but that was barely half the truth. The other half was a faint hope that my assistance would lead to overtures in another vein.

Maverick spun around, crowing. "Yes! See?"

"As generous as that is," Matthew said with a smile in my direction, "I don't think it's a good idea."

"Come on, Dad! Please?" She clasped her hands together, pleading. "Please, please, please?"

"Liam is busy; we shouldn't impose. Speaking of which, we had better leave him to his work."

Maverick heaved a theatrical sigh.

"*Now,*" he said sternly. "Liam." He snuck a wink over the head of his daughter.

"Have a good day, Dr. Collins," I said. I couldn't bring myself to call him by his name.

Jutting her bottom lip out, Maverick allowed herself to be steered away, but she waved goodbye to me before vanishing around the corner. I smiled, shaking my head. My amusement was short-lived; returning my attention to the inventory record, I found myself wondering if Matthew's politeness had actually been marching orders in sheep's clothing.

RAINEY

Life thus far hadn't given me the tools to handle rejection. Both my parents had spent my formative years telling me what a lovely, bright girl I was, encouraging me with adages like, *you can do anything you set your mind to.*

Well, obviously not.

I'd learned this the hard way at the age of seven when I'd fallen off my bed trying to levitate. Now I was having to adjust to the harsh reality that life really wasn't like one of Lisa Oswell's books, that I was not Rosalind with her dainty wrists and heaving bosom who miraculously made men fall over themselves in adoration. (My bosom was decidedly unimpressive.)

The thing was, I couldn't make my mind up how I felt about it. One moment I wanted to burst into tears, and the next I wanted to flip Liam the bird. And not just a tiny sparrow. No, the whole damn turkey.

Dad must have told Mom that I was going through boy trouble, because she bought a tub of cookie dough ice cream and watched K-dramas with me Tuesday night after Maverick had gone to bed.

"Do you want to talk about it?" she asked after we'd watched several episodes of *Boys over Flowers*, her slender legs folded gracefully under her.

"I'm not sure what there is to talk about. It's not like we broke up. We weren't even dating." Saying this made me feel even worse. Why couldn't I just brush this off and move on with my life? Don't you have to actually have something in order to lose it? I scraped the bottom of the tub with my spoon, trying to scrounge any last morsels of ice cream.

"Rejection is a bitter thing to swallow, no matter the timing," Mom said. Bracing her elbow on the back of the couch, she laid her head against her hand, looking like the subject of a nineteenth-century painting.

"How do you know?" I asked sourly. "You have Dad."

Mom laughed. "Children always think the world began when they were born. I'll have you know I was twenty-one when I met your father, and reeling from heartbreak."

"You're kidding." Mom had loved someone other than Dad? But they were soulmates. How could she have been with anyone else? I tried to picture it and couldn't.

"His name was Peter Chandra. He was my dance partner, and don't tell your father, but he was the most beautiful man I've ever seen. He moved so gracefully and had the most intoxicating laugh." Mom's gaze softened as she spoke, a smile on her face that made me feel like a voyeur, intruding on something extremely private and poignant, and yet I couldn't look away.

"There was something about him," she murmured. "A sense of mystery that drew people in, like he had all these secrets you'd die to discover. We danced together for three years. I dare say, I loved him almost as much as he loved himself, and that's saying something."

"What happened?"

Mom sighed. "He found another partner. One he thought was more talented and had a better chance of helping him audition for the Mariinsky Ballet in Russia. His parents wanted him to be the next Rudolf Nureyev, and it became his life's dream. My point is rejection is a part of life. No one gets through it without being hurt at one point or another. And even though it took me years to realize it, I eventually came to understand that what happened between Peter and I had less to do with me and more to do with him and his ambition. The same probably goes for you and Liam. Whatever happened between you two, you shouldn't take it too personally."

"Did Peter ever make it to Russia?" I asked.

Mom's smile stretched into a grin. "No, last I checked."

It was comforting to know that even my mother—the kindest, most caring person I knew—had been jilted too. However, I couldn't figure out how I was supposed to take Liam's ruthless rebuke if not personally, and while Mom championed the emotional high ground, her grin made me think she had taken Peter's betrayal more personally than she wanted to admit.

I sighed, dropping my spoon into the empty ice cream tub. Sometimes it didn't matter what we told ourselves, feelings had a sneaky way of prevailing over cooler heads.

* * *

We moved on to stoichiometry in chemistry on Wednesday, much to Carson's dismay. "I just figured out ionic and covalent bonds. I can't even pronounce stomach-try. What the hell does that even mean?"

The volume of his grievances was starting to annoy the other students in the library. The toad-like Mrs. Spielman pinned us with her bugging eyes and cleared her throat loudly.

"Don't worry," I whispered. "You'll get the hang of it. We're just starting, remember?"

"What the hell, Carson!"

In unison, Carson and I swiveled around to see Becca standing a few feet away, hands perched on her hips, lips drawn into a furious line.

"What are you doing?" She shot me a look that epitomized the phrase *if looks could kill*, the desire to dissect me with a scalpel burning in her eyes.

Mrs. Spielman cleared her throat again, throwing us another volley of reproving looks.

"Studying?" I whispered. I thought it was obvious given the books spread out across the table.

"I wasn't talking to you, slut," Becca snapped.

"Don't talk to her like that." Carson's voice was needle sharp. I'd never heard him speak that way before, and judging from the horrified look on Becca's face, neither had she.

Over by the checkout desk, Mrs. Spielman was overcome with a spell of insistent throat clearing.

"Shut up!" Becca screamed at her. The librarian stared at the girl with an open mouth, adding to the impression of a warty toad.

"Maybe I should leave you two to talk things over," I murmured. Collecting my things as quickly as I could, I shuffled off towards the library doors, casting Carson an apologetic look as I abandoned him like a fallen soldier.

I wasn't entirely sure why Becca was so angry, but during PE, she and several of the other girls targeted me with a vengeance during our game of dodgeball. I was hopping to and fro, trying to keep out of the way, when I saw Becca and Val advance on me, both armed and ready. It was impossible to dodge both missiles at once. Thrown simultaneously and with deadly accuracy, the balls hit me square in the face with enough force to make my eyes water.

"Christ, girls, this isn't ten-pin bowling!" Coach Gardiner shouted from the sidelines. "Ease up!"

I walked over to the end zone where my fellow outed teammates were waiting, gingerly rubbing my nose. The following three games ended in much the same fashion, and by the time Coach Gardiner dismissed us for the changerooms, I was sweaty, exhausted, and more than a little irritated.

I caught Becca and Val whispering to each other and tried my best to ignore them. Grabbing my towel and my bag of toiletries, I headed to the showers so I could get cleaned up. Pulling the curtain across the cubicle, I shimmied out of my wet gym strip and hung it on the hook next to my towel.

The hot water felt blissful against the back of my neck, the warmth easing the tension building up around my shoulders. After I was done, I pulled back the curtain and reached for my towel. It took me a moment to realize there was nothing there. For a good long moment, I stood dripping water onto the tile floor, too stunned to speak.

This had to be a dream. The same dream I'd had of going to school and realizing halfway through my English lit class that I was naked. Maybe if I just closed my eyes, I'd wake up in bed? But no matter how many times I tried, I remained where I was, standing in the shower in the girls' changeroom, sopping wet with no clothes and no towel.

"Ha, ha. Very funny, guys," I called out. "Now can I please have my stuff back?"

There was no response.

"Hello? Is anyone there?" I waited for half-muffled titters of laughter. "Hello?" I called out, louder this time. My voice echoed strangely through the changeroom. My heart, recognizing that this was most certainly not a dream, thudded painfully against my chest. I stepped tentatively out of the cubicle, arms strapped tightly across my chest.

The changeroom was empty. I ran to my gym locker, but whoever had taken my gym strip and towel had also taken my clothes.

"Oh my God, oh my God, oh my God. Okay, breathe. You'll figure this out," I said to myself. Frantic now, I tried every locker door in the changeroom, hoping to find a spare set of clothes. I didn't care if they were dirty or didn't fit. Anything would do.

Tragically, all the lockers were either empty or securely locked. Ripping some paper towel out of the dispenser by the sink, I dried myself off as best I could, but that did nothing to change the fact that I had no clothes.

Overwhelmed, I burst into hysterical sobs. I barely heard the last bell of the day ringing, then realized I was probably going to miss the bus home on top of everything and wailed even harder. *Why was this happening to me? If everything happens for a reason, what was the reason for this? Please, God, explain it to me.*

Gasping for breath, I sat down on the bench and tried to think through my predicament. If I waited long enough, eventually all the students and teachers would leave, and I could run to my locker, get my phone, and call home. But how long would that take? Mom and Dad were bound to panic if I didn't show up at home on time. They would call the police, who would then commence a nationwide search complete with helicopters and sniffer dogs. My face would get plastered all over the news, and I, Rainey Collins, would go down in history as the girl who caused a cataclysmic uproar because she was stuck naked in the girls' locker room.

I started to sob again, so hard it hurt.

Over my heaving, gurgling wails, I heard Nan's voice in my head. *You won't find the answer to your troubles at the bottom of a Kleenex box, darling girl.*

Hiccoughing loudly, I fought to gain some control. *Think. This isn't as bad as it looks.*

Yes, yes it was.

Oh God, what was I going to do?

I wiped my tears with another wad of paper towel and threw it into the garbage bin under the sink. Struck by sudden inspiration, I pulled the bag out and lifted it up. Sure enough, the custodians had stored spare black bin liners in the bottom of the garbage. Taking one, I opened it and ripped a hole in the bottom for my head and two more in the sides for my arms. Another perk to being short, legroom aside, was that I could wear a bin liner and it came down to my knees.

I looked in the mirror. My eyes were red, my face blotchy, and my hair clung like seaweed to my neck. I looked like a soggy, miserable, paper-bag princess, but it was better than nothing. I still couldn't bring myself to leave the changeroom until I was sure the buses had left. I probably could have made a break for my locker after fifteen minutes, but I waited nearer to an hour before poking my head out of the changeroom door.

"Hello?" My voice echoed through the empty gymnasium. I strained to hear if there was any noise coming from the hall beyond and snuck out.

I opened the gym door the tiniest of cracks and peeked around the corner. The cafeteria was empty except for the custodian who was sweeping up the day's refuse. He was facing away from me, humming softly.

Holding my breath, I ducked and ran down the deserted hall, my bare feet slipping on the cold tiles. I skidded to a halt just as Mrs. Burt came out of her classroom, but she turned the other way, heading towards the teacher's lounge with her empty coffee cup, desperate for her afternoon caffeine fix.

I spotted my locker. One quick dash and I'd have my cell phone to make a call home. I ran, head down, but just as I passed a corner, I struck something large and solid.

"Ouch! What the—"

I rubbed my nose, bruised for the second time in the space of an hour, and looked up to find Liam staring at me with a perplexed expression I knew would haunt me until my dying day.

"Oh God, kill me now."

"Rainey? What . . ." he glanced down at the garbage bag. "What are you doing?"

There was nothing else for it. Jerking my chin up, I gathered the remaining dregs of my scattered dignity and said, "I am trying to get to my locker. If you would be so kind as to step aside, I'll just . . ." I tried to shuffle around him, but he turned and started to follow me down the hallway. I could feel the heat in my face; I probably looked like I'd just stepped out of a tanning booth after falling asleep for five hours.

"Do you mind me asking why you're wearing a garbage bag?"

I closed my eyes. He just couldn't let it go, could he? "Long story. Explaining would require talking, and I know you don't want to talk to me. Right now, I don't want to talk to you either. So can we just pretend this didn't happen?"

As I spoke, hot tears started to prick my eyes. Damn it. Just how much humiliation was I expected to endure? I'd thought last Friday had been the worst day of my life, but I was now recalibrating.

"Rainey—"

"I need to get to my locker and get my phone. I need to call my parents."

"Rainey!"

I stopped walking. Liam's brow was creased with concern, his eyes searching my face like a doctor assessing the status of a critical patient. "Where are your clothes? Are they in your locker?"

"No." My voice cracked. "They were taken."

"Taken?"

"Some of the girls in my PE class stole them while I was in the shower."

Liam exhaled slowly through his nose, something I was beginning to recognize he did whenever he was trying to control his anger. "Come with me." He took my hand and led me in the opposite direction. Too defeated to put up a fight, I followed.

When we came to his locker, he opened it and reached up to the top shelf, pulling out a pair of grey sweatpants and a T-shirt. "Put these on. They'll be a little big, but they're clean."

"Are you sure?"

He thrust them into my arms. "Put them on," he repeated.

"Thank you," I said, and meant it.

He opened his mouth to say something but seemed to change his mind midtrack and just said, "I'll wait here."

I shuffled into the bathroom, discarded my woeful garbage bag, and got dressed. I had to roll the pant legs up several times so I wouldn't trip on them, and the T-shirt almost came down to my knees, but I felt infinitely better with proper clothes on. Burying my nose into the shirt, I took a deep breath, appreciating the smell of laundry detergent and old textbooks. I also caught the slight whiff of cigarette smoke. I wondered fleetingly if Liam smoked, but I didn't think so. An image of the man at the trailer barged into my mind with his yellow teeth and greasy fingers, and suddenly a part of me wanted to take the clothes back off.

"You okay?" Liam called from outside.

"Yes."

His eyes swept over me as I came out. I became stupidly conscious of the fact that I didn't have my push-up bra on under the large shirt and probably looked like a twelve-year-old boy in his father's clothing, but his gaze settled on my bare feet; having traipsed through the school, they were now filthy.

"Do you need anything from your locker?" he asked.

"My phone."

He escorted me back to my locker. I was surprised that he'd refrained this long from commenting on my makeshift garb. Anyone else would have split a gut laughing at my expense, and while I appreciated his tact, the militant silence was making me just as uncomfortable.

"What are you still doing at the school?" I asked while opening my locker and taking out my bag.

"I tutor Rosie's son every Wednesday at five. I usually stick around here for an hour or so before heading to the diner."

I remembered him mentioning he tutored Rosie's son. I checked the time on my phone. It was half past four. "You'd better get going," I said.

"May I borrow your phone?"

"Er . . . sure?" He took it from my hand and dialed a number. Someone picked up on the fourth ring.

"Hi, Rosie, it's Liam. Something has come up. Can we reschedule today's session for tomorrow? Great. Thank you." He ended the call and handed back the phone before I registered what he'd done.

"Why did you do that?"

"I wanted to," he said simply. He paused then, considering his next words. Whatever they were, he was having considerable difficulty formulating them. He dragged his hand through his hair, pulling it askance.

"Look, I've been meaning to talk to you about . . . about what happened the other day."

"You don't have to," I said quickly. Rehashing it would only hurt, like picking at a barely healed scab.

"Just hear me out. Please?"

He waited for a response, but all I could manage was a small nod while staring at his left ear.

"What I said before, about feeling like scum when I'm around you . . . it's not true. Not exactly, anyway. It's just . . ." He sighed, struggling as if each word was a weight he had to heave out of a chasm from somewhere deep within.

"My family . . . it's a mess. And I'm not talking minor dysfunction. I mean seriously fucked up. My father is in prison. He killed a man five years ago in a bar fight with the broken end of a beer bottle. He didn't even feel bad about it, and my stepdad . . . well, you met him. He makes honey badgers look like goddamn chipmunks, and I'm not so different from them. So when I see someone like you, someone who comes from a respectable family, someone honest and decent—" His voice caught on each word, like they hurt to say aloud. "I feel worthless. But that's no excuse for how I treated you the other day. It's not your fault. It's just . . . I never wanted you to see that part of me because I was afraid of what you might think."

Mute, I let Liam's words sink in. I wasn't sure what to say or what to think, but looking into his eyes, I felt my bones go all soft and mushy. I desperately wanted to touch him, to trace the lines of his face with my finger, along the sharp edge of his jaw, down his nose, and over his brows, so I could imprint this moment and the way he was looking at me into my soul.

His gaze dropped and his lips thinned. "Anyway, I just wanted to tell you that in case I didn't get another chance."

"Thank you." It felt a little inadequate after everything he'd said, so I blurted out, "And you don't have to worry about what I think. Because I think you're pretty amazing, and I don't care about any of that other stuff. Nobody's family is perfect anyway, right?"

His eyes were wide and solemn. "Yours seems to be."

"Yeah, well, I have a crazy great-uncle who has an attic full of these old wooden marionettes. That's Norman Bates levels of creepy if you ask me. Maverick and I think he might be a serial killer."

"That does sound creepy."

"I know, right?" I grinned, then bit my lip. "But just because I have a crazy uncle doesn't mean I'm crazy. And I don't know your dad or your stepdad, but based on what you've told me, I don't think you're like them at all."

Liam didn't look wholly convinced, but I thought perhaps some of the grimness eased from his face. "Thanks."

"Does this mean we're on talking terms again?" I asked, keeping my tone light.

"If you want to be." There was no mistaking the trepidation in his voice.

"Well, I'll need to see you again if I'm going to return these clothes."

This brought Liam's attention back to my current situation. "Did you want to call your parents and have them come pick you up? Or I can take you home if you want. Whichever you'd prefer."

I hesitated only for a second. "I'll go with you."

Liam nodded. "Okay." Without warning, he turned and crouched down in front of me. "Climb on."

It took me a moment to realize what he meant, and when I did, my heart gave a funny twinge. "I'm too heavy," I protested. I was short, but I wasn't built like a twig.

"I doubt that."

Holding my breath, I wrapped my arms around his neck and held tight. He stood, circling his arms around my legs, and proceeded to carry me all the way to his truck while I buried my face into his shoulder and melted.

LIAM

Rainey felt warm and solid against my back. Her breath was soft against my neck, and I could feel the gentle thump of her heart. Her feet swung out in front of me, bouncing with each step I took, her toes covered in dirt. I carried her as gently as I could, as if I was carrying the most precious thing in the world.

I knew better than anyone that high schoolers could be assholes, but stealing someone's clothes from the locker room was a social crucifixion I found viciously unsettling. The fact that it was Rainey raised my hackles and made me want to punch whoever was responsible.

"I haven't been at the school this late in years," she said suddenly, her voice muffled against my shoulder. "It's strange seeing the halls all empty."

"I like it," I admitted. It was probably the only time I liked being here.

"It reminds me of *Romeo and Juliet.*"

"It does?" I failed to draw the connection. "How?"

Rainey shifted on my back. "It's sort of embarrassing."

More embarrassing than being caught wearing a garbage bag? I thought it but didn't say it; I didn't want to remind her of such a recent trauma, not when she sounded so happy. I was surprised at how happy she seemed, as if she'd completely forgotten about it.

"Do the hallways somehow remind you of the streets of Verona?" I asked, coaxing an explanation.

Rainey laughed softly. I felt the soft reverberation of it and wondered if that was what joy felt like. I couldn't say, having never felt it before.

"No, it's not that." She hesitated. "Promise you won't repeat this."

"I promise."

"Back in ninth grade, my parents made me join the drama club. I think they were worried I wasn't making friends and figured it would help me gain some confidence. I had to stay after school on Thursdays, but I was way too shy to participate in the group. I'd sneak into the costume room and hide out until Mom came to pick me up. Sometimes I got bored, so I dressed up as Juliet and acted out the scenes. I was a total sucker for tragic love stories."

I lurched to a stop. I couldn't believe it.

"That was you?"

"What?" Rainey stiffened like a startled hare and slid off my back. "What do you mean?"

"I remember you! I was in the costume room one day and heard someone reciting the death scene."

"No!" Rainey gasped, burying her face in her hands. "No, that's not possible. I was alone."

I couldn't keep the smile off my face. "I didn't want to interrupt, so I ducked behind a box of old coats. I never saw who it was."

"Oh my God." Her cheeks were red behind her hands.

"Your performance was excellent. Very committed."

"Shut up."

"I'm serious." I was, too. "You should consider a career in acting."

"Now you're just making fun of me."

"I'm not." I pulled her hands away from her face so she could see the sincerity in my face. I was smiling, but not because I found it funny. That day had been terrible. It had snowed, and the temperature had dropped below minus twenty. Mom told me she'd pick me up after school, back when we owned an old '89 Pontiac, but she never showed up. I went to the costume room looking for a jacket because we had no money for winter clothes, and I figured no one would miss a dusty old overcoat from the back closet. Hiding behind that box, listening to Rainey re-enact Juliet's histrionic heartbreak, I forgot about my own misery for a while. It was a little funny. After she left, I found her Romeo: Mr. Bones, the school's skeleton, lying prone on the couch, covered in a pale pink shroud.

I turned around and crouched down so Rainey could climb onto my back again. She hesitated before wrapping her arms around my neck.

"You shouldn't spy on people," she murmured. "It's rude."

Now that she couldn't see my face, I grinned. "Next time I'll announce myself."

"It was a one-time performance."

"Shame."

I felt her laugh, and my grin widened.

I carried her out to the parking lot and helped her into the front seat of my truck so the gravel wouldn't cut the bottoms of her feet. She was quiet as I started the engine. I blasted the heat to keep her feet warm, wondering desperately what was going through her mind. She was looking out the window, her hands curled up in her lap, her bottom lip trapped between her teeth.

"What are you thinking?" I asked.

She looked at me, her eyes bright and unobscured. I was no

poet, though I'd read a lot of the romantics, from Byron to Keats, and looking at her, I was reminded of Edgar Allan Poe's "Annabel Lee."

For the moon never beams, without bringing me dreams
Of the beautiful Annabel Lee;
And the stars never rise, but I feel the bright eyes
Of the beautiful Annabel Lee

I considered most of the romantics to be melodramatic milksops, so I'd always read their work with a sort of tired resignation, but perhaps there was something to their work I hadn't previously appreciated.

"I was thinking that I want to hold your hand," she said at last.

The artless proclamation sent a shot of adrenaline through my body, leaving it tingling and warm. Reaching over, I picked her hand out of her lap and wove my fingers through hers, letting our hands rest on the seat between us. "Better?"

She smiled. "Yes."

I pulled out of the parking lot and headed towards her house. "Do you mind me asking why someone would want to steal your clothes?" I asked.

"I don't know," she said, but I could tell from the slight tilt of her head, this wasn't entirely true. "Becca found out I was helping Carson in chemistry. We've been studying during lunch, but I don't know why that would bother her so much."

"You don't?" I'd seen the way Carson looked at her, and I could hedge a guess or two.

"No, but I'm glad you found me. I don't feel nearly as bad as I did before." She smiled again, looking down at our hands.

This won't last. It can't. You don't belong with her.

The unwelcome thought crawled like a poisonous root through my mind, but Rainey's smile was so bright, I didn't want to mar the moment with thoughts of doom and gloom. When we got to her house, I looked down at our interwoven hands. I wasn't sure I could bring myself to let go just yet. I also knew that the longer I held on, the more painful it would be when I had to.

"I'll see you tomorrow?" I asked.

"I'd like that," she said, smiling again. Knowing I would talk to her the following day made it a little easier to let her go now. I released her hand, its sudden absence sending a chill from my palm all the way up my arm.

"If you need help hatching a revenge plan, you can count me in," I said as she got out of my truck.

"Tempting, but I'm okay. Really." She sounded like she meant it. How was that possible? Anyone in their right mind would be ready to make even. "Today has actually turned out kind of nice."

Before I could respond, she ran up the steps of her house and disappeared inside.

* * *

I rolled the window down as I drove home, letting the wind ruffle my hair. The sun was still warm, but the air was cool. It smelled of damp earth and hay, baking in the sun. I crossed the cattle guard and pulled up in front of the trailer, my hand still tingling from Rainey's touch.

Mom was still at work, but she'd left a note on the kitchen

table saying there were pork chops in the fridge. I poked my head into the fridge but couldn't find any pork chops. Clearly, Ray had beaten me to them. I rummaged through the cupboard and found some stale saltine crackers and a jar of peanut butter. Digging a cracker into the jar, I scooped some out and popped it into my mouth. It wouldn't completely abate my hunger, but it would do.

Sitting down at the table, I continued eating the crackers and peanut butter. Something felt off, and I couldn't put my finger on what. It took a moment, but I finally decided I felt hopeful. It wasn't quite happiness, but maybe happiness adjacent.

Closing my eyes, I tried to picture Rainey's face. I managed to summon a few fractured details, like the way her hair curled around her ears when it was wet, and the round curve of her cheek when she smiled, but the whole remained elusive.

I decided to pay closer attention the next day, because as long as I had a picture of Rainey Collins and her bright eyes in my mind, Ray could eat all the damn pork chops and I wouldn't give a shit.

* * *

The following morning when I walked into math class, Rainey turned and smiled at me, and I noticed the way her chin dimpled. I smiled back reflexively. I wasn't used to smiling—not without forcing it. It felt strange and unfamiliar, accompanied by a pleasant warmth in my chest.

I sat down at my desk. "Hi."

"Hi," she answered, still grinning.

I wasn't sure what MacAlastair taught that day. I was too busy trying to memorize Rainey's face: the pattern of freckles across her nose, the way her bottom lip pouted over her short chin. There was a pencil smudge on her cheek where she'd absently wiped her hand—a downside to being left-handed, I realized.

When the bell rang, she waited for me to collect my things, and we walked together to her next class. I didn't particularly care if I was late to mine.

"I've been meaning to ask . . ." Rainey started. "Are you ever going to tell me what happened to you last week?"

"Oh, that." There was a lot I hadn't told her, I realized. "That was Chase."

"What?" Rainey stopped so suddenly, I walked past her. I backed up.

"Chase did that to you?"

"Him and five other guys on the football team," I clarified. I didn't want her thinking one guy had inflicted that much damage on his own.

Rainey's freckles stood stark against her now chalky face. "Was Carson involved?"

"Yes."

Mouth hanging open, Rainey stood in the middle of the hall, oblivious to the students trying to skirt around us. I pulled her over to the side, afraid she'd get knocked down or stepped on. "Oh my God, I can't believe I helped him!" She said this so loudly, several students around us turned to stare. This didn't seem to bother her though. "That no-good, lying, piece of shit! I'm going to . . . to . . . urg!" She stomped her foot.

I couldn't help it. I laughed. "Did you just stomp your foot?"

"Yes," she snapped, still fuming.

The fact that she was this upset over me was unexpectedly touching.

"You have to tell Principal Jenner," she said. "They have to pay for what they did."

"I thought you didn't subscribe to revenge."

"Not revenge. Justice. There's a difference."

"Maybe, but I'm not going to Jenner, and neither should you."

"Why not?"

"Because if I go to Jenner, I'll be signing up for another beatdown. Chase won't let something like that go, and Jenner made it clear that any more violence on my part will result in my immediate expulsion," I said, quoting his threat.

"That's totally unfair. Chase can't get away with this! He can't still be angry about what happened by the bleachers?"

I glanced around. A girl was getting her books out of her locker only a few feet away. As much as I trusted Rainey, I couldn't tell her about Chase's mom, not here where people could hear. I hated the guy, sure, but that was one secret I didn't want to be responsible for leaking.

"We'll talk more later," I promised just as the second bell rang. I was definitely going to be late.

10

RAINEY

I ROUNDED ON CARSON THE MOMENT I sat down in chemistry. "Liam told me what happened last week. How could you! I thought you were one of the good guys!"

Two spots of colour appeared in Carson's cheeks. "It wasn't my idea," he said. His voice was absurdly child-like given his massive size.

"And that makes it okay?" I snapped back. "Because Chase made you do it, you're absolved of responsibility, is that it? If Chase told you to jump in front of an oncoming train, would you do it?"

Carson lifted a shoulder. "He's family. And we're a team. We stick together. You wouldn't understand."

"No, I don't. Whether they're family or a teammate, when someone is doing something wrong, you don't just go along with it. That's not loyalty; that's blind servitude," I said angrily.

"Quiet please," Ms. Bierman said. "I'd like to get started."

The legs of my stool shrieked as I dragged it as far from Carson as I could get while staying at the same table.

Carson leaned over to close the gap. "I felt bad, really, I did," he said through the corner of his mouth. "I didn't sleep for days, but I saw him on Monday, and he looked okay."

Seriously? Liam had recovered, so it was okay? I remembered how haunted Carson had seemed last week. I'd tried to *console* him. I rolled my eyes. "If you really felt bad, you'd turn yourself in to Principal Jenner."

Pausing in the middle of writing a chemical equation on the board, Ms. Bierman looked over her shoulder. "I can still hear people talking. If you're talking, you're not paying attention!"

We started to copy down what she was writing, but after a few seconds, Carson whispered, "If I turn myself in, the whole team gets in trouble. I can't."

"You can't, or you won't?"

Carson sighed. "If it was just me, I would, okay?"

"And if Liam says something?"

"He won't." He said this confidently but shifted nervously in his chair. "He won't, right?"

I wasn't going to give Carson the satisfaction of that certainty.

"We're still meeting at lunch, right?"

I nearly choked, dropping my pencil on the floor. Swooping to pick it up, I shot Carson a furious glower. "You're kidding, right?"

"But—"

"Rainey and Carson, am I going to have to split the two of you up?" Ms. Bierman asked, earrings swishing as she rounded on us. Today was a pair of dangling pineapples.

"I'd like to move, actually." Grabbing my things, I took myself over to an empty stool near the front.

Ms. Bierman blinked like a startled, colourful owl. Clearly, she hadn't expected me to respond. "All right then, let's carry on, shall we?"

* * *

Even though Carson had deceived me, and I wanted Chase's head on a pike, I felt blissfully, invincibly happy. Like nothing could go wrong. So much so that when I saw Becca and Val in the hallway, I grinned and waved cheerily at them. They stared at me like I was some circus freak who'd escaped her cage, their faces matching spectacles of confusion.

I almost wanted to thank them. If it hadn't been for their little prank, I wouldn't know what it felt like to be carried on Liam's back or to hold his hand. I wouldn't know the smell of his shampoo or the fact that I could fit two of me in one of his T-shirts. There was a lot to be thankful for.

Liam was waiting for me outside Mr. Greene's classroom right before lunch. The unexpected sight of him spurred my heart rate to a rapid pounding. Was this going to be normal now? Would he always come and find me? It seemed far too good to be true, but I was way too chicken to ask.

"Hi," I said again.

"Hi," he echoed.

Marco.

Polo.

Like a bird call, I thought stupidly.

"Are you busy?" he asked.

"No," I said, grinning.

"Would you like to—"

"Yes."

Liam's brows shot up. "I didn't even finish what I was going to say."

"Whatever it is, my answer is yes."

He smiled. "All right then." We headed to one of the benches near the football field after I retrieved my lunch from my locker. Mom had made a caramelized onion risotto and creamy garlic chicken for dinner last night. I'd made a sandwich with the leftover chicken and had packed a container of risotto, along with one of the brownies Maverick had made for dessert. Liam didn't have anything.

"Where's your lunch?" I asked.

"I ate already."

"You did?" I looked down at my plethora of food. "You don't mind me eating in front of you, do you?"

"Not at all," he said, waving at me to proceed.

I took a bite of my sandwich, but it felt weird, him sitting beside me, watching me eat.

"Would you like some?" I asked, holding out the other half of my sandwich.

Liam shook his head. "I'm good. Like I said, I already ate."

"Are you sure? I won't be able to finish this all by myself. Here." I handed him the second half. "You have to try it. I added romaine lettuce, cranberry sauce, and a bit of herbed goat cheese. It's the best sandwich you've ever tried, trust me."

Liam looked down at the sandwich. I saw the ball in his throat bob.

"You'd be doing me a favor," I cajoled. He finally capitulated and took a bite. I watched his eyes widen appreciatively.

"That is amazing," he said around a full mouth.

"Just wait until you try the risotto. Mom also makes an amazing potato dauphinoise. I'll ask if she can make it tonight so I can bring you some tomorrow."

"I'm not sure what potato dauphinoise is, but it sounds fancy. I wouldn't want your mom making it on my account."

"Oh, she won't mind. She loves making things for people." Mom always joked that she'd won Dad over by cooking for him. *The best way to a man's heart is through his stomach*, she said. I was eager to test the theory.

I'd also been thinking about the upcoming football game and how much I was dreading it. It had crossed my mind that maybe it wouldn't be so terrible if Liam was there too. I just didn't know how to ask him to come without making it look like I was asking him out on a date.

I looked up at the clouds, sweeping across the sky like a giant ship plowing the ocean, and swallowed the last of my sandwich.

"I was wondering . . ."

"I was thinking . . ." I stopped.

"You first."

"No, go ahead," I said, chickening out.

"I noticed you like hummingbirds."

Was that really what he wanted to ask? I masked my disappointment, grateful for the redirection.

"They remind me of Maverick," I said. Small, colourful, and

feisty; even though they could weigh as little as a ping-pong ball, they would still attack larger birds who infringed on their territory. They were fearless.

Come on, ask him already! What's the big deal? I heard her say.

Shooting Liam a quick look before returning my gaze nonchalantly towards the sky, I said, "I was thinking maybe, if you had nothing else going on, you could come to the football game tomorrow and we could hang out?"

"Oh."

My heart stuttered. That hadn't sounded like the good kind of 'oh'. "I understand if you don't want to," I said quickly. "I know you don't like football. It's just, they're having a party in the park afterwards. There will be firepits and a wiener roast. I thought it might be fun if we went . . . er, together."

"That does sound like fun. It's just . . . after everything that's happened between Chase and me, I don't think it's a good idea for me to show up at one of his games."

"Right. I mean, that makes sense." I forced a smile to my face so he couldn't see that I'd just died a little on the inside. "Maybe some other time then."

After finishing lunch in a stilted silence, I started to clear up my things. While putting my plastic container back in my lunch bag, I caught Liam looking at me, the faintest trace of a smile on his mouth.

"What?" I asked.

"I really would like to hang out sometime."

I nodded. "Okay."

"Really," he assured. "Also, you've got chocolate on your lip."

"What?" My hand flew to cover my face, and I rubbed my

sleeve frantically across my mouth. "Is that better?" I asked.

He was trying very hard not to smile. "No, not quite. Here." He reached out and brushed his thumb across my lip. I dissolved like cotton candy on the tip of a tongue.

LIAM

True to her word, Rainey brought some of her mom's potato dauphinoise on Friday, and we sat on our bench over lunch eating it. I quickly discovered that potato dauphinoise was my favorite dish of all time, and tried not to look like I was auditioning for the role of a starved orphan in *Oliver Twist* while eating it.

"Is your mom a professional chef or something?" I asked, licking my fingers, my excuse being we didn't have napkins.

"No. She just loves to cook, and ever since Maverick was born, she's spent a lot of time at home looking after her. She makes up recipes as a way to pass the time between appointments and homeschooling."

I wanted to ask how sick Maverick really was, but that seemed like an impertinent question. I then realized I'd never told Rainey about seeing her father and sister at the hardware store. When I told her, she looked mortified.

"She never told me! Oh my God, she didn't . . . she didn't say anything to you, did she?"

"Like what?"

"I . . . never mind." Rainey's cheeks turned pink. "How did it go?"

"Meeting your sister? It was the best part of my day," I said honestly. "She's very . . . spirited."

"A stick of TNT in a jack-in-the-box, as my dad puts it," Rainey said, then looked down at her lap. "I wish I was more like that."

"You're more alike than you think."

Rainey's mouth popped open in surprise. "You think?"

I remembered the rage on her face when I'd told her about Chase's ambush, and grinned. "Definitely."

A part of me regretted not agreeing to come to the football game after school. If it meant spending time with Rainey, I would have endured watching Chase and his teammates hog the attention of the entire school for three hours without complaint. However, the fact remained that I couldn't afford a run-in with Chase.

I could not, *would not* get expelled.

* * *

My regret increased tenfold as soon as I got home that afternoon. I shouldn't have been surprised. It was Friday, and hunting season was about a month away, and the one thing Ray, Wes, and Paul loved doing more than shooting back beers was shooting rifles. The three of them were out in the front yard, balancing empty beer bottles on the fence posts, a couple of Remingtons and Ray's Marlin balanced against the log pile by the firepit.

I figured I had a fighting chance of sneaking into the trailer without being noticed, but Ray caught me before my foot touched the porch step.

"Hey, kid, get over here."

"I've got homework to do," I said. Like Ray would care.

A hand landed on my shoulder. "It can wait ten minutes. We need some help. You want to help us, don't you?"

"Help doing what, exactly?" I asked, jerking away from Ray. He stank of beer and chew and gun oil. "Finding your dignity?"

"Hey now." Ray's voice dipped to a dangerous whisper. "Quit giving me lip, boy, or I'll knock you into next week." He dragged me over to where Wes and Paul stood.

Wes snorted. "You've got a rope tied around his balls, my friend."

"I sure do." Ray tossed his empty bottle into the grass.

If I'd had a rope, I would have wrapped it around his neck and choked him until he couldn't talk anymore.

"I have an idea." Wes grabbed me around the back of the neck with a calloused hand, pinching hard. "How about junior stands over here and balances one of 'em bottles on his head like . . . like . . . shit, what's that story with the apple?"

I doubted any of these men knew who William Tell was. I also doubted their marksmanship was up to par, even if they had been sober. I wrestled free of Wes's grip.

"Ho! Easy does it, kid. We're just having a bit of fun," he said, raising his hands. His eyes were cold as he spat a wad on my shoe. I kicked it off.

"You're low on beer," I said through my teeth. "I'll go bring you some more."

"Now there's an idea! Kid's smarter than he looks, ain't that right, Ray? Go on then, boy. Off you get!" As I turned, Wes chucked his empty beer bottle. It whipped past me, missing my head by a mere inch, and shattered as it struck an old tree stump. I flinched but kept walking. After a moment, I heard them resume their conversation and veered around the corner of the trailer. The second I was out of sight, I sprinted across the field towards Mercy's.

I didn't stop until I reached the fence, my breath coming in short, sharp gasps. I gripped the barbed wire until the spikes cut into the palms of my hands. There was no pain, only the hot lick of blood dripping down my wrist and the violent howling in my ears.

I struck the fencepost with my fist, then struck it several more times, bruising my knuckles. The pain was distant but there, calling me back and tethering me down. I started to count, first up to ten, and then back down to one, until the howling started to fade. When at last it was gone, I sat down, wiping the blood from my hands off on the grass. The pain was sharper now, my palms stinging. I considered staying where I was until the sun went down, just counting. I could count the blades of grass, or the ants crawling by, or the ways I wanted to kill Ray and his friends.

Instead, I got back up and continued on to Mercy's.

Flea greeted me at the barn, tail whipping around in a frenzy. I knelt down and let him lick my face and sniff my pockets in search of a treat. "Sorry, boy, I don't have anything." As if wishing to voice its own indignation at this, my stomach growled. To make matters worse, I could smell Mrs. Ramos's famous *bulalô* coming from the house.

"I thought that was you." Mercy came jogging over. Judging from the untied laces, she'd thrown her shoes on in a rush. "I saw Flea running towards the barn from my bedroom window. You want to come in for some supper?"

"Your parents won't mind?" I asked.

"Of course not. Come on."

Escaping into the Ramoses' home was exactly what I needed, its clutter, noise, and warmth a barricade that would block out the howling of the wolves in my head. Keeping my hands in my pockets so Mercy wouldn't see the cuts left by the barbed wire, I followed her back.

Mr. Ramos was sitting in his recliner watching golf when we came inside, a bowl of soup in hand. "Liam. Quick, come see. Im Sung-jae is putting for an eagle!" He waved me over with his spoon, his eyes barely deviating from the screen.

Mrs. Ramos tutted from the dining room table. "My mother never let us eat in front of the television. Meals were always eaten around the table. That is what they are for!"

"Relax, Mom. If he spills anything on that chair, you can finally throw it out," Mercy said. "You hate that thing."

Mrs. Ramos's face brightened at the possibility, her demeanor changing to one of hopeful anticipation as she watched her husband balancing his bowl at an ill-advised angle. "Liam," she said, noticing me. "The pot is on the stove, and there is bread in the pantry."

"Thank you, Mrs. Ramos."

Mercy and I ate quickly. They had a porch at the back of their house with a pair of wicker chairs and a couple of weathered foldout tables where we sat looking out into the yard. Just off the porch, next to the fence, was a pile of wood.

Taking note of my curiosity, Mercy said, "Mom asked Dad to knock down the back fence. She said it was blocking the view, but I don't think she wanted him to leave it here like this either. If he doesn't clear it away soon, she'll be slipping pins into his porridge."

A thought niggled at me. "I could use it."

"Really? What for?"

"A treehouse."

"You want to build a treehouse?" Mercy's tone was incredulous. "Aren't you a little old for that kind of thing?"

"It's not for me."

"Please don't tell me it's for that girl from your school."

"Rainey? No, her sister."

"You've met her sister?"

"She and her dad came by the hardware store."

Mercy didn't say anything for a moment, and I figured she wasn't interested in hearing more. Suddenly, she jumped to her feet. "It's Friday. I feel like we should have some fun, don't you?"

"Fun?" The word never sat easily on my tongue. "What did you have in mind?"

She shrugged. "I don't know. We could nab a couple of beers from the fridge and head out to the pond."

There was a pond at the back of the Ramoses' property where Mercy had hung a dartboard and stashed an old CD player, along with her Misfits and Black Flag CDs, which Mrs. Ramos had banned from the house.

"Yeah, maybe," I said.

Noting my lack of enthusiasm, Mercy shrugged. "What do the kids at your school usually do on a Friday night?"

"Tonight is the Mustang football kickoff game. Everyone is at the school. I think there's a party afterwards."

"And you're here because?"

I snorted. "Really? Football? Come on, you know me better than that."

"I don't know," Mercy said with a lopsided shrug. "It could be fun. Rainey will be there, right?"

I nodded. "She has to take pictures for the yearbook."

"So? Let's go."

"I don't know, Mercy. I don't think it's a good idea to break my self-imposed restraining order against Chase and his friends. I'd rather not spend the weekend in a jail cell."

"But this is the perfect opportunity to exact your revenge! Those assholes need a lesson in karma," she said, eyes gleaming with righteous fury.

"No. I'm not going there." I had too much to lose.

"So you're going to let them get away with what they did? I saw you that day. You were a mess! They could have killed you, for Christ's sake. How can you not be pissed?"

"I am pissed. I just . . . I can't."

Hands on her hips, Mercy blew out a long breath. "Well, I can't just let it go." Her mouth formed a thin line, then split into a wide grin.

"What?" I asked, feeling uneasy.

"What if I told you I had an idea?"

"I'd be worried that it involves legally dubious activity."

"What if I promised you no one will end up in jail or get hurt . . . badly?"

"Mercy—"

"Hand on heart. You won't even have to lift a finger. You'll have zero accountability, I swear. Please." She tugged on my arm. "Pretty please?"

I sighed. "What kind of plan?"

RAINEY

As president of the student council, Jo was tasked with organizing the kickoff party, which meant she spent Friday afternoon agonizing over the lemonade order and spewing vitriolic complaints against hot dog companies who insisted on selling eight hot dogs per package while buns were sold by the dozen.

"It's a conspiracy to make more money," she ranted while I helped her string lights around the refreshment stand.

"Where do you want the sound system?" Troy, Springbank's in-house tech guy, was carrying two speaker stands and had cables lassoed around his shoulders like a rodeo cowboy.

"Over there." Jo pointed to the edge of the trees. She bit the end of her pen as I shifted the ladder over and climbed back up, tying the lights to the pole on the other side of the lemonade stand with a twist tie.

"I wanted to end the night with fireworks, but Jenner kiboshed the idea. He said the school would never get the permit. Do you think people will be disappointed?"

"I think we'll manage," I said, stretching out a stitch in my side. "Is this okay?"

Jo studied the fruits of my labor. The lights drooped in the middle, but if I had to climb the ladder one more time, I was going to scream.

"I guess that will do."

I didn't want to think about how I looked after we finished setting up. My hair was a mess, and I'd spilled ketchup on my boob. Maybe it was better that Liam wasn't coming. I could hear the clamor of slamming doors and the blare of an air horn from across the street where the school parking lot was starting to fill with spectators. There was only half an hour until kickoff. I suspected Coach Gardiner was giving the boys an inspiring pep talk in the changeroom right now.

I had to get my camera before the game started. "I've gotta run. See you there!" I shouted to Jo before dashing off towards the school.

* * *

Jo and I found seats near the front of the bleachers, with a clear view of the field so I could take my shots without worrying about getting blocked by a Mustang flag or giant set of horns. (The defending team was the Vikings, and many of their supporters insisted on wearing horned helmets of varying size and absurdity.)

I snapped several pictures of the crowd waving banners, and of spectators who had painted their faces red and white in support of Springbank High. Our mascot, Bucky the Horse, broke out into a dance in the middle of the pitch when "Cotton-Eyed Joe" came on over the speakers, and was joined by the cheerleading squad. I caught as much as I could and was almost starting to enjoy myself when Jo nudged my arm.

"I thought you said Liam wasn't coming," she shouted into my ear.

"He isn't."

"Isn't that him?" She pointed to the edge of the bleachers. Looking over the heads of the crowd, I followed the line of her finger until my eyes landed on the person in question. It was definitely Liam. Unlike the rest of the crowd, he wasn't wearing a Mustang jersey, just his usual jean jacket over a plain white T-shirt.

"Who's that with him?" Jo asked.

Standing next to him was a girl with curly black hair. Her head was bent towards Liam, her shoulder brushing his in a way that hinted at intimacy without being overtly couple-ish.

She was stunning.

As I watched, she nudged him with a hip sheathed in a pair of skin-tight jeans. Her teeth flashed white against her brilliant bronze skin as she laughed.

"I don't know," I said, my mouth suddenly dry.

"Are you going to go find out?" Jo asked, brows raised in a way that told me in no uncertain terms I should do just that.

I didn't want to. Doing so would necessitate finding out why Liam had shown up at a game he'd told me he wasn't coming to in the company of another girl who he clearly knew quite well. And as desperate as I was for an answer, I was equally as desperate to avoid the inevitable destruction of my already fragile ego.

"Do you want me to come with you?" Jo asked, reading my hesitation.

I shook my head. "I'll be right back." Clutching my camera, I shimmied along the bleachers, trying my best not to knock someone's drink or tumble into anyone's lap.

"Er . . . hi. I thought you weren't coming," I said when I got close enough to be heard. It was hard not to stare at the girl by his side. I kept focusing on the long curl of her lashes, the swell of her cleavage, and the narrow curve of her waist above the flair of her hips.

God.

Liam looked pleased to see me. At least I thought he did. His eyes brightened a little, and he took a step closer to me.

"I wasn't planning on coming, but Mercy convinced me. Mercy, this is Rainey. Rainey, this is my friend Mercy."

"So this is Rainey." Mercy stepped forward as well, moving closer to Liam. Her eyes were the most startling shade of green. I felt them drift over my face and body in a cursory sort of way. "I've heard a lot about you."

"Nice to meet you too." Still holding my camera, I waved awkwardly, then realized that's not what she'd said. She'd heard about me, but I hadn't heard anything about her? I looked at Liam, hoping for some kind of explanation, but he was busy scanning the crowd. "I don't think I've seen you at Springbank before."

"Oh, I don't go to school here. Liam and I are neighbors."

Her words nudged a memory. "You're Joshua's sister?" I asked.

"That would be me," she said brightly. "I hope you don't mind me crashing your party. I convinced Liam to come so he could observe justice in action. Speaking of which, I'd better hurry."

"Be careful," Liam said.

"Don't worry. I'll be back before you can say blueberry pie." Mercy winked at him and disappeared into the crowd.

I felt like I'd swallowed something large and spikey, like a massive durian fruit. "Where is she going?"

"To slip laxatives into Chase's water bottle."

I felt my eyes pop. "Right before the game?"

"Her idea, not mine." Despite this fact, Liam didn't seem at all bothered by the savageness of her plan. I guess the name was a misnomer; there was nothing merciful about her.

"Are you sure you want to do that?"

"The guy broke my ribs. I'm not all that sympathetic right now."

Neither was I, but something about this felt wrong. I opened my mouth, then shut it again; I already felt at a disadvantage with Mercy here. I didn't want to argue with him. "Do you want to sit with me and Jo?" I asked.

"Sure."

He followed me back to my seat, and we all shuffled down to make room.

"Glad you could join us, Hayes!" Jo shouted over the blare of another air horn. Liam's response was swallowed up by a clamor of cheers as Bucky did a backflip.

Jo nudged my leg. *Who was she?* she mouthed. I waved my hand in an I'll-tell-you-later sort of way.

Ten minutes later, Mercy came back and sat down beside Liam, displacing me along the bench. Two guys in front of us turned around to stare at her. Feeling like a twelve-year-old, I fought the urge to dump my popcorn over her head.

Jo didn't hold back and scowled openly at her, which I found assuaging.

"Done! Now all we have to do is wait and watch!"

"How did you do it?" Liam asked.

Mercy snorted. "Easy. I went up to him in the locker room and asked him for his autograph. Then I told him what an amazing star quarterback he was and how strong his throwing arm was." Mercy caressed Liam's arm in demonstration. Jo made a gagging motion behind Mercy's back. I didn't want to know what my face looked like. An avocado, if I were to hazard a guess.

Liam shifted his arm out from under Mercy's hand, but she didn't seem to notice. "And then I just asked if I could fill up his water bottle for him. He practically threw it at me," she said, laughing.

Just then, a whistle blew, and the two teams came running out onto the pitch. The crowd stood and cheered, or at least most of them did. Liam remained firmly seated, his gaze locked on the players as they made formation.

I tried to focus on taking some decent pictures, but I found my attention continually drawn to Mercy and Liam and my burgeoning jealousy. I turned, adjusting my lens until Liam's face came into sharp focus. He was leaning forward over his knees, his hands folded loosely together. I noticed several shallow scrapes across his knuckles as if he'd hit something. What—

The thought broke off as shouts of confusion rose from the crowd. Several people jumped to their feet, and one boy pointed across the field. I turned and saw a single uniformed figure running across the pitch, the ball tucked under his arm. Only he wasn't heading towards the end posts; he was heading towards the school.

"Buckner, where the hell are you going!" Coach Gardiner yelled.

Chase dropped the ball and continued to beeline it for the school. Halfway there, he wobbled and sank to his knees, his head bowing to the ground.

"Ha!" Grinning ear to ear, Mercy nudged Liam in the ribs. "He's never going to live this one down. You know that, don't you? From now on, everyone will remember Chase Buckner as the kid who shit his pants in the middle of the homecoming game. Layup. Who is the greatest friend who ever lived?" She raised her hand for a high five.

A reluctant smile flickered across Liam's face, and he clasped her hand, but he didn't say anything. Instead, his eyes rose and found mine. For a moment, it felt as if we shared the same terrible thought: as bad as Chase was, as much as he deserved to pay for his crimes, this public humiliation tasted less of victory and more like malicious cruelty.

Was this really what Liam wanted? I hadn't thought of him as cruel, but maybe . . . maybe I didn't know him as well as I thought.

* * *

The rest of the game was a disaster. Springbank had to bring in their backup player to fill Chase's spot, and we lost catastrophically as a result. Afterwards, I dropped my camera off at my locker and rejoined everyone as they trooped across the street to the park in the gloaming light. Despite the loss, people were buzzing, the atmosphere one of jocular hilarity as they ran to claim the best campfires.

"Oh my God, can you believe it? Chase Buckner literally shit his pants in the middle of the season's kickoff game."

"Did you see him waddling back to the locker rooms? Someone followed him and saw everything!"

""Springbank's hustling Mustang? More like Springbank's hustling Mustank!"

The conversation fizzled around us like champagne, warming the blood, but the only member of our group who seemed to be enjoying herself was Mercy.

"Best comeback ever!" she crowed, dancing along the park

path, her long curls flying in the wind. Even though I didn't like her, I still felt a pang of envy. "Reminds me of the time you beat up Zack after he cheated on me," she said. "You scared the shit out of him."

Liam was walking slowly, keeping pace with me and Jo. He smiled half-heartedly at Mercy but didn't say anything.

Heedless, Mercy carried on. "Hey, can you remember when I first dropped out of school? Dad grounded me and took away my car keys and my cell phone." She turned and smiled at me, skipping backwards while she told her story. "Liam helped me sneak out of the house using a ladder from the barn. I climbed out my bedroom window, and we spent the whole night in that old hunter stand eating corn chips and watching the stars. It was so cold, we had to spoon just to keep warm."

Beside me, Jo scoffed and hugged my arm. I leaned against her, taking in Mercy's words like a sucker punch to the gut. I knew I shouldn't be bothered; Liam and I weren't together. We weren't anything, really. The fact that this gorgeous *caliente* creature had a history with him could hardly be construed as a betrayal. And yet . . .

I peeked at Liam out of the corner of my eye. A line had formed between his brows; there wasn't a single trace of a smile on his face now.

"How about this one?" Jo asked, pointing to a fire pit whose only occupants were two female freshmen. "Do you mind if we join you?" she asked them. They shook their heads shyly. "Great. Rainey, why don't you get close to the fire? Your hands feel like they've been dipped in frozen lake water. I'll go get us some wieners."

"I'm not that hungry," I whispered. I reached my hands out to the fire, keeping my eyes fixed on the flaking coals.

"How about a drink, then?" Reaching into her bag, she pulled out a bottle of tequila.

"Jo! What the hell?" I looked up at the two girls on the other side of the fire who were staring at Jo like a pair of startled raccoons.

"You can't say you don't need one. I know I do." Without further ado, she pressed the bottle to her lips and tipped it back. She smacked her lips, wincing. "God, that is foul."

"I'll have some," Mercy said with a grin. Jo passed over the bottle reluctantly.

"Mercy—" Liam reached to stop her, but he was too slow. She took a long drink and wiped her mouth.

"Wow, that is some high-grade shit." She studied the bottle appreciatively. "Way better than the stuff my dad has in his liquor cabinet."

"It's Gran Patrón. Sells for around five hundred dollars a bottle," Jo said, taking it back with an uncharacteristically haughty arch to her brows.

Mercy snorted. "Fuck me. I usually avoid entitled rich bitches, but there are perks to hanging out with them."

"Mercy, can I talk to you?" Before she could answer, Liam grabbed her arm and dragged her out of earshot.

Jo watched the two of them through poisonously narrowed eyes. "I do *not* like that girl." She looked at me, and seeing the defeated look on my face, came over and gave me a big clumsy hug, the bottle of tequila knocking my head. "You are way prettier than that low-class cow. Come on, I think I saw someone with some marshmallows over there. Let's make a flaming marshmallow cocktail."

While this didn't sound like the best idea, I felt it was better than sitting about like a pitiful third wheel, watching Mercy and Liam chat it up for the rest of the night. If Liam came back to find us gone, that was his problem. Arm in arm, Jo and I wandered off through the trees, Jo singing the lyrics to "Boys Are So Ugh" in such a pitchy, off-key tone that even though I wanted to cry, I couldn't help but laugh a little.

LIAM

"What the hell was that?" I snapped.

"What was what?" Mercy asked. She was laughing like this was funny to her and she was waiting for me to clue in on the joke.

"Entitled rich bitches? You didn't have to call them that. They're nice people. And what's with all this?" I waved my hand at her.

"What are you talking about?"

"Cut the crap, Mercedes." I never called her by her full name. She hated it, but I was too angry to care and was gratified to see her wince. Her smile tapered into an ugly sulk.

"You're acting weird," I said. "And why did you have to mention that night in the hunter stand?" I'd seen the look on Rainey's face when Mercy had brought that up. Mercy might as well have spat in her face. Were it not for our long-standing friendship, I would have throttled her.

Mercy stuck her chin out. "So what if I brought it up? It

happened, didn't it? At least I didn't tell her what you told me, that it was one of the most memorable nights of your life."

I remembered saying that, and it was true, too, but not because I'd harboured feelings for Mercy. That night had been the first night in a long while that I'd felt some semblance of peace, that I'd felt the cold ache of loneliness ease away in the presence of friendship. Had I really misled Mercy all this time? Was I that blind?

"That's what this is about. You're jealous."

Mercy didn't respond.

"You said you were fine with all this. Why would you lie to me?"

"I didn't lie!"

"Then why?" I asked. "Why hurt her? And don't tell me that wasn't your intention."

Mercy crossed her arms over her chest and scoffed.

"Well?" I pressed.

"Because you don't belong with her!" she said furiously, throwing her arms out. "Jesus, Liam. You don't belong with those people. They drive Audis and drink five hundred dollar bottles of tequila on a Friday night. You might think you like her, but she's just a shiny bauble in a store window that's caught your eye. If you spent more than a second being honest with yourself, you'd see that."

Mercy stepped closer, her face lit by the last remnants of the sun, her cheeks flushed from the tequila. "But you and me? We're the same. I love you. You know I do, and I think deep down, you love me too."

I stepped back, feeling suddenly a hundred years old, my soul hunched and arthritic and too tired to carry my anger. "I don't."

"Oh please. And you call me the liar!" The sound of her voice, almost frantic, wrenched at something deep in my chest.

I ran my hand through my hair, shaking my head. "Mercy, I'm not lying. You and me . . . it would never work."

"What do you mean it would never work? We haven't even tried." She reached out to touch me, but I caught her hand and moved it aside.

I wanted to be honest with her, but I couldn't bring myself to tell her the truth. That I saw a part of her in me, the untameable, angry part that sparked itself into a burning passion more quickly than nitroglycerin. The part that had enjoyed Chase's humiliation, had relished it even. The part that would inevitably fall from grace and drag everything within reach down with it. I didn't blame her for its existence, but I didn't want to give it air to breathe either. I didn't like that side of me, and I didn't like how I'd seen it in the cool reflection of Rainey's gaze when our eyes had met during the game.

"I can't, okay?"

Mercy glared at me, arms once more crossed as if she were protecting herself. "I don't understand. Why not? What did I do that was so wrong?"

"Nothing. It's what I did."

"You didn't do anything!"

"Yes I did. I became someone tonight I didn't like, and I hurt someone I care about." I rubbed my eyes with the balls of my hands. I wanted to go home. I couldn't stand being here anymore.

Mercy was quiet. "You mean Rainey."

I scowled at the way she said her name, like she was some

third-string fiddle. "Yes, Rainey."

"What about me? What about my feelings? Don't they matter to you?"

"Of course they do. You're my only friend, and I'm sorry, but I can't tell you something that isn't true, even if it hurts you."

"You came to me tonight, remember?"

"I know. And I'm sorry if that gave you the wrong impression, but I didn't have a choice."

"Sure you didn't." Her eyes were wet, but the tears didn't fall. Mercy never cried if anger was an option. "You always had a choice, Liam. You're just telling yourself you didn't so you don't have to feel bad about the fact that you've been using me. You owe me."

I stood in shocked silence, hardly aware of the laughter levitating over the dusky shadows of the park, or the sudden chill as the sun dipped below the horizon. I could tell from her face that she regretted the words as soon as they were spoken.

"Is that really how you feel?" I asked.

Her lashes lowered over her eyes, and her shoulders drew in like paper curling under the heat of a flame.

I swore quietly under my breath. "See? Together we will tear each other apart."

Mercy blinked, looking anywhere but at me. "Fine," she said. "Maybe you're right. Maybe we would be bad for each other. Or we might be the best thing ever. I guess we'll never know. Your new friends can take you home." She stalked past me and ran towards the road where she'd parked her car, leaving me standing alone on the fringes of the revelry, wondering if I'd just lost the only friend I'd ever really had.

RAINEY

I leaned my head against Jo's shoulder as we wandered along the path, my eyes following the dotted line of fires speckled throughout the trees, the redolent smoke carrying with it the smell of sizzling hot dogs and burnt marshmallows.

"Want some?" Jo asked, holding up the bottle of tequila.

"You'll be in trouble if someone catches you with that," I warned. But whether it was out of a sudden rebellious curiosity or a need for some kind of distraction, I took the bottle and drank the tiniest sip.

"Urgh! That's disgusting!" I wiped my lips, desperate to get the foul remnants of the tequila off them. "How can you drink that?"

Jo laughed. "It gets better after the first try."

I doubted that.

A familiar, worried voice caught my ear. "Have you seen him? He disappeared after the game, and I haven't seen him since."

"He'll be fine. He's probably getting drunk with some chick."

Weaving around a patch of trees, I spotted Carson and Becca. They were standing around a campfire among a familiar group of people, the boys still wearing their jerseys and the girls in knee-high boots and skirts that barely came down over their asses. I stopped, dislodging myself from Jo's arm.

"What's up?" she asked.

"I don't want to see them," I said.

Jo looked over to the group in question. "Why not?"

Becca had moved away from Carson to join Val by the fire, their bare legs and crop-top midriffs sacrificial lambs to the altar of fashion. One of the football players, Toby Thomas, juggled marshmallows under their critical observation, no doubt hoping to prove himself. What juggling marshmallows proved, I had no idea.

"I just don't, okay?" I said, avoiding Jo's inquisitive stare.

"Rainey Collins, you're not telling me something. What is it?"

Knowing Jo wouldn't let it go, I caved and told her what had happened in the girls' changeroom. Her face darkened into a furious glower.

"Why the hell didn't you tell me this sooner?"

I tugged sheepishly on the end of my braid. "I was embarrassed. And they're your friends, and they're on your volleyball team. I didn't want to make things awkward."

Jo rolled her eyes. "Geezus, Rainey. Sometimes you can be really thick. Come on."

Before I could object, she grabbed my hand and marched over to Becca and Val, dragging me with her. I shrank back, wanting to disappear.

"Hey." Jo gathered their attention with a snap of her fingers as if she were speaking to a pair of misbehaving dogs. "So Rainey here told me about how you two stole her clothes out of the girls' changeroom. What's the deal with that, huh? Did your dads take away your credit cards so you couldn't go shopping, and your sticky little fingers just couldn't resist?"

Becca glared at me. "Oh please. Like we'd want to look like that frumpy dud."

"It was a joke, Solano," Val said. "Where's your sense of humor?"

"I see," Jo said. "So you find public humiliation funny. I'll have to remember that next time I'm in the mood for a little joke.

In fact, here's one right now. Who here knows that Becca Montgomery—"

"Jo, stop!" I said. Becca's snarky expression had deflated into a pale contortion of fear. There had been more than enough humiliation going around tonight. I had had enough.

"Fine," Jo said. "But as captain of the volleyball team, I have the authority to kick you girls off the team whenever the hell I want. Monday morning, I'm writing to tell Coach Gardiner that you two are resigning from your positions."

"You can't do that!" Val screamed. "We're your best players!"

"I don't care. There's more to being on a team than skill. I'd rather Rainey be on the team than you snollygosters, and she can't even reach the top of the net. No offense," she added as an aside to me.

"None taken," I murmured.

Not to be cowed, Becca rounded on me. "That bitch tried to steal my boyfriend!" She jabbed an accusatory finger at my chest.

Jo looked at me, then back at Becca. "Your boyfriend? You mean Carson?"

Staring at the scuff mark he'd worried into the dirt, Carson refused to meet my eye.

Jo laughed. "I think you have your wires crossed, Montgomery. Rainey is head over heels in love with someone, but he's no dumbass football player."

"Jo!" I winced. Carson's cheeks flush red with embarrassment.

"What? It's true. She likes Liam."

"The Hayes kid?" Toby Thomas had been listening to our exchange with rapt attention.

Jo ignored him. "If you're worried your boyfriend is straying, maybe you should take a good look in the mirror and ask yourself why, rather than shove the blame off on someone else."

Becca looked on the verge of tears. "You really are a bitch, Solano."

"No, I'm just a teller of unfortunate truths," Jo rejoined blithely.

"Well, at least I *have* a boyfriend, which is more than you can say."

Jo snorted. "Who says having a boyfriend magically makes you better than the rest of us?"

"You're just saying that to make yourself feel better. The truth is, you're afraid no one likes you. Little Miss Perfect with her four-point-oh GPA," Becca scoffed. "Reality check, Solano: no one likes you. Even your parents couldn't give a shit about you."

Jo stiffened as if she'd been struck.

"When was the last time they actually checked that you were still breathing?" Becca persisted. "I doubt they would even notice if you got hit by a bus; they'd just leave you in the gutter to rot and send flowers to the driver with a note of apology for the blood spatter."

"What the hell, Becks," Carson muttered.

"Stay out of this, Carson," Becca snapped, her eyes sparkling.

I looked at Jo. She was staring at Becca with a strangely vacant expression, as if her soul had been sucked out, leaving behind a frozen waxwork doll. The thought disturbed me so much, I tugged on her arm. "Jo . . ."

Finally, she blinked and opened her mouth. "I would slap you, Montgomery, but shit splatters. Let's go," she said to me.

"Jo . . ."

"Come on." And with one last look back at Becca and Val, she led me off into the night.

LIAM

Rainey was gone when I got back to our campfire. Jo too. I asked the two girls who were still sitting there with matching cups of lemonade where they'd gone, but they just shrugged.

Swearing, I headed towards the food tables and the lemonade stand. A lineup of people was waiting to load their charred wieners up with pickled onions and relish, but I couldn't spot Rainey's dark braid or Jo's blond head among them. I circled back to the campfire, checking the other sites along the path with no luck.

They were gone.

I couldn't blame her, but I was still angry that Rainey hadn't given me the chance to apologize or explain, and on top of everything, I was now stranded with nowhere to go. Shoving my hands into my pockets, I started walking. I didn't want to stay, surrounded by people laughing and hanging out with their friends, their happiness an irritating mockery of the bruised and wretched night.

Dusk was settling into night, and the temperature dropped. I hugged my jacket close to me, trying to keep out the wind as I walked along the road. I wasn't wearing a watch, and I didn't have a phone to check the time, but I figured it had to be nearing nine. Walking home would take hours, and I was exhausted.

Maybe, if I was lucky, Rosie's would still be open. Maybe in exchange for a few extra tutoring sessions, she'd let me sleep in one of the booths. Maybe.

I broke into a light jog, cutting across someone's yard in the hopes of getting there before she locked up. I was crossing the street when I heard the shriek of squealing tires. It all happened in a matter of seconds, and yet I could remember each moment with perfect clarity, as if my brain had captured crystal clear pictures at lightning-shutter speed.

A bright yellow Porsche shot past me at what had to be nearing eighty clicks, nearly clipping me with its wing mirror. I leapt out of the way and watched it swerve, hitting the corner of a parked white van with an ear-splitting screech. Caught by its own momentum, the Porsche spun out, flipping end over end until it struck a light pole, the body crumpling like a paper bag.

I stared at the wreckage, breathing fast. The alarm was blaring from the van, but nobody came. I looked both ways down the street, hoping to see someone so I could tell them to call 911, but it was empty, and the house next to me was completely dark, with several newspapers shoved into the mailbox.

"Shit." I ran over to the Porsche. The back wheel was still spinning, and I could smell gasoline. Crouching down, I peered through the cracked driver window into the crumpled interior. The driver was hanging from his seatbelt, arms flopped over his head like a grotesque marionette, blood dripping from a gash in his forehead.

"Hey!" I called. "Hey! Can you hear me? Chase!"

Chase's head turned slightly, his eyes fluttering. I looked around, thinking frantically. The house next to us had a low retaining stone wall that framed a neatly landscaped flower bed under the front windows. I ran over and kicked at it until one of the stones came loose, and picked it up.

Through the spiderweb of glass, I could see Chase tugging at his seatbelt.

"Don't move, okay? Hold on. Can you cover your face?" I mimicked hitting the window with the rock so he knew what I was going to do. I saw him nod once and waited until he turned his head away from the glass. Bracing myself, I smashed the stone against the window until the glass shattered. It crunched under my weight as I lay down on my stomach and crawled forward.

"Hey, you okay?" I asked, panting.

Chase turned back to face me, groaning. I caught the stale smell of beer on his breath. The cut on his head was bleeding profusely, but it looked superficial. However, now that I was closer, I noticed another cut on his arm. The blood coming from here was a brilliant, garish red.

"You're going to be okay," I said, more to reassure myself than Chase. I wasn't even sure he could hear me. "We need to stop the bleeding." Undoing my belt, I ripped it out through the loops of my jeans and wrapped it around Chase's arm, cinching it as tightly as I could. He gave the strangled yelp of an animal in pain, his body jerking.

"Okay, okay. It's okay. I know that hurts." Placing one hand over the wound on his arm, I used the other to feel around in his jacket pocket until I found what I was looking for. I pressed the button on the phone, and it lit up, asking for a password.

"Chase. Can you hear me? Chase, what's your password? I need to open your phone so I can call an ambulance."

"2-5 . . . 4-2-3."

The phone unlocked. "You're doing great. Just hang in there."

I dialed 911 and waited for the operator. A woman's voice answered. I told her there was a car crash a couple of blocks east of Springbank High. "The driver is in bad condition and needs to be taken to the hospital."

"There will be emergency personnel with you in five minutes," she said. Sure enough, a few minutes later, I heard the blare of the approaching sirens. Police and firemen converged on us, and I was asked to step aside, which I did, feeling dizzy. They broke the doors off the Porsche and loaded Chase into the back of an ambulance. The paramedics looked at the cinched belt around his arm and the blood on my hands.

"You do this?" one of them asked. He was young, maybe twenty-five, with the inky curve of a tribal tattoo rising over the collar of his shirt.

"Yes."

"Nicely done. This young man saved your life, my friend," he said, patting Chase's shoulder.

Chase's eyes flickered in my direction. Lying on the gurney, his face as pale as chalk that had been ground across fifty yards of asphalt, he looked like someone trapped in the clutches of a nightmare.

"You coming to the hospital?" the paramedic asked me. "You can ride with us if you want."

I hesitated, but I had nowhere else to go, and deep down—deep, deep down—I knew I was standing before the altar of my revenge, bearing witness to its ugly aftermath. I couldn't just walk away. I jumped up into the back of the ambulance just as the paramedic slammed the doors shut, and we took off, the siren screaming into the night.

I stayed out of the way while the paramedic worked, checking Chase's vitals and setting up an IV drip. Chase was quiet, his eyes closed, a sweaty sheen covering his face. There was a brief moment of chaos when we arrived at the hospital—the paramedics wheeled Chase into the emergency room, relaying the situation to the doctors in a quick-fire exchange of numbers and medical jargon—and then it was quiet.

I stood frozen in the middle of the emergency waiting room, adrift and numb. A nurse told me to take a seat on one of the blue vinyl chairs in the waiting room, but my body didn't want to sit. My hands were spattered with Chase's blood and felt hot and sticky, so I went to the bathroom. I washed up, the water swirling pink against the white porcelain. Finally, I turned off the tap, leaving my hands dripping and heavy against the sink. Every part of me felt heavy, especially my head. Still, I forced it up and looked into the mirror. My face stared back at me, pale and accusing.

Are you happy now?

But the dark, angry Liam who had secretly revelled in his revenge didn't answer. Instead, all I could hear were excuses. It hadn't been my idea. I hadn't put the laxatives in his water bottle. I hadn't forced him to drive drunk.

I felt sick.

Eventually, I returned to the waiting room. I sat for a couple of hours before a doctor came out and told me that Chase was in the recovery room. "He's lost some blood and has a minor concussion, but he's stable, and his vitals are good. He asked to see you."

"He did?" Why? Did he know? Did he want to blame me for what had happened?

My feet dragging, I followed the doctor to the recovery room and found Chase lying in a bed, the curtains half drawn around him.

I stopped several feet away and cleared my throat.

Chase didn't quite look at me, his eyes glazed from the pain meds. He didn't say anything for a while, and I wondered if he was even lucid. "About what the paramedic said . . . I wanted to say thanks," he said at last.

"Oh." The fact that he felt grateful after what I'd done made me feel even worse. And yet I was relieved too. "Don't worry about it. I'm just glad I was there."

Chase swallowed and nodded. "Rough night."

Whether he meant it as an explanation for the accident or as a general grievance, I couldn't tell.

"The thing is . . ." Chase bit his lip, plucking at the bedsheet. "The thing with my mom . . ."

"You don't have to explain," I said.

"It's hereditary." Chase finally met my eyes; stripped of his cockish bravado, I saw the dark shadow of fear in them, stark and exposed like a leering demon.

"Do you . . . ?"

"I don't know."

Just then, Robert Buckner strode past me and descended on his son like a raging bull. "Good God, Chase, what the hell were you thinking? I just got off the phone with the police. They said your blood alcohol level was a point two. You could have killed someone!"

"I'm sorry."

"Sorry? What good is sorry? You've disgraced us! If your mother were here, she would rip her hair out in shame, damn it!

I've got to call the lawyers, but then I'm calling the board of governors at Wycliffe. You'll be on the first plane tomorrow morning."

"Dad, please—"

"No. I've had enough of this foul behavior. I can't deal with it any longer. You need help." Robert Buckner tugged at the cuffs of his shirt, the artery in his neck pulsing visibly against the tight band of his collar. He looked around, suddenly distracted. "I need to speak with the doctor here. Where are the nurses?"

Noticing me for the first time, Robert blinked in momentary confusion. I could see the thoughts pass clearly across his face as he registered my attire and age, dismissing me as a member of the hospital staff. "Who are you?"

I'm the one responsible for this.

"He was the one who called the ambulance," Chase explained, not quite meeting my eye.

"Oh, I see." Robert cleared his throat. "I take it you're looking for some kind of compensation?" Reaching into his jacket pocket, he pulled out a leather wallet two inches thick with cash and dispensed one crisp hundred dollar bill.

"Dad, don't—" Chase started.

"I don't need your money," I said.

Robert waved my objection away like an inconsequential gnat. "Oh, come now, no need to be self-conscious about it. You did a service for my son. You should be recompensed."

"No, thank you." I stepped away as he held out the money.

Robert shrugged and tucked the bill back into his wallet. "Very well then. Is there something else you want? It's late. Do you need a ride home? Let my man give you a lift."

At this point, I would have rather eaten my shoes and walked home than accept anything from Robert Buckner, but it was nearing midnight, I was twenty miles from home, I and had no money for a taxi. Cursing Mercy for leaving me stranded, I accepted the offer and was hastily directed out front where a man in a chauffeur's cap stood next to a black Lincoln Continental. He held the door for me as I got into the back seat.

As we left the hospital, I stared out the tinted windows, marveling at the fact that through the tangle of guilt and shame and regret, I felt a sharp and unexpected pang of sympathy for Chase Buckner.

RAINEY

I ran through the grass, the long blades brushing against my legs, trusting nothing but my balance in the endless darkness. Around me, crickets hummed a string symphony while the sounds of the campfire celebration faded behind, and up ahead, I could hear Jo laughing, her deep whoops leading me onwards like the luring melody of the Pied Piper.

"Jo, slow down!" I yelled.

I was running so hard, my lungs felt like they were about to burst, and my throat ached each time I sucked in the night air. It engulfed me, smelling of damp earth and decaying leaves. Then the grass fell away, and I felt the earth turn to gravel under my shoes. My toe caught on something sharp and hard, and I pitched forward.

"Ow!" I hopped on my good foot, trying to shake the pain out of my bruised toe. I'd tripped over the elevated iron rails of train tracks.

"Jo?" I looked around. It was almost too dark to see her, but I could just discern the curves of her silhouette against the inky blue line of the horizon. She was walking along the train tracks, balanced with her arms out like a prima ballerina, the sloshing bottle of tequila in one hand. I ran to catch up.

"What the hell, Jo? Didn't you hear me calling?"

"Shhh! Listen, can you hear that?"

"Hear what?" All I could hear was my labored breathing.

"Be quiet." She wobbled dangerously, giggling. "It's the sound of the cosmos, the sound of life, barreling towards us. Swoosh!" Swinging the half-empty bottle, she lost her balance and tipped sideways into me. Tequila splashed down my pant leg, the smell burning my nostrils.

"Careful!"

Jo sobered, her giggles cutting off abruptly. "Do you ever wonder about that?"

"About what?" I needed to get her off the tracks. This wasn't safe.

"About the fact that life is coming at us so damn fast? And we're . . . we're racing towards it with our heads down, and we're so busy running that we won't even notice when it hits us? I wonder what happens to us when it does. I mean, what if the impact completely annihilates us, and we just disappear into dust without even realizing what happened?"

"I think you need to stop drinking," I said. I made a grab for the bottle of tequila, but Jo swerved onto the tracks, holding it high over her head and out of my reach.

"And I think you need to chase me!" she crowed, and took off straight down the middle of the tracks. Cursing my short legs, I followed after her.

I heard another whoop of laughter ahead of me, followed by a second, this one more distant.

"Okay, this is getting old fast," I shouted. "I'm done." I slowed to a walk, my feet dragging. Swatting at a cloud of gnats, I thought longingly of my bed, wishing I were tucked under the covers with a cup of hot water sweetened with honey and lemon. Another deep hoot of laughter echoed through the night, but it didn't sound quite right, more like a deep wail that reverberated through the ground in a great tremor.

The hair on the nape of my neck rose. "Jo!" I broke into a fresh run. I nearly collided with her. She was standing perfectly still in the middle of the tracks, head tilted back, gazing up at the stars overhead.

"There's a train coming. Come on. Let's get off of here." I took her hand and pulled, but she wouldn't move.

"Can you hear it now?" she asked.

"Jo, this is not funny." I looked down the tracks, but all I could see were shadows upon shadows. I could hear it, though, and felt the rumble of its implacable approach through the soles of my feet.

"I wonder what would happen if I just . . . stopped, you know?"

"Sounds great. Let's stop somewhere else, shall we?"

"Do you think it's too late? Do you think life will still annihilate us?"

"No one is getting annihilated," I said firmly. I could see the beam of the train's headlight now, hurtling towards us at fifty miles an hour like a proverbial light at the end of a dark tunnel. Horrible images of bugs getting splattered across a windscreen filled my mind. I pulled hard on Jo's arm, but she resisted. What the hell did they put in that tequila to make people so strong?

Panic rose in my chest, prickling and painful. "Josephine Solano, you get off these tracks right now, you hear?"

"You go. I'm staying here."

"Like hell you are." I realized the more I fought with her, the harder she would resist. Typical lawyer, I thought acerbically. "Fine," I said. "I'll stay here with you." I stepped up beside her and turned to face the approaching train. My body was not on board with this plan. My heart was pulsing at the same tempo as the train. Du-dun, du-dun, du-dun. Despite the cold night air, a trail of sweat rolled down the curve of my spine.

The train was less than a kilometer away, Jo's smile a fierce flash of white teeth against the dark. The train was now close enough that the arc of its headlight was starting to climb up our legs, revealing our mud-spattered shoes and grass-stained jeans. The train's horn blared loudly, reverberating through every bone in my body.

Suddenly Jo jerked my hand, and we dove headfirst off the tracks, screaming. I struck the ground, a whoosh of air rushing over me as the train barreled past us. The ground shook, and all I could do was lie with my face pressed against the cold shale, gasping for air, a blade of grass stuck to my lips.

Several long minutes after the train passed, I rolled onto my back and looked up at the stars. Every inch of me tingled as if my body wanted to remind itself that it was still alive.

"Rainey? Are you okay?" Jo's voice sounded from somewhere

to my right. I could hear her breathing heavily, her cold hand still clinging to mine.

"No," I said. The tingling sensation had turned into full-on tremors that ran from the crown of my head to the tips of my toes, shaking loose a geyser of tears. "No, I am not okay! What were you thinking?"

I felt her squeeze my hand. "I'm sorry." Her voice trembled, as if the blast of the train had blown away all her brash confidence, leaving her just as scared and sober and I was.

But the small apology wasn't enough to quench my anger. "Goddamn it, Jo. What was that?"

"I don't know," was her quiet reply.

I placed my other hand on my chest, trying to soothe my frantic heart, and turned my head to see Jo staring up at the sky, tears leaking out of the corners of her eyes. Suddenly my anger drained away.

"Oh, Jo. Don't listen to Becca. What she said . . . it isn't true. Not a word of it."

"You don't know that," Jo whispered. Now that I'd had time to calm down, I could feel her shaking with silent sobs. "My parents barely notice me. It's like I don't even exist some days. Like I could just fade away and they wouldn't even realize it; they'd just wake up one day and wonder who used to sleep in the spare room with the crepe walls." She whimpered. "I'm sure they wish I'd never been born. Nobody . . . nobody loves me."

"That's rubbish. I love you! You're my best friend, Jo. I love you to the moon and back, and if anything were to happen to you, I'd be devastated, and so would your parents! I know they're busy and always working and travelling, but they are so proud of you."

Jo sniffed and wiped her nose but didn't answer, so I continued, huddling closer and tucking my head under her chin, as much for comfort as for warmth.

"Your dad frames all of your awards and hangs them in his office, and your mom always wears that locket you gave her with your picture. I've never seen her take it off. Of course they love you! You're a fierce queen, Jo Solano. Don't let the rabble knock your crown off."

"Thanks, Rainey," she whispered.

We lay there in the grass, our clothes slowly growing damp. I started humming songs we both knew, and Jo slowly joined in. Eventually, we crawled to our feet and headed back towards the park, leaving the half-empty bottle of tequila in the grass.

"I'll drive us home," I said. I wanted nothing more than nine uninterrupted hours of sleep on my pillow-top mattress right now. "By the way . . . what's a snollygoster?"

11

RAINEY

THERE WAS A WOODPECKER OUTSIDE my window, rapping against a tree. I squeezed my eyes shut, as if doing so would block out the noise as well as the fresh sunlight floating through the lace curtains. Why wasn't there a switch that could just turn off the world for a while? I wanted to sleep, to block out my tangled feelings for Liam and my concern for Jo in the vapors of inarticulate dreams.

A hurried thumping of feet approached my bedroom.

"Rainey! Rainey, get up!" A cannonball struck my bed, bouncing me awake.

"Seriously?" I groaned, burying my head under my pillow. "I'm trying to sleep!"

"Liam is building me a treehouse!" Maverick squealed.

"That's nice," I said drowsily.

"Didn't you hear me? I said Liam is building me a treehouse! He's in our backyard, like, right now."

Her words sunk through the murky waters of my conscience until they landed with a heavy thud, dispelling all the cobwebs in my head.

"What?" I sat up so quickly, my head felt like it pirouetted off my shoulders and bounced onto the floor. I rubbed my eyes and climbed out of bed. Ripping the curtains back, I blinked against the painfully bright light and peered down into our backyard. Sure enough, Liam was on the lawn in his white T-shirt and jeans, hammering two-by-fours into a square frame.

"What the . . . ? Do Mom and Dad know about this?" I asked.

"Duh." Maverick shimmied herself between me and the window so she could oversee the construction of her castle. "He came by an hour ago with all the stuff in the back of his truck."

I looked at the fluffy blue clock on my bedside table, the hands pointing to nine and twelve. "I don't understand. Liam came here at eight in the morning on a Saturday to build you a treehouse?"

"That's what I said. Geez, you need a coffee."

"I didn't sleep well," I grumbled. "Wait. I'm confused. Why is he building you a treehouse?"

"Because I asked if he would help, and he said he would."

"You didn't! Oh my God, Maverick." I backed away from the window and sank onto my bed, horrified.

"I like him," Maverick said. "He's nice, and he said he can probably finish it by tomorrow. How awesome is that?"

I barely heard her. I was too busy registering the fact that Liam was here. On a Saturday morning. Building Maverick a treehouse.

Had I somehow woken up in an alternate universe? Was I still dreaming? I pinched my arm, and sure enough, it hurt.

Maverick waved her hand in front of my eyes. "Earth to Rainey! Are you coming down to say hi?"

Geezus. I felt my hair, which was still in yesterday's braid, the strands drooping like sad tulips that hadn't been watered in weeks, then looked down at my unicorn pajama pants and the old shirt I'd thrown on, stained with cereal milk.

"Um . . . maybe in a bit."

"Okay. I'm going down to supervise. I want to make sure he builds a trapdoor."

"Maverick, don't you dare be bossy! He's doing you a huge—" my throat closed around the word, and I had to swallow a sudden lump in my throat, "—a huge favor. Just be polite and grateful, understand?"

Maverick threw me a salute. "Yes, sir! Can I still ask for a trapdoor?"

"Maverick!"

"Fine." Throwing her head back, she marched out of my room.

I returned tentatively to the window and peeked around the curtain, hoping Liam wouldn't turn and catch me spying on him. He was bent over, a nail pinched between his lips, a carpenter's belt slung low on his hips. The back of his neck was red from the sun.

After everything that had happened last night—namely meeting Mercy and my subsequent disappearing act—the last thing I expected was to find Liam in my backyard. I was still unsettled and hurt by the fact that he'd shown up to the game with another girl after telling me he didn't want to come. I mean, what was I supposed to take away from that? He'd wanted to come, just not with me?

And then there were the things Mercy had said. I couldn't stop picturing the two of them cozied up under a blanket of stars. My imagination ran wild with the unspoken possibilities of what had happened in that hunter's stand.

She'd called me and Jo entitled rich bitches. Was that how Liam saw me too? Being a long-standing acquaintance of Denial and her circumspect relative Avoidance, I'd planned on putting off these questions for as long as possible, but I couldn't very well spend the whole weekend locked away in my bedroom.

I showered and picked out a pink cable-knit sweater dress from my closet. It would have looked better if I'd had long, tanned legs with toned calves and a full C-cup chest, not pasty, short legs and a pair of ambitious but uninspiring As. Still, it was better than my usual Saturday ensemble of sweatpants and fuzzy socks.

When I came downstairs, Dad was standing by the double glass doors overlooking the back deck, a steaming cup of tea in his hand. I came up beside him and looked out onto the lawn where Liam was busy working. Maverick sat on the edge of the deck, 'supervising'. I could hear her muffled treble voice chirruping away.

"What's going on?" I asked.

Dad shrugged. "You tell me. He came by this morning and asked if he could build Maverick a treehouse. Had all the supplies and everything. I couldn't really say no, and you know your sister." He shrugged and took a sip of his tea. I caught the pleasant whiff of bergamot. "He's a hard worker. Very motivated."

It was impossible to miss the note of wry humor in my dad's

voice or mistake the implication. My cheeks heated. "He's probably hoping to include it as volunteer work on his college application," I hedged.

"Mm, perhaps," was his mild reply.

I opened the doors and stepped out onto the deck, shutting them carefully behind me. Liam looked up at the sound of the latch. Seeing me, he stopped and hooked his hammer through the loop of his belt.

"Hi."

"What are you doing here?" I asked. I wasn't in the mood for niceties.

"Your sister wanted a treehouse. I figured I could build her one."

"It's going to look amazing!" Maverick said. "These are the support beams, and that over there will be the roof. There's going to be a window with shutters too!"

I smiled at Maverick, but it faded as I moved closer to Liam and lowered my voice. "I can see you're building a treehouse. My question is why."

"I was hoping it might make up for last night," Liam said.

"You mean when you came to the game with Mercy?" While I'd intended only to state it as fact, I couldn't hide the hurt in my voice.

"About that . . ."

"After you said you didn't want to go with me."

Liam winced. "It sounds bad when you put it like that."

"I'm not sure how else to put it."

"I hadn't planned on going. It's just, Mercy can be very persuasive."

Was that supposed to make me feel better?

"And the thing with Chase . . ." Liam sighed. "It was her idea, and I know I went along with it, but I wish I hadn't. I should have stopped her." He looked down at his hands, absently rubbing the dirt and grease smeared across his palms. "I hadn't even planned on seeing her last night. I had a run-in with my stepdad and needed a place to go. Mercy lives next door, and we've been friends for a while. She convinced me to go to the game. But really, I wanted to see you."

"Have you always been just friends?" I asked, aiming for nonchalance. After everything Mercy had said, their relationship sounded like a lot more than friendship to me.

Liam nodded. "If we're even that now. I was furious at her for what she said to you."

I wasn't sure what to say, so I looked down at my toes.

"I'm sorry. You're the last person I ever wanted to hurt. I hope you don't mind my coming here like this. I just . . . I wanted to see you and explain. I was worried I wouldn't get a chance after you disappeared last night."

"I shouldn't have gone without telling you." His apology had eased some of my hurt pride, enough to earn this small admission.

"I don't blame you. You had every right to be upset."

"So to earn my forgiveness, you decided to enslave yourself to my sister?" I asked, looking over at Maverick, who was plucking blades of grass out of the lawn with a suspicious eavesdropping tilt to her head. "Traitors and murderers don't deserve such a punishment."

Liam followed the line of my gaze, and I saw his mouth give a humorous twitch. "It's no trouble."

Play it cool, Collins.

"If she starts to bother you, you have my express permission to tell her to buzz off." I raised my voice so she would hear. Maverick stuck her tongue out at me.

"Every tradesman needs a good foreman," Liam said. "Anyway, I should get back to work if I'm going to finish this by tomorrow night."

"Right. Of course. Let . . . let me know if you need anything," I said awkwardly.

Liam walked back to the frame he was constructing, pulling a measuring tape out of his belt. He checked the width of the frame while Maverick buzzed about him like a fly. A fly with some express opinions on the quality and design of his construction. He didn't seem to mind though. He let her hammer a few nails, making adjustments to her grip, explaining why the angle had to be just so, and listening carefully as she told him how nice it would be to have a pulley with a basket to help her carry things up.

"I think I can manage that," he said, squinting up at the tree to calculate the possibility. "I might have the perfect basket for the job too. How about I bring it tomorrow and you can test it out?"

Responding to the alarm bells in my head that were heralding an imminent swoon, I left Liam and Maverick to their devices. I didn't want Liam knowing just how quickly he'd broken through the gates of my boys-are-so-ugh-never-again defenses. Like seriously, if winning over jilted Juliets was a sport, he'd just executed the pole vault of the century. The judges were holding up tens across the board, and children were laying wreaths upon his podium. Not that I was going to tell him that.

As I returned to the kitchen, I felt my phone buzz. It was Jo.

Sorry again about last night. Didn't mean to freak you out.

No blood, no foul, I texted back. How you feeling this morning?

Like my head is stuck in a compressor. Drinking a coffee, and then this fierce queen is going back to bed. What's with the racket btw? Is that Liam in your backyard?

Yup. He's building Maverick a treehouse to make up for last night's fiasco.

Well played, Hayes.

Well played indeed.

* * *

At noon, I brought out a plate of sandwiches and a pint of iced tea, setting them down on the patio table. Maverick had retired to the bench by the lilac bushes and was dozing in the shade, one bare foot perched on the armrest, the other dangling over the grass.

Balanced on a ladder, Liam hammered a two-by-four across the support beams, sweat beading along his hairline, his sinewy arms covered in a layer of sawdust and dirt. My eyes wandered over to the lawn hose beside the deck, and my errant imagination started playing out a scene from one of my romances in which the hot next-door neighbor gets sprayed down with water while wearing a white T-shirt, only with Liam playing the star role.

"Is that for me?"

"What?" I nearly knocked over the pitcher of iced tea as my hand flew out in surprise. Liam came down from the ladder and nodded towards the pitcher. "Oh . . . er, yes," I stammered. "You must be thirsty." I poured him a glass, sloshing tea over the rim in my haste.

"Thanks." He wiped the sweat from his brow and downed the entire thing in a series of desperate gulps. Before he could catch me ogling his body, I turned my attention to his hands, which were still bruised and scraped. As he placed the empty glass down, I spied evidence of deeper cuts across the palms of his hands.

"What happened?" I asked, alarmed.

He looked at his hands with mild surprise. "Oh, this? It's nothing. I cut them on some barbed wire is all."

"That doesn't look like nothing. Here, let me look." I took hold of his hands and gently inspected the wounds. They had crusted over, the skin an angry red. It looked painful. "It doesn't look like you cleaned them very well. I'll get you some Polysporin. Dad probably has some bandages in the bathroom."

"It's okay, really," Liam said, brushing off my concern.

I was less than convinced. "How can you hold a hammer? Doesn't it hurt?"

"It barely itches."

"Are you sure?"

"Trust me, the only thing giving me grief right now is my stomach. I'm starving." He pulled his hands away and stepped closer to the sandwiches, redirecting the conversation.

I was supposed to be taking it cool, I reminded myself. I cleared my throat. "I hope you like ham and cheese."

"I'd chew a strip of leather at this point." He grabbed one of the sandwiches off the plate and ate it without appearing to stop for breath.

"Easy there," I joked. "You'll choke eating that fast."

Liam smiled, shrugging. "Sorry."

Keeping him company during his lunch break was keeping it cool, right? I wracked my brain for a safe, totally cool topic of conversation and decided to stick with the matter at hand.

"You're good with your hands."

"What?"

Realizing the ambiguity of this statement, I fumbled to clarify, "Building things, I mean." My cheeks burned. *God, Rainey.* "Do you build a lot of stuff?"

"I worked construction over the summer," he said. "And my dad used to be a framer. He taught me a few things when I was young."

I hesitated, wondering if I dared ask. "When was the last time you saw your dad?"

"Seven years ago." Liam's gaze dropped. "Before he went to prison."

"Do you miss him?"

Liam lifted a shoulder. "Sometimes."

"I can't imagine not being able to see my father."

"Yeah, well, it's probably a good thing my dad is locked away."

"What was he like?" I asked before I could stop myself. I was asking too many questions, and it was clear from the look on his face that Liam wasn't eager to answer this one.

"I don't have many memories of him, to be honest. He had a temper. He always wore these dungarees and had a Carolingian cross tattoo on his arm. I remember one day, he took me to see the Calgary Flames playing the Boston Bruins at the Saddledome. We ate hot dogs and drank hot chocolate and cheered when Iginla came onto the ice."

"That sounds nice."

Liam grimaced, his gaze fixed on the empty glass in his hand. "After that game, he drove us to a seedy part of the city and left me in the truck while he went off on some business." Liam's voice turned cynical. "When he came back, he had a black eye and a bag of drugs hidden in his jacket pocket."

"Oh." It was my turn to look down.

"Just our luck, a cop pulled us over for a broken taillight. My dad told me to hide the drugs in my backpack, so I did."

"Were you caught?"

Liam shook his head. "But I remember wondering what would happen if we were. I was afraid my dad would try to cover his tracks and tell the cop the drugs were mine since juvies have an easier time in the courts than adults with criminal records. No cop would believe him, but I was young and scared. Nowadays, I feel like I'm just fighting fate."

"What do you mean?"

He shrugged. "Like it doesn't matter how hard I work or how good my grades are, I'm never going to escape my life. People look at me and see my dad. It's like a self-fulfilling prophecy, and it doesn't matter how hard I try, it won't make any difference."

"How can you say that? Of course it makes a difference," I said. "Trying is what matters most."

Liam didn't look convinced. "That's what people say when they haven't had to fight tooth and nail just to get by."

Entitled rich bitches. The implication lurked behind his words, and maybe he was right. Maybe I was naive, but that didn't mean I was wrong.

"It's like Horatio in *The Depraved Duke*," I explained. "He was kidnapped as a kid and sold as a slave. He escaped by killing the man who owned him, and spent years surviving as a thief and sleeping with rich women who paid him in exchange for . . . well, you get the idea." I felt my face redden. "Anyway, he thought he was beyond redemption when he saw Rosalind in the street. She was the youngest daughter of a wealthy noble, and he wanted to be worthy of her, even though he felt he never could. But she fell in love with him rather than his rival, Count Montrieve, who was rich and handsome and had everything handed to him on a silver platter, because she saw how hard Horatio worked despite his misfortune."

Having talked all the air out of my lungs, I took a deep breath and blew it out. Later in the story, Horatio had found out he was actually a duke, richer and more powerful than the count, but I doubted Liam was a secret duke, so I omitted that detail.

Liam's mouth was clamped shut, and I could tell he was trying very hard not to smile.

I blushed. "You think I'm being naive and stupid, don't you?"

"No," Liam said, his smile creeping up despite his efforts. "I was just thinking maybe I've been reading the wrong books."

I grinned. "You don't know what you're missing."

Liam cracked, laughing. "Revelations of the highest order, apparently."

"Don't forget the sex," I said before I could stop myself.

Liam's ears turned pink, our eyes locking. "Right, well, I should get back to work," he said, throat working. "There's still a lot to do."

The moment he turned his back, I slapped my hand over my mouth to contain a shriek of mortification and sank into the nearest chair before my knees could give out.

* * *

Liam worked all day and well into the evening. The next morning, he came back shortly after eight, this time with a large wicker basket decorated with orange and pink ribbons.

"Oh my God, it's perfect!" Maverick's eyes looked ready to pop out of her skull. "Where did you find it?"

"One of the ladies at work had a baby shower. The basket came with one of the gifts, but she didn't want it." Liam smiled, his eyes meeting mine over Maverick's head.

"How could she not?" she asked, taking off with it to the backyard.

"Thank you," I said. "Really. I don't think I've ever seen her this happy."

Liam shrugged. "I'm glad I could help."

Watching him head out, I pressed my hand against my chest, trying to keep my heart from being reefed out along with him.

"He's cute." I jumped as Mom came up behind me. "You should ask him to stay for supper."

"I should?"

Mom looked at me with an expression identical to the one Dad had worn the previous morning. "Uh-huh."

LIAM

I stood back to appraise my work. It wasn't bad, all things considered. The door was a little crooked and the rope stuck in the pulley if you tugged on it too quickly, but the foundation was sound, which was the most important thing.

I headed up to the house and knocked on the glass doors. Rainey was sitting at the oak dinner table, her school books splayed out in front of her, one cheek cupped in her hand, a pencil caught between her teeth. She dropped it at the sound of my knock and hurried to open the door.

"It's done," I said.

"You're kidding?" Rainey grinned. "Maverick! Come see!" she called over her shoulder. I heard an excited whoop from inside the house, and Maverick came skidding around the kitchen island, her pale face flushed with excitement. Without stopping to put on her shoes, she darted onto the lawn and scrambled up the ladder onto the platform above. She looked around, surrounded by the brilliant yellow foliage, bright as a sunbeam.

"You think she likes it?" I asked.

"Are you kidding? You've struck her speechless. Do you know how hard that is?" Rainey said, nudging me playfully with her elbow. "By the way, you've been invited to stay for supper."

I looked down at my torn, grass-stained jeans and my filthy shirt covered in sawdust, then past Rainey, through the french double doors, to the polished tile floor, the massive hardwood staircase, and the floor-to-ceiling stone fireplace next to a pristinely arranged leather sofa.

Jesus Christ.

"Thanks, really, but I don't want to impose."

"It's not an imposition. My parents are insisting that you stay."

"I don't have anything nice to wear."

"What you're wearing is fine. This isn't the Ritz."

I begged to differ.

"Mom is making a roast, and Maverick spent the morning baking a blueberry crumble for you. If you don't stay, you'll hurt her feelings."

"That all sounds delicious, but—"

Rainey took my hand and pulled me into the house.

"Wait, let me just—" I scrambled to kick off my shoes.

"Welcome." She spun around, waving her arm over the general splendor like it was a fort made of sheets and cushions. "I'd give you a tour, but there's not much to see."

Not much to see was the bathroom in the trailer with the cracked toilet and chipped mirror, but I didn't want to draw attention to the stark differences of our respective environments right this minute.

"Hello, Liam." I turned to see a stunning woman standing next to the counter. The first thing I noticed was her hair, which was the same apricot colour as Maverick's. At a glance, she looked young—maybe twenty—but as she came forward to greet me, I noticed faint laugh lines gathering in the corners of her eyes.

"Liam, this is my mom, Coralie."

"Please, call me Cora," she said with a smile. "I can't thank you enough for what you did for Maverick. My little girl is over the moon. Matthew is still at the hospital, but he should be home soon. Dinner will be ready in ten minutes. I hope you're hungry.

Do you like prime rib?"

"That sounds delicious," I said, even though I'd never had prime rib before. Was it similar to corned beef? It felt stupid to ask.

"Can I eat in my treehouse?" Maverick shouted from outside.

"Incorrigible, that one," Cora said with a roll of her eyes. "Rainey, why don't you show Liam your darkroom?"

"Oh." Rainey looked a little taken aback by the suggestion. "I don't know. It's kind of boring."

"I'd like to see it," I said.

"Rainey is quite the photographer," Cora said to me. "You should see her pictures."

Rainey bit her lip, clearly uncomfortable.

"Go on," Cora encouraged.

"Okay." Rainey took me down the sweeping carpeted stairs to the basement. I tried not to stare at everything, but it was hard not to. A massive pool table took up the middle of the main room next to a bar with marble countertops and mahogany cabinets. There was a giant plasma television on the far wall opposite a leather sectional and a treadmill. Everything from the thick plush carpet to the velvet throw pillows looked incredibly expensive.

Rainey led me into a room off to the right. It was pitch dark inside; the moment she closed the door, I couldn't see my hand in front of my face.

"Hold on," she said. I heard the click of a light switch, and an eerie red light flooded the small space.

"What—" I spun around. There was a tall table along the far wall stacked with several shallow, rectangular trays, and strings ran from one side of the room to the other with an array of black-and-white photographs hanging from wooden pegs.

Letting go of Rainey's hand, I walked up to take a closer look. The picture nearest to me was of Cora. She was bending over Maverick's bed, kissing her daughter's head. Looking at the display of maternal tenderness, I felt the jagged pain of some gaping absence inside me, an absence long since forgotten. It was so painful, I had to look away.

The next picture was of Maverick blowing bubbles on the grass, her cheeks puffed out like she'd swallowed a balloon. Maverick playing in a creek, splashing water at the person holding the camera. Maverick hanging from the branches of the tree in their backyard, barefoot with her pants rolled up to her knees, legs dotted with angry-looking mosquito bites.

There was one of Rainey's parents, dancing in the kitchen, her father dipping her mother back as she laughed. I tried and failed to remember a time when my mother had smiled like that. All her smiles were like faded watercolours, barely there, and washed out at the first hint of tears.

Rainey rocked from foot to foot as I studied her collection, her eyes following my progress with wary apprehension. "They're nothing special," she said shyly. "Not compared to professionals like Lee Jefferies or Annie Leibovitz. Their work is amazing . . . the way they capture emotion. I try, but I'm nowhere near as good."

"I don't know who those people are, but I think these are amazing." I tore my eyes away from her dancing parents to look at her. Her face was glowing with bashful pride. She couldn't see it because she was surrounded by it, but her pictures *did* capture an emotion, and I, the deprived refugee to it, stood like a beggar in the street, looking through a window to a smorgasbord of warmth and love and happiness.

"What made you want to be a photographer?" I asked, swallowing a sudden lump in my throat.

Rainey shrugged. "I guess I like the idea of capturing time. It never stops. It's always slipping through our fingers. Photography is my way of trying to slow it down, you know?"

I didn't know. For me, time couldn't pass quickly enough, but then, I didn't have a sister living on borrowed time.

"You probably want to wash up," Rainey said suddenly. "I'll show you to the bathroom."

The bathroom was huge, with stacks of fluffy white towels and soap that smelled spicy and exotic. The faucet sparkled—there wasn't a speck of dust anywhere. I turned the water on with my elbow, afraid to leave grimy fingerprints everywhere, and washed my hands and face. After I was done, I cleaned up carefully behind me, wiping down the surface of the sink with a tissue that I tucked into the pocket of my jeans rather than leave in the empty wastebasket; I wasn't even sure if it was a wastebasket.

When I came back to the kitchen, Rainey was busy bringing plates and cutlery out to the table. The smell coming from the oven was glorious. I could hear the sizzling of the meat and the gravy bubbling in a pot over the stove. My mouth was suddenly swimming.

Matthew was standing by his wife, his hand gently touching her lower back. As I watched, he leaned over to kiss her head and murmured something softly into her ear. She smiled back.

I started to wonder if maybe, within the species of homo sapiens, there were subspecies. Particularly those who possessed the gene to express love and affection, and those who didn't. It would explain why I felt like such an imposter, like an alien species studying the unfamiliar behaviors of normal humans in their natural habitat.

Matthew spotted me and smiled. "Cora told me Rainey roped you into staying for supper. I'm glad you can stay. I also saw the treehouse. That's some pretty impressive craftsmanship. I hope you'll let us compensate you for the materials."

"It was no trouble. The wood was recycled, so it didn't cost anything."

"Let's eat, shall we?" Cora asked, squeezing her husband's hand.

We gathered around a dining table set with taper candles, wine glasses, and heavy white cloth napkins. Why you would use something one step removed from a Persian rug to wipe your mouth was beyond me. I followed Rainey's lead and dropped it over my lap, feeling like a complete fraud. I should have told Rainey my mom was expecting me home, or that I had an essay to write, or had a shift at the hardware store. (Why were the excuses coming to me now?)

"Rainey tells us you're top of her class," Matthew said, dishing himself some buttered green beans. "What are your plans for after graduation?"

"Oh come, Matthew, it's a little early for an interrogation, isn't it?" Cora chided. "Here, have some potatoes, Liam." She passed me a dish piled with roasted potatoes crusted in garlic. I could have eaten the entire dish but took only two before handing it to Rainey. She smiled warmly at me, her eyes glowing.

That, I thought. That was why I'd resigned myself to sitting here feeling ten thousand degrees of uncomfortable.

"It's not an interrogation. I'm just making conversation,"

Matthew argued.

"I don't know," I said, answering his question. "I haven't given it much thought." This was a lie. I'd given it a lot of thought. However, every covetable course that had presented itself in my mind was barred by one insurmountable obstacle: I didn't have the money.

Matthew poured himself a glass of red wine from the decanter, frowning slightly. "What are you interested in?"

"A lot of things, I guess."

"Like?"

"Science, literature, philosophy." The collar of my shirt was starting to feel tight and itchy.

"He's reading Aristotle," Rainey said as if this were some amazing feat. "I can't remember the title though," she added apologetically. "And *Moby Dick*, and something by Stephen Hawking."

"That's an impressive reading list," Matthew acknowledged. "Which schools are you looking at?"

The school of hard knocks. "Nothing yet. I was thinking of working for a while first. Earning some money." I wished he'd stop asking questions long enough for me to start eating. I decided to go on the offense. "How did you end up choosing medicine?"

Matthew chewed thoughtfully on a piece of prime rib before answering; I took the opportunity to shovel a piece of potato into my mouth. "My father was a psychiatrist. He had all these textbooks in his office about brain circuits and chemicals. I used to read them when I was young and developed a curiosity for the structure of the brain and the nervous system. Of course, now I wish I'd gone into cardiology, but we can't always know the future, can we?" A shadow passed over his face as he spoke, and his gaze shifted to Maverick.

"I think you should become a professional treehouse builder," Maverick said.

"That sounds like an excellent idea." Rainey grinned at me.

"I'll take it under advisement." I smiled, but Cora and Matthew remained stoic.

We polished off the rest of the food, the conversation remaining light for the remainder of the meal. Cora noticed that Maverick didn't eat much and asked if she was feeling okay.

"Just not very hungry," she said.

We finished with bowls of warm blueberry crumble served with vanilla ice cream. I'd never eaten so well in my entire life; my stomach felt like it was fit to burst.

Afterward, they pulled out a deck of cards and we played go fish. I started to relax, lulled by the atmosphere of laughter and familial teasing. I felt like I'd drunk a potion and was caught in a bizarre but beautiful dream. Was this what life was supposed to be like? Was this what contentment felt like? This warm, comforting sense of satiety? It was so foreign to me, I didn't immediately recognize it for what it was, accompanied as it was by the familiar sting of envy.

I knew I shouldn't be envious. The Collins family had their own cross to bear, and it was by no means light. Maverick had to go to bed early, worn out from the excitement of the day. Her father carried her up the stairs, her eyes bruised with an unhealthy fatigue, and Rainey went quiet. She followed me out onto the front steps as I readied to leave, closing the door behind her.

It was dark out. Only a few stars were visible through gaps in the clouds, and the temperature had dropped. Rainey hugged her body, rubbing her arms to keep warm.

"Thank you," she said. "It was very sweet of you, what you did for Maverick. She's been wanting a treehouse for years."

"I had fun," I said truthfully.

"I know you did it to make up for the football game, but I feel like I owe you. I really want to pay you back somehow."

I was about to tell her it wasn't necessary but changed my mind. "How about a date?"

The offer caught her by surprise. "A date?"

"If you want to."

"I'd like that," she said quickly.

"Would Friday work?"

"Okay." Her shy smile did something funny to my heart, like the corners of her mouth were attached to a fishing hook lodged in my chest, making it twitch.

"Okay then."

"Okay." It happened so fast, I had no time to react. Coming up onto her tiptoes, she leaned forward and kissed me. It was quick, just a brief pressing of her lips against mine, leaving the impression of warmth and the faintest taste of blueberries.

I caught one glimpse of her giant, terrified eyes before she spun around and ducked back into the house. My lips tingling, I stood frozen in the middle of the driveway. After a moment, the world started to go fuzzy around the edges, and I realized I'd stopped breathing. Sucking in the fresh, cold night air, I walked slowly back to my truck. I might have convinced myself I'd imagined it, but all the way home, I could still feel the tingling remnants of her kiss on my lips.

You're playing with fire, Hayes, I thought, but at the moment, I didn't really care if I got burned.

12

RAINEY

I COULDN'T BELIEVE IT. I'd kissed Liam Hayes. I'd actually kissed him. What had come over me? Was Maverick finally rubbing off on me?

Lying in bed, I wiggled and kicked my feet, flopping about like a fish on dry land, then buried my head into my pillow and squealed.

"Is everything okay in there?" Dad's muffled voice came from behind my closed door.

"Yes!" I called, trying to compose myself, but I was completely wigging out. I rolled onto my back, clinging to my pillow, and waited to hear the soft footsteps of my father's retreat before letting out a soul-quivering moan.

I seriously needed to get a grip. As far as kisses went, it suited the chill stark walls of a nunnery, not the torrid bedchamber of a French courtesan. Still, I couldn't help but grin and touch my mouth, remembering the feeling of his lips, surprisingly soft, against my own.

Tomorrow was going to require a lot of coffee because there was no way I was falling asleep tonight.

* * *

I pretended to be busy with the zipper of my backpack when Liam came to math the next morning. Apparently, twelve hours is the exact amount of time it takes for elation to fizzle into embarrassed self-consciousness. My brain kept replaying the kiss, only now it played out less like a dream and more like a shipwreck. My first kiss with Liam should have been an Oscar-winning lip-lock, preferably in the rain after some heated argument spurred by insatiable passion. Instead, I'd attacked him like a dive bomber.

What was I going to say to him?

Before I could devise a recovery strategy, Liam slid into his chair, leaned across the gap between our desks, and slipped his hand through mine. I must have made a sound of surprise because several people near us turned to look at me. Blushing, I looked down at my desk.

"Hi," he whispered.

I smiled nervously. "Hi."

"Did you ask your parents about Friday?"

Damn. "Not yet. It should be fine though." Dad had said he didn't want me dating Liam, but that was before the treehouse, and

I couldn't see Dad objecting now after Liam had gone to such lengths to apologize.

To my delight, Liam never once let go of my hand during class. I caught Mr. MacAlastair regarding us with a singularly disapproving look on his face at one point, but he didn't say anything. Maybe because Liam was at the top of the class. In all of our assignments, I hadn't seen him get a single wrong answer. It pays to be brilliant, I thought a little sourly.

After the bell rang, Liam walked me to chemistry. We didn't say anything. I was too preoccupied with our hands; they felt fused now, and it made me wonder what would happen when we finally broke apart. Would my hand die like a plant ripped from the soil? I paused outside the door to the lab, reluctant to let go.

Before I could carefully disengage, Carson came around the corner and walked right between us, ripping our hands apart.

"What the—"

"Just trying to get to class," he muttered. I stared after him as he stalked to our table and slumped into his chair.

"I could always skip economics and sit in on your class," Liam suggested, his eyes fixed on Carson.

"It's fine. He's probably just in a bad mood because they lost the game on Friday. I'll come find you at lunch."

Leaving Liam, I took my seat beside Carson. He didn't look up as I sat down or say hello. "Have a good weekend?" I asked.

"So you and Hayes are dating," he said, disregarding my question.

"I guess we are." I didn't like his tone.

"I told you he's bad news."

"He is not. And why do you care anyway? What's he done to

you?"

"Nothing, I just . . . I don't like him is all."

"Well then, it's a good thing you're not the one dating him. You're with Becca, remember?"

"Becca and I broke up."

"Oh. I'm sorry." I wasn't really, but it felt like the only thing I could say under the circumstances. As far as I could tell, Carson was better off without her.

I was glad when Ms. Bierman started class and gladder still when it ended so I could get away from Carson's incessant scowl.

* * *

When I got home that afternoon, I asked Mom if Liam could take me out for supper Friday night.

"Like on a date?" Maverick asked, abandoning her English reading list.

"That is the term people generally use," I said, still looking at Mom as I waited for an answer. She was reviewing Maverick's appointment schedule on her tablet.

"I don't see why not," she said. "As long as you're home before eleven and you let us know where you're going."

"Of course," I said quickly.

Maverick whooped. "This is awesome! Can I pick out your outfit? Please? I don't want you dying an old maid, and if you wear another one of your turtlenecks, Liam might leave you for a bathing suit model with glorious long legs."

"Gee, thanks for the vote of confidence."

"Please, please, please," she begged, clasping her hands.

"You can pick something out, but I have veto power," I warned.

"Yes! You won't regret it!"

Later that night, after Maverick had gone to bed and I was finishing up the last of my homework, I heard the purr of Dad's car coming up the driveway. I listened as he came into the house and dropped his keys on the counter by the door. I got up to wish him goodnight, but when I opened my bedroom door, I heard the soft murmur of Mom's voice. Something about the tone of it made me pause and step quietly out onto the landing above the stairs.

"Should we talk to her about sex?" Mom asked.

"God, Cora, I'm not ready for this."

"You think I am?"

"We're always looking after Maverick; I didn't even realize Rainey grew up."

"I'm sure it will be fine, love. It's only dinner."

"You can remember being seventeen, right? Being a slave to your hormones? And I'm not sure about this guy Liam."

"Oh please, a few days ago you were saying what an upstanding young man he was."

"He is, as far as I can tell."

"Then what's the problem?" Mom pressed.

Dad was quiet for a moment. "What do we know about his family? Are they good people?"

"I don't know. I never thought to ask, but Liam seems like a nice kid."

"I know, it's just . . . it's obvious they don't have much money, and the other day I noticed a cut on his lip, and I don't think it was from falling off a skateboard or fumbling a football."

"You think he's dangerous?"

"No, not exactly . . . I don't know, Cora. I'm just worried."

"You wouldn't be a father if you weren't. It's just one date, Matthew. Let's not get ahead of ourselves."

Before I could hear more, I retreated quickly back to my bedroom, my ears ringing and my mouth suddenly drier than the Atacama Desert. I felt unaccountably angry at my parents for judging Liam based on something as superficial as his family's income. I didn't think they were the kind of people to hold prejudices like that. Why couldn't Liam stand on his own merit? And did they actually think I was going to have sex on our first date? God, is that what *Liam* thought? What was I going to do if he did? Was I ready for that? My body suddenly broke out into a cold sweat. I couldn't have sex! I didn't know how. I mean, I knew *how*, but I'd never actually worked through the precise logistics. Where did my legs go, exactly? In movies, they always focused on the actors' faces, and while I respected people's privacy, I was now prepared to argue it was irritatingly uninformative.

Just when I thought I'd gotten a handle on things, I was back to knowing absolutely nothing.

LIAM

After my shift at the hardware store Monday night, I stopped by Sean's office and asked if I could pick up a couple more shifts before Friday. "And is it possible to get paid up front?" I didn't have high hopes he'd say yes but asked anyway.

Sean's narrow mouth pinched. "Sorry, we have a no-advance

policy. You know that."

"I know," I said. "But I'm in a bit of a tight spot. You'd be doing me a huge favor. I can even throw in a couple hours of overtime."

Sean's frown did not let up, his arms folded across his chest. The worn line in his belt exposed the fact that he'd gained some weight recently. I waited while he made a show of considering the offer. I knew he wanted to take advantage of the extra hours' work, but didn't want to step outside the bounds of protocol. I was a good worker, one of their best, and one of our clerks, Mindy, had just gone on maternity leave, leaving us shorthanded.

"Fine," he said at last. "But I can only pay you half up front. You'll get the other half next week."

"Thank you, Sean. I appreciate it." I tried not to punch the air and whoop as I left his office.

* * *

It was both the longest and slowest week of my life. I worked an extra shift on Tuesday and Thursday and tutored Casey Wednesday night over a turkey bacon club sandwich with extra fries. When I woke up on Friday, my feet were sore with blisters, my eyes itched from lack of sleep, and I was completely bushed, but lying in bed, looking up at the cracked plaster over my bed, I couldn't keep the grin off my face.

Today I was taking Rainey Collins on a date.

Bent on making it as perfect as possible, I'd planned everything meticulously. The washing machine in the hallway closet was broken—it had been for months—and ever since my blowout with

Mercy, I'd stopped going over to borrow hers, so on Wednesday, before meeting Casey, I took my jeans and the nicest shirt I could find and dropped by the laundromat near the diner. After the tutoring session, I picked them up, fresh and clean, careful to hang my shirt from the hook on the back of my door when I got home so it wouldn't get wrinkled.

Including the money Sean had lent me, I had a hundred and twenty dollars. This, I had calculated, would pay for the nicest items on the menu at Vero Bistro, including a generous tip, and a bouquet of roses from the florist, which I planned to pick up after school. After dinner we would take a walk along the Bow River pathway, cross the Peace Bridge and stroll through Prince's Island Park, maybe stopping for ice cream before heading home. If the weather was too cold, I could take her to the Plaza Theatre and we could catch an old film, but according to the weather report, it was going to be a mild fifteen degrees centigrade. If she remembered a jacket, she would be fine.

I was contemplating bringing one of my spare hoodies, just in case, when Mom knocked on my door. "Liam?"

Something in the tone of her voice made all the happy globes of light floating through my mind flare and pop like exploding light bulbs. I sat up and opened the door.

"What is it?"

She brushed a tangled strand of hair back with an irritated swat of her hand. "It's nothing. It's just . . . don't overreact, okay? There's no need to—"

"Mom! Just tell me."

She sighed. "It's about that dog."

"That dog? You mean Flea?"

"He's hurt. Pretty bad, I think."

"What happened?"

"Ray caught him sniffing around the porch this morning. Kicked him pretty hard."

"He *what?*"

Mom flinched. "Liam, please."

The circuits in my mind sparked with bolts of electric anger, stiffening every muscle in my body. "Where is he?"

I wasn't referring to Flea.

"Don't." Mom blocked the door with her arms. "This isn't worth the fight. Besides, Ray left a few minutes ago. He's driving up to Lloydminster."

She had waited until he was gone to tell me. I wondered just how far he'd driven, and if I could catch up to him.

"And Flea?" I asked through a clenched jaw.

Mom looked down. "He's out front. Wouldn't leave, the dumb thing."

I pushed her out of the way and ran outside. Flea was lying on the gravel, his breathing fast and shallow. When he saw me, he moved to get up, then lay back down with a whimper, his tail wagging feebly.

"Hey, boy, it's okay. It's okay, I got you." I knelt down beside him and rubbed his ears, murmuring comforting words, my anger quietly charging. I ran my hands over his belly, checking for any obvious injuries. He let out a soft whine as my hand brushed against his left side.

"Okay, good boy. Let's get you to the vet. Come on. I got you." I lifted him up and carried him to my truck. I laid him down on the front seat as gently as possible, then ran inside and grabbed my jacket and keys. Driving with my left hand, I kept my right on Flea's back for comfort, kicking myself the entire way. This was my fault. He would never have come looking for me if I hadn't been so intent on avoiding Mercy. "I'm sorry, buddy."

My eyes stinging, I rubbed them on the sleeve of my jacket, then rolled down the window, figuring Flea would like the smell of the fresh air. We hit the edge of the city, and I pulled into the parking lot outside the vet.

Leaving Flea in the truck, I ran in and explained the situation to the receptionist at the front desk, saying that some asshole had kicked my dog and he was hurt. The lady was very kind and said she could squeeze us in to see Dr. Huber before his first scheduled appointment. Thanking her profusely, I brought Flea in, and we waited until the vet entered the examination room.

"Let's take a look, shall we?" Dr. Huber was a tall, skinny man with thinning grey hair and a soft German accent. After I lifted Flea onto his table, he made a quick inspection, his large, long-fingered hands probing and prodding with methodical scrutiny.

Flea didn't like most people, but he tolerated Dr. Huber and tolerated him even more after the vet slipped him a couple of liver treats from the pocket of his white overcoat.

"There's no swelling in his abdomen, which is an excellent sign, and his breathing sounds clear, which suggests his lungs are good, but I think one of the lower ribs has a fracture. I won't know until we X-ray."

"How much will that cost?" I asked.

Dr. Huber regarded me with kind brown eyes under a pair of truly spectacular eyebrows. "It depends on if we need to sedate him. If he can stay still, which I think he might, it will cost around eighty dollars." He didn't ask, but I could tell he was waiting for me to give some indication of consent.

"Do whatever you have to," I said, swallowing hard.

Sure enough, Flea had a fractured rib. "It's his left T12," Dr. Huber said, pointing to the X-ray with the tip of his pen. "Luckily, it's not displaced, and there doesn't appear to be any shards that could result in a punctured lung."

"That's good, right?"

Dr. Huber smiled. "Yes."

"So what do we do now?"

"You need to make sure he gets plenty of rest. A fracture like this, even though it's minor, can take up to eight weeks to heal completely. Limit his exercise. If you notice any changes in his appetite or behavior, bring him back immediately. I will prescribe some oral medication to help manage the pain."

I nodded, my fingers curling into Flea's hair.

Dr. Huber patted my shoulder. "He's going to be fine, son. You did well, bringing him in. Some cases like these can be much worse."

After loading Flea back into my truck, I went to the receptionist. The bill came to one hundred and twelve dollars, including the pain medication. My stomach dropping, I paid and drove Flea back to Mercy's.

I knocked on the door when I got there, wondering if anyone was home. Mercy might be at the garage, working. I wasn't sure if I wanted her to be home or not, but before I could figure that out, the door opened.

"Liam." Mercy looked surprised to see me. She was wearing sweatpants and a hoodie, her hair piled up into a messy bun on top of her head. "What are you doing here?" she asked, her tone edged. "Shouldn't you be at school?"

"Flea came by my place this morning looking for me. Ray found him and kicked him pretty hard."

The wariness behind Mercy's eyes vanished, overcome by genuine concern. "Is he okay?"

"He will be." I explained what Dr. Huber had told me, handing her the paper bag with the pain medication. "Can I bring him in?" Mr. and Mrs. Ramos had a rule about dogs in the house. I hoped they would make an exception.

"Of course. Do you need help?" She threw her shoes on and followed me out to my truck. I carried Flea inside while she held the door open, and brought him into the kitchen where she laid down a pile of blankets.

"Good boy," I whispered, scratching his neck. The pain medication the vet had administered was kicking in; he wasn't breathing as hard, and his eyes were starting to droop. "You rest up, okay? Mercy will take good care of you. You might even get some grilled chicken for supper." I looked over at her as I said this and smiled a little.

The corner of Mercy's mouth twitched in response. "I'm sure Joshua will feed him plenty. And thanks for taking him to the vet."

"Of course. Keep an eye on him, okay? Make sure he doesn't stress his ribs too much."

"I will."

She petted Flea's head, her eyes concealed behind her long lashes. I got to my feet and headed back to the front door. Mercy followed. I wondered for a moment if she was going to bring up the fight we'd had; she kept opening her mouth as if to say something, but every time she changed her mind and clamped it shut again. I wondered if I should say something, too, but I wasn't sure what to say or how to say it. *I'm sorry. I can't help the way I feel. Can we still be friends?* Even I winced at this last phrase, knowing it would only hurt her more.

Eventually, I left without saying anything, and neither did Mercy.

* * *

"You missed math. Is everything okay?" Rainey asked when I found her at lunch. We were sitting at our bench even though it was cold and there was a fine drizzle falling. I hoped the weather would clear before tonight, but a bit of rain was the least of my concerns.

"Not really," I said. "I had to take my dog to the vet."

"You have a dog? Is he okay?"

"He's technically Mercy's. We sort of share custody." As soon as the words were out, I knew Rainey would take them amiss. Sure enough, her hands curled into a knot in her lap, and her chin dipped towards her chest.

"You two have a dog together?"

"It's complicated. I found him abandoned in a ditch about a year ago, but I couldn't keep him, so Mercy took him instead. She looks after him, but we, I don't know, bonded, I guess. Maybe because I was the one who found him."

"Is he okay? What happened?"

"He'll be fine." I didn't elaborate, not wanting to bring up Ray.

"We're still on for tonight, right?" Rainey asked.

Despite the explanation I had ready on the tip of my tongue as to why we had to cancel, my head nodded again. "I'll pick you up at six." It was as if someone else was talking. A plucky optimist who was determined not to let the girl sitting beside him down.

The bell rang. I opened my mouth in a final attempt to reschedule, but Rainey's wide smile plugged my throat.

"See you at six then."

I watched her head to class, wondering what the hell I was going to do with only six dollars.

* * *

Skipping biology, I went to the AV room where the film club held their meetings and asked the kid there if I could borrow one of the film projectors for the night.

"AV equipment can't leave the school premises," he said, regarding me through purple-tinted glasses. I wondered how long it had taken him to gel his black hair into that douchey angle.

"I'm not taking it off school premises," I lied. Thanks to ample practice with Ray and my mom, I was good at it. "I'm working on a final project for Mrs. Mason. I'm staying here after school." I said it smoothly and with confidence, holding his gaze.

"Oh . . . okay. You'll have to sign it out." He handed me a form and a pen. I scribbled my name down and handed it back.

"By the way, which films do you have that will play on this thing?" I asked.

"We have . . ." He opened a cupboard beside the projector carts and pulled out a box of reels. "*Casablanca* or *Psycho.*"

"That's it?"

The boy shrugged.

I didn't have much experience when it came to dating, but watching a horror film seemed like a bad idea. "I'll take *Casablanca*."

13

RAINEY

I KNOCKED ON MAVERICK'S DOOR.

"Hey," I said, coming in after I heard her call. "You want to help me get ready?"

My sister was lying on her bed, one arm suffocating Carrots and the other draped over her face. She looked like a miniature Ophelia, lamenting Hamlet's fatuous preoccupation.

"You okay?" I asked.

"I'm fine." Maverick threw off her arm and sat up, assessed me with blatant judgment. "And it's not that I want to help. It's that you *need* help."

"Gee, thanks." As if I wasn't nervous enough as it was.

"Where is he taking you?"

"I don't know." I hadn't thought to ask, being far too

overwhelmed with the fact that I was going on a date at all.

"He hasn't given you any clues?" Maverick tutted like a disapproving Korean *ajumma*. "How are you supposed to know what to wear?"

Muttering her frustrations, she climbed off the bed and went to my room, where she proceeded to pull out every piece of clothing I owned, tossing the rejects willy-nilly on the floor. At long last, she laid my outfit over my duvet: a yellow polka-dot skirt and a dark blue sweater with silver moons sewn across the front. The kaleidoscopic colours were bound to induce a seizure in any susceptible bystander, but after I put it on, I had to admit that the motley arrangement actually worked. Maybe it was because it reminded me of Maverick, and being a little bit more like my sister was probably a good thing right now.

I thought about the conversation I'd overheard between my parents about sex. Okay, I wasn't *that* brave.

"Will you let me braid your hair?" Maverick asked.

"Sure." I sat down on the floor and let her brush out my hair. She was quiet as she twisted the strands; even when she wasn't talking, Maverick usually hummed to herself. The silence felt strange. I tilted my head back to look at her. "You're quiet."

"I'm fine."

"What are you thinking about?"

Her small hands stopped moving.

"Bean?"

I felt the whisper of her breath against the back of my neck. "I was thinking . . . I was thinking about all the things I'm afraid I'll miss."

"What do you mean?" I turned, my hair falling loose.

Maverick's freckled face was tilted down. I tried to see it, but she turned away. "I wonder if I'll ever have a first date."

My mouth went dry. "Of course you will, silly." Miraculously, my voice didn't waver. In no conceivable universe could Maverick *not* have a first date. I could picture her dressed in her brilliant lime-green shorts over her favorite purple stockings, walking up to some poor kid who had no clue how he'd managed to win over such an exotic, rare creature. They would go rock climbing, or bungee jumping, or climb the Calgary Tower and look out over the city at night because that was Maverick. "And I'll be there to help you get ready," I said, tickling her feet in an attempt to make her laugh. "I'll dress you up in a grey turtleneck and black slacks."

Maverick snorted. "No one says slacks."

"Nan does."

"She's sixty-seven."

"What can I say? I'm an old soul."

"You're a fossil."

"Don't tell Nan you said that."

* * *

I waited by the door, tucking a strand of hair behind my ear and fidgeting with the loose button on my jacket.

"Stop that; you'll tear it off," Mom chided. She had picked up crochet over the summer and was currently working on a hat for Maverick. At least, that's what she said it was. I thought it looked closer to something removed during an autopsy.

It was a quarter after six. Liam hadn't shown up yet. I couldn't help but wonder if he'd changed his mind or been beset by bandits and dragged off into a ditch somewhere.

"I think you've been stood up," Maverick said, echoing my thoughts.

"He's just running late," Mom reassured me.

"Or maybe you were too eager," Maverick continued. "I read that guys like to chase girls who aren't interested in them. You should have set him a list of tasks to complete before agreeing to a date, like bringing you the tooth of a lion. Heroes always have to battle dangerous animals."

I was too nervous to respond but feared she might be right about the eager part.

Two minutes later, the doorbell rang. I felt a jolt of electricity shoot through me and fumbled to open the door. Liam's eyes widened a fraction at the sight of my yellow skirt, and the corner of his mouth twitched.

"Hi."

I grinned. "Hi."

Marco.

Polo.

"Sorry I'm late. It took a little longer than I expected to set things up."

"Set things up? Aren't we going out for dinner?" I had a sudden flashback to seventh grade when I'd prepared a presentation on beluga whales, but the teacher told me the smart screen wasn't working, so I couldn't read off the slides I'd prepared. I'd stammered through what little I'd memorized and then hid in the bathroom for the rest of the class.

"About dinner . . ." Liam rubbed the back of his neck nervously. "I was wondering if maybe we could do something a little different?"

"Like what?" I hoped he wasn't about to say something crazy like MMA cage fighting or a monster truck rally.

"It's sort of a surprise."

"Oh . . . er . . . okay."

After several reminders to drive safely and be back by eleven (Mom) and not eat anything that could get stuck in my teeth (Maverick), we managed to extract ourselves from the house and got into his truck. A moment of awkward silence fell. I peeked at Liam from out of the corner of my eye, suddenly feeling self-conscious.

"You look lovely, by the way," he said.

"Maverick helped pick the outfit." I splayed my fingers and smoothed out my skirt. My palms were sweaty.

"It suits you."

"It does?"

"You remind me of the moon."

"I do?"

He nodded, and taking my hand, entwined his fingers through mine. We drove west out of Springbank along the highway, leaving behind the streetlights and sidewalks until we were passing open fields dotted with hay bales. Eventually, we turned down a narrow gravel road.

"Should I be worried?" I asked, only half joking. I'd seen plenty of movies where the killer took the victim to a remote area and murdered them with a hacksaw.

"We're almost there." He pulled into a small side road—it was more like a pair of muddy ruts in the grass than a road—and stopped in front of a hay bale covered with a white sheet. Metal posts marked the corners of a large square around which hung strands of miniature lights.

"What's all this?"

"Get out. I'll show you."

He brought me around to the back of the truck, and I noticed he'd lain out a thick wool blanket in the bed of the truck. He jumped into the back and helped me up—it was a little awkward wearing a skirt.

"I thought we could start with a picnic," he explained, kneeling down beside a couple of boxes tucked in the back corner. He looked at me apprehensively. "You're not disappointed, are you?"

"Disappointed? Why would I be?"

Liam gestured to the box. "It's not exactly a Michelin Star restaurant."

I knelt beside him. "It's perfect. It's beyond perfect."

"Do you mind me asking what you were expecting?"

I laughed nervously. "Er . . . a cage fight?"

I was afraid he'd take this wrong, but after a moment, he threw his head back and laughed. I'd never heard him laugh so hard. It was a great barking sound of surprise that brought a reluctant smile to my face.

"What's so funny?" I asked, my cheeks flushing.

His laughter subsided, but his cheek-splitting grin remained firmly in place. "For one, the thought of taking you—" his eyes swept over my brilliant outfit and braided hair "—to a cage fight. It's just so disconsonant, like bringing a butterfly into a coal mine."

I didn't know what disconsonant meant, but I got the idea, and while I didn't wholly disagree, I couldn't help but feel a little defensive. I didn't want Liam to think I was some wilting, delicate flower. "I think a cage fight would be cool to see," I said with bravado.

Liam continued to grin. "I'll remember that for next time."

I liked that he was already thinking about a next time. "And your other reason? You said 'for one'."

"For another, I appreciate your honesty. You are unapologetically you. Do you know how endearing that is?" Without warning, he leaned forward and cupped my face in the palms of his hands. As gently as if he were holding a dove, his thumbs caressed my burning cheeks. He looked different from the Liam I knew at school. He looked . . . *happy.*

My eyes shut as he leaned forward, and I might have stopped breathing as I felt the soft pressure of his lips against my brow. I blinked as he released me, at once light-headed and disappointed.

"Are you hungry?" he asked, his voice a little rough. He cleared it before opening the box and pulling out a pair of hot dogs and a couple cans of soda. "As I said, it's not exactly high class."

"Are you kidding? I love hot dogs."

We ate in the open air, watching the clouds drifting overhead. I was glad for the blanket, which I used to cover my legs to keep warm. When the sun started to set, Liam turned on a small generator next to the hay bale. The string of lights flickered and blinked on. I suddenly felt like I was surrounded by fireflies.

"We'll have to wait until dark before we can start the movie."

"Movie?"

He pointed to the second box. "I took a film reel out from the film club at school. Do you like *Casablanca*?"

"I've never seen it," I admitted. I watched him set the reel up, an uneasy curiosity bubbling. "Have you taken a lot of girls out like this before?" I asked, unable to contain the question any longer.

He looked at me in surprise. "Why do you ask?"

"You just seem to know what you're doing. You seem to know what you're doing about a lot of things." I looked down at my hands. "It's a little intimidating." I was starting to wonder if he really did expect the night to end in sex.

The same bemused line I'd seen on our first day in math class appeared between his eyes. "Really? Because today has been a disaster, and I'm seriously making this up as I go."

"You could have fooled me," I said.

Liam shook his head, smiling crookedly. "The one benefit of being a Hayes, I guess. We have lots of practice dealing with disasters. To be honest, I've never taken anyone on a date before."

My mouth dropped open. "You haven't?"

"You sound surprised."

"I am. You're so . . ." I struggled to find the word. "Mature?" It wasn't exactly what I was going for. For the most part, being a teenager felt like you were constantly off-balance. You spent most of your time trying to figure out up from down and left from right and right from wrong. It was like being trapped in a bizarro funhouse full of trick floors and distorted mirrors.

To me, Liam felt grounded. Like he'd somehow gotten through the funhouse and had solved the puzzle to understanding everything.

"My Nan would like you," I said. "You're what she'd call a catch."

"Me?" Liam plucked my soda out of my hands and sniffed it.

"What are you doing?"

"Smelling to see if there's alcohol in here."

I grabbed it back, flushing. "I'm serious."

"I know. That's what I find so unbelievable." Liam shook his head. "I brought you out here because I couldn't afford anything else, despite working my ass off all week. My parents are a mess, and I can't afford to go to a technical college, never mind university. You still think I'm a catch?"

I looked around at the wide, cloudy sky, slowly turning the colour of sangria, and the string of lights twinkling around us. I thought of the long hours I'd watched him working in our backyard, listening with unending patience to Maverick's endless chatter. How he'd stood up for Joshua even though it had gotten him into a world of trouble with Chase. Against an unfair world, Liam was the heavyweight champion of the world.

"Of course. You're the best person I know, Liam Hayes. You're like Clark Kent without the cape and the flying."

Liam laughed, shaking his head.

"What? Is that so funny?"

"Sorry, it's just . . . I was picturing Superman wearing a hardware-store apron."

"Aprons are just backwards capes," I said, grinning.

* * *

After it got dark, we watched *Casablanca* against Liam's makeshift screen while sharing a bag of Twizzlers. The whole time, I was aware of his legs stretched out next to mine under the blanket, so close that I could feel the warmth coming from him. Eventually, I found the courage to rest my head against his shoulder. It felt nice. It made me think of how it felt when we held hands or when he'd cupped my face. How perfectly we fit together, like peanut butter and jelly or tomato soup and grilled cheese.

Halfway through the film, I smelled the rain.

Liam must have as well. He peered up into the darkness and raised his hand just in time to catch the first drop.

"Uh-oh."

In seconds, the clouds opened up and it started to pour. Liam jumped up to cover the projector. I tried to help him put it back in the box without getting it wet and packed up the food while he ran to get the generator.

"What about the lights?"

"I'll get them tomorrow. Get inside!"

I jumped into the cab of the truck, my teeth chattering and my skirt plastered to my legs. Grabbing the sheet from the hay bale, Liam threw it over the boxes in the back of the truck and jumped into the driver seat with the blanket. He started the engine and turned the heater on.

"It's a little wet," he apologized, wrapping the blanket around me and rubbing my shoulders to warm me up. He was so close, I could see the individual droplets of water caught in his eyelashes and smell the faint scent of cherry soda on his breath. He really was beautiful. The desire to touch him was so dizzying, I thought maybe there had been alcohol in my soda after all. My fingers twitched, brushing the soft, damp wool.

He finally looked at me, his hands pausing. I couldn't say if I leaned in or if he pulled me towards him, but suddenly his lips were against mine, and it wasn't like last time. Not even close.

Because he was kissing me back in a way that was turning my bones to butter. His hand came up to cup my face, pulling me even closer, and my lips parted under his.

When he pulled away, he was smiling. "I should take you home," he whispered.

"Right now?" I asked. We both heard the disappointment in my voice, because Liam's smile widened.

"Yes. I promised your mom I'd bring you back by eleven, and if I don't drive you home now, I'm not sure I'll want to."

"Oh." I felt my face flush red.

We backed out of the field and rolled back onto the road. When we hit the highway, I felt my phone buzz in my pocket. I pulled it out and checked the screen.

"What the—"

"What is it?"

"Ten missed calls, all from Mom's cell." The fluttering sensation that had lingered after Liam's kiss turned to something hard and cold in the pit of my stomach. I hit the notification to hear the voice message Mom had left and listened to her tight, frantic voice.

Where are you? Maverick collapsed. We're taking her to the hospital. Come when you get this message.

I dropped the phone as everything inside me crumbled. Hands shaking, I ducked to retrieve it.

"What's wrong?" Liam asked.

"It's Maverick. C-can you take me to the hospital? Please?" Tears burned my eyes, the world around me swimming. Oh God, oh God no. Please no.

Liam hit the gas, and the truck roared and shot forward.

LIAM

Rainey was silent as I drove her to the hospital. I knew she was worried, but I didn't try to fill the quiet with empty words of comfort and reassurance. I wasn't confident I could say anything helpful, so I just held her hand, tracing the lines of her bones with my thumb while she stared out the rain-spattered window.

The moment I pulled into the parking lot, she jumped out and ran towards the giant automatic glass doors. After paying the meter, I went in and found her at the admitting desk talking with one of the clerks.

"Her name is Maverick. Maverick Collins. Her doctor is Mitchel Carter, the pediatric cardiologist. Can you tell me where she is?"

The clerk typed something into the computer while Rainey scanned the waiting area, searching for her parents. She saw me and made a bleak attempt at a smile.

"She's on the tenth floor, unit 103A," the clerk said.

"Thank you." She turned to me. "You don't have to come."

"I want to."

We got into the elevator beside a middle-aged woman in a wheelchair. Rainey hit the button, shifting her weight from side to side with restless energy. I couldn't believe twenty minutes ago I'd been kissing her and thinking this was quite possibly the best night of my existence. Now she wouldn't even look at me, her eyes locked on the ascending floor number blinking on the digital display.

The elevator dinged, and Rainey veered around the woman in the wheelchair, her head swiveling left and right, looking for the right room.

When we found them, Rainey gave a single, heart-wrenching sob. "Mom!"

Cora and Matthew were perched on the edge of Maverick's bed. They looked up at the sound of Rainey's voice.

"Rainey! There you are. Oh my God, I was worried when I couldn't reach you. Where have you been?"

"I'm so sorry. My phone didn't have reception. What happened?"

I hung back, giving Rainey and her family a moment to convene. Cora had tied her hair back in a scrunchy, but flyaways were poking out every which way from being dragged through with anxious fingers. Matthew's tie had been tugged loose, his hand gripping his wife's shoulder.

Rainey sank down beside her sister. Propped up by a balustrade of pillows, Maverick was sleeping, her tiny body hooked up to various cables and machines that beeped and blinked around her. Her cheeks looked pale and sunken. "Hi, bean," Rainey whispered.

"Liam." Matthew saw me and beckoned me over. Feeling like an intruder, I inched forward. "Thank you for bringing her."

"I'm sorry we couldn't get here sooner."

Rainey finally looked at me, her beautiful eyes drained of the light I'd seen in them while we'd sat talking in the back of my truck. How could that have been less than an hour ago? "You should go," she said softly.

The dismissal hurt more than I expected. I knew she was right: I would only get in the way if I stayed. And yet, I desperately wanted to be there for her, to be someone significant and involved enough to stay, who *needed* to stay. I didn't want to be extraneous.

"Are you sure?"

"Yes. I . . . I'm sorry. I just need to be with my family right now."

"Of course." I wished then that I had a cell phone. I'd never been able to afford one before, but it would have been nice to tell her to text me if she needed anything, to call, even if it was in the middle of the night: *I'll answer, no matter what.* But I didn't have a phone, and if I left now, there was no way for Rainey to reach me.

"Can I give you my home number? Just in case?" I asked.

"Of course." She handed me her cell so I could enter the number of the trailer's landline.

"If you call and Ray answers, just hang up, okay?" I said, handing her phone back.

"Okay."

I was finding it hard to move, but Rainey had already turned back to her sister, leaving me standing on the perimeter of the room, alone.

I left.

RAINEY

Mom and Dad were talking to the doctors. Dad asked if I wanted to come and hear what they had to say, but I said no. I wanted to stay with Maverick. Now that I was here, I wasn't going to leave her side if I could help it. Truthfully, a part of me didn't want to know what was happening. If I didn't know, I could pretend it wasn't bad. That come tomorrow, or maybe the day after, we'd go home, and Maverick and I could sit up in her treehouse eating Fuzzy Peaches and listening to Bob Seger's greatest hits. By then, this would all be over like a bad dream.

But that future in my head kept getting blocked by the image in front of me: Maverick, lying still and tiny under the starched white sheets of the hospital bed, like a baby bird fallen from its nest. I blamed it on the sheets. The main entrance and public areas of the hospital were painted a multitude of brilliant colours to make the place a little less daunting for the patients and their families, but up here in the CCU, the rooms were stark and sterile, filled with beeping machines and fluorescent lights. A token stuffed bear sat on a shelf in the corner holding a giant heart. Way to rub the problem in.

If this was going to be a long stay (which it wasn't, I kept telling myself), maybe I could bring Maverick some of her things from home, just to have a little more of her around to brighten the place up. It wouldn't be against code, right?

I kept expecting Maverick to open her eyes and start babbling away about the latest thing she'd seen on *National Geographic*, or the friend she'd made in the park while swinging on the swing. *He was a really nice old man with a brimmed hat and a little schnauzer dog named Randall. He offered me a Werther's candy.*

I could also picture my response. *You shouldn't accept candy from strangers, dummy! What if he wanted to kidnap you?* She'd roll her eyes and accuse me of being a ninny.

Eventually, the silence became so overbearing, I started to talk, keeping my voice low so I didn't wake her. "You're probably wondering how my date went. It went better than I expected; you'll be happy to know I didn't get anything stuck in my teeth." I leaned in conspiratorially. "I really like him. Like, a lot. I think you know that, though, or else you would have told me you were feeling sick. You wanted me to go, and you knew I'd cancel if something was wrong." I squeezed her hand. "You should have said something, bean."

I looked up at the ceiling, clenching my jaw to keep from crying. Not that I didn't want to, but there weren't any tissues around, and I didn't want to have to wipe my nose on the sleeve of my sweater. Crusty sleeves were the worst.

"I haven't thought about where my life is headed. Jo asked me if I'd thought about what I wanted to do after graduation, and I couldn't say. I was too afraid to imagine it, afraid you might not be there to share it with me. It felt selfish, I guess. But tonight, when I was with Liam . . . I think I found something I want badly enough to actually risk *wanting* it. I just hope . . . I just hope you get to come along for the ride, you know? Could you do that for me? Because I really need you to stick around."

Even though I wasn't crying, my nose started to drip. I sniffed loudly, trying to swallow around the giant rock lodged in my throat, and started to hum the melody to "Against the Wind". I was starting it over for the third time when Mom and Dad came back. They didn't look relieved, just tired. My heart sank.

"Come on, sweetheart, I'm going to take you home," Dad said.

"What about Maverick?"

"Maverick has to stay here for a while. The doctors need to

keep a close eye on her stats. Mom will stay here and call us if anything changes."

I didn't like the way he said *if anything changes.* "But I want to stay."

Dad squeezed my shoulder. "I know, sweetheart, but there are only so many cots available for family members, and I think it's best if you get some sleep in your own bed. We've called Nan. She's flying in from Kelowna and will be here in the morning."

"You called Nan? Why?" I could hear the rising panic in my voice. If Nan was coming, did that mean they thought things were going to get worst-possible-thing bad?

"She's just coming to help your mom and me out. We're probably going to be here at the hospital a lot for the next couple of weeks, and we need someone to look after you and the house."

"I'm fine," I said. I didn't need anyone to look after me; I wasn't five. "And I'll be here with you."

"It's just for peace of mind, Rainey." Dad looked exhausted, the bags under his eyes more pronounced by the bruises under the nose pads of his glasses. As terrible as I felt, I knew my parents had to feel worse, so I let it go.

Dad whispered something in Mom's ear and kissed her cheek. She nodded and took a seat in the chair beside Maverick's bed, her back as rigid as a soldier on sentry duty.

"Come on, kiddo." Dad drew me out of the room, and we took the elevator back down to the hospital lobby. On the drive home, Dad explained Maverick's condition.

"Her heart went into sudden failure. They inserted an IABP into her aorta, which will help her heart pump, but it's a short-term treatment. Carter has her on the transplant list, but he says there is no guarantee we'll get a match. If a heart becomes available, they'll perform the surgery immediately. If it's successful, our greatest concern will be potential graft vasculopathy and renal complications, but chances are high she could live a healthy life for another fifteen years."

I think it helped him to talk it through, relaying the facts through the medical lens of a doctor, rather than as a parent. I just wanted him to tell me Maverick was going to be okay. The fact that he didn't made my panic swell until I felt like I was drowning in it.

The moment we got home, I shucked off my shoes and ran upstairs to Maverick's room. It looked exactly like it had before I'd left earlier that evening, the 2:00 a.m. darkness turning the bright yellow walls into bleak grey stone. The bed with its sunflower comforter sat empty and neatly made, the pillows carefully arranged.

Grabbing the pillows, I proceeded to chuck them one after another across the room using every ounce of strength I possessed. They bounced feebly against the wall. Unsatisfied, I ripped back the comforter and mussed up the sheets until the whole thing was a scrambled mess. Then I lay down on top of it, breathing hard, clutching Carrots to my chest.

Dad had brought me home so I could get a good night's sleep. Did they honestly think that was possible? It was so late it was practically early, and I could not get my head to settle. Every surface in my mind was painful, so the ball kept bouncing, never staying in one place too long.

I finally grabbed *Peter Pan* off the bookshelf and started to read. I read aloud, just to fill the silence. "All children, except one, grow up." I'd read it so many times my eyes barely followed the words across the page.

I must have fallen asleep at some point because I woke curled up on my side in a pool of sunlight, *Peter Pan* stuck to my cheek. Rubbing the sleep out of my eyes, I crawled off Maverick's bed and went to the bathroom to brush my teeth. I was still wearing my yellow skirt and blue sweater from the night before. They were wrinkled and smelled, so I threw everything into the wash and had a quick, scalding-hot shower.

I came downstairs to the sound of bacon sizzling in the pan, the smell of pig fat wafting through the house. Dad thought bacon was as good for your heart as a two-pack-a-day smoke habit was for your lungs, so I wasn't surprised when I came into the kitchen to see Nan wielding a spatula over a griddle of pancakes and a frying pan spitting grease.

"Morning, sleepyhead," she said. I came over and wrapped my arms around her waist, breathing in her familiar rose perfume. Her arm came around my shoulders, and she gave me a tight squeeze. "I've made you some chocolate chip pancakes for breakfast, complete with bacon and orange juice. You need some meat on those bones of yours."

"Thanks, Nan, but I'm not hungry."

"I thought you loved chocolate chip pancakes." When I didn't respond, she gave my shoulder another squeeze. "Not eating isn't going to help Maverick, darling girl."

"I know," I whispered, but the thought of eating made my throat close up. "Is Dad awake?"

"He left for the hospital an hour ago, right after I arrived."

Why hadn't he woken me? I would have gone with him. Did

they think I'd get in the way?

Nan must have read something of my thoughts in my face because she said, "He wanted you to get some rest, and he's right. The greatness of our troubles diminishes significantly after a good night's sleep and a hearty breakfast. We must rally our strength before we go to battle."

"I just want to be where Maverick is."

"I know, darling girl, and I'll take you to the hospital, but you have to eat something first."

I managed to chew my way through one pancake and a couple strips of bacon while Nan cleaned up. Despite the wrinkles and the pure grey of her hair, she held herself like a war general, always lauding the importance of a steady gaze and good posture. "People respect you only as much as you respect yourself," she always said. Hearing this in my head, I realized I was slouched over in my chair like a defeated recruit. I straightened up.

"Your father said you had a date last night," Nan said. "What's the lucky man's name?"

I shifted in my chair, swirling the last piece of my pancake around in a pool of syrup. "Liam." Saying his name was like holding a small flame in my hands, a comforting warmth that reminded me of a time when everything had been utterly, transcendently perfect.

Then the universe had come along and torn it all apart.

Did the universe have a beef with perfection or something? If there really was a God, was he the bitter and jealous type that went around upending people's happy moments?

"I can see from the look on your face that things are serious."

"Not that serious," I said. "We've only been on one date."

"I knew I was going to marry your grandfather after our first date."

"You did?"

"Certainly. I was supposed to meet a young man named Simon Walsh at La Grenouille in New York for dinner, but he never showed. Your grandfather came to the restaurant with some friends and saw me sitting by myself at the table. He asked if he could join me; he had the kindest eyes." She shook her head, a reminiscent smile lingering on her mouth. "At any rate, I should be very pleased to meet this Liam of yours, whether it's serious or not. Now, I know you're eager to go, so if you're done, I'll get my keys."

I sprang out of my chair. "Just a second." I ran upstairs and selected a few of Maverick's books, including *Treasure Island* and *The Hobbit*, as well as her pillow in its purple casing. Finally, I grabbed Carrots, because every soldier needs a brother-in-arms.

* * *

Maverick was awake when we got to the hospital.

"Bean!" I ran over to her and gave her a big hug, mindful of the IV attached to her arm along with an unnerving number of tubes and cables. "I brought you something," I said, holding up Carrots.

Maverick's eyelids looked like bruised flower petals, and her fingers were cold when they brushed against me as she took him. "I'm too old to need Carrots," she said, but she tucked the rabbit under the covers beside her anyway.

"Good morning, sweet pea." Nan kissed the top of Maverick's

head. "How are you feeling?"

"She's a little out of breath, and the furosemide is making her dizzy, but the IABP is working, so her heart has stabilized," Dad said.

Nan raised her brows, wearing the same expression Mr. MacAlastair used whenever a student spoke out of turn, but my father was busy scanning the chart at the end of Maverick's bed and didn't notice. I winked at Maverick. She smiled wanly.

"I'm okay. The hospital food sucks though," she said. "The Cream of Wheat tastes like a hockey player's sock."

"Want me to go hunting for some of the good stuff?" I asked. There was a coffee shop on the second floor that made delectable croissants. I'd found it the last time Maverick had undergone a round of tests.

"She should stick to the food provided by her doctors," Dad said, kiboshing my most brilliant plan. I noticed he was wearing his lucky tie.

"Where is Cora?" Nan asked.

"She's getting some sleep," Dad said. "She was up all night." They started talking in low adults-discussing-important-things-voices, so I crawled onto Maverick's bed, making sure not to jostle or bump her, and started to read her *The Hobbit*.

It was a long day. Dad got angry at one of the nurses for not checking Maverick's legs for signs of edema even though they'd checked an hour before, and Mom got angry that Dad had lost his temper, and no one was very hungry, but everyone was hangry and on edge, and while I didn't want to leave my sister's side, the tension was suffocating, and I wanted so very badly to see Liam.

During one of the cardiologist rounds where the doctors came into the room to poke and prod, I escaped to the hospital lobby and tried calling the number Liam had entered in my cell. No one answered, and there was no voicemail, so I couldn't leave a message. When I came back up, I found Mom and Dad sitting on the bench along the wall outside Maverick's room. Dad was bent over, his elbows braced on his knees, his hand clasped around Mom's. She was hunched beside him.

I froze.

They were both crying. I knew it wasn't the-worst-possible-thing. I could see Maverick sleeping in her bed, her fragile chest rising as her heart continued to fight.

But seeing my parents—my strong, beautiful, loving parents—bowing under the insurmountable weight of impending agony turned my blood cold. It occurred to me how strange and selfish it was that we would do anything to save ourselves from the blistering pain of losing a loved one, even if that meant praying and hoping another child would die. Because as tragic as it was, at least it wasn't *your* child. And Maverick needed a heart.

Did that make us monsters?

I looked back at Maverick and thought of a quote Liam had scribbled in one of his notebooks: *What is done out of love always takes place beyond good and evil.* I thought maybe whoever came up with that understood sisters had to protect each other no matter what. Even if she always ate the last Fuzzy Peach. Even if she woke you up before your alarm with her ice-cold feet. Even if she made fun of your complete lack of fashion and drove you totally bonkers.

No matter what.

LIAM

Saturday afternoon, I headed over to Mercy's to check on Flea. He'd graduated from the kitchen floor to the sofa—Mr. Ramos was willing to overlook the dog hair in exchange for a fellow golf enthusiast—and looked much like a retiree enjoying the finer pleasures in life, including the leftover crusts from Joshua's grilled-cheese sandwich.

"Now that he's come inside, he won't leave. Mom isn't too happy, but I caught her rubbing his belly when I came down for breakfast this morning, so I think he's well on his way to winning her over," Mercy said.

"Thanks for taking care of him."

"He's my dog, too, you know. But I'm glad you came. It's been quiet around here without you dropping by," she admitted. "Mom even asked if we should call the police. She was worried something had happened to you."

"It's only been a week."

"Yeah, well, you know Mom."

Mrs. Ramos could be a little histrionic at times.

"And me," Mercy said, nudging my arm. "I've missed you."

I'd missed her too: the old Mercy who told me when I was being a brooding curmudgeon and would die alone if I didn't come over and help her pick raspberries from their raspberry patch. The Mercy who got back at the guy who brought his Corvette into the shop and said the only place a girl should be was in the passenger seat of his car. She'd hidden a dead mouse under the driver seat before he'd come to pick it up.

I wanted to tell her everything that was happening with Rainey and her sister and how shitty it had felt when Rainey had brushed me aside after I'd brought her to the hospital. Mercy would probably tell me to stop being a selfish jerk.

"Things have been busy," I said instead.

Mercy expelled a sharp breath of air and squared her shoulders the way people do before giving a difficult speech. "Look, about that night at the football game . . . I'm sorry about what I said." Her voice was firm and steady, and I knew she'd practiced saying this. "You don't owe me anything. Anything I did for you, I did out of friendship . . . and maybe because you're cute, but that's your fault, not mine."

I was still too angry to smile at her attempted humour, but my mouth might have twitched a little.

"I was just scared of losing you," she continued. "For as long as I can remember, I've been your person, you know? And then I saw the way you looked at her, and I freaked. I would plead temporary insanity, but that's just an excuse, and I hate excuses. And I don't expect you to forgive me. I just wanted to let you know that I'm going to earn your trust back even if it takes years."

"Decades," I corrected, smiling now.

"The rest of my life," she countered. "Because you're that important to me, Liam Hayes. Seriously. I need you around to tell me when to shut up because I say a lot of stupid shit that I don't mean, and it gets me into trouble."

"I can't argue that."

I knew Mercy meant what she said, but our argument was still present in the space between us, and like a determined poltergeist, it would take more than one paltry sage burning to exorcise it from my mind.

"It's too soon," I said.

Mercy nodded. "I know. But I'm not going to stop trying."

I hoped she wouldn't.

* * *

Ray came back from Lloydminster Saturday night. He was in a foul mood, which was no surprise, having spent the previous night in a roadside motel and the last five hours on the road. Lying on my bed, one arm tucked under my head, I heard him stomp into the trailer and head straight for the fridge.

"Fuck." The fridge door slammed shut. The dial tone stuttered as he picked up the phone. After a few seconds, he said, "Hey, I'm back. No, the bitch is working, but the kid is here. Come over and bring some beer, would you?" The phone slammed down.

A few seconds later, a fist pounded on my door, rattling the lock. Gritting my teeth, I opened the door. Ray grabbed me by the front of my shirt, his foul breath stinging my eyes.

"Where the fuck is my beer?" he snarled.

"I have no idea what you're talking about," I said, smiling thinly.

"Piece of shit." He shoved me, and I stumbled back onto the bed. "You better have it, kid, or I'm gonna loosen some of those teeth of yours."

"I took it as payment for the vet bill you cost me." That morning, I'd poured three six-packs of beer down the sink. It sure as hell didn't compensate for the bill or atone for what he'd done to Flea, but watching the amber liquid disappear in a funnel down the drain, knowing how much it would piss Ray off, had been hugely satisfying.

Ray's face twisted in confusion; I could hear the grinding of the gears in the rusted wreck that was his brain. Finally, his eyes cleared and he snorted. "This is about that damn dog? You're not serious."

I stood so that we were eye to eye. "You're lucky I didn't call the cops."

"You took my beer because of a *mutt*?" Ray snorted. Then before I could brace for it, he drove his fist into my stomach. I doubled over, gasping for air. "You so much as lay a finger on my beer again, and I'll drive more than a fist into your gut, you hear me?"

Winded, I couldn't answer.

Ray kicked open the porch door and left to wait for Wes and Paul out front. As soon as he was gone, I collapsed onto my bed, hoping that at any moment, the phone would ring, and it would be Rainey, asking me to come to the hospital. I knew she was going through the worst possible time with her family, but I wanted more than anything to see her, to remind myself that the world wasn't complete shit, and while there were people like Ray walking around polluting everything, there were also people who made you feel lucky to be alive just because you could hold their hand.

RAINEY

It was Sunday morning, and Maverick was showing no signs of improvement. The doctors had to increase her dosage of furosemide to mitigate the edema in her legs, and her feet had started to hurt, which Dad said was a sign of ischemia caused by inadequate blood supply to her extremities.

I sat beside her and read. I put extra effort into performing all the different voices and acted out the parts the way Maverick liked, just so I could do something other than sit and wait and watch while my beautiful little sister fought a battle I could not fight for her no matter how much I wanted to.

When the doctors came for their rounds, I went outside for some air. It was cold out for the first day of October, maybe only a few degrees above zero. I started to shiver almost immediately, but the chill was bracing, and I didn't want to go back inside just yet.

There was a small courtyard outside the day ward with a tree and a low stone bench. I sat and tried to call Liam again. This time, the phone rang only once before a husky voice answered.

"Hello?"

I'd heard that voice once before, and I would never forget it. I hung up without saying anything. Less than a minute later, my phone buzzed.

"Hello?"

"It's me. I'm sorry about that. I heard the phone ring, and Ray was right there. He's gone now, and he won't be back until later tonight. Is everything okay?" Hearing Liam's voice was like feeling the warmth of the sun directly on my heart. My lip began to wobble as I pressed the phone against my ear.

"Maverick isn't doing well," I whispered. "I'm scared, Liam. What if . . ." I couldn't bring myself to say it out loud. Someone like Maverick wouldn't die—dying was too mundane. No, she would disappear with a snap of her fingers in a cloud of fairy dust.

"What will I do if she . . . ? I mean, she's so young, she's barely had a chance to live. It's just so unfair."

"I know."

"I'm not sure I can bear it, Liam. I'm afraid. I'm afraid I'll just crumble into a million little pieces and get blown away by the wind, and all the king's men won't be able to put me back together again."

It was quiet for a moment, the enormity of my looming grief pulsing like a living beast, waiting to burst out of my chest.

"If that happens, and you crumble into a million little pieces, I'll pick up every single one, and I'll hold you in my hands so you don't get blown away."

Hot tears spilled down my cheeks. I sniffed loudly. Just then, I saw Nan coming out the doors of the hospital, holding a pair of Styrofoam cups. "I have to go." *I love you*, I wanted to say, but didn't. "I'll call you again soon."

"I'll be here."

I hung up just as Nan sat down. She passed me one of the cups. "It's hot chocolate. Or at least that's what they charged me for. Tastes like tap water filtered over a single cocoa bean. Do hospitals have something against sugar?"

"I think so," I said, wiping away my tears.

"They shouldn't. Miserable places should at least try to compensate for their existence by providing sustenance palatable enough to be distracting. My mother understood this and made the most exquisite meals whenever people came to visit."

We sat, quietly drinking the hot chocolate. It was bland and too hot, and I burned my tongue, but it gave me something to hold onto, and I needed something to hold on to, something to anchor me to the present.

"Was that Liam you were talking to?" Nan asked.

I nodded.

"Good. At times like these, it's important to remember that the world hasn't stopped turning."

"What do you mean?" I was too tired to make sense of ambiguous speeches right now.

Nan sighed. "When your grandfather died, I was devastated. I thought I'd never feel happiness again. For days, it felt like I was trapped in a spell where time moved differently or didn't exist at all. I felt lost, and I didn't know which way was up or down, but eventually, I woke up. I realized that, with or without your grandfather, life had carried on, and I had no choice but to carry on with it. I had to jump back into the fray, so to speak. At times like that, it's always best to have a hand on the other side to help you keep your balance. I had your mother. She kept me steady long enough to get my bearings. She reminded me that there were people who needed me, that I still had a purpose. I'm not saying you have to move on, or forget, but you learn to keep moving forward."

I thought of how it felt when I held Liam's hand, and I felt a little better knowing he'd be there to hold on to.

"Do you think Maverick will die?" The question tore itself out of my chest, leaving a throbbing hole where it had been growing.

"I don't know, darling girl. I wish I could say no, but I don't know."

I laid my head against Nan's shoulder as the wind teased my hair. Why couldn't she lie to me? Why couldn't anyone just lie to me?

"Let's go back inside before we catch our deaths," Nan said, patting my knee. "The doctors are probably finished."

Maverick was awake when we returned. Her doctors had told her to lie as still as possible, but she managed to lift her head a little and smiled as I came in. Dad had been called to see a critical patient in neurosurgery, but Mom was fussing over her, arranging the pillows around her head.

"Are you comfortable, sweetheart? Do you need another pillow? How about another blanket? You look cold. Or maybe a heating pad. I'll get you one, just a second."

"Let me, Cora," Nan said. "You sit down. You look exhausted."

Even though Mom wasn't usually one to let others do the heavy lifting, she collapsed into her chair as if her legs were about to give out while Nan went to ask the nurse for a heating pad.

"Hey, bean," I murmured, perching myself on the edge of Maverick's bed. Her hand reached for mine across the blanket. She held it with what I knew to be most of her strength. *Don't let go.* The words were there between us, quivering and desperate.

It occurred to me that, as scared as I was, Maverick had to be terrified. How could she look so calm? How could she lie there and smile when she didn't know if things would get better? My body felt like it was being torn apart, and I was on the brink of screaming.

"Are you okay?" I asked.

Maverick peeked quickly at Mom, who had closed her eyes and was now sleeping fitfully in her chair. She had a tissue shoved into the sleeve of her sweater, and I could tell from the redness around her eyes that she'd been crying.

"I don't think she knows that pillows aren't going to fix my heart," Maverick whispered.

It hurt to smile. I didn't have to tell Maverick that Mom was just doing what she could so she didn't feel useless like the rest of us.

"Have you heard from Liam?" she asked.

"I called him while you were with the doctors." I shot another look at Mom, and lowering my voice even further, whispered, "I think I love him, bean."

Maverick responded with a look: *Duh.*

"Hey, it's hard to say."

"Why?"

"Because it's just so . . . so big." My inner critic was slow clapping at my amazing choice of words. "And I'm not sure he feels the same way."

Maverick gave me another look: *You're an idiot.* "You should tell him."

"It's a little early for that, I think."

"No, you should tell him. Now."

"Are you kidding? He'll think I'm crazy. I *am* crazy. And I can't say something like that over the phone."

Maverick rolled her eyes. "No, dummy. Go see him. He won't think you're crazy."

"I can't. No. I'm not leaving."

"Please, Rainey. Go. Then come back and tell me about it. It will be a good story."

"What exactly do you expect will happen? I tell him I love him, birds will start singing, and he'll carry me away on a white horse like *Snow White*?"

"No, you'll probably mess it up."

"Gee, thanks."

"But it doesn't matter. You just have to say it."

"No."

Maverick continued to stare at me with *the* look—the beseeching puppy-dog look that I could never say no to.

"Why?"

"Because it's important, and you won't do it unless I make you."

And I might not be around much longer to make you, I heard and flinched.

"You have to, Rainey. It's not scary, telling someone how you feel."

"Oh yes it is! It's possibly the most terrifying thing in the world."

Apart from losing you.

"But if you can do this, you know you can do anything, right?"

Goddamn it.

I looked down at our hands, aware of Maverick's eyes on me. There was another reason for my hesitation: the last time I'd gone to Liam's unannounced, things had gone horribly wrong. He'd been furious at me for coming, but that was because his stepdad was home. Hadn't Liam said Ray was gone and wouldn't be back until later tonight? If I left now, I would reach Liam's place well before suppertime. That was plenty of time to say, "I love you," and leave before Ray showed up.

"Please, Rainey."

I waffled, then finally capitulated.

"Okay, but you have to promise me you'll be here when I get back," I said.

Maverick gave me another choice look: *Like where am I gonna go?*

Somewhere she wouldn't be able to hear the story, I thought with a painful tremor. "Just promise me, okay?"

She held up her pinkie finger, and I wrapped mine around it just as Nan came back with the heating pad.

"Nan, can I borrow your car for an hour?" I asked. "I need to see Liam, if that's okay."

"I don't see why not," Nan said, handing me her car keys. "Maverick is only allowed two visitors at a time anyway. Just wear your seatbelt and don't speed, whatever you do. I don't want to get a ticket on a rental."

"Don't worry. Rainey drives like an old lady," Maverick said with a grin.

"I take offense to that," Nan chided.

"I'll be careful," I promised and blew Maverick a kiss. "Love you, bean!"

14

LIAM

SUSAN DROPPED MOM OFF after her shift at the grocery store with a paper bag.

"Where's Ray?" Mom asked as I took the bag from her and put it on the counter. She'd bought a loaf of bread and a can of beans.

"Out with Wes and Paul. They spotted coyotes over the hill and took the guns out."

"Hunting season isn't for another month though." Mom sounded like a prisoner who had just heard their execution date got moved up.

"Call the Canadian Wildlife Service."

"And get a fine? We can't afford that."

Hunting season was the worst time of year. Wes and Paul were over every night, drinking themselves pissed after tracking game all day. Last year, Ray had put Mom in the hospital with a broken arm after she had knocked over the rifle he'd left leaning against the kitchen wall.

"Hungry?" I asked.

Mom looked at the can of beans. "Not really. You?"

"Not really." We sat down at the table and looked out the window into the bleak October.

RAINEY

I didn't know how to get to Liam's place without following Joshua's bus route, so the drive took a little longer than it should have. I made one wrong turn and ended up on an unfamiliar road with nothing in sight except a few spruce trees and an old barn, but eventually, I found the driveway with the red mailbox and the neglected planter box and pulled over into the shoulder.

"You can do this," I muttered to myself.

I did the top button of my jacket up and shoved my hands deep into my pockets to keep them warm. My breath fogged in front of my face as I exhaled my nerves, then forged ahead through the tall grass and onwards towards the trees.

I love you.

Three little words. I said them to Maverick and my parents all the time. How hard could it be to say them to Liam?

The wind picked up, and I felt a soft flutter against my cheek. Looking up at the thick wall of cloud, I grinned.

Snow.

According to every K-drama I'd ever watched, it was a good omen. They believed that true love would blossom if you were with the person you liked during the first snowfall, and if you made a wish, it was bound to come true. Figuring I had nothing to lose, I sent up a prayer for Maverick.

Please let her be okay. Let her grow old and fall in love and do all the things she wants to do.

The tiny flakes continued to fall, tickling my nose in answer.

I knew it was ridiculous. I knew the snow wouldn't answer my prayers, but I wanted so badly to believe it would work. So much so, I convinced myself that if I held up my end of the bargain, if I told Liam I loved him, she would be okay. That was the deal.

I broke into a run, giddy with nerves. I could do this. I love you. I love you. I love you. Just three little words. It was easy.

But what if he doesn't say it back? What then? What if he thinks you're crazy?

I nearly stopped, my mind spiralling around all the what-ifs. But then I heard another voice, Maverick's voice. *It doesn't change how you feel, does it?*

No, it didn't.

Be brave, Rainey.

Maverick was right—I couldn't do this without her, but I could do it for her. Was this the reason? The mysterious *why* I'd struggled so long to understand? Did Maverick have to fight for her life just so that I could be brave enough to say three little words?

I was nearing the trees when something struck me with an ear-splitting crack. The force of it knocked me backwards, and the world spun in a kaleidoscope of sky and earth.

I stared up at the sky, my ears ringing as the snow drifted

down. What had just happened? Why was I lying on my back? Where had that sound come from? Thoughts sparked in bright bursts like fireworks against the dark fog of my vision. I felt a strange, uncomfortable heat burning across my temple. Then, over the ringing in my ears, I heard voices.

"I think I got it!"

"Where is it?"

Someone was walking through the grass. Then a face loomed over me, pale and sunken. I saw the whites of his eyes as he looked down at me, a rifle in his hand.

"Shit!"

"Paul, what is it? Did you get it!"

"Shit! Fucking hell." The man buried his hands into his hair, nearly ripping it up from the roots. "It's . . . it's a girl. What do we do?"

"Jesus Christ." Two others came up behind him. My vision was starting to blur, dark spots blooming across the watery sky. This man had shot me, I realized. The thought felt distant and strange. I couldn't figure out if I was afraid or indignant, or anything for that matter, apart from the numbness spreading through my body.

"I . . . I heard something and just turned and . . . oh God . . ."

"Let's get out of here!"

"Are you kidding? We can't just leave her!"

"We call the cops, and we'll go to prison."

"Can't we just say we found her like this?"

"You think they'll believe that?"

The voices swam around me, fading in and out. *Don't go. Please.*

But they left.

I tried to move, but I couldn't feel my hands or my feet, so I lay still, listening to the wind whistling through the grass. It was otherwise quiet: there were no birds. I couldn't even hear the buzz of insects.

I wondered if I was dying but thought, of course not, that was impossible. How could I be dying? Maverick needed me, and I needed to tell Liam that I loved him. We'd only gone on one date. One perfect, beautiful date. But I wanted to go on a second date, and a third, and a fourth. I wanted to have sex, for Christ's sake!

I realized the future I'd been so afraid of was something I now desperately wanted. I wanted to see Liam. I wanted to see him, and I called his name, but no one was coming, and I wasn't sure if I was even saying it out loud.

I love you.

LIAM

Ray came barreling into the trailer, the door slamming against the opposite wall, making the two of us jump. His face was the colour of arsenic, a pale grey tinged with yellow.

"We're leaving," he snapped. "Get your things. Now!"

I looked at Mom, dumbfounded, then back at Ray. "What?"

"You heard me!" He ran towards the bedroom. I heard the thud and slam of drawers opening and closing as he started to pack his things.

"Ray, what happened?" Mom rose from the table and followed after him.

"I told you to pack, damn it!"

I came up behind Mom and watched Ray shovel clothes into a bag; he wasn't even bothering to remove the hangers from his shirts. Sweat was pouring down his face.

"What did you do?" I asked.

Ray spun around and glared at me. "I did nothing! It was Paul. He—" Ray froze, suddenly quiet. I heard it then: the distant sound of police sirens. "Fucking moron called the police."

"Ray, what's going on? What happened?"

"Forget it! I'm leaving." He shoved my mother aside. I caught her as he ran for the door. He didn't even bother shutting it behind him as he left.

I looked at Mom. "Are you okay?"

"I'm fine. What was that about?"

Ray's truck peeled away down the gravel drive as the sound of the sirens grew louder. I ran to the window and watched two police cars swerve in the middle of the highway, giving chase after Ray as he sped off in the opposite direction. A third cruiser turned into our driveway and pulled up to a stop in front of the trailer. A female officer got out of the car. Her cap was pulled low, shielding her eyes. Her mouth was set in a grim line. She knocked on the side of the trailer, peering cautiously through the open door.

"Can I help you?" I asked, stepping out onto the porch.

"Good afternoon. I'm Officer Barrow with the RCMP. Is this the home of Raymond Cote?"

"It is."

"Are you his son?"

"His stepson."

My mother shuffled around the edge of the door, her arms

curled around her waist as if she were anticipating a beating. "Ray is my husband. Is . . . is there something wrong?"

"Was that who left just now in the grey Buick?" the officer asked.

"Yes," my mother answered.

"And did he tell you where he was going?"

"No, he didn't. What is this about?"

The officer pressed the call button on her radio. "This is Barrow. Affirmative on the Buick."

"Copy that," a voice answered.

Barrow looked back at my mother. "We received a call from a Paul Davis. A seventeen-year-old girl was shot with a Ruger hunting rifle about a kilometer south of here. We're trying to track down those involved. Do you know anything about this?"

"No. I'm . . . I'm sorry, did you say a girl was shot?"

"Yes, ma'am. Over that way." She gestured towards the Ramos property.

My mother's hand flew to cover her mouth. "Oh God."

I was still struggling to make sense of the police officer's words. A girl, shot? But there weren't any girls out here. The nearest was Mercy, and Mercy was nineteen, and she never came this way. She wasn't allowed. Had the officer gotten her age wrong?

"The girl . . ." My mouth had gone dry, and the words stuck in my mouth. "What was her name?"

"I don't know," the officer said. "The ambulance took her to the hospital. She was in bad shape."

"What did she look like?"

"Caucasian. Reddish-brown hair. She was wearing a red wool coat."

The world spun around me in a sickening blur.

I stumbled over to the phone and dialed Rainey's number. "Pick up, pick up, pick up." It rang five times, then went to voicemail. I hung up and tried again. My hands were shaking so badly, I had to dial her number three more times before I could get it right. Again, it went to voicemail.

It wasn't her. That description matched a lot of girls. And why would she come here? She was at the hospital with her family. She wasn't picking up her phone because her battery was dead or because she was in a no-call zone. That was it. Of course. I'd go to the hospital and she would be there, sitting next to Maverick, and she'd see me, and her eyes would light up, and I'd wonder how I could have ever imagined this absurdness.

"Liam, where are you going?" my mother yelled as I ran past her and the officer. The wind had picked up, and it had started to snow, but my body didn't register the cold. I jumped into my truck and headed for the hospital, my foot slammed against the accelerator.

It was hard to focus on the road. My heart was pounding so loudly, I couldn't hear anything over the rush of the blood in my ears and the hollow gasp of my breath. She was going to be there. She was going to be there. She *had* to be there. The needle on the speedometer wavered as I hit my truck's top speed.

When I got to the hospital, I ran up to the Intensive Care Unit, taking the stairs three at a time, nearly bowling over a young couple walking past the stairwell.

"Watch it!"

"Sorry!" I gasped, hands raised in apology.

I spun around and turned the corner, skidding to a halt. Two other police officers were talking to Rainey's parents. I'd read books where the writer used the phrase "my heart stopped beating" to convey feelings of shock and horror, but that isn't what happens. Your heart keeps beating painfully, loudly, defiantly, drawing out the moment you wish you could somehow escape. *I'm sorry but you have to bear this*, it whispers to you.

Cora and Matthew looked haggard and exhausted, holding onto one another as if they were propping each other up. One of the police officers said something, his voice a soft, apologetic murmur. And then I watched Cora's face crumple as she sank to her knees, clutching her chest. Matthew let out a deep wail, a sound that sought to tear the fabric of reality apart in a powerless attempt to unmake it, and I knew she was gone. Grasping the wall, I bent over, my empty stomach heaving while the tile floor spun before my eyes, and my heart kept beating as the world came crashing down.

* * *

I sat on one of the benches outside the CCU, vaguely aware of the doctors and nurses working around me. I knew I didn't belong here. I was the cause of this unbearable pain. How could I even show my face? And yet I couldn't bring myself to leave. I kept looking up, expecting to see her walking towards me with that quiet smile on her face. Someone would come around the corner with brown hair, and my heart would leap. *There she is! See, this was just a misunderstanding.* But it was never her, and I knew it never would be her, and I felt sick because I would never see her bright, beautiful eyes again, and it was my fault. It was all my fault.

Why had she come?

Why hadn't she called?

How could this happen?

I kept asking myself the same questions over and over in dizzying succession, but there was never any answer, only the ringing phone behind the call desk, and the beeping of machines, and the phantom voice of the intercom paging Dr. Chen to the OR.

I couldn't say how long I sat there, but at some point, a woman approached me. I'd seen her with Rainey's parents and thought perhaps she was Rainey's grandmother. She had Cora's high cheekbones and long nose. I could see from the redness around her eyes that she had been crying.

"Are you Liam?"

I nodded. At first, I was afraid she was going to ask me to leave, but she sat down beside me, folding her hands over her knees. "I'm Marjorie, Rainey's grandmother. I've been watching you. You've been sitting in this same spot for hours. You must be tired." Her voice was soft and ragged from weeping.

I couldn't bring myself to respond. I wasn't tired. Tired didn't begin to describe what I was. I was lost in the chaos beyond sense and perception. But Marjorie didn't wait for a response. She dabbed her nose with a wrinkled Kleenex, sniffing.

"You know, I always told the girls you can't fight your battles on an empty stomach and poor sleep, but I find I don't have an appetite, and my heart has been shaken too deeply for my body to rest. I suspect you feel the same." She paused. "Are you waiting for Maverick?"

"Maverick?"

"Yes. She went in for surgery after they brought Rainey in. She was a match. Has no one told you?"

Oh God. I managed to shake my head.

"She held on long enough to get to the hospital, but they couldn't do anything about the bleeding in her brain. A small miracle, the doctor said." Marjorie grimaced. "I think he intended to give Cora and Matthew some pittance of comfort, but the deliverance of one child doesn't diminish the pain of losing another. It doesn't work like that." Tears rolled silently down her face.

I hadn't realized it, but I was crying too. A tear dripped from my chin onto the back of my hand. I looked down at it, and the words of Melville came to my mind, "From beneath his slouched hat Ahab dropped a tear into the sea; nor did all the Pacific contain such wealth as that one wee drop."

"Do you know . . . do you know if . . ." The words kept failing. I took a deep breath, but it didn't help. "Did the doctors say if she . . . if there was any pain?"

Marjorie stared at the ceiling for a long moment. "I don't know," she said at last. "I'd . . . I'd like to think she didn't suffer. I pray she didn't. And I'd like to think that maybe, wherever she is, she knows Maverick will be okay. I think that would make her happy."

How would you know? I thought unkindly. Maybe Rainey would have railed against the injustice of it all. Maybe she would have been devastated that we'd never gotten the chance to say goodbye. But these were my thoughts, I realized, and if there was anything in the world Rainey loved more than air itself, it was Maverick.

About an hour later, Matthew came by. The calm, collected man I'd seen last week looked hollowed out, as if he'd drunk a draught that had aged him ten years in a single night. "Maverick is out of surgery. She's awake."

He didn't look at me. From the angle of his hunched shoulders, it was clear he didn't want me there, and this announcement was for Marjorie.

"Thank God," she said. "Oh, thank God. How is she?"

"Physically, she's stable. But Cora and I had to tell her . . . we had to explain . . ." Matthew let out a ragged breath that shook his whole body. "She's devastated. She's barely said a word."

I stared down at the floor, waiting for him to turn to me, to haul me to my feet and pin me against the wall and scream at me. *This is all your fault! She would never have been there if it hadn't been for you! You killed my baby!*

I wished he would. I'd read a book about a mountain climber who fell and crushed his leg. Blood had built up in the calf muscle, causing him an excruciating amount of pain. He'd cut his leg with a utility knife just to relieve the pressure. Matthew's rage would have been my utility knife, cutting an exquisite release. I almost begged him to hit me.

"She asked to see you," I heard him say instead. I thought he was still talking to Marjorie, but when she didn't answer, I looked up. Matthew's eyes—so like his daughter's—stared at me coldly. "Maverick," he clarified. "She wants to see you."

No, I thought, I can't. I can't do that.

But I didn't dare ask Matthew for the mercy of an excuse. Instead, I nodded and got to my feet. I had been sitting for so long, the blood rushed to my head and my knees nearly gave out, but I managed to follow him down the hall. We didn't go to the same room as before, but walked through a pair of sliding doors and down another hall to the recovery ward. It was quieter here. There was less beeping, and the rooms were dimmer and more peaceful. Maverick's room had a large window looking out towards the parking lot.

It was dark out. For the first time, I wondered what time it was. Nearly dawn?

Maverick was lying in her bed, her head turned towards the window. Cora lay beside her, her arm wrapped around her daughter, one hand gently stroking her hair.

"Cora," Matthew whispered.

She turned at the sound of her husband's voice, and seeing me, rose slowly from the bed. Maverick turned too. Seeing her was a shock. There were bruises under her eyes, and the burning brightness that I'd come to associate with Rainey's indefatigable little sister had drained away down the glistening tracks of her tears. And yet there was a flush of pink in her cheeks that had not been there before, proof of her sister's heart beating strong and steady in her chest.

As Cora passed me, she touched my shoulder. "Thank you for being here," she murmured. The words tore at me. How could she say that? How could she not hate me as much as I hated myself?

She and Matthew stepped out of the room leaving me and Maverick alone. I moved closer, my feet propelling me along like an unwilling hostage, and I sank onto the chair next to the bed.

Maverick was quiet, gripping her stuffed rabbit as if she were caught in the rapids of a river and it was her only life raft. My eyes fixed on the gauze visible above the neckline of her hospital gown, and I pictured the heart beneath trying to adjust to its new surroundings. I knew it was just a heart, a beating muscle driven by electrical impulses, but I couldn't help but wonder if maybe there was some small essence of Rainey locked inside.

Maverick bit her lip. The mannerism was so much like her sister, it hurt to see. Tears pooled and slipped from the corners of her eyes. "I'm sorry," she whispered.

I blinked, too stunned to comprehend. "What are you apologizing for? This wasn't your fault."

"Yes it is. I . . . I told her to go see you. I told her . . . I made her promise." The tears came more freely, and she wiped them away, sniffing. "She told me she loved you, and I told her she had to tell you. I made her promise." She stared at me beseechingly, willing me to understand. And I did, and it felt like a knife had just slid through my ribs, straight into my heart.

Maverick started to sob. Without thinking, I reached forward and held her, her narrow shoulders shuddering and heaving against my chest while I murmured incomprehensible sounds of soothing, worried her incision would open.

Eventually, she pulled away from me, her nose dripping. I offered her a tissue that she used to wipe her nose. She looked at me then, her face filled with more pain than it could possibly hold, and whispered, "Do you hate me?"

"I could never hate you."

"You promise?"

"I promise."

* * *

I stayed with Maverick until she fell asleep, her cheeks still wet from her tears, then quietly got up to leave. I would have stayed longer—Maverick had asked me to—but Matthew had made it clear he didn't want me around, and I didn't blame him.

I didn't know where to go and considered driving to the police station. I wanted to find out what the police had done, and if they had arrested Wes and Paul, or if they had caught Ray. I pictured his face when he'd arrived at the trailer, sweaty and panicked, demanding we leave. That had been just minutes after they'd shot her.

And he'd left her, bleeding in the grass . . .

I was no stranger to anger, but the rage I felt was different from the bitter hate and frustration I'd felt before. It was cold and calm. I realized with a chilling detachment that if I saw any of those men again, I would kill them without a moment's hesitation.

However, as I walked by the recovery waiting room, something caught my eye. The television was on, airing the morning news. *Police chase of murder suspect results in fatal crash.* The large bold words glared at me along the bottom of the screen. Ears ringing, I walked over to try to hear better.

"Can someone turn up the volume?" I asked. A nurse behind the desk took a remote out of a drawer and adjusted the volume until I could hear the dispassionate tones of the presenter's voice over the coughing of the person in a nearby chair.

"Pursuit of a murder suspect has ended in a fatal crash. At approximately five o'clock last night, police apprehended two individuals involved in a shooting that killed a seventeen-year-old girl. A third suspect was seen fleeing the scene in a grey Buick heading west down Range Road 52. During police pursuit, the vehicle struck a utility pole, killing the driver on impact. Alcohol may have been involved."

I stared at the camera shot of the mangled Buick that appeared on the screen. The front end was completely annihilated, its wheel ripped clean off, exposing the bent front axle like a rusty compound fracture. I could imagine the force with which the truck must have hit the pole to produce that kind of damage.

It felt strangely decisive, and for a moment, I wondered if more than alcohol had been involved in sending that Buick into that pole. Something powerful and righteous. I looked up, seeing nothing but fluorescent lights and gypsum ceiling tiles, and thought, *You're too late.*

15

LIAM

I FOUND MY MOTHER SITTING at the kitchen table next to Susan when I got home. Two mugs of tea steamed between their hands, and a heap of used tissues was piled next to an empty box. Knowing these tears were for Ray made me want to puke, and I looked down at my mother, hating her to the marrow of her bones for being weak.

"Liam! Where have you been?" she choked.

"I've been at the goddamn hospital. Where do you think?"

Susan stiffened at my tone. "How dare you yell at your mother! She's been through hell. Her husband has just died."

"I wasn't talking to you!" I snapped, my anger breaking free of its tether. Susan's eyes bugged out. It was the first time I'd spoken directly to her. "Do you honestly think Ray deserves another wasted breath? We should be celebrating, for Christ's sake."

"Liam, please!" My mother started to cry again. I used to feel bad whenever she cried, but I was too angry now.

"God, Mom, look at yourself! You're grieving for a man who beat you, for fuck's sake! He and his friends shot an innocent girl and ran. They fucking RAN!" I was yelling now, my voice shaking with rage.

"You're being unfair. Love does not discriminate. Love—"

"Oh, shove your preaching up your ass, Susan." That shut her up. Her vacuous mouth snapped shut with an audible click. I rounded on my mother. "You know it, and I know it. That bastard got exactly what he deserved, and if he wasn't dead, I would kill him myself. You want to talk about love? The girl he shot. Did you know I loved her? Do you even give a shit about the hell *her* parents are going through?"

My mother's blotchy, creased face paled. "Liam, I . . . I didn't know—"

"Of course you didn't know! You're blind to everything but your own suffering, for Christ's sake! The only thing you love is suffering, and you're so fucking besotted with it, you refuse to consider the collateral damage of your blindness. As far as I can tell, you're as guilty as Ray. You might as well have gotten in that goddamn Buick with him." The words burst out of me, raw and ugly, leaving me hollow and panting.

My mother let out a small gasp as if I'd physically struck her, leaving her choking on her tears, but now that I'd started, I couldn't stop.

"You never did anything. Why didn't you do anything?" I asked, begged. "And now it's too late! It's too fucking late!" I was vibrating. I picked up the empty chair in front of me and smashed it against the wall. It gouged a hole through the panel, bits of gypsum scattering across the table.

Susan cleared her throat. "I-I'll go wait in the car," she stammered. She snatched up her purse and scooted around me, giving me as wide a berth as the small kitchen allowed.

My mother's hands shook, the hot liquid in her cup sloshing. "Liam, I couldn't—" she began.

"No!" I growled. "No, you don't get an excuse." And neither did I. I was just as culpable. I never should have left her; I never should have left the hospital. Goddamn it, why had I left? I felt like I was going to throw up again.

"I'm going to go stay with Susan for a while," my mother said quietly. It was as if I hadn't said anything, as if she'd blocked out the last five minutes and I'd just walked in and asked politely what her plans were.

"Do whatever the fuck you want. I'm done with you," I said, and I went to my room, slamming the door behind me.

* * *

Looking back, it wasn't the day she died that was the worst. It was the day after. C. S. Lewis once wrote, "No one ever told me that grief felt so much like fear." I'd never understood that. What was there to fear in grief? But that day, lying in my bed, wearing the same rumpled clothes I'd worn for the past twenty-four hours, I figured it out.

The fear was moving forward without them.

I remembered the first time I noticed her; it hadn't struck me then, but a part of me must have thought, *her*, and fixed the compass of my being on its course to salvation like a ship sets its course on the stars. But now the stars were dark and the waves were crashing down all around me, and I couldn't tell which way to go, and I was just lying on my mattress with its broken spring, drowning in darkness.

I'd never felt so lost, or so terrified.

The following day, I managed to get showered and changed into some fresh clothes. The effort this took was exhausting, and I ended up crawling back onto my bed afterwards and falling into a semi-conscious state. I could never fall completely asleep because every time I closed my eyes, I saw Rainey lying on the ground, her lips cold, her eyes staring towards the sky, screaming in pain, and I would jerk awake screaming too.

I kept expecting to hear a knock at the door and find the police there, waiting to arrest me. *You have been found guilty of destruction.*

Destruction of a life that should have been lived. Destruction of joy and innocence and beauty. But no one came to relieve me from my tortured conscience, and I continued to lie on my bed in the silence of the trailer, frozen in time and pain.

Eventually, I fell asleep, but my dreams offered no respite. I walked in a dark forest, wreathed in fog, unable to see anything but the flickering, dim glow of fireflies darting through the shadows. I heard her voice, calling to me from a distance.

Wait! Don't go!

But no matter how fast I ran, I couldn't catch up to her.

* * *

It was Wednesday. At least I thought it was Wednesday. I went to school, not because I wanted to, but because I needed to do *something*, and school was the only thing I could think of. However, being there was almost worse than the silent confinement of the trailer. Everyone had seen the news. Those who hadn't had heard it from their friends or their parents. Eyes followed me as I walked down the hall towards my locker, heads turning conspicuously.

Did you hear? His stepdad killed Rainey Collins.

Oh my God. Is he even allowed to be here?

Weren't they dating?

That is fucked up.

The speculations buzzed around me like a swarm of gnats. I did my best to tune them out, but I wasn't able to tune out the teachers. MacAlastair approached me after class and told me in an uncharacteristically soft voice how sorry he was. Mrs. Burt burst into tears in the middle of her lecture and tried to hug me.

I didn't want their sympathy. I didn't deserve their sympathy.

I passed Rainey's locker at lunch. People had posted notes and left flowers, turning her locker into a memorial. Carson stood in front of the display, head and shoulders above everyone else, a bag of Fuzzy Peaches in his hand. He knelt down and placed it next to a bouquet of wilting roses, his eyes swollen and his nose red.

For one horrible moment, I wondered what might have happened if Rainey and I had never met, if I had picked some other seat in math class. Such an inconsequential decision, and yet it had come with such devastating repercussions. Rainey would have been alive. She might have fallen in love with a guy like Carson. Someone uncomplicated, maybe a little misguided, but well-meaning. She would have graduated, gone to college, gotten married, and had children.

Instead, our worlds had collided, and I had mangled her future irrevocably.

But what about Maverick? a small voice asked. Would she have died instead? Is that what you would have wanted?

The question hung in my mind, waiting for an answer, but there was no answer, only a jumble of *ifs* and *could have beens* and a wordless sense of injustice.

Carson spotted me as he turned. Twin spots of red burned his cheeks. "What are you doing here?" he snarled. "You have some nerve coming here, you bastard!"

He lunged towards me, but a hand caught him by the wrist before he could take hold.

"Don't." Chase's grip on his cousin's wrist tightened.

"Let go of me," Carson warned. The muscles in his arm flexed; I had no doubt he would bulldoze Chase against the wall of lockers if push came to shove.

"Let it go, Kozlowski. It's not his fault."

"Like hell it isn't! If it weren't for him, she'd still be alive!"

Chase's grip didn't let up. "Let it go, man."

Carson's nostrils flared. "I backed you when you wanted to take him out. Now you want to let him go?"

When Chase didn't respond, Carson shook his head. "Whatever." He ripped his arm free and stormed off towards the cafeteria, nearly knocking down a terrified-looking sophomore standing next to the memorial.

My eyes met Chase's.

"You can't choose your family," he said quietly enough that

only I could hear, and walked away.

Coming here had been a mistake. I turned to go and nearly ran into Jo. She wasn't wearing her usual designer dress or three-inch heels, just a pair of coveralls and a T-shirt, her long blond hair tied back into a careless ponytail. She looked like she'd slept about as much as I had, and was looking over my shoulder at the memorial like she wanted to rip it down and set it on fire so she wouldn't have to keep passing this obtrusive reminder that her best friend was gone.

"Want to get out of here?" she asked me.

"Yes," I said with some relief.

I followed her out of the school to the bench Rainey and I had appropriated during our lunch hours. It was cool but bright, the sun beaming down on us with callous indifference. How fucking impertinent, I thought.

I half expected Jo to round on me like Carson had and blame me for Rainey's death, but she didn't. She just sat beside me on the bench, looking out over the empty football field, and cried. I felt too dead inside to cry with her. My insides were a husk, burned clean by my anger.

"The funeral is next Thursday," she said after a time. "Did her parents tell you?"

"No. I haven't spoken to them since . . . since I left the hospital."

"The service is being held at the Dignity Memorial Funeral Home. One o'clock. You're coming, right? Jenner gave all of us permission to attend."

I closed my eyes, trying to block out the sun. "I don't know."

"What do you mean, you don't know?" Jo demanded,

sounding a bit more like her old self.

"I don't think her parents want me there."

"That's bullshit. You have to go. She loved you, for Christ's sake."

And here it was again, someone confirming what was still unbelievable to me. It was like being told the earth was flat or the moon was made of cheese. And I never got to hear her say it, and I never got the chance to say it back, and the pain of that was so utterly excruciating, I wanted to scream.

"I can't, Jo."

"I don't care. You're going. She would want you to be there. You don't have to say anything, but you damn well have to show up."

I didn't answer, but Jo took my silence as tacit compliance.

"It's just so fucked up," she whispered. "A week ago, I was drunk out of my mind, wondering if anyone would care or even notice if I was gone. I actually thought it would be better if I were dead. How fucking stupid. How goddamn self-absorbed. I mean, she was right there. She was right there, and I took her for granted, and now I won't ever see her again." She started to cry again, sniffing loudly.

My head was throbbing, and all I could think about was how much I wanted to be sitting here with Rainey, not Jo. I tried to picture Rainey's face in my mind, the line of her nose, the faint specs of green in her grey eyes, and the way the sun caught the red tones in her hair. I was terrified to realize some of the details were already hazy. Over time, would I completely forget what she looked like? I couldn't be sure. All I knew was that I'd never forget the way her smile had made me feel like maybe the world wasn't quite so shit after all.

Would I ever feel that way again?

"By the way," Jo said, "I'd extend my condolences for your stepdad, but I can't. Sorry."

I snorted. "Don't be. I only wish the other two had died with him."

Jo smiled wanly. "I knew I liked you." After a while, she sighed. "I have to go. I'll see you at the funeral next Thursday. One o'clock. Don't forget."

It wasn't a question.

* * *

Mercy came by the trailer that evening. It was the first time she'd ever visited, so it was a shock to see her standing under the flickering porch light, moths fluttering over her head.

"I heard what happened," she said softly. "Are you okay?"

I stepped out, shutting the screen behind me to keep the bugs out, and sat on the top step. The current state of the trailer was unsuitable for company; I hadn't patched the hole in the wall from when I'd thrown the chair, my room was a pile of dirty clothes and unwashed sheets, and the kitchen was a mess.

Was I okay?

"No," I said honestly.

Mercy sat down beside me, looking almost as lost as I felt. "I'm so sorry, Liam."

"Are you?" I asked. It was unfair of me, but my anger was so close to the surface these days.

To Mercy's credit, she took the lash without flinching. "I wish there was something I could do. What can I do?"

Nothing, I thought. There is nothing anyone can do.

"Where is your mom?" She looked towards the window, searching for a light or some sign of movement from inside.

"Gone."

"Gone? Gone where?"

"She's staying with one of her friends."

"She left you?" Mercy swore under her breath. "She's coming back, though, right?"

"I don't know." I didn't care either. I'd been looking after myself for most of my life. Not having to worry about my mother made life easier, not harder.

I could tell Mercy was more perturbed by my mother's absence than I was, but she refrained from going off on her with what I imagined to be a considerable effort. "What are you going to do?"

"I don't know. Stick around until I graduate, I guess. I was thinking about joining the army."

"The army?" Mercy's voice betrayed her shock. "What about..."

I smiled grimly as she struggled to finish the sentence. "There's nothing here for me, Mercy. Even you're planning on leaving."

"You could come with me," she whispered.

"Thanks, but I need to figure some stuff out on my own."

Mercy didn't say anything for a time, her gaze locked on my face. Finally, she asked, "Is joining the army really your plan, or are you just trying to punish yourself?"

I shrugged in response. Did it matter?

Mercy rested her head against my shoulder. "Whatever you decide to do, don't just disappear, and don't give up, okay? I know it's cliche, but you are meant for way more than this shithole trailer or some part-time gig at a hardware store. I know it. I've always known it."

I made an indistinct sound of derision. "I'm not sure what I'm meant for anymore."

Crickets hummed and chirped in the impregnable darkness beyond our little island of light, and somewhere far off, I heard the sharp bark of a coyote. Behind us, the trailer sat empty and silent as a crypt.

"Not this," Mercy whispered.

*　*　*

The funeral home was a large A-frame building with massive windows that looked out over the hills, fenced in on the north and east sides by towering spruce trees. I stood across the street directly opposite, watching the people in their funeral-appropriate attire walk in silent procession up the gravel path scattered with wet leaves, their heads bowed against the wind.

I didn't own a suit. The realization had come to me that morning when it first crossed my mind to wonder what one was supposed to wear to a funeral. I'd never been to one before, so I'd donned my nicest shirt—the same one I'd worn on my first and only date with Rainey—and my cleanest pair of jeans. Only now I realized I was horribly, unpardonably underdressed. There was no way I could go in as I was and stand amongst all those people in their crisp suits and couture dresses and not feel like a scab, ugly and festering and offensive.

I saw Jo. She arrived ten minutes before one o'clock in a slim black dress with two people I guessed to be her parents. Her father had his arm around her shoulders while her mom held her hand, both of them offering what support they could for a daughter who had lost her best friend. No doubt they were counting their blessings that it wasn't their child who had died.

A few minutes later, Jo came back out of the funeral home alone. I wasn't sure if I wanted her to notice me or not, but I couldn't make myself move either way.

She finally spotted me, and after waiting for a cab to pass, crossed the street, running with surprising agility in her high heels.

"There you are! What are you doing out here? The ceremony is about to start."

"I can't."

"We've been through this already—"

"No, I mean, look at me. I'm not presentable."

"You're fine. Seriously, no one cares what you're wearing."

"I do!"

Jo sighed, assessing me with a tilt of her head. "I have an idea. Come on."

She pulled me across the street and up the gravel path. There was a small coat room next to the chapel door. Jo went in and reappeared a few seconds later with a very expensive-looking suit jacket. "Here," she said, thrusting it into my hands.

"Whose is this?"

"It's my dad's. He gets hot easily, so he took it off. You can borrow it. I promise he won't mind. Now hurry up."

We entered the chapel, which was now packed with people. Rainey's parents, Marjorie, and Maverick were sitting in the front row. I intended to stay near the back, not wanting to intrude, but then I saw the casket at the front of the room, raised on the platform, the polished maple glowing under a profusion of fragrant lilies.

The lid was open.

Unable to help myself, I walked forward. I walked all the way up to the casket without speaking or looking at anyone, not even Matthew or Cora. She looked like she was sleeping, eyes closed, hands folded neatly over her stomach. This was the last time I would ever see her. How long would they let me stand here, I wondered, before they dragged me away?

I gripped the edge of the casket. I wasn't sure if she was looking down, or if she could hear me, or if she was just gone, but I said it anyway.

"I love you too."

A hand touched my shoulder, and I turned to see Marjorie, her eyes soft with concern.

"Come sit with us," she said. She guided me to a chair next to Maverick, who sat still and silent next to her mother, staring at something only she could see. She was gripping something tightly in her lap. It was Rainey's camera, I realized. I couldn't think what to say to her, but there was no time because the minister stood and walked up behind Rainey's casket. He started to talk about the tragedy of losing one's child and how we had to pray that her soul was in heaven.

I blocked most of it out. I didn't want Rainey's soul to be in heaven. I wanted it down here, in her body, so that I could hear her laugh and cry and scream. I wanted her back, and the wanting kept hitting me in the gut like a physical blow over and over again.

After the service, I went outside, eager to get away from the suffocating press of bodies, the mournful looks, and the token phrases of solace that crowded my ears until I thought I might punch the next person who said, "God just needed another angel in heaven."

It was bullshit. It was all bullshit, and the last thing the Collins family needed was the deranged boyfriend (did I even have a right to call myself that?) starting a brawl in the middle of the chapel.

There was a stone bench behind the funeral home under the boughs of a large spruce tree. I sat down, relishing the bite of the wind on my face. There was no one here, just the wind and the swaying branches overhead, and if I closed my eyes, I could picture Rainey sitting next to me, humming softly. Another invisible fist hit me in the gut, and I bent over, wondering how long this unbearable pain would last and if I had the strength to bear it.

Eventually, I became aware of a presence just beyond the tree. He came over and sat next to me, folding his hands gently in his lap. I kept my gaze fixed on the hole in the toe of my shoe. I couldn't bring myself to look at him. Just now, if I didn't move, if I barely breathed, I could bear the weight of my guilt, but only just. To look into his face now, knowing I would see the mirror of my own grief in the lines of his face, in the bruised circles under his eyes and the slump of his shoulders, it would bear down and crush me.

"I'm sorry," I whispered.

"It wasn't your fault." Matthew's voice was soft. "You might have been the reason she was in that field, but you weren't the one who pulled the trigger."

My hands clenched into fists, my knuckles turning white. I just had to keep breathing, in and out, in and out.

"God knows I wanted to blame you," he murmured. "I did at first, but blaming you was unfair, and it didn't bring her back or ease the grief, and the angrier I got, the more it hurt Maverick. She's dealing with more than anyone right now, thinking her life came at the cost of her sister's. I don't want to add my bitterness to that."

I had sat beside Maverick through the entire ceremony, too lost in my thoughts to consider what she must have felt attending a funeral that would have otherwise been hers. I'd been too preoccupied to even say hello. "Do you hate me?" She'd asked me this in the hospital. Did she think I wished she had died instead? Did she think her parents felt the same way?

I buried my face in my hands. "I don't know what to do. I'm just . . . I'm so angry and lost, and I keep thinking back to when I drove Rainey to the hospital. I should have stayed. I should never have left."

I heard Matthew breathe a deep sigh. "You can torment yourself with a million should-haves. Believe me, I've had plenty of my own to contend with. But they don't serve any purpose and will only drive you mad if you let them."

It started to snow. Light, small flakes floated lazily through the air, disappearing the moment they landed on the path.

"Rainey said you read *Moby Dick*. Perhaps you're familiar with the line, 'Give not thyself up, then, to fire, lest it invert thee, deaden thee, as for the time it did me. There is a wisdom that is woe; but there is a woe that is madness'. It's a good warning, don't you think?"

I shrugged, too weary to think.

"Anger is a part of grief, but I think Melville saw the danger in letting it consume you. If you don't overcome it, it will lead you down a path so dark you won't be able to find your way back. You're better off turning that anger into defiance and fighting for the best possible life you can live. That's the only way forward."

"It's not that easy."

Matthew smiled bitterly. "Nothing worthwhile is easy. That's what makes it worthwhile. We have to fight for it, and the fighting makes us stronger, and the more we suffer, the stronger we become. Truthfully, I don't think we can achieve greatness without suffering. We can be good, maybe, but not great."

I would have settled for good, I thought.

Matthew must have read this in the tenor of my silence because he said, "You have a lot to offer, Liam. Anyone can see that. I would hate to see you waste it, and so would Rainey."

It surprised me that the man upon whom I'd carved the greatest wound anyone could possibly bear could bring himself to care about me. "I don't deserve greatness," I said at last.

Matthew pushed his glasses farther up the bridge of his nose. "I know I'm not your father, but if it's not too out of turn, do you mind if I impart a little piece of wisdom?"

I nodded.

"I think you're laboring under a grave misconception that there are good people and bad people and that, because of your circumstances in life, you belong among the bad. But the truth is, no one is wholly good or wholly bad. We all have a bit of both in us, and we all struggle to find our way. From what I can tell, you were dealt an unfair hand in life. You've struggled more than most. And I know there are days you probably want to give up, but you can't. You have to keep fighting, because it's worth it. You might not be able to see it now, but one day, you'll notice that even though it can be painful, life can also be beautiful. I saw it when Rainey was born. The nurse put her in my arms, and when she looked at me . . . it was like being pierced through the heart by pure divinity. They may be rare, but those beautiful moments . . . they make everything worth it."

Matthew reached into his jacket pocket and pulled something out. "Rainey was the photographer. She was always behind the camera, so we don't have many pictures of her." He made a sound in the back of his throat, a small gasp of grief not quite contained.

"Here," he said, handing me a slip of paper. It was a photo of Rainey smiling widely, her arm wrapped around her sister.

"I can't take this," I gasped.

"I think you should have it." His tone brooked no argument, and despite my words, I was already gripping the picture too tightly to let go. "Let it serve as a reminder of what you're fighting for."

I tucked the picture inside my jacket pocket before the snow could ruin it. "Thank you," I said. It couldn't have been easy for Matthew to part with it.

"I should get back. Cora is probably wondering where I've gone." Matthew stood up, but before he left, he paused and said, "If you need anything, anything at all, call us. I know things aren't great for you at home. If you need a place to stay, our door is always open."

"I appreciate it, but I'll be fine," I said. It was a bold statement, one I wasn't entirely sure was true.

"Even so. I want you to know you're not alone."

I watched him head towards the chapel doors, a faint dusting of snow coating his shoulders and speckling his hair. Truthfully, I'd never felt more alone in my life, but in one respect, Matthew was right. My anger could become my defiance. If I gave up now, I was letting Ray, my mother, my father, and that goddamn trailer win. They had destroyed enough. I couldn't let them take anything else from me, not now, not ever, and if I had to fight every day of my life to ensure they didn't triumph, I would do it for her.

If everything happens for a reason, Rainey would be mine, now and always.

EPILOGUE

MAVERICK

SIX HUNDRED AND FIFTY-FOUR STEPS down, only ten more to go. Our heart was beating loudly, and I was starting to sweat a little, but we were so close! I climbed the last ten steps and looked out over the rooftops of the cafes and shops of Paris and the sprawling green carpet that was the Champ de Mars one hundred and fifteen meters below me.

I grinned, running to the edge of the viewing platform. "Isn't it beautiful?" Our heart answered by slowing to a steady beat, as if wanting to appreciate the view with an equivalent serenity. Having waited until this moment atop the Eiffel Tower, I took the letter I'd received that morning out of my pocket. The return address was visible under the ink of the airmail stamp: Taitou-ku, Tokyo, Japan. Ripping open the envelope, I pulled out the piece of paper inside and unfolded it.

I winced, thinking of yesterday's incident when I'd corrected Monsieur Armand on the proper way to make hot *espumas* using a siphon. He'd looked like he'd wanted to throw his hat at me. I sighed, returning to the letter.

show me all the best cafes and we'll walk along the Seine.

Let me know, and I'll make the arrangements.

Love,

Liam

I read the letter three more times, drinking in every word. It had been four years since I'd last seen Liam. He'd come to my high school graduation, as promised, bearing an orchid corsage as spectacular as my fuchsia skirt. It was the first time he'd been home in years, but even then, he'd only stayed for one day—coming home was hard for him.

I missed him. I think a little part of me loved him even, but I never tried to make him stay. As long as he was happy, and as long as I got to see him every once in a while, that was good enough for me.

I carefully folded the letter and put it back in my pocket, our heart pounding joyfully as I looked out upon the glorious prospect, feeling Rainey was right there with me.

Acknowledgements

I would like to take a moment to thank all the people who helped me on this epic adventure. First, to my beta readers, the people who helped shape the book in its early stages: Kelsey, Jericho, Lisa, Tara, Laurie and Alison. Your advice and encouragement kept me going—thank you, as ever, for your honesty. Thank you to Dr. Michele Novak for answering my many questions and my editor Stacey for her keen eye. Finally, and most importantly, thank you to my husband who has cheered for me since the beginning—I couldn't have done this without you, love.